THE GIRLS
ARE NEVER GONE

THE GIRLS ARE NEVER GONE

SARAH GLENN MARSH

RAZORBILL

RAZORBILL

An imprint of Penguin Random House LLC, New York

First published in the United States of America by Razorbill,
an imprint of Penguin Random House LLC, 2021

Visit us online at penguinrandomhouse.com.

Library of Congress Cataloging-in-Publication Data
Names: Marsh, Sarah Glenn, author.
Title: The girls are never gone / Sarah Glenn Marsh.
Description: New York : Razorbill, 2021. | Audience: Ages 12 and up.
Summary: Seventeen-year-old Dare plans to spend her summer debunking a
haunting at an historic estate with a dark past, but she finds herself
in a life-or-death struggle against a malignant ghost.
Identifiers: LCCN 2021020274 | ISBN 9781984836151 (hardcover)
ISBN 9781984836175 (trade paperback) | ISBN 9781984836168 (ebook)
Subjects: CYAC: Dwellings—Fiction. | Ghosts—Fiction. | Diabetes—Fiction.
Podcasts—Fiction. | Bisexuality—Fiction. | Horror stories.
Classification: LCC PZ7.1.M3727 Gi 2021 | DDC [Fic]—dc23
LC record available at https://lccn.loc.gov/2021020274

Printed in the United States of America

1 3 5 7 9 10 8 6 4 2

SKY

Design by Rebecca Aidlin
Text set in Garamond Premier Pro

For Mom, who believes.

For Erin, who sees.

And for those who went before me,
who walk beside me still.

ATTACHMENTS

S1, E1

Intro music fades in. Violins play a slow, eerie melody.

DARE CHASE (voiceover): Imagine: you're on a vacant highway in the murky dark, gas tank on empty. Desperate, you take the first exit you finally see—that is, if you have enough privilege to think you'll be safe there. But to your dismay, the tiny two-pump station closed hours ago, even though it's just past ten p.m. As you look around, you see a few other buildings, their windows boarded up, the only light coming from the glow of the familiar Golden Arches. You seriously consider getting some hot, greasy fries to ease the pain of being stranded until morning. But even the McDonald's has been closed for an hour already, its sign a beacon for disappointment.

That's life in New Hope, Virginia, population 4,602. It's the kind of place where you'd never want to insult your neighbor in public, because his first-grade teacher is standing behind you in the grocery checkout line, and that teacher also happens to be your cousin who you pissed off last Thanksgiving by challenging their racist politics.

The town sprang up around a paper mill, which produces a strong rotten-egg smell throughout the area—talk about tourist repellent. But even more remote and unloved than the town itself is the Arrington Estate. Built in 1870 for Lou and Jane Arrington, the estate lies a desolate ten miles outside of New Hope, accessible only by a one-lane bridge and bordering a large lake. Shrinking from the sun and buried in weeds, it's the kind of place where vampires would feel more at home than the living. But it's where I'll be spending a month this summer instead of getting sunburned on a beach with my best friends—anything for a good story. For the truth.

I suppose it's time to introduce myself: I'm Virginia Dare Chase, but you can call me Dare. Most of you likely know me from my ghost-hunting YouTube channel, Strange Virginia, but this summer, I hope you'll join me in trying something new. A podcast, focusing on one story over the whole season: the mysterious death of Atheleen Bell. This is *Attachments*.

I've put a picture of Atheleen on our official Instagram account, so be sure to check it out and follow us for more updates. For now, I'll describe her: long, wavy brown hair frames a pale oval face and a pixie-sharp nose and chin. Her eyelashes are thick behind slightly crooked gold-rimmed glasses. Her big, goofy smile as she hugs a black-and-white cat against her chest tells me she had no idea what fate awaited her at the Arrington Estate when her family moved in.

Now, if you haven't heard of Arrington, you're not alone. I first learned about the estate a few weeks ago from a Strange Virginia subscriber: shout-out to Kiwi-LovesMango! According to Kiwi, the place is as haunted as it looks. There are reports of objects moving on their own, phantom smells, feelings of being watched—a ghost hunter's dream. And it just so happens this lucky ghoul will be staying there for the entire month of July, volunteering with the town's historical society to help renovate the estate as a museum.

I suspect the ghostly activity there is related to Atheleen, the seventeen-year-old girl who supposedly drowned in the lake in the summer of 1992. Foul play was quickly ruled out, and her parents left in a hurry. It seems Atheleen was homeschooled, so no one knew much about her or her family other than that they were brave enough to move into Arrington in the first place. The estate has cast a shadow over the town since long before the Bells arrived, and has continued to do so in the years that followed.

Now, maybe Atheleen really did drown, and maybe it was an accident. New Hope doesn't have much crime to suggest otherwise. Maybe I'm heading to the Arrington Estate based on a bunch of spooky rumors born out of the doldrums of small-town living. But there are a couple reasons I think there's more to Atheleen's story. First, while the lake *is* massive, conditions were calm on the day of her death. It was eighty-five degrees, sunny, no wind. An ideal time for an avid swimmer to cool off in the clear waters of Paradise Lake. Second is the state of Atheleen's body. Only one news article mentions the coroner's findings: that her remains were sunken and skeletal, suggesting rapid decomposition in the span of hours. I'm no doctor, but something doesn't add up here. I want to know what the estate is hiding.

Could Atheleen herself still be there, waiting for someone to listen so she can tell her story? What really happened to her before she wound up in that lake? Over the next month, I intend to find out whatever I can, to shed light on a restless spirit's final days.

Secrets always surface. And if the Arrington Estate has any, I'm going to sweep its darkest corners until I dredge them up, kicking and screaming.

Once again, this is *Attachments*. Stay tuned.

ONE

I'VE ALWAYS BEEN DRAWN to the dark. I've never seen a ghost, or a body, or known someone who's gone missing, but when bad things happen, I can't look away. And in just a few hours, I'll be standing on the shore where Atheleen Bell spent her final moments. The thought makes my stomach churn around the remnants of breakfast, the tall, weathered house casting a long shadow across my mind. Funny how it's even bigger in my imagination than it seems in pictures.

Rolling green fields dotted with sheep flash by the car windows, but I barely spare them a glance as I check the subscriber count on my new podcast, *Attachments*, for about the millionth time today.

"Any new subscribers?" Mom asks. She knows me too well.

I shrug. "Not today. Not yet." I try to sound like I don't care, but I really wish the count were higher already. This is my first big solo project, and I want to get it right. On my last ghost-hunting project—Strange Virginia, the YouTube show I made with my boyfriend, Joey—everything seemed so easy. We never had trouble getting viewers, comments, even sponsors. But that all ended when Joey broke up with me at the beginning of the summer, right after our junior year. So now I'm going to prove to myself that I can do this on my own—I hope. Because without listeners, I just might prove the opposite.

From the back seat, Waffles whines, startling me from my thoughts. I half turn in my seat and meet my dog's sincere shiny-copper eyes, which he takes as an invitation to lick my cheek, coating me in slobber.

"Gross," I moan. "You're a mess, buddy. You got your paws all wet, too. And the seat. Do all dogs drool this much, or do you need to see somebody about that?"

My teasing aside, either he's alerting me to my blood sugar going low, or he needs a potty break—and we only left DC two hours ago.

Behind her large tortoiseshell sunglasses, Mom's eyes haven't left the road; I think she was hoping a four-hour drive would mean no stopping, especially in a strange area. She gets turned around easily, always in her head thinking about work, and the signal out here is patchy. I only have one bar right now.

"Blood sugar or bathroom?" Mom asks, sounding a little ex-asperated.

Waffles is my very best friend, but he isn't very good at his diabetic alert dog duties—signaling to me when my blood sugar is dropping. His slimy cheek kiss probably means nothing, but I still glance at the continuous glucose monitoring app on my phone to check in. Straight from a thin wire under my skin to an app via Bluetooth, my CGM tells me that my blood sugar is 180 mg/dL and climbing. Not cool—prolonged high blood sugar can eventually lead to organ damage and other complications—but not what Waffles is alerting me about. It's not surprising, though; I ate a bagel for breakfast, after all.

Plus, okay, I'm a little nervous. Usually around this time, I'd be packing a bag for a week at the beach with my friends—Amanda,

Deitra, and Lindsey. It's been tradition since we were little to go to Ocean City in July.

Instead, this year I'll be in a new place, faced with unknown internet quality. Potentially crappy food. New people who might not get my fascination with all things dark and unexplained. Not to mention new people whose only reference to diabetes is an elderly mustached man on a drug commercial.

I'm not bitter, I swear, but sometimes it gets exhausting, having to teach everybody the basics of my disease.

Like how being nervous can lead to high blood sugar—what's happening right now. I grab my insulin pump from my jeans pocket and give myself a dose with the push of a few buttons. The plastic casing around the small pump is electric blue, matching my latest hair color. My hair used to be rose gold bordering on pink, but since this summer will be different—hopefully, my best one yet—I figured I might as well try out a new look.

Waffles whines again, louder. He's not a barky, growly sort of dog; he's usually a quiet dude, so that whine means he urgently needs a pit stop. "Bathroom break," I tell Mom, and she sighs.

Outside, we pass more white barn churches, precarious wood fences, and a brick chimney whose house crumbled to dust long ago. Mom taps the brakes, parking us in the grass alongside a cow pasture.

"We probably shouldn't have given Waffles his whole breakfast before we left," Mom says, beating me to it. We're usually on the same wavelength, and today is no exception.

"No one can resist those eyes!" I laugh, opening the door so the dog can barrel out to freedom. I'm glad he'll be staying with me this month—thank goodness for service dog laws—even if he isn't exactly the hypoglycemia-sniffing machine we were promised when he was a puppy. He's the best partner in crime I could imagine, unafraid of whatever life throws at him.

Cows flick their tails lazily at swarms of flies, not even glancing up as Waffles sniffs around for the perfect potty spot. There's a ramshackle fence between us and them, but it's not enough to keep anyone—let alone an eighty-pound Labrador retriever—from getting through if they're determined. But maybe the cows don't realize that.

As Waffles does his thing, I pull out my phone again and—I can't help it—check the subscriber count for *Attachments* again. Still less than two hundred. Ouch. Very few of our Strange Virginia fans have followed my solo project so far, almost like they were only watching the old vids for Joey's icy blue eyes and the edgy attitude he put on for the camera.

Hopefully, once I'm at the estate and post another episode, I'll start getting more listeners. The Arrington Estate hasn't been explored by other ghost hunters yet, and it's barely been written about online—its past, and its spirits, are mine to discover. I have all the necessary ghost-hunting equipment, and a bunch of experience in old, spooky places. I know how to establish baseline readings of a building, and what to look for during an investigation: the drops in temperature, an electric feeling brushing across the skin, the softest noise set apart from the background creaks and groans of life in an aging house. If Atheleen Bell really has lingered after her untimely drowning at seventeen, I'll find her.

Privately, I'm willing to bet she hasn't. The rumored haunting is the result of an overactive imagination and too much spare time, with a side of not understanding the mechanics of old homes with bad plumbing and weatherworn boards.

I know it's weird for a ghost hunter to be this much of a skeptic. For most of my life, since my grandpa died when I was in kindergarten, I've wanted nothing more than to see a ghost. To know beyond a shadow of a doubt that there's something more after death. My life-changing type 1 diabetes diagnosis only made me need some proof of the afterlife more; there's nothing like being confronted by your own mortality at fifteen, holding a syringe of life-saving hormone in your shaking hand and knowing that while it's necessary to push that needle into your stomach and get your insulin, taking too much could be the last mistake you ever make. My need for proof is why I started hunting ghosts, and why I'm an avid Insomniac, a proud Gravekeeper—you name the spooky fandom, I'm part of it.

But in all the allegedly haunted sites where I've sat for hours, the digital camera counting the minutes of my boredom, I've seen nothing. Heard nothing. Felt no stray chills. I'm a far cry from the hoaxers and conspiracy theorists willing to disregard the scientific because they *need* something more. But since I crave that something more, too, I'll keep stalking the dark and searching for answers—for myself, and for my listeners. If I ever get them.

Waffles grabs a large stick, more like a fallen branch, between his teeth. Tail wagging, he scampers in circles around me, inviting me to play. But before I can try to snatch the stick out of Waffles's mouth and run with it, Mom opens the back door of the Jeep and makes a sweeping gesture.

"Next stop, Arrington!" she declares cheerfully but firmly.

AKA no one else better need to make a pit stop between here and there. Can't argue with that—it was really nice of her to take a day off work and drive me in the first place. I wasn't sure my old car was reliable enough to make even a four-hour trek out of the city.

As the Jeep kicks to life, resuming our steady drive southwest toward the blue-green foothills of the Blue Ridge Mountains, I'm hit with a welcome rush of AC. It must be pushing ninety degrees today; just ten minutes outside the car and I'm already sweating hard enough to loosen the tape around the infusion site on my right hip—the spot where my insulin pump connects to my body. I'm glad I piled my neon hair into a high ponytail before we hit the road, making it easier for the cold air to reach the back of my neck.

My phone pings twice.

"Is that your brother?" Mom asks knowingly. "Does he need something?"

Good luck, Ghost Bait! Max says. *If you need me, I'll be at the beach with your friends. Speaking of, I think Lindsey blocked my number. Talk to her? You know she can't get enough of my sick GTA skillz.*

I roll my eyes and grin. Seventh graders, am I right?

"He's fine," I assure her. She hates leaving him home alone for the day, even though we both know he won't move from his gaming chair where he's playing *Grand Theft Auto* with his merry band of would-be NASCAR drivers.

"Okay," Mom says hesitantly, her lips pursed like she's holding something back. A moment later, she draws a certain sharp breath that tells me what's coming next. The Talk. "You have your emergency card and your medical alert necklace?"

"Yes, of course. Not that I've ever needed them." I dutifully produce a bright-red business-card-shaped paper from within my phone case. It lets first responders know I'm wearing an insulin pump and what to do with it, as well as how to reach my doctor. "See?"

"Good." She nods, as if reassuring herself. "Make sure you drink lots of water—your CGM readings aren't as accurate when you're dehydrated—and use those pump features I've been asking you to read up on forever if you eat any heavy carbs like pizza." She frowns. "I'm guessing there will be lots of pizza at something like this."

"Actually, Cathy emailed earlier—the volunteer coordinator from the historical society, remember?—and she says we're having filet mignon with roasted rosemary potatoes and crème brûlée for dessert to kick things off," I deadpan in response.

That does it; Mom finally cracks a smile. Victory. "You know you can call if you need anything, though, right? I can be there in four hours flat, especially without Waffles as my copilot." She shakes her head. "And if you go into town, take someone with you. You're still planning to take a break from boys this summer, right?"

"Don't worry, Mom. If I want to have a wild night while I'm here, it won't be with a boy—it'll be with a Ouija board and a couple of dead Victorian girls whose idea of *wild* is putting a splash of liquor in their tea." I snicker at her bemused expression. "Seriously. It'll just be me, my fellow volunteers, and the ghosts."

The road forks, and as we veer left, the tall pine trees open up to give us our first glimpse of Paradise Lake and the narrow bridge across.

Deep blue water fans out on either side of us, stretching to the horizon out the driver's side window. Waffles grumbles a complaint as the bridge bumps and jostles our car. There are small gaps between the wood slats, and I force myself to shut my eyes when I realize that looking through them is making my stomach churn.

Once we've crossed the bridge, we take another dirt road, this one less traveled. The path ahead is studded with the occasional rock that makes Mom gasp when it plinks against the windshield. At last, we reach the base of the gentle slope up to the house and begin a slow crawl along the driveway. Paradise Lake looks murkier up close, less pristine than it did from above on the bridge, as it laps at the shore to our left.

You'd think the water in a lake called Paradise would be a little less muddy.

Out my window is a wooded field. Most of the trees have been reduced to stumps poking out of the earth like jagged teeth, no doubt waiting to be ground to dust to make way for a visitors' parking lot.

The house itself watches our approach through shattered eyes, having taken a few rocks to its front windows. It's just as big as the beast it appeared to be in pictures, though less polished. It crouches against the trees that flank it on either side, as if trying to disappear into the sprawling woods, afraid of someone seeing the slight sag in its double-story columned porch, the lingering graffiti stark on its white, peeling sides, the overgrown lawn, the moss that clings patchily to its shingles. Behind the house, farther away than they appear, the mountains, those huddled blue giants, see everything.

Was Atheleen Bell happy to see this place when her family arrived? Did she flash her wide, carefree smile, imagining the summer adventures she'd have on the grounds? Did she—like I soon would—shoulder her bags and stride eagerly toward the porch, her little black-and-white cat at her side? Or did she shrink back from the sight of the neglected building starved for love? Perhaps it looked less forbidding in her day, even though it was old back then, too.

By the time Mom stops the car as close to the front door as she seems willing to get, the afternoon clouds covering the sun have stained the mountains the deep plum of a bruise. I lean against her, inhaling the familiar scents of coffee, dog dander, and spring meadow fabric softener—of home.

"You're sure you want to do this, baby girl?" she asks softly, frowning up at the house.

"You're just salty because you're going to miss my cooking for a whole month, and you'll have to order takeout every night," I try to tease, but as I follow her gaze, my voice gets smaller until it vanishes altogether.

There are secrets in that house, concealed by cracked paint and faded grandeur. Who knows what I might dig up during the renovation process ahead? Perhaps evidence about the life and death of a girl my age—and I'm ready to explore. I'm not leaving without some insight into Atheleen's final days and a bigger follower count.

The Arrington Estate is a dark place, but I like the dark. It's content, it's quiet and empty. Just as I've done so many times before, I'll reach out into the darkness, safe in knowing nothing ever reaches back.

TWO

THE PORCH CREAKS IN protest under the combined weight of Waffles and me. I'm sure it will hold us—the historical society wouldn't have asked for volunteers if the place wasn't structurally sound—but a few of the boards have just enough give to make my stomach flip.

A june bug throws itself against the door in a vain attempt to gain entry, its glittering green shell audibly connecting with the wood as it bounces off.

Next, it's my turn. I bang the heavy brass door knocker shaped like a stag's head, but no one appears. I shouldn't be surprised; they're expecting me by six p.m., and it's not yet three.

I turn to wave goodbye to Mom one last time, but all I catch is a glimpse of the back of her head, phone pressed to her ear, the Jeep's taillights like glowing red eyes as they retreat into the distance.

There's only one car parked near the house now, a shiny silver Lexus convertible looking out of place among the dandelions and unkempt clover.

Past the fancy car, the lake laps sluggishly at a narrow strip of sandy shore, the closest thing to a beach I can spot from here. It must be where Atheleen took her last breaths before the murky blue water closed over her head. Suddenly cold, I tear my gaze away. When my friends and I take our annual beach trip, I stay under the umbrella, or in the nearby community pool. I've never been much for swimming in murky water, not quite sure how to move my limbs, too focused on what could be reaching unseen for my feet.

A mosquito whines in my ear. I must have several bites already; there's nothing those suckers love more than my sweet blood. I take one last gulp of hot, muggy air and brace myself for whatever awaits me inside the estate. Based on what I've seen so far, it's going to be damp, musty, and outdated.

The door gives easily at my touch, and as it swings open, a low rumble of thunder warns me I'd better hurry inside.

No. Not thunder.

It's Waffles.

He stands at the edge of the porch, as far as he can get from the door without falling down the steps or breaking off part of the fragile wood railing.

I follow his gaze through the open door into a dimly lit foyer that oozes with dampness, just as I expected. The antique-looking carpet laid across the wood floor must be trapping the smell of the lake indoors. Overhead, a brass-capped chandelier gives off a faint glow, a few of the bulbs flickering as if close to death. Its many crystal-studded tendrils drip down from a vaulted ceiling toward the floor, giving it the appearance of a jellyfish.

"Come on, buddy, there's no one here, see?" I plead. "And we're letting all the cool air out—do you want them to hate us from day one?"

Waffles usually likes to dart ahead of me when we're out

walking together, so I step to one side, shuffling my luggage around, and show him the entrance like I'm his butler or something. "Sir, your accommodations await," I joke.

Instead of trotting forward, Waffles sits back on his haunches and continues growling, the sound scraping my nerves raw.

"Dude. What's with you today?" Seriously concerned about the old house's AC, I unzip my duffel bag and grab Waffles's leash, clipping it to his collar. "There's a hot dog in it for you," I sing-song, hoping the society ladies won't mind parting with a little of whatever meat they've stocked in the fridge.

But Waffles won't budge, even with me pulling as hard as I dare on the lead.

"Fine," I sigh, removing the leash and resigning myself to what will come next.

Leaving my luggage in a heap on the porch, I bend my knees and scoop the large dog's bulk into my arms. Together, we stagger forward like an awkward top-heavy monster with too many limbs, Waffles's deep growls continuing all the while.

The instant I set Waffles down on the antique carpet, he whines softly, then falls silent. He licks his whiskery muzzle and looks at me expectantly—he must have understood the part about the hot dog.

"Soon," I promise him, returning to the porch to pull my bags inside.

"Need some help with those?" a soft voice asks.

I look up to see a girl standing at the bottom of the stairs. I must have been so busy with Waffles and his drama, I hadn't noticed her approaching. Because any other time, I would have noticed her right away.

"Welcome to Arrington," she says, red lipstick gleaming against her white teeth as she smiles curiously at me. She flips a wave of black hair over her shoulder and grabs the rolling suitcase full of Waffles's kibble and toys, hauling it inside.

As I set down the rest of my stuff and shut the door, the girl moves toward Waffles, extending a manicured hand for him to sniff. His tail starts wagging so hard that it beats against the handsome cherrywood grandfather clock in the foyer like a drum. Laughing, the girl kneels, seeming unconcerned with the short skirt of her floral dress, and throws her arms around him. "Hi, Waffles," she says, reading the tag on his collar. "I'm Quinn Reyes, your new friend. And *you* must be Dare." Her deep brown eyes, a rich, warm color I could get lost in, search my face from behind stylish cat-eye glasses. "Nice to meet you."

It takes me a minute to find my voice, distracted by the girl's flawless light-brown skin and my dog's apparent love of her. "Yeah! Hi. How do you know—?"

"My mom's the one who bought Arrington. She's an interior designer, so she'll be working on the museum with us. You'll meet her soon," Quinn explains, still kneeling on the floor with Waffles. He's got her giving him belly rubs already. "She and Cathy went into town for some more supplies before dinner—food and stuff, no Instacart out here—so you're stuck with me for now. Hope that's okay."

I swallow over a dry throat. "Of course." I've mostly emailed with Cathy, the historical society's volunteer coordinator, but someone named Rose has always been cc'd—she must be Quinn's mother. "You're here for the month, too?" I grin at Waffles, whose tongue is lolling out of his mouth as Quinn lavishes attention on him.

"Yep!" she says. "And my college is even giving me internship credit for it." I'm a little surprised—I had assumed she was my age. She continues, "I was a freshman this year at Savannah College of Art and Design. I'm trying to get into the industry—interior design, like my mom." She stands after giving Waffles a final pat, seeming reluctant to stop petting his thick glossy fur. "We should get your bags up to your room," she declares, grabbing the heavier suitcase again without waiting for direction. "Sorry—I don't usually talk this much, and I'm sure you're tired from the drive."

"I'm fine," I assure her, though perhaps the sweat that's soaked into the collar of my T-shirt tells another story. "Ready to paint some walls and refinish some furniture—just point me to it." I'm mostly being honest, though my heart is beating a little faster than I'd care to admit, sometimes a sign of high blood sugar. And sometimes a sign of talking to a really cute girl.

As Quinn rolls my suitcase toward the emerald-green carpeted stairs straight ahead of us, I sneak a glance at my phone to check my sugar: 160. Finally, the number is coming down a little, the insulin taking effect. So I guess this time, my heart is just excited about the cute girl.

I turn to take a final look around the foyer, getting familiar with my surroundings. My gaze sweeps over a painting of a cargo ship sailing toward ominous-looking waves under a leaden sky; a potted fern, its leaves heavy with dust; old water damage creeping out from under the antique rug, staining the floorboards like dried blood.

"What's that?" I ask, spotting a glassed-over wooden box of numbered brass bells in neat rows at the base of the staircase. There are fourteen bells in all.

"Oh, that's the servant call box system," Quinn answers with a glance over her shoulder, already partway up the first set of stairs. "It's not original to the house, but close; the family who lived here after the Arringtons installed it, but it doesn't work anymore. The wires have all been cut." She sighs. "It would have been so cool to give demonstrations on tours, right?"

"And this?" I point to a dark-coated metal trumpet thing sticking out of the wall nearby.

"That's a speaking tube you'd use to tell the servants what you needed; the Arringtons built that into the original design. There's another tube in the dining room, and one in my mom's room as well—she's staying in what would have been the owners' suite." Quinn seems completely in her element explaining all of the details of the old house.

She bounds up the stairs, and Waffles follows, breezing past me. Whatever was going through his little brain earlier has clearly disappeared, replaced by happy thoughts of belly rubs and new friends.

The stairway is long, my feet sinking into the plush carpet—it must be somewhat new, unlike the one in the foyer downstairs.

There are portraits in heavy gilt frames lining the walls, oil paintings of what looks to be a family—mostly young women—in Victorian clothes, their faces pale and expressions bored. Between them are flickering lights in glass sconces that emit a low static hum as I pass—I'm willing to bet they give off a high EMF reading, as old electric fixtures are prone to do. High EMF, or electromagnetic fields, can give someone feelings of nausea and paranoia, of being watched—exactly as KiwiLovesMango described in their YouTube comment.

I make a mental note to do an EMF sweep of this whole place later tonight. Given the estate's age, those fixtures probably aren't the only appliances giving off high readings.

The only trouble with always debunking claims is that my listeners—all 197 of them, as it were—are expecting a thrilling podcast, and here I am already ruining their scares. There had better be more to Atheleen's story than what was in the papers, or my podcast is sunk.

Quinn leads me into a hallway with three doors on each side at staggered intervals. There's an antique cherrywood wardrobe shoved against a narrow section of wall where the hall dead-ends to the left, and at the opposite end, a trio of stained-glass windows surround a strange glass box that seems to be fixed to the floor by a pipe as thick as my forearm.

"Ah, you've noticed the aquarium," Quinn says eagerly. "It's original to the house—isn't it neat?" She leads me there first, pointing to a toy-sized man in what looks like an astronaut's outfit—an old diver's suit—sitting alone in his empty prison. "He's the only Arrington left in this place," she adds, admiration softening her features. "Since the aquarium won't be part of the museum, Mom doesn't think it's a priority to get it working, but . . . maybe someday. Okay—now to your room," Quinn says, giving the ancient diver a final glance before setting off again.

There's no musty smell up here. The metallic tang of new paint tickles my nose as I follow Quinn; this level of the house has already been renovated. The freshly laid carpet, continuing the emerald theme from the stairs, is tender and pliable as we move down the hall toward the last door before the dead end where the tall antique wardrobe towers imperiously over us.

The sconces lighting our way up here are clearly newer, imi-
tation Gothic designs with an antler motif that calls to mind the
old brass door knocker. They must be Rose's choice. When I stand
near one, there's no obvious buzz to signal potential EMF issues,
though they don't shine bright enough for a place with such dark
wood trim and too few windows. Wherever Quinn walks, the
hall's shadows seem to converge on her, as if hungry to consume
her light.

As I take another step after Quinn, a strange feeling comes
over me. This seems like a house in want of something. I don't
know where the impression comes from—I know a house can't
want, it's just a thing someone made, wood and metal studs devoid of emotion—but the boards creak and the air ripples with an
undeniable emptiness like the hollow ache of hunger.

My fingers toy with the two beaded bracelets on my wrist, a
good-luck gift from my BFF Deitra yesterday before I left. She's
into horoscopes and crystals, and she swears the polished amethyst and obsidian beads she gave me will ward off any negative
energy at the estate—not that I really believe that. At least they're
pretty. She and the others must be on their way to the beach right
now. I'm sure my phone will soon be flooded with pictures of
white-capped waves and toes in the sand.

Something hits the top of my head, cold and sharp, startling
me into looking up.

Unlike the walls with their smooth white paint, the ceiling is
as stained and faded as the downstairs carpet, and above me is a
particularly soggy patch that's bloated like dead flesh left too long
in the heat. Have the dark clouds I saw on my way in finally burst?
Rain must be seeping through a crack in the roof somewhere.

"Dare?" Quinn calls. "Where'd you go? What—?" she stops short as she sees me wiping away the water that tried to roll down my forehead. Wincing, she says, "Sorry. I told my mom not to paint until we had all the plumbing issues worked out. You'll notice that leaks are a regular occurrence around here. We're . . . working on it."

Waffles gives a short, impatient bark, tired of waiting on me. I hurry toward the sound, taking in an unremarkable bedroom with a simple double bed and quilt, its pattern a rippling blue like the lake. There's a small shag carpet on the wood floor, white as the walls, and a dresser. Quinn has already set up Waffles's favorite sleeping cushion across from a small black marble fireplace streaked with gold, a relic from the days before central air and heating.

As I move toward the window to check on the storm and take in the lake view, Quinn slams the door shut behind us. The lock clicks into place.

Confused, I whirl around to face her.

"Took you long enough," she says seriously, perching on the end of the bed and patting the space next to her. "We have business to discuss." Her doe-brown eyes roam over my face as she lowers her voice. "I'm the one who asked you to come. I'm the one who's been haunted since we got here."

She has her hands folded in her lap, and she starts absently chipping at her perfect manicure as she waits for me to say something, but I'm at a loss for words.

"You're KiwiLovesMango?" I say at last.

Quinn's lips curve in a reluctant smile. "Right. I got the name from my two lovebirds. They're at my dad's right now. Mom can't stand the noise while she's working. She's the best, but she's also kind of a lot—you'll see when you meet her."

She speaks softly, and I can smell something earthy and sweet—rosemary and lavender?—surrounding her as she leans closer. She's acting as though she trusts me already. I feel a twinge of guilt at how quickly I had dismissed the claims from her YouTube comment. "Okay," I say. "Tell me what you've been experiencing. Give me every detail."

"The first thing is the dreams about the lake—I've been having them since we got here three weeks ago. It's especially weird because I usually *never* remember my dreams. Sometimes I'm swimming in the lake, and other times I'm on the dock, with shadows moving in the water below me—shadows way too big to be fish," she adds, gouging another fleck of red polish off her thumbnail.

"Are you a good swimmer?" I ask. There are many reasons why someone might have nightmares about a lake the size of Paradise.

"I was on the swim team for years," Quinn answers with a slight frown. "I love the water. But it's more than just dreams— at night, I've heard knocking coming from somewhere upstairs when I *know* Cathy and my mom have been asleep for hours. I've had some weird things happen in the shower, too. Like, a couple times now, the water has gone from cold to scalding for no reason. And I've felt—well, I think I've felt someone tapping me on the shoulder in there."

I hesitate. "Well, we'll definitely want to check the walls—it sounds to me like we might have mice. As for the shower, you said yourself the place has plumbing issues," I point out gently.

Quinn looks a little hurt, but then she nods. "That's fair. And I know how you work—I've seen every episode of Strange Virginia.

You have to try to debunk the claims before you look for supernatural explanations."

Despite her steady voice, there's no mistaking the fear in her eyes. I'll have to check the bathroom for high EMF readings, too. That will be my first priority.

"Look," I say, hopping off the bed and unzipping my duffel. I start pulling out my equipment: a K2 meter, a thermal camera, an EMF meter, a digital camera, and a voice recorder to capture any phantom sounds not heard by human ears. "I've brought everything I need to figure out what's going on, and I won't stop until I get answers."

Quinn's shoulders visibly relax. "Great. There's just one more thing—you can't tell my mom any of this. She doesn't believe in things like ghosts, and I need her to take me seriously on the renovation if I want her recommendation, her contacts in the field. And she has very high expectations."

"Got it," I say as Waffles hops up from his cushion to join Quinn on the bed. He's good at sensing when someone's on edge.

Quinn continues while I unpack. "I had a hard enough time convincing her to let me come here. She wanted me to spend the summer with my dad; and don't get me wrong, I was tempted, especially since he moved back home to Bayamón to take care of my abuela. Mom's white, Dad's Boricua." I nod, but she must be used to clarifying. "Puerto Rican. Anyway, old houses are my thing, so I insisted on coming. I love the stories these places tell if you know how to listen."

As I shove my diabetes equipment into the top drawer of the dresser—extra syringes, alcohol swabs, infusion sets, and reservoirs for the pump all moving from my bag to their new home with practiced speed—something keeps drawing my gaze back to Quinn, and it's more than her red lipstick.

It's not just that she's the daughter of the estate's new owner, either, or that she's supposedly experienced the paranormal firsthand—though there's no denying how much interest that could add to the podcast. Maybe it's how much Waffles seems to like her. He's a pretty solid judge of character.

A moment later, Quinn leaps to her feet and declares, "It's nearly four. I should give you a quick tour before Mom and Cathy get back. And our other volunteer should be here soon, too." She arches a brow and nods to my faded crimson shirt. "What's that mean?"

The faded white text proudly proclaims VAMPIRE'S FAVORITE DESSERT beneath a silhouette of a bat—a little type 1 diabetes humor.

"I, uh, love Halloween," I say lamely. Doesn't she know about my disease? I had to tell Cathy and Rose about my condition before making arrangements to stay here. Did Quinn's mom fail to mention, perhaps, that Waffles is a service dog? I shouldn't be lying to Quinn, but now I don't have to explain, or deal with the popular misconceptions that always crop up. For the next few hours, we can just hang out. I can just be.

As Quinn unlocks the door and steps into the hall, trailed by Waffles, I finally glance out the window, which offers an expansive view of the shore and lake, as well as the forest that borders part of the lake's edge. It isn't raining yet after all.

But when I step into the hall, the leak in the ceiling has grown more persistent, weeping a puddle onto the new carpet.

I hope Quinn's mom has the number for a good contractor.

THREE

OUR FIRST STOP IS Quinn's room, just across the hall from mine. It's got the same basic setup, though its window overlooks the side lawn, the mountains just peeking over the distant trees. For one wild moment I can't explain, I wish we could trade views.

The main difference in here is the walls: they're covered in paintings, most on watercolor paper. There are a couple of colorful birds—the famous Kiwi and Mango?—schools of little fish, and scenes of the lake and forest at Arrington. There are also a few photographs, including one of Quinn outside her dorm room with a frail-looking woman sporting a flowered dress and a cloud of white hair sitting regally in a wheelchair.

"That's Nana Olsen," Quinn says softly, tapping the picture. "She died a few months ago. She was an artist, too—runs in the family—and she's the reason Mom wanted to buy this old place so badly. Before she was born, my grandparents used to live in New Hope. Nana never wanted to talk about her time out here, though." She turns away from the picture and sighs, putting a hand down to scratch Waffles under the chin. "Mom hasn't said as much, but I think she's hoping this project will help her feel close to her mom again. I guess it's part of why I wanted to come here, too."

"I'm sorry to hear that," I say as I try to take in the rest of Quinn's art. She's really good. "My grandpa died when I was pretty young, but I still miss him all the time." A poster above Quinn's dresser catches my eye, and as I move closer, my heart skips: it's a *Gravekeepers* TV promo poster for season two, signed by the whole cast. "What? Where did you get this? This is *amazing*!"

Quinn gives me a dazzling smile. "You're a Gravekeeper, too? No way! Britt, my ex-girlfriend—we're still friends—got this for me. Her uncle works on set. And she's not even a fan, can you believe it? That should be a crime or something."

"What's your favorite case from season one?" I ask, aware of the stupid grin on my face but unable to hide it. "Please don't say the one about aliens. They give me the creeps."

Gravekeepers covers true scary stories: mostly mysterious deaths, often highlighting cases of missing Black and Indigenous women that don't receive mainstream coverage, but they take on other types of mysteries, too.

Quinn considers for a moment. "The supposed drowning of that college student, Cassie Carroll—the one who was found in the swimming pool of a hotel when she should've been studying for finals. I still can't figure it out."

I remember that case—and my friends' weak attempts at interest when I tried to discuss it with them over lunch last year. Talking about it with Quinn is much more fun. "You don't think her boyfriend did it?" I counter.

"Reasonable doubt," Quinn says, pushing up her Kate Spade glasses a little higher. "Have you turned up any suspects in Atheleen's drowning yet?" she adds eagerly. "I listened to the first episode of *Attachments* the day it dropped. Duh. Let me know if I can help with anything while we're here—like, I don't know, holding a camera or something."

It's a generous offer. I want to jump at the chance to say yes, but just the thought is giving me butterflies, and that's not a sensation I enjoy. Taking her help would mean spending even more time with her outside my volunteer hours. Alone. Together. At night, with a cute girl who loves mysteries and my dog and who paints a beautiful version of the world in vibrant color.

Is this a crush? I've known I liked girls for years now, but it's not something I've ever gotten to explore. And even if I do like Quinn, I need to stay focused on why I'm here: the podcast. Atheleen's death. It's probably too soon to jump into something new—Joey and I didn't break up that long ago—and maybe this is all wishful thinking, anyway. She might not see me as anything more than an answer to her ghost problem. The thought stings more than I expect it to.

"Sure," I agree, forcing a bit of cheer into my voice. My feelings will just have to shut up and take a back seat while we work on this project. "Thank you. I'd love to start by interviewing you about your experiences here, everything you told me back in my room. But I'm warning you—the hours will be late."

"My insomnia says bring it on." Quinn beams. How is anyone that pretty *and* nice?

Continuing our tour, we retrace our steps downstairs, where the jellyfish chandelier's tendrils of crystal sway slightly at our passing. There are two hallways leading off the foyer, one on either side of the staircase, and we head to the left side first.

"That's the Mako room," Quinn says as we pass a study with an antique writing desk.

Next is a family room with an old TV and a battered leather sofa. Behind it, open boxes are stacked haphazardly, full of tools that must belong to Rose. "The Sunfish room," Quinn announces. "Mom's going to have us tear apart this room last so we have somewhere to hang out." Nodding to the boxes, she adds with a slight grin, "We have enough gloves, Clorox wipes, and hand sanitizer to supply an army. Mom keeps a stockpile of *everything* these days."

From somewhere in the room comes a faint scratching sound, a shiver of claws on wood. It wouldn't shock me if this place had its share of wildlife taking up residence in its walls.

I start toward the next door, but Quinn puts a hand on my arm to stop me. "That's a sunroom, but it's full of broken glass. We shouldn't go in."

We cross the foyer with Waffles sniffing along at our heels. The first door off this hall leads to what must have been a formal parlor. "The Blue Marlin room," Quinn says as we breeze past. "And this is the Kraken room."

We enter a mostly empty room where an eight-armed chandelier of some brassy metal stretches down toward a scratched wood floor now devoid of the table and chairs that marked it. Water stains darken several uneven patches of the tray ceiling, creeping steadily down the walls. Whoever owned the house before Quinn's mom really let this place go.

"What's with all the sea creature stuff?" I ask as a little shiver passes through me.

"Apparently, Mr. Arrington was a navy captain and avid fisherman, both at the lake and at sea," Quinn explains. "Thank goodness none of his trophies survived."

I squint at one of the many discolorations on the wall, picturing the corpse of some poor fish mounted to a board on this very spot, forced to spend its afterlife being gawked at by Captain Arrington.

Our tour leads outside next, behind the house, to an orchard of stunted apple trees. Their bark is a scaly gray, each fetid limb bearing clusters of withered green fruit. "I haven't figured out what's wrong with them yet," Quinn admits. "They don't seem to be getting enough water, which is odd because I've been making sure they get the recommended amount. But—"

"Whoa, what's that?" I interrupt. Beneath one of the trees, flush with the dirt and so faint I almost missed it, there's a grave marker.

Of course this house would have a random gravestone.

Together, we kneel and try to make out the timeworn letters. They appear to say SAM. That's it—no dates, no other information that might tell us who's resting here. I know it's most likely a pet's grave, but I can't help wondering if it might belong to a person just like I can't help the shiver that ghosts across my skin.

"Poor Sam. I can't believe I hadn't noticed it before," Quinn says, laughing lightly to disguise a quiver in her voice. "Anyway, this is where I've spent most of my time since we got here; I thought I could turn it into a community garden of sorts— something visitors to the museum can enjoy, too."

She shows me a neatly weeded patch of dirt where lettuce, onions, radishes, and herbs are growing strong. There are tomatoes supported by cages, and expertly trellised squash just developing their signature bright-orange blossoms.

No wonder Quinn smells like rosemary and lavender, working out here often.

I hastily shoo Waffles away from a ripening tomato. "What will you make with them?"

Quinn laughs. "Nothing. I can't cook, seriously. Just ask my mom."

I don't know what's wrong with me, why I can't resist showing off to this girl. I mean, she's already excited about the podcast. I don't need to impress her. And yet. "Well, if you let me pick a few things, I'll make us something good. I do most of the cooking at home."

As we head down the sloping lawn toward the lake, the sun peeks from behind a menacing cloud; the storm seems to be skirting around us, the faint and occasional rumbles of thunder not worth a second thought.

The ancient pines and other trees standing sentinel along the shore all seem to lean toward the water, as though the lake has its own gravitational pull. A few trees stand in the lake itself, their branches bare, their roots flooded. Nothing but skeletons now.

From the opposite shore, near the tree line, a lone heron watches us with a disapproving yellow eye as it bends its long neck toward the brownish water at its feet.

Just to the left of the narrow strip of beach, if you can call it that, there's a girl sitting on a weathered dock that juts far into the blue, her pale blonde hair hanging in a braid down her back. The water level in the lake is so low that her legs don't reach far enough for her to soak her bare feet, but she seems content to dangle them over the edge, above the small rowboat tethered to the dock. She's wearing lululemon leggings and a tank top, her cheeks pink as if she just finished a run. Sure enough, discarded sneakers and athletic socks are nestled on top of the large duffel bag at her back. This must be the other volunteer.

The girl turns at the sound of our approach—our steps are muffled by the overgrown grass, but Waffles's excited panting would startle anyone.

"Are you Holly?" Quinn asks.

"Yeah. I knocked about a hundred times." Holly nods to the house, then glances curiously between Quinn and me. "Guess you two were busy."

"I'm so sorry!" Quinn gushes. "I was just showing Dare around—I hope you weren't waiting too long. You're local, aren't you?"

Holly crinkles her nose. "Not for much longer if I can help it." There's a hint of a Southern twang in her voice, almost musical. I like it. "I live with my parents a few miles from here. They run the antiques shop in downtown New Hope—now, I can tell neither of y'all are from around here, so before you ask, we *do* have a downtown. It's just one street, but the café is pretty cute. Anyhow, my parents are kinda hoping I'll find some cool stuff while I'm here." She shrugs. "And I guess this sort of internship looks good on a college application. I'm . . . taking a gap year first. Figuring some stuff out."

Waffles sniffs hopefully at the lake, lowering his muzzle for a drink. It must not taste very good; he spits everything out and shakes his head, showering Quinn and me with lake water. "Go play over there!" I urge, pointing down the shore, but he suddenly sits at my feet and starts pawing at my chest: his signal that my blood sugar is dropping.

Sure enough, as I reach for my phone to check my CGM, it gives a sharp wailing noise.

"You caught it this time!" I tell Waffles encouragingly, rubbing his head. "Good boy, thank you." My blood sugar is 70 and dropping; the walk must have sped up the insulin already in my system. Soon, my hands will start shaking, but I've got a sleeve of raspberry-flavored glucose tablets—think Pixy Stix in a harder, quarter-sized form—in my pocket for just such emergencies.

I shove three in my mouth and chew quickly, my face burning with more than the unexpected blast of summer sun as the clouds roll back. I don't mind educating, but I'm not sure I have the energy right now to give the Type 1 Diabetes 101 lecture.

"You're diabetic?" Holly asks, meeting my eyes with her bright blue ones as Quinn and I join her on the dock. I wince, but Holly doesn't seem to notice my reaction as she continues, "So is my uncle."

I somehow keep my groan silent. She's going to tell me about some relative who lost a foot due to type 2 diabetes, which is a disease of insulin resistance, not the insulin deficiency that is type 1. Anytime someone learns about my diagnosis, they tell the same story I'd rather not hear. My pulse jumps beneath my wrists as if urging me to flee the dock.

"Type 1?" Holly guesses as I take out my pump and press a button to suspend insulin delivery while my blood sugar tries to rise. I nod. "Just like Uncle L! That's cool. My mama's an army nurse, and she's taught me plenty since he was diagnosed. Let me know if you ever need anything, okay? I know I only just got here, but give me five minutes inside and I'll figure out where the society ladies keep the chocolate." She grins. "I've sworn off it for the summer, but that doesn't mean you can't enjoy it for both of us."

I smile in answer, which is surprisingly easy. While I wouldn't call my disease "cool," it's nice to know there will be someone else in this massive tomb of a house who knows the signs of high and low blood sugars, and who can probably fill an insulin syringe or mix a glucagon shot for a severe low in a pinch.

"So what brought y'all here?" Holly asks as we dangle our legs above the water, dragonflies darting around our toes. "Trying to get into college, too?"

"My mom's the one who bought this place," Quinn explains. She smiles shyly as I look her way, making me regret my earlier white lie when she asked about my T-shirt.

"Whoa!" Holly gasps. "My friends and I have been trying to sneak onto the grounds since we were in middle school. Just, like, to take a couple selfies and look in the windows. But the old owner, everyone called her Miss E—well, she was so paranoid, she had all these security cameras and stuff. I'm pretty sure she even had cops patrolling for a while after this dumbass from my grade threw some beer bottles onto the lawn freshman year. You couldn't get near this place when she was alive." She half turns and cranes her neck up to regard the estate. "This is the closest I've ever been to Arrington—my friends gave me such a hard time about this internship, too. I think they're just jealous," she confides with a grin.

"Jealous of wallpapering and dusting and sorting through old stuff no one wanted?" I laugh. There's something about Holly that makes me comfortable enough to make jokes around her already. With her laid-back manner and a hint of mischief in her eyes, she reminds me of my friend Amanda. Of home. And knowing I won't have to explain why my body stopped making insulin or how I have to calculate my doses at each meal is a big relief.

"More like jealous that I might see a ghost," Holly says, her voice casual but her gaze betraying her interest. "I always thought there was something weird about this place, and I want to find out what it is while I'm here. See, I grew up with stories about a girl who drowned in the lake before we were born."

Quinn and I exchange an excited glance.

"Dare plans to find out exactly what happened to that girl— Atheleen Bell," Quinn confides, leaning closer to Holly. "She's making a podcast about it. She used to be the star of Strange Virginia—have you seen it?"

"Costar," I correct automatically.

Quinn shakes her head. "I said what I said."

"That's amazing!" Holly says. "My friend Sean loved that show. He was pissed when it ended out of the blue." She sounds slightly distracted as she gazes up at the house again. "I don't really think it's haunted, even if it is butt-ugly. Oh, shit, sorry," she adds with a guilty look at Quinn. "Didn't mean to insult your mama's taste. I just think whatever happened to that poor girl wasn't as simple as everyone makes it out to be. People get kind of strange when they talk about her, like it's some dirty subject, when they have no problem discussing all the grisly murders we see in the news. I just want the truth."

I like Holly's honesty. "Me too. Maybe you could help us look into things while we're here, if you want."

"Dare brought all her equipment," Quinn says eagerly. "We plan to set things up tonight."

Holly glances between us, her lips quirked. "Y'all are kind of weird, you know that?"

"We all are," I shoot back, which makes her grin. "Or we wouldn't be here."

We laugh, but a crash of thunder directly overhead sends us scattering off the dock, Waffles in the lead as the rest of us each grab one of Holly's bags. The storm hasn't spared us after all; the mountains in silhouette seem to scrape the bottoms of the thunderheads as the clouds march steadily closer.

"That house better not be full of spiders or bedbugs or anything!" Holly yelps as we try to outrun the rain. She's right behind me, bringing up the rear of the group, which is surprising given that she seems to be an athlete—though to be fair, she's hauling the biggest bag. We still have to tackle the distance between the lake and house, but thankfully my blood sugar is back in the 80s, safe.

"Shhh, you'll hurt the bedbugs' feelings," Quinn teases from up ahead.

Holly grabs my shoulder, her grip surprisingly firm, as a gust of wind whips across us.

I turn to her in time to see her face fall. "Sorry," she says quickly. "That was dumb. I thought I saw . . . never mind."

Quinn drops back. "What's up?" she asks, looking from me to Holly.

"Nothing," Holly assures her. "Just admiring the grounds."

I let the others hurry ahead of me with Waffles, glancing back at the lake one last time as the first raindrops fall, wondering what Holly really thought she saw.

There's the faintest green glow emanating from the center of the lake, far in the distance. Cold swirls down my back—how can anything be glowing in the complete absence of the sun?

Forcing myself to look closer as the others rush toward the house without me, calling my name, I decide the glowing spot is a little fuzzy at the edges, like an algae bloom caught in a stray beam of light. There must be a break in the storm I can't see from here. That, or some type of rare bioluminescent creature. Weird, but not impossible. Because otherwise, it doesn't make sense.

FOUR

THE KITCHEN, TUCKED AWAY at the back of the house, clings to its shadows. Even the window above the farmhouse sink seems reluctant to let light in—not that there is any tonight.

A ceramic rooster, its once-white feathers turned a sour yellow, glares at us from its perch atop the wooden cabinets to the left of the sink as we put plates and bowls on a large picnic-style table at the back of the room, its surface pockmarked with the uneven grooves of old knife marks.

I might have spent the meal wondering who made those marks, if not for the conversation happening around me, livelier and louder than the thunder still rattling the windows. Cathy actually did cook instead of ordering pizza—baked chicken, macaroni and cheese, and green beans.

Quinn's mom, Rose, puts a basket of cheesy garlic bread on the table to appreciative murmurs from everyone but Holly, who seems to be avoiding everything with a carb in it. Well, not me. Like many type 1s, I can have carbs if I choose, and I love them—I just have to give myself the right amount of insulin.

Waffles, hidden beneath the table, scoots closer to Quinn and farther away from his duties to me, having already figured out that she drops the most crumbs.

As we feast, Quinn and I groan about Holly's love of reality TV, which only makes her determined to convert us. We agree to watch some show about hot people on a beach if she watches one season of *Avatar: The Last Airbender*—something else Quinn and I both enjoy, apparently. It's a fair deal, in that all of us are skeptical about the other's choice.

"More chicken, anyone?" Cathy asks from the head of the table.

If I had to guess, I'd say she's in her sixties, her neatly bobbed blonde hair streaked with gray. She seems to be the sort of person who's always cold, dressed for dinner in a long-sleeved cardigan despite the day's heat.

Once she's sure everyone has a full plate again, she clears her throat softly and says, "Now, I want you all to consider to-night your orientation. This program isn't too strictly structured, mind—our goal for you is to spend these next four weeks clean-ing and sorting through all the objects left behind at Arrington over the years so we can get this place fit for public tours of the downstairs." Her green eyes shimmer with a hint of amusement as we agree that sounds easy enough. "Come talk to me at the end of the day tomorrow and see if you haven't changed your minds about how much work there is to do around here. Not that you'll be responsible for any hard labor, of course—that'll be done by contractors—but it's our aim to give you a feel for how organiza-tions like ours preserve and display antique items."

Quinn, who must have heard all this already, cuts a small piece off her chicken and tosses it to Waffles, whispering, "Catch!"

I grin as I watch them, but suddenly, she looks mortified.

"Oh my god," she stammers, causing the rest of the table to fall silent. "I just fed your service dog. I just—I wasn't thinking. That was beyond rude of me. I'm so sorry."

"It's fine. *Really.* I feed him bits of people food sometimes, too. And he's not exactly good at his job; what you saw earlier was a fluke." I stop there, embarrassment washing over me. In my haste to reassure Quinn that she hasn't made a mistake, I just admitted that I don't actually rely on Waffles in front of the people who only allowed me to bring him here because he's a service dog.

The table falls silent, letting the thunder and pounding rain take center stage.

As my face starts to burn, Rose smiles at a memory and says, "Our dog Bella loves peanut butter. And cornbread. Crazy girl." And just like that, the tension is gone. It's clear I'm not in any trouble, at least not with her.

It's almost hard to believe that Rose is Quinn's mom, not her older sister or a young aunt; there are no lines on her professionally tanned face, and her shoulders haven't yet bowed under the weight of adult responsibilities. She sits tall, shoulders back, in a boutique dress with a statement necklace of polished gemstones glittering at her throat, like a queen receiving her subjects. She doesn't even seem aware of the way she commands the room when she starts talking—which just makes her cooler. She picks up where Cathy left off in our orientation speech, telling us all about the project and the house as we finish our dinner.

"I've always wanted to work on a historical preservation project," Rose admits as she stands and digs out a container of ice cream from the small freezer once we're done eating. "Usually I design office spaces and things like that—yawn." She winks at us, then turns to grab some chocolate syrup. "I want this house to be a piece of living history, a place where visitors can actually touch things, feel connected to the past and their community.

I'm hoping a laid-back and welcoming atmosphere will convince people this place is worth the drive."

"That's smart," I say, and Rose flashes a smile that makes me giddy. I don't know why I want her approval, but I do. I want to show that I've done my own research, that I'll work hard to help this place, too. "Your parents used to live in New Hope, didn't they?" I ask. "Did your mom ever make a painting of Arrington? Quinn mentioned she was an artist. I was sorry to hear about her passing."

Rose's salon-sleek brows shoot up, and she glances curiously at her daughter. "Quinn told you about her nana?"

I quickly give Quinn a questioning look of my own, but she seems to be avoiding my gaze as she pets Waffles.

Rose runs a hand through her razor-straight reddish-brown hair, then puts on a determined smile. "Yes, that's exactly how I knew about this place—my mother's work. When I saw the house listed for sale a few weeks after we lost her, I jumped at the chance." She sets five ice-cream bowls on the table, then glances around the kitchen, her hazel eyes lingering appraisingly on the original cabinetry, on the bubble-glass transom above the door to the butler's pantry. "Old places like this have seen so much, they could write better novels than most writers. That's why I'm here—to help the house tell its story. There are several changes I plan to make, but even if I remodeled the whole interior, this house wouldn't forget a thing. That's what gives these kinds of places so much personality— almost like they have minds of their own, no?"

I meet her eyes, and for a moment, we share an understanding. In my years of searching for spirits, I've learned there are certain things that will always mark a house's age, things human hands can't change or erase: echoes of laughter, late-night secrets shared, wishes made, arguments had, all absorbed into the walls. A house remembers everything it witnessed, down to its very foundation. And Arrington seems to have a particularly long memory—of what, I'm not sure yet.

I reach for a bowl, now equal parts nervous and excited for what tomorrow will bring. I'm here for my podcast first, but after hearing Rose's love for the estate, I'm also ready to do my part as a volunteer. She has high hopes for the renovation—more so than Cathy, who seems content with us simply being here—and I want this to go well for her. Still, I can see what Quinn meant about her mom expecting a lot from her. She seems like the sort of person who expects a lot from everyone.

"I always feel that in places with a lot of history, like this one. Maybe we can put up some sort of memorial marker for Atheleen Bell near the dock," I suggest as I help myself to the ice cream. I want to get a feel for whether Rose or Cathy knows anything that could point me in the right direction with my research.

"Oh, my," Cathy gasps. "That was a long time ago, and terribly sad. How do you all know about Atheleen?" Her gaze lingers on Holly, which makes the most sense; Holly is local, after all, and said she grew up with the story.

Before any of us can answer, Rose says, "Thank you for bringing that up, Dare. Since we don't have a lifeguard, one of the few rules we'll have for you here is no swimming in the lake. Parts of it are much deeper than they look, and no matter how strong a swimmer you think you are . . . Atheleen is proof that accidents happen, no?"

The three of us reluctantly mutter our agreement as Cathy starts clearing away plates and bowls.

"I'd better get to work—tomorrow's going to be a long day," Rose declares, rolling up the sleeves of her nice dress and reaching for a sponge. The last owner hadn't bothered adding a dishwasher to the array of outdated kitchen appliances.

"I'll do those," I offer quickly, grabbing a dirty plate off the stack. Rose looks slightly confused, but appreciative. "Orientation's over, so I might as well dive in," I add, hoping to prove what a hard worker I am.

"Thank you, Dare," Rose says, turning to clear the last few glasses on the table.

It takes a minute for water to begin crawling through the pipes. The spigot burbles and gasps before spitting out a wave of green gunk as thick and dark as the algae in the lake, splashing the back of my hand. Gross.

"Hey, look at this!" I urge whoever might be listening.

By the time Rose sweeps over and peers into the sink, the water is running clear. "We're on a well system here," she explains. "If the water looks off to you or smells bad, don't drink it. We have filtered water in the fridge, and—"

The single bulb over the sink sputters and dies, plunging us into a cocoon of shadow. Rose and I gasp at the same time, the darkness hitting us like a wave of cold. Though it's only a few feet to the kitchen table, where the lights of the overhead fixture blaze steadily, the distance seems stretched and distorted, the house consuming the glow before it can reach us.

Glancing up, Rose half smiles despite having flinched as the bulb blew. As she starts to unscrew the dead light, it blinks on again, bathing us in dusty yellow. "Remember what I said about old houses."

They have minds of their own. This one's personality seems to be geriatric and slightly feral, unused to company, or perhaps preferring to be left alone. But we'll have to get used to each other—after all, I'm here to see what it's been hiding.

After dinner, I take a shower in the claw-foot tub in the bathroom I'm sharing with Quinn and Holly, paying attention to the scent and color of the water, the ebb and flow of the pressure, and the temperature—all while trying to ignore the rust stains that tell the tub's age. I hope there's no lead in the pipes; that would be just my luck. By the time I finish, nothing strange has happened, but I'm determined to figure out what's been making Quinn feel uneasy in here.

Wrapped in a towel, I use my EMF meter to take readings of the light fixtures on either side of the mirror—0.2 milligauss. That's nothing. The rest of the room reads at 0 on the little machine. Maybe Quinn is so worried that this place is haunted—or really wants it to be—that she's manifesting these things herself. Some people seriously underestimate the power of wishful thinking. Still, the EMF reading alone isn't enough for me to declare this place ghost-free. I have work to do tonight.

When I get back to my room, I check my phone. My blood sugar is too high—163—so I give myself a small correction dose with my pump. Then I scroll through my texts: Mom checking in, the latest scandals and rumors about our classmates from Amanda, a few artsy pictures of the beach and boardwalk from Lindsey, and Deitra begging me to keep my gemstone bracelets on. Apparently, she's already listened to the first episode of *Attachments*, and she loved it. But I guess it freaked her out a little, too.

I lean back against the bedframe, my damp hair slowly leaking a puddle onto the crisp white pillowcases, and open the podcast page.

The first episode has a decent number of downloads, considering that subscribers don't always play an episode right away—120 so far—and a couple of comments. Most are just the usual: Chills! And When's the next episode?! But there's one from a now-familiar username that makes me smile.

KiwiLovesMango: Great stuff. Keep it up and this will be bigger than Strange VA.

I hope she's right. I've only got twenty-seven days left to learn all I can about this place, which means sleep will have to wait. It's already ten p.m., and I told Quinn I'd interview her tonight before we turn in.

I finish reading through the comments before closing the page—there aren't many, so it doesn't take long. But the most recent one catches my eye.

SewSweet412: Miss E saw everything that happened at the lake. She never missed her afternoon walks around it—before or after that poor girl died. If you ask me, she's the only one who's ever haunted its shores. She put in a bid for the estate the day the Bells moved out, and after that, she hardly left.

The comment sends my pulse racing. I don't recognize the username, and their picture isn't any help either—the generic silhouette means they didn't bother to upload something more personal. I wish I had some way to find them because this could be my first big lead.

Miss E is what Holly said everyone in town called Arrington's last owner, the one who took it over when Atheleen's family left in a hurry. A quick search through my notes on the estate's history tells me the former owner's name was Eileen Brown. She sold the property to Rose Olsen Reyes earlier this year.

Quinn knocks softly on my door, ready for our interview. My listeners will love this, so I try to push aside my impatience to learn more about Miss E in order to pay attention to Quinn. Luckily, she makes it easy to listen. She sits on Waffles's cushion with him while recounting her experiences in the house so far— we go through her nightmares about the lake, the water temperature changing suddenly and the phantom tapping on her shoulder, and the knocking at night—and then she helps me set up a digital camera in the hallway, nestling it within a fake potted hibiscus tree near the old wardrobe in the hope that Rose and Cathy won't notice.

Quinn adjusts a drooping silk-petaled flower around the lens and then steps back to admire her work, brushing against me in the process. Her damp hair smells like lemons, like summer—she must have taken a shower after me, though if anything strange happened, she didn't mention it. Maybe knowing that someone's looking into the haunting is enough to put her mind at ease and stop her from perceiving things that aren't there.

I hope so; I don't want her to worry, especially over nothing.

Back in my room, I invite Waffles up onto the bed and shut off the lamp on the nightstand. The darkness out here is deeper, more complete than it ever is in my bedroom at home, where neighbors' porch lights and security lights peek through the blinds at all hours, and the sound of late-night motors running soothes me to sleep. The silence is greater, too, despite the untamed woods breathing down the house's back. I had expected a chorus of frogs, cicadas, and other nocturnal creatures, but tonight, perhaps because of the storm, no one's singing.

There's only the rhythm of the house, popping and creaking like old bones as it settles in for the night. That is, until a stray branch scrapes along the wall by my head. Funny, I didn't notice any trees that seemed close enough to touch the walls on this side of the house, but the wind must be tossing them around.

I toss and turn for half an hour, watching through my window as distant lightning stabs the empty sky over the lake, but I can't sleep. It's not unusual for me to lie awake at night, my anxiety forcing me to relive little moments from the day, worrying over things I might have said or done wrong, like a scab I'm always picking at so it can never fully heal. But my wakefulness tonight is different. My mind is still racing from the comment about Eileen Brown. I remember Holly saying she had passed away, but maybe she has family in the area still, a relative who can tell me about her. I pull up my laptop and start searching. Eileen must have known something about what happened to Atheleen; the commenter implied that Eileen was there the day the girl died. But Eileen has no hint of an online presence—either she never did, or a family member deleted her accounts. Either way, she seems to have been quite a recluse—the house probably liked that. It doesn't feel like this house would want many visitors, preferring to be left alone.

I blink, rubbing my temples. I don't know where those thoughts came from—watching too many scary movies before I came here, maybe. I've got to stop thinking of this place like it's a person, or I'm going to make myself start jumping at every shadow.

Frustrated with my search leading nowhere, I wander toward the large picture window. Waffles, his leg twitching in the grip of a doggy dream, doesn't follow.

The glass could really use some cleaning; there's a thin film of mold growing over it. I ease the window open and stick my head out to face the night. The air is still charged, restless, though the storm has passed. Beneath the pungent odor of decaying plant matter, the lake's signature smell, the air is thick with another scent, too. Something familiar, sweet like overripe fruit, though I can't quite place it.

I narrow my eyes at the water's surface, searching the horizon for the strange green glow I saw earlier. But the lake is flat and utterly still, a sheet of unbroken obsidian glass twinkling where it reflects the silver-white stars.

I should have expected as much. It was nothing more than a clump of algae—not proof of anything supernatural. But no amount of disappointment has managed to kill the stubborn hope that rises in my chest every time I think, *What if?* Not yet, anyway.

As my gaze roams over the lake, a faint sound scratches at the corners of my awareness, rhythmic and insistent. It's coming from behind me, not in my room, but close. Grabbing my digital recorder, I open my door and step into the shadowed hallway. It's almost like rain, a soft patter of water. Has the leak in the bloated patch of ceiling gotten worse since the storm?

I shuffle slowly up and down the hall, using my bare feet to search for the puddle I stepped in when I first came up here. I can't find it. The noise continues, its rhythm as regular as the ticking hands of the old grandfather clock downstairs. There's no mistaking the soft plink of water. I just need to find where it's coming from, or else I'll never get to sleep.

The steady drip beckons me to the very end of the hallway, where the antique wardrobe leans against the narrow dead-end wall. Up close, I notice the wardrobe's brass knobs are shaped like lions' heads, pull rings dangling from their small but ferocious snarling mouths.

My right foot squishes into wet carpet as I step into the wardrobe's long shadow. Using the gentle light of my insulin pump's screen, I examine the floor. There's water seeping from under the wardrobe—no, from under the wall itself.

Quietly as I can manage, I push the wardrobe aside. It's surprisingly light; it must be empty. Then I run my hands along the wall, not really sure what I'm looking for. That water has to be coming from somewhere, though. My callused fingers roam over smooth, inoffensively patterned fleur-de-lis wallpaper until they catch on a slight indent, a seam.

There's a door here.

A door leading to a water-damaged room or passageway.

A door someone went to great lengths to hide.

FIVE

THE HOUSE FEELS STRANGELY empty without the sounds of coffee brewing or Max's video game explosions—the sounds of my home—when I head downstairs for breakfast after posting my first episode since arriving at Arrington. Episode two ends with finding the secret door—listeners love a cliff-hanger.

As I help myself to a few pieces of toast and a yogurt, Quinn appears in the doorway, smoothing the skirt of her kitten-patterned dress. She looks amazing as ever, but not like she's ready for a day's work.

As she slides into the space across from me at the table, putting peanut butter and slices of banana on toast, she says, "It's stupid that you can't be a pilot." She glances up as Waffles sniffs hopefully in her direction. "Because of your type 1," she clarifies, seeing my expression. "I have no idea if you like planes. But still, it sucks."

It takes a moment for me to catch up. I like flying—I want to see the world if I can ever afford it—but type 1 diabetics aren't allowed to pilot commercial planes. No one will ever have to trust their life to my hands, no matter how capable they might be. This isn't exactly the breakfast conversation I was expecting, but I don't mind. "People think it's too risky, just because my cells started attacking some random organ I never knew I needed. I mean, who the hell takes time to appreciate their pancreas?"

Quinn laughs a little. "I do now."

"So were you hoping to sign the two of us up for flying lessons after the renovation, or—?"

Quinn watches Waffles eat his kibble as she quietly confesses, "I . . . sort of googled a bunch of stuff last night. I just didn't want you to have to answer all my questions. There are some great type 1 YouTube channels, by the way." She reaches out, lightly touching my forearm. Yesterday's chipped manicure has vanished. "I didn't realize how hard it was," she adds suddenly, still too embarrassed about her Google deep-dive to hold my gaze. "It's cool that you don't seem to let it stop you."

We both stare at her hand on my arm as the house seems to hold its breath. My face flushes at the thought of it watching us— a ridiculous thought, and quickly dismissed. The result of having Rose's speech from last night stuck in my brain, that's all.

Quinn opens her mouth to say something as Holly breezes into the kitchen wearing lime-green yoga pants and a New Hope High varsity track team shirt, her braided hair a mess.

"Has anyone seen my sneakers?" she grumbles, her voice thick with sleep. Quinn and I shake our heads, and she groans. "Is there green tea, at least?" She starts digging through the cabinets. "Please say there's tea."

She heats a mug and plops onto the bench beside me, a box of cherry Pop-Tarts in hand.

I must look confused—after all, she skipped everything with a carb in it at dinner last night—because as she rips into the silver pastry sleeve, she says, "Technically, I started cutting sugar two weeks ago when I picked up running." She takes a huge bite. "I also started playing *Pokémon Go* thanks to my brothers. I contain multitudes, okay? But since I didn't sleep much last night, I need this sugar rush to get going. Speaking of—where are our fearless leaders?"

"They left an hour ago, around seven," Quinn says, finishing her toast. "One of the downstairs windows broke in the storm last night. Some kids had thrown rocks at it, so it was already in bad shape." She shrugs. "Anyway, they went to town because the antique desk in the Mako room got damaged, and they need an emergency consult on the restoration. Cathy also wants to get more light bulbs and rat traps from the Walmart in the next town, so they'll be gone until at least six, which means we're in charge of dinner."

Rats—like I thought, that explains the occasional scratching I've heard throughout the house, and the knocking Quinn heard, too.

"Sounds like pizza night." I add a dollop of plain yogurt to Waffles's bowl because he, too, is a health-conscious eater. "Assuming anyone delivers out here. We should probably get started on clearing out the attic or something while they're gone, huh?"

"Or," Holly says, the excitement in her eyes swiftly spreading to her whole face, "hear me out: we can have a little summer kickoff party down by the lake. Nothing big—I'll just invite a few friends. Willa from pottery, Alec from soccer, Jess from volleyball. Y'all get the idea."

I laugh. "How many hobbies do you have, exactly?"

Holly's expression falters a bit. "I've tried a lot of things since starting high school. The trouble is, nothing's stuck yet." She shakes her head as if clearing it, and looks to Quinn. "So, what do you think? It's everyone's dream to party on the grounds at Arrington."

"I don't know." Quinn wrings her hands. "You heard what my mom said about not swimming in the lake. And if she finds out, I'll be the one who pays for it."

"No, you won't!" Holly puts her hands on her hips, looking like my mom. "Like I said, it'll just be a few people. And if we get caught, y'all can blame me." She's already texting someone. "Besides, who said anything about swimming? We can keep everyone on the dock and the shore; keeping track of three or four extra people won't be that hard."

"Maybe . . ." Quinn says, still unsure, her eyes searching mine.

"Look." Holly puts down her phone. "Full disclosure? And keep this to yourselves, because I haven't told anybody else." She sighs. "But I'm not really taking a gap year. I didn't get into the only college I applied for because my grades sucked. So I *do* have something riding on this internship. And now that y'all know my secret, maybe you'll trust me when I say I don't want us to get caught either."

There's a pause in which the house creaks, boards shifting as it digests this revelation.

"It could be interesting to interview a couple people our age for the podcast. Find out what they've heard about Arrington," I say at last. It's not how I planned to spend the day—I'm hoping some of Atheleen's belongings are stashed in the piles of junk waiting to be sorted in the attic—but maybe one of Holly's friends remembers something about Eileen Brown.

After a moment's thought, Quinn shrugs. "I guess."

Waffles, sensing the excitement in the room, thumps his tail against the cracked tiles.

Holly's eyes widen. "So you're saying . . . ?"

"Let's do it."

"Yes!" Holly leaps up from the table. "Do you hug? Please say you hug." When Quinn nods, Holly almost knocks her glasses off with an enthusiastic squeeze. "You're the best!" She disappears behind her phone again.

Holly's friends show up with several more friends in tow, despite her warnings not to tell anyone what we were up to. By noon, it seems like half the teens in New Hope have come to Arrington, littering the narrow shore with foam pool noodles, a rainbow of umbrellas, and coolers of beer. Most of the people who turned up are older, or have older siblings who don't mind buying whatever they want to have a good time. A giant unicorn float, big enough to seat six, sails around the lake with half the local high school's volleyball team crammed on the back—once the alcohol started flowing, people seemed to have forgotten about the no-swimming rule. So much for a small, safe gathering with a few trusted people.

There's even a couple making out in the dilapidated boathouse to the left of the dock, seeming unaware that people can see them through gaps in the worn blue-painted boards.

A few girls stand with their backs to the house, arms linked, taking group selfies with the estate looming over them. I can imagine the hashtags trending already.

Someone blasts music from their car speakers loud enough to make my heart thump to the beat, and at some point this morning, I must have turned eighty, because I'm so relieved when one girl produces a portable Bluetooth speaker with way less bass.

The blaring music also makes it hard to interview people about Eileen, though I do manage to talk for a few minutes with Willa, a pretty Black girl who works at the Mystic Teacup, the café downtown. Holly sent her my way since her aunt was the Realtor who sold the place last time.

"I think Eileen was a photographer or something!" Willa shouts over the music. "She was nuts about this place way before she bought it. She used to come up here all the time and wander around the lake, snapping pictures, poking through the woods— I wonder if that freaked Atheleen's family out."

"My mom wouldn't like it," I agree, thinking of the security cameras Holly told me Eileen had installed. "Eileen seemed to work hard at keeping people away herself after she bought the place—any idea why?"

Willa shrugs and pulls up the slipping strap of her pink bikini—she's just come in from a turn on the unicorn float. "My aunt said Miss E was, like, really protective of the house even before she signed the contract. Aunt Mae came back a couple times to check on her after the sale, too. I guess she didn't feel right about an older lady being out here alone, y'know?" Willa shields her eyes from the glare of the sun as it emerges from behind a passing cloud. "Anyway, she said Miss E had all kinds of plans for this place. She wanted to put a stone wall around the property and turn the house into a bed-and-breakfast, but she could never get the funds together."

When it's clear she doesn't know much else—and would rather dance than talk about real estate at a party—I thank Willa for her help, but decline the beer she offers me. Type 1 and drinking don't mix well. My endocrinologist says a little should be fine—when

I'm of age, she's quick to add—but I don't know how it'll affect me until I try it. And in a new place with way more new people than we planned for, the last thing I want to be is not in control of myself and my surroundings.

Quinn waves me over toward the end of the dock where she and Waffles have set up camp with two folding chairs.

Waffles doesn't even look up to greet me; he's too focused on staring at the water through a hole in the worn boards, watching schools of green-yellow perch chase each other back and forth.

"I think he wants to apply for a fishing license," Quinn says, grinning at the lab.

She's wearing a daffodil-yellow one-piece and big, dark sunglasses that hide her eyes, but I don't need to see them to know she's happy I came over. Her smile says enough. Like me, she's drinking from a water bottle, though I assume hers is filled with something more exciting than my ice water.

"Can I get you anything?" I ask, slipping into the empty chair beside her.

Quinn shakes her bottle, which rattles with ice. "Nope, still have plenty of lemonade, but thanks. I'm not much of a drinker—not with the kind of grades I need to keep getting."

"Me neither, for obvious reasons." I point to the outline of the insulin pump clipped inside my teal bikini bottom, and we exchange a grin. Pointing to shore, where several people have started a volleyball game with a makeshift net, I add, "Everything okay? You're missing all the action back there."

"I'm fine. I suck at sports—I'm always the one who gets hit in the head with the ball—and besides, someone has to play lifeguard." Quinn nods to the group on the unicorn float, Holly among them, who are alternately laughing and screaming as they try to shove each other into the water near the middle of the lake. "They say alcohol and pools don't mix, and this is basically a bigger, deeper, more dangerous pool." Lowering her sunglasses, she leans toward my chair and says, "I'm not much fun at parties, am I?"

"I think you're fun," I insist, my mouth going dry as she puts a hand on my arm.

"Well, then, here's my next fun suggestion: sit with me and soak up some sun," she says breezily, tipping her head back.

Pulling off my T-shirt to reveal my bikini top, I realize my CGM is showing. And I don't care as much as I usually do. I'm too distracted by Quinn to be self-conscious as I take the empty chair beside her. The smell of her coconut sunscreen surrounds me, overpowering the earthiness of the lake. Her lips, coated with watermelon gloss and gleaming in the sun as she turns to me, make it hard to remember why being alone with her is a bad idea.

"Did you watch this week's *Gravekeepers* yet?" she asks, clearly not realizing where my thoughts have strayed. "Who do you think took that little boy? There's no way he actually ran away from home."

Thanks to the breeze blowing toward us from shore, I catch snatches of conversation from the partygoers about school, someone bragging about a new car, people comparing how much they can drink. Holly's friends and former classmates seem nice, but I'm pretty sure I'd be ruining their good time if I pulled any of them aside to talk about true crimes and unsolved mysteries.

But not Quinn. She gets it. Talking about these things is our way of coping with how messed up the world is.

We must be on the same wavelength, because she suddenly stops telling me her theory on the case, and says, "I've missed this—talking about the show with someone, I mean. Not many people get it. Britt does, but since we broke up, it's not quite the same even though we're still friends." She pulls off her sunglasses to look at me. "You and Joey must talk about this stuff all the time, though, right?"

"We're not together anymore, actually. That's why we quit *Strange Virginia.*" I'm amazed we've been able to keep it quiet this long. We just posted a message about deciding to pursue separate creative projects. Of course, I've seen the speculation in the comments section, but maybe Quinn has better things to do than read what trolls are posting.

"I'm sorry," she says after a moment. "I didn't know. Are you okay?"

I nod. "It was a couple months ago. Trust me, there's nowhere I'd rather be right now than here. At the lake, I mean. Er—at the house. You know, working on my podcast." Heat rises to my cheeks. I didn't know I could get this tongue-tied around someone.

Quinn's smile sends a thrill all the way down through my toes. "Good to know," she says. "This is exactly where I want to be, too."

I didn't feel beautiful when I came to the lake in a faded T-shirt meant to hide the infusion site on my hip and the continuous glucose monitor on the back of my arm, but I do now, even with all my scars showing and the T-shirt discarded on the dock. Because of the way Quinn is looking at me. It's new and strange, and I like it—I more than like it.

Quinn lets her sunglasses fall into her lap and leans toward me as a cloud once again obscures the sun. I'm not cold, though. We seem to make our own heat.

As she closes the distance between us, all thoughts of why this is a bad idea disappear. Her breath, citrus-sweet from the lemonade, brushes over my lips and makes me shiver as she whispers, "May I—?"

A scream from the middle of the lake drowns the rest of her words.

It's Holly.

"Something's got my leg! I can't—it's too strong!" she shouts before disappearing beneath the lake's green-blue surface.

Someone cuts off the music.

The other girls on the float start to panic, their reactions delayed because their heads are so clouded from too much beer and sun. They flee clumsily, pulling each other down as they struggle to be the first to shore. They've got a long way to swim, and not one of them sticks around for Holly, even though it's her party they crashed.

Her hand resurfaces, just the tips of her fingers. If she's crying out, the lake is smothering the sound.

I've already disconnected from my insulin pump so I can go after her, my distrust of murky water be damned, but Quinn moves even faster. She dives off the end of the dock, and I recall her saying something about being on the swim team.

I'm about to jump in when Waffles rushes to my side and paws insistently at my thigh, barking and panting. I don't feel low—my hands were shaking a moment ago, but only because I was about to kiss Quinn. But I have to check my blood sugar on my phone all the same, or there's a chance neither Holly nor I would make it back to shore.

130 and steady. I should be fine to swim out to the middle of the lake. But as I dive after Quinn's increasingly distant figure, Waffles growls deep in his chest.

Maybe he's confused by the shrieks and cries of the girls just beginning to stagger to shore, sobbing into the arms of their friends, but I don't have time to reassure him as I tread in dark water up to my chin.

My fingers brush one of the dock supports, and it's all I can do not to cry out; the wood is slick with feathery green algae that clings to me like a second skin. Suddenly, I remember the shadowy shapes Quinn described in her nightmare; if they're below me, I can't see them. I can barely see my calves, a flash of pale against the grime.

Holly's hand breaks the surface again, urging me forward, and my discomfort is momentarily forgotten.

I've only gone a short distance when Quinn reaches Holly and—though it's hard to tell from several feet away—seems to pull her above water with little effort. I turn around and head to shore, going slow enough that eventually Quinn and Holly catch up with me.

As we emerge onto the muddy, pebble-strewn shore, Holly recovers herself enough to snap at the guy who tries to hand her a beer, "Go home, Josh!" She then glares at the group who left her stranded; one of them managed to bring the unicorn float to shore, and is hugging its neck like a favorite pillow. "Go," she repeats, breathing hard. "All of you, just go. Party's over. The lake isn't safe!"

Willa approaches despite Holly's temper, her brown eyes narrowed in concern. "What happened out there?"

"S-something grabbed m-my leg," Holly stammers as I wrap a towel around her shoulders and hand another one to Quinn.

"Like a hand?" Willa asks, glancing not at the lake, but behind her, at the house.

"No," Holly says firmly, though she's still so shaken that she sinks to her knees in the wet sand. "More like a rip current in the ocean, if you've ever felt one. The water was being sucked down, and dragging me with it. I couldn't fight it."

Quinn flops down on one side of Holly, and I sit on the other with Waffles as the people Holly invited—and the majority who invited themselves—quickly pack up their things and head to their cars, leaving behind a few discarded Solo cups and a pair of abandoned sunglasses for us to remember them by.

I gaze out across the lake, chilled by the near miss, Holly's scream echoing softly in my mind. I can't help wondering if that was how Atheleen died. Alone, pulled under by an invisible current that caught her feet and wouldn't let go. Maybe Atheleen liked it here. Maybe she loved to swim. A current like Holly described could get the best of anyone. Maybe her death really was a tragic accident.

But then, why were her remains described as skeletal after mere hours in the water? At the very least, someone did something to her before she died. And yes, thirty years is a long time, but someone who knows what happened could still be out there.

For a while, I stay lost in thought, none of us saying a word as we sit shoulder to shoulder in the wet sand, shivering slightly each time the wind blows.

Eventually, the sun reappears from behind the clouds, and I leap to my feet to snatch an empty cup away from a curious Waffles.

Quinn sheds her towel and helps me pick up the rest of the trash and clear the dock until there's no evidence of the party. Of our almost kiss.

"Good thing I've already had my time as prom queen," Holly says weakly as we return to shore to check on her. She's staring out across the blue horizon, even though there's nothing to see but a thick smudged line where the water meets the sky. "After today, my popularity has to be at an all-time low."

"Screw them, then," Quinn says. "Those girls didn't even try to help you. Do you really care what they think?"

"No," Holly admits. "I'm sick of all of this. Them. I'm gonna leave this town behind as soon as I can and never look back."

"Where will you go?" I ask.

"Dunno. I don't even know how I'll get there. I just . . ." She shrugs, seeming lost in thought as she twists her long blonde braid around her fingers. "I'm sorry," she says after a time. "I had no idea my friends sucked that much at keeping a secret, and then I let them convince me to get in the lake after Rose and Cathy said it was dangerous. I was so stupid."

"We're cool. Stupidity happens." Quinn hugs her knees to her chest and laces her fingers together as she studies Holly through her thick sunglasses. "But . . . I have to admit, I have a bad feeling about all of this. On top of everything I've already experienced here, this really freaks me out. I feel like . . . there's something wrong with this place. The lake. The house. Maybe both. I don't know. Someone could get hurt—someone nearly did," she corrects, putting a hand on Holly's shoulder.

Feeling Quinn's eyes stray to me, seeking my opinion, I say, "It's possible." She's just starting to like me; I don't need to challenge her worldview by pointing out that the only unnatural thing to occur this afternoon was a bunch of people mixing drinks with a deep and unpredictable body of water. It was scary, just not for the reason Quinn believes.

"Maybe, but I don't think we should say anything to Rose or Cathy. We'll just stay out of the lake from now on," Holly says firmly. "Otherwise, it's goodbye internship, and we're barely getting started."

"I agree," I say quickly. I can't go home yet. If Rose and Cathy learn we broke their golden rule, I'll never get any closer to telling my listeners why Atheleen might be lingering after her untimely death. "If we leave, we'll never get to the bottom of what's happening here. But if we stay, and if the three of us work together, we can uncover Arrington's secrets—and I do think there are secrets."

"Fine. We won't say anything—for now. But we have to look out for each other," Quinn says. "And not just near the lake. In the house, too." She rubs her shoulder, clouds gathering in her eyes as she turns toward the estate.

"Look, Q, accidents happen—" Holly begins, trying to soothe her.

"That's what I'm worried about." Quinn cuts her off. "What if next time, somebody dies?"

SIX

AFTER DINNER, I SLIP up to my room despite the offer of ice cream, eager to review footage from the camera Quinn and I set up last night. At the very least, maybe the recording will show where Holly left her sneakers. But all it reveals is my own shadowed figure, recorder in hand, creeping toward the end of the hallway. I set it up to run again tonight from its hiding place, and on a whim, I also set up my thermal camera. It detects heat signatures and shows them on a color scale in real time, so a warm body appears in fiery hues of orange and red, while a spirit—if they existed—would show up in cool tones, bruise-purple and frosty blue.

My eyelids are so heavy, I expect sleep to come quickly after I finish setup, but instead, Waffles and I lie awake together and listen for phantom sounds.

The house is dark, too quiet, infused with a watchful still-ness that presses down on us, holding us hostage on the bed as branches scratch at the window like skeletal hands asking to come inside.

In the hush, I notice a smell, something besides Waffles's usual doggy musk and the Band-Aid scent of the insulin vial on my bed-side table. It's damp and earthy, like algae gathering on the surface of the poorly maintained pond adjacent to our neighborhood's cul-de-sac. It must be related to the water stain still occasionally weeping from the ceiling in the hall, as I can't find a new leak any-where, at least not by the light of my phone.

As I'm giving up and climbing back into bed, unexpected footsteps groan against the hall's worn boards, sending a jolt of cold down my back. At first, I think it's Quinn or Holly on their way to the bathroom, but the steps don't grow more distant like they should.

Instead, they get louder, stopping just outside my closed door.

There's no light streaming in from the window thanks to the heavy clouds that seem reluctant to leave, and no night-light in the hallway—nothing to help me pick apart the shadows that fill the one-inch gap beneath the door.

Silence falls over the house again.

The only sound now is the blood pounding in my ears and Waffles panting. I run my fingers over the amethyst beads from Deitra, thinking about my friends a state away, laughing and hav-ing fun without me, safe.

My doorknob rattles and slowly begins to turn.

"Hello?" I rasp, my mouth bone dry. Quinn's stories about knocking on the walls and someone tapping her shoulder race through my head as the door creaks open, and for a moment, I think my heart is going to burst through my ribs, leave me for good.

"Dare," a muffled voice says, sounding closer to my ear than is possible, and my heart kicks into overdrive.

"It's just us," Quinn whispers, shuffling into the room with Holly in tow. She swiftly shuts the door.

Relief washes over me, along with a hot rush of embarrass-ment. I can't believe I let Quinn's stories get to me. I pat the bed in invitation, and they both pile on between Waffles and me as Holly explains, "We couldn't sleep. We bumped into each other in the hall—I guess we both had the same idea, coming in here."

I feel a little thrill deep in my stomach at the idea that Quinn wanted to come here, in my room, when she couldn't sleep.

"Today was . . . a lot," Quinn adds. A faint scent of lavender clings to her, but there are things not even aromatherapy can fix, like watching your new friend almost drown. One thing I will say for the experience, though—it definitely brought us all together.

"Stay, then," I urge, hoping they can't sense my slowly receding panic as Quinn nestles her head on my shoulder, setting off more butterflies in my stomach, and Holly settles on my other side, her back against mine. "We can all suffer together."

My limbs are boneless with relief, but I feel like an idiot. I've been in supposedly haunted hospitals, an asylum, graveyards, an old battleship rumored to be infested with demons, and I've never seen so much as a phantom shadow. Who was I expecting on the other side of that door?

Not Atheleen, her skeletal body dripping lake water and reeking of decay.

But perhaps a small part of me, the part that's at home slinking around in the dark after midnight, was expecting someone else who's at home in the shadows—like whoever wallpapered over that door at the end of the hall. Whoever's been keeping secrets. Someone who knows something.

After a long morning of working to fix the water damage in the study, Rose declares we're on break until after lunch. Dressed this morning in a Lilly Pulitzer blouse and high-waisted khaki shorts, her hair gleaming in a high ponytail, she once again looks like she just walked off the set of a magazine shoot. She doesn't break a sweat despite fixing breakfast for five and laying new tile in the downstairs bathroom, and shows no signs of being ready to take a break herself. No wonder she's so successful; she's a machine. And we're lucky she is, because we're taking advantage of her distraction to do a little project of our own.

"Remind me again why you didn't tell us about this sooner," Quinn says through gritted teeth as she cuts away strips of wallpaper from the hidden door with her mom's tools.

We've positioned ourselves in the upstairs hallway, Holly at the top of the stairs keeping lookout. I sit against the wall near the dead end where I found the outline of the door, working on editing the latest content for *Attachments*, my laptop warm against my legs.

Quinn and I moved the wardrobe so she could better access the wall where she now crouches, frowning at the puzzle before her. Waffles curls up inside the deep cupboard of the empty wardrobe like a bear in a cave, watching her work with one eye half open.

"Oh, I don't know—I was just a little distracted by Holly almost dying," I answer at last. "I didn't realize we were throwing a party at Camp Crystal Lake."

Only Quinn laughs.

"What do you think really happened out there yesterday?" Holly asks softly. "Do lakes even have rip currents?"

I pull up the browser on my laptop. "National Geographic says they do. So does the National Weather Service."

"Then why didn't I feel anything when I pulled Holly out?"

Quinn asks as she peels away another thin strip of wallpaper, carefully confining her work to a narrow area that the tall wardrobe will conceal when she's done.

"National Geographic doesn't have an answer," I tease.

There's no humor in Quinn's reply. "Maybe that's because there isn't one. Maybe what happened yesterday wasn't . . . normal."

"The current could have stopped by the time you reached her. Currents do that. But—I guess there's a chance we'll never know," I quickly conclude as something further down on the site I'm reading catches my eye.

According to this, rip currents don't pull people under; that's a common misconception. They simply pull you away from shore. Maybe that's what Holly felt, but then why did she plunge straight down, her hand grasping desperately toward the clouds? I don't have an answer, so I lock the question away in the basement of my mind; we have more pressing things to deal with right now.

"Well, we *are* going to find out what's behind this door," Quinn declares, a now-familiar determined gleam entering her eyes as another scrap of wallpaper falls to the floor. "I bet it's something Eileen wanted to keep hidden."

"Maybe it's the reason she had all those cameras and security," Holly adds, glancing up from her phone. "When I went for my run this morning, I saw two extra windows on the second level that don't seem to match up with any of the rooms we know about. They must belong to whatever room is behind this door."

"What, you think Eileen hid some kind of treasure in there?" I shut my laptop, too distracted to keep working. "Wouldn't she have taken it with her when she moved out?"

"Dare's right," Quinn agrees. "It's probably not anything

valuable. I guess it could be something she felt protective of. Didn't Willa say that Eileen used to be a photographer? This might have been her darkroom."

Holly throws up a hand, a warning signal, and we all tense.

If Rose or Cathy starts heading up the stairs, we'll push the wardrobe back to cover our work and all head for my room, where we've set out some chips and other snacks to make it look like we're hanging out, killing time.

Just like what happened at the lake yesterday, the three of us agree there are certain things neither of the adults needs to know about until we have answers.

A moment later, Holly lowers her hand, and my shoulders relax. "Maybe the room was boarded up before Eileen even moved in," I suggest.

Quinn's face brightens. "Dare, you might be right. Look!" She steps back to reveal the square of wall that she's uncovered, but instead of part of the door, there are several strips of plywood hammered over it. "These seem pretty old," she says, pushing on the boards. "Could be Captain Arrington who sealed it up . . . like a time capsule."

"If some crazy old Victorian guy hid his riches in there, it'll be the most interesting thing that's ever happened in New Hope," Holly says doubtfully. "I'm so over this place, not even a pile of gold could get me to stay."

"Any sign of water damage?" I ask Quinn, since it was the dripping that led me here.

"Nope. But I'm no expert. The window seals could be bad, and maybe they let in water during the storm. Whatever's in that room could be covered in mold."

"Good thing your mom brought extra masks," I say, thinking of the box of N-95 respirators downstairs in the Sunfish room. "No matter how moldy it is, I still want to check it out. Whatever's in that room might help us figure out more about Atheleen's time here."

"Or what happened to Holly in the lake," Quinn says through gritted teeth, throwing her strength into demolishing the wood barrier.

As she pries off the first piece of board, Waffles growls a low, choppy warning.

Startled, I follow his gaze to see what his mysterious doggy brain has decided is dangerous this time.

It's Quinn.

She slowly lowers the board and extends a hand to Waffles, hurt glistening in her eyes. "I thought we were friends, buddy. Did you forget who's been giving you all those belly rubs?"

When his growling only grows louder, she retreats until her back is against the exposed boards barring us from the hidden room.

"Come on, buddy," I urge softly, trying to project calm. "You know her."

He doesn't seem to hear me. He flashes his teeth at Quinn, his gaze unblinking.

"I'm sorry," I say quickly. "He doesn't usually growl at anything. Not even strangers. He's only three—maybe he's going through some kind of moody phase." I move between him and Quinn, but the growling continues as he peers around me.

"Maybe he smells something we can't?" Holly suggests from the top of the stairs. "Like that mold Q was talking about. I mean, think about it; he's trained to sniff out low blood sugar. I'm sure his nose is a million times better than ours."

I'm about to lead him to my room when suddenly, the growling stops. He whimpers softly, sounding almost confused, and nudges my hand, asking for ear scritches.

"Here—let me," Quinn offers, moving away from the wall so she can pet my usually happy-go-lucky dog. "We clearly need to start over. Isn't that right, sweet guy? I heard you like hot dogs, and guess what? I know how to open the fridge for you."

Waffles thumps his tail eagerly against the back of the wardrobe as she approaches, coming out of his hiding place to lean against her legs.

"Wait—look at this." I lean toward the wood panel for a closer look. There's a glint of metal where Quinn pried the board loose that's caught my eye. A gold-plated keyhole. I pick up a thin screwdriver and shove it into the opening, wiggling it around as the others look on.

I keep shimmying and twisting the metal, with no results. "This works in the movies, okay?" I sigh, flustered that I'm doing such a bad job when I want to impress Quinn.

"Let me try," she offers.

As she pulls out another tool, Holly throws up her hand again.

"Someone's coming," she hisses.

I hastily shove the wardrobe back against the wall while Quinn grabs her tools and the largest wallpaper scraps. It's like we were never here. Almost.

We dash into my room and throw ourselves onto the floor, Waffles at our heels, as the stairs creak with the weight of someone ascending.

"Hey—my shoes!" Holly gasps, grabbing her sneakers from under Waffles's bed.

I should have known; he has a thing for collecting people's footwear.

As Holly inspects her shoes for teeth marks, I snatch a handful of chips from the bowl we put on the floor, tossing one to Waffles. Quinn cracks open a book on gardening and hides her guilty eyes, and Holly pops in some earbuds. The footsteps grow louder.

Trying to breathe as quietly as possible despite the rush of activity, I listen as whoever just came upstairs heads toward the hall's dead end.

The steps pause.

Something rustles softly—the potted hibiscus near the wardrobe being moved?

I thought we'd done a good job of hiding our discovery, but I guess I was wrong. We should have tried to pick up every last splinter and scrap around the wardrobe. I exchange a worried glance with Quinn and Holly; there's no time to get our story straight.

As my heartbeat thuds in my ears, the footsteps beat a hasty path to my room, and Cathy pushes open the door.

She's not smiling, but her eyes aren't unkind, either.

"Ladies," she says in a slow Southern drawl. "Next time you want to hide something, I'd make sure the lens isn't sticking too far out of the fake leaves. People are bound to notice." She opens her clenched left hand to reveal the small digital camera I set up with Quinn and passes it to me.

I don't know whether to be alarmed or relieved; the secret room is still just between us, but Cathy is frowning like she's just caught us smoking on top of old, dry, valuable furniture.

"It was all me," I blurt quickly. "Quinn and Holly had nothing to do with it, so don't—"

"I'm not mad," she gently interrupts. "I just thought you'd want this back before Rose finds it. She wouldn't be happy at all. I still remember the look she gave me when I hung a cross on my wall; she called it mysticism, if you can believe that." She presses her lips into a thin, unamused line at the memory. "She isn't much for religion or superstition of any kind, and she especially doesn't want to hear about ghosts, even if finding one would mean figuring out what really happened to the poor Bell girl."

As my fingers curl around the camera protectively, I catch Quinn's eye, wondering if she's thinking the same thing as me—how did Cathy know the camera was mine before I claimed it? And how did she know I was looking for ghosts? Or that I want to piece together what happened to Atheleen?

I search Cathy's face for some hint, but her green eyes, crinkled kindly at the corners, reveal nothing. "Now, if you girls don't need anything before I go, Rose and I will see you downstairs in an hour to start painting the dining room."

"Don't you mean the Kraken room?" Holly's voice is shaky with relief as she twists the cord of her earbuds around her hands.

Cathy laughs softly. "Silly names, aren't they? Good thing Captain Arrington is past caring if we change them." She turns to go, but pauses in the doorway. I'm pretty sure she makes the sign of the cross over herself before she adds, "There's leftover pizza if anyone's hungry."

I have much more important things to worry about right now than food. I need to be able to run my equipment if I'm going to catch anything worth mentioning on the podcast. I'll just have to hide the camera better next time.

The instant Cathy closes the door, Holly leans toward me. "You know what's coming," she warns, "unless you don't like hugs. I know Cathy wasn't mad, but if she had been, you'd have saved my ass just now."

As Holly throws her arms around me, Quinn adds softly, "And mine. *I* was the one who helped you, after all. And I wouldn't have denied it." She brushes her fingertips across my hand that still holds the camera. "Thank you. Did you catch anything on there yet?"

"Not yet. But I plan to make a habit of reviewing it every morning," I promise, though privately I'm not looking forward to watching hours of mind-numbing footage of an unmoving, unchanging hallway. This place seems about as haunted as the Walmart where Cathy bought the light bulbs and catch-and-release rat traps.

"Hey, I was thinking of taking some pictures of the house if either of you want to come with," Quinn says, closing her book. "It's going to be my next painting."

"I'll pass," Holly says, pushing herself up off the floor and heading to the door. "I'm going to try to catch up on sleep."

Quinn looks hopefully at me. "What do you say—buddy system?"

I grin. "Waffles and I will be your bodyguards, sure. Ghosts and criminals roaming around in broad daylight, look out."

She grins back, making heat rise to my cheeks, and then I have to look away as my expression falters. Maybe I shouldn't have agreed so quickly—being alone with her could be all kinds of awkward. I haven't stopped thinking about our almost kiss. I don't know if she's been thinking about it, too, or if maybe she's even regretting it.

I glance at Holly's closed bedroom door as we head toward the stairs, Waffles in tow. I'm used to being up late, and with her insomnia, Quinn must be, too. But for anyone used to getting up at dawn to run like Holly, the restless nights in a new place have got to be taking their toll.

Waffles jostles past me, catching up to walk beside Quinn.

"So, you like me again, huh?" she asks him, putting a hand on his back as they descend. "You're a little like my ex—hot and cold, playing hard to get," she teases the dog, smiling at me over her shoulder.

My heart flutters, confused and daring to hope.

I pause on the landing to study the oil paintings—it's colder than I expected on the stairs, but drafts are common in an older place like this. The Arringtons' smooth, pale faces gaze down impassively from their portraits as though they're a jury and I'm on trial. Captain Arrington, the only man in the group, is easy to pick out—an unsmiling dark-haired soldier in a stiff uniform, sporting sideburns and a mustache that I'm sure were fashionable back in his day. His wife is a blonde wisp of a woman, a living ghost, her features thin and pinched. Of course, I don't think I'd look happy either if I were trapped in a house with my ten children all the time, miles from town and my friends. Seven girls and three boys complete the family portrait collection, all but one with their father's dark hair and strong features. One of the girls seemed to have taken after her mother, with her smoke-pale hair and birdlike build.

Quinn's head appears at the top of the stairs; she must have gone all the way to the bottom before realizing I wasn't following. "Aren't they neat?" she asks, following my gaze to the portraits. "The Arringtons didn't live here long—only for about a decade— but Mom was able to borrow these paintings from a private collector. We're thinking of hanging them in the dining room once we've finished in there."

I nod, rubbing my arms to banish the lingering chill. "I wonder why they left—ten years isn't a long time to spend in your custom-built dream home. The fishing wasn't what the captain hoped?"

Quinn shrugs. "That, or maybe they all died of smallpox. My mom would know more. To be honest, before you came and told me about Atheleen, I thought one of them might be my ghost." She points to the family portrait with all the children. "These were all painted on the grounds, by the way. The artist was local. Speaking of which—" She holds up her phone, the camera app opened and ready.

We hurry outside, walking partway down the long dirt drive so Quinn can fit the whole house into the frame.

But as she raises her phone again, she pauses, her breath stilling in her chest.

"You okay?" I ask.

She nods. "It's just . . . I've never seen it from this exact angle. It's really beautiful, isn't it?" There's a tenderness in her voice and her face that I can't believe anyone would have for a musty old building full of leaky pipes and odd noises.

Yet as I follow her gaze, I see it, too: a palace ravaged by time, the cracks of its age masked by a combination of afternoon shadows and sun. I see the house's desperation to salvage its fading beauty, yearning for the love and care that went into building its proud columns and porches. I see weeks and months of careful hands sculpting trim and railings, swinging hammers, laying boards, their hard work on the verge of being lost to history. I see why people like Rose and Quinn are drawn to these places, to the stories swept under their moth-eaten rugs.

"I love it here," she murmurs, her eyes straying from the phone to me.

"You—you do?" I stammer, totally lost. "I thought you had a bad feeling about this whole place, the lake and everything."

She shakes her head, her brows lifting slightly, then drawing together. "You're right. Of course, you're right. I don't know what came over me just now. The house is just really beautiful in good lighting, I guess."

The clouds in her eyes seem to roll back as she turns away from the estate, her expression becoming thoughtful. "Go lean against that tree." She nods to the wide arms of an old oak.

"What? Right now?" I protest, swatting at a stubborn mosquito. I don't exactly feel photo-worthy in my faded *Hamilton* T-shirt and shorts.

"Yes, now. The lighting's perfect," Quinn insists, making a shooing motion with her free hand as she adjusts her phone camera's settings. "I want to remember every part of our time here. That means you."

The bugs and humidity combined make it tempting to say no, but something in the way Quinn looks at me gets my reluctant feet moving toward the oak.

I turn my head this way and that, striking poses at Quinn's urging, laughing because I feel silly, but also because I'm having more fun than I thought.

After a few minutes, I say, "What happened to the buddy system? Get over here!"

She flips to the front camera on her phone and we start taking selfies together, arms slung over each other's shoulders, still laughing. She kisses my cheek in one, making my heart flutter wildly again like beating wings. Her lips leave a perfect red print on my skin, and if it weren't for Rose waiting inside, I wouldn't wipe it off. I can't remember the last time I smiled this much.

I tuck a strand of hair behind her ear, an excuse to get closer, and her breathing quickens—maybe she's as nervous as I am.

"So, um, about the other day—" she says, but Waffles drowns her out with sudden barking.

Right away, the subject of his attention is obvious: a bird, flying erratically, far above his head. It's slightly round, its feathers shades of mottled gray—a pigeon, far from the bustling places they usually inhabit. Before either Quinn or I can react, it dives toward us, plummeting like a puppet on a taut string being yanked down against its will.

Waffles leaps high, trying to bite the bird out of the air on its descent, but it clears his open jaws by a hair as I instinctively duck, pulling Quinn down with me before covering my head. I brace for the bite of its beak or the sting of its talons digging into my back, or maybe tangling in my hair.

A moment later, Quinn cautiously lowers her arms. A bit breathless, she says quickly, "It's—it's okay. It's gone. You can look."

I glance up as the bird jerkily launches itself higher, cartwheeling through the air away from us. But rather than soaring toward the trees, it crashes into the attic window with a sickening thud.

Quinn gasps and grabs my hand as ash-gray feathers rain down on the porch roof.

She doesn't have to explain why she's shaking even though the threat is gone; I've read enough paranormal threads online to recall the omen right away. A pigeon hitting the window means someone is going to die.

SEVEN

THE ATTIC IS DIM even with the two bare bulbs switched on, just as Cathy warned us it would be. Armed with trash bags and flashlights, Waffles in tow, Holly and I follow the older volunteer up the stairs and into the musty, cavernous room. The murky glass of the sole window mutes the early-morning sun, and a closer look reveals a smear of the remains of yesterday's erratic pigeon along one of the lower panes.

I swallow past the lump forming in my throat and hastily look away. Quinn's been on high alert ever since it happened, and not even the evidence I've gathered so far—that is, hours of static silence on my digital recorder and even more hours of footage of an empty hallway on camera—has been enough to reassure her that the five of us are alone here.

Last night, as I headed to bed, she was still at the kitchen table, sipping old, tasteless tea of Eileen's while trying to place an online order for quartz crystals, a Himalayan salt lamp, and an essential oil diffuser.

As Cathy, Holly, and I begin setting up our three piles in the center of the cavernous room—keep, toss, and donate—I sneak a glance at my phone. Ever since we stepped into the attic, something doesn't feel right, like my skin is a little too sensitive, my stomach uneasy. Maybe it's high blood sugar from the Pop-Tart of Holly's I ate. My CGM app says I'm only 119, but it can be wrong.

No device is perfect. I know I should listen to my body and prick my finger to verify the number on a glucose meter, but I use my blood sugar testing supplies so little that they're downstairs in my dresser.

And maybe, if the CGM is right . . . maybe it's the attic. I felt fine before. I glare at the mountains of junk surrounding us. It's just a room. A room that's making my hands clammy and my mouth dry—but still, just a room. I shake my head at myself; I need to keep it together.

Before I put my phone away, I notice I have a few texts waiting.

The first is from Quinn: a series of memes, most starring funny dogs or other animals. There's also one about low blood sugar cravings that's legitimately funny.

The other text is from Deitra. *What do you think is behind that door? We've been listening while we sit on the beach and whine about how much we miss you. I don't care if you inherit a whole haunted hotel next summer, you're ours in July!*

Despite the work ahead of me, I smile. It's good to be missed.

Another message comes in while I'm typing my reply: *Seriously, though. Any ghosts, or did you miss vacay for a mysterious room and a cute girl?*

I might have told her about Quinn, which means the whole group knows.

No ghosts, I confirm. *Wearing my bracelets though. As for the cute girl, can I just remind you that you let a cute boy dictate all your electives freshman year?*

Whatever, Deitra texts back. *Go find that key!*

Raising the flashlight I brought to help with our search, I head toward the back of the attic, where the shadows are harder to pierce. "I'll start over here," I announce. If there's any evidence of what happened to Atheleen in this house, I'm willing to bet it's buried deep in the piles of broken toys and moth-eaten clothes. The key to the hidden door could be here, too.

Holly follows me, taking the left side while I set up a few trash bags on the right. I nestle my EMF meter into the threadbare cushion of a child-sized rocking chair, out of Cathy's sight.

Waffles watches us from what he clearly deems a safe distance—the top of the attic stairs. He's panting slightly, though it's not nearly as hot up here as I expected. In fact, a tendril of cold snakes down my back as I wade deeper into the mess.

Cathy takes the front of the attic, near the window. I'm hoping that later in the day I might get her alone, but now is clearly not the right moment. There's a lot of work ahead of us here. She pulls up some soft music on her phone and snaps on a pair of gloves as Holly and I gaze around the miniature landfill.

There are so many things jumbled together that it takes my eyes a moment to make sense of them. Furniture with sheets over it makes ghostly silhouettes among cheap-looking mirrors, an old Singer sewing machine, a broken typewriter, boxes of costume jewelry, and haggard seasonal decorations that have become homes for spiders.

I pull out a wreath of leaves in autumn shades, curious what's cushioned beneath it, only to be showered in tiny crawling bodies.

Holly screams, causing Cathy to drop a snow globe. It shatters at her feet, and the older woman groans as she realizes there's no danger.

Apparently, Holly really doesn't like spiders. "Chill," I urge as

I swat them away. "They eat other bugs—that's not so bad, right? And they weren't even on *you*!"

"I hate all bugs equally." Holly shudders, retreating farther into her side of the attic in case I missed a spider. She opens the next box more carefully, and with gloves on, and frowns when she notices my amused look. "Come on, doesn't anything freak you out?"

"Of course." I wince as I uncover a bunch of rusty nails at the bottom of a bin of Christmas decorations. Toss pile for sure. "Needles, for one thing. Or at least they used to. Right now, my biggest fear is crashing and burning with this podcast." I'm only half kidding.

Holly grimaces, holding up a lacy baby's christening dress that was once white, but has turned a vivid yellow and falls apart at her touch. "This could've been a nice display piece if anything had been done to preserve it." It disappears into a trash bag.

She sighs as she digs into her next mission: a box of old shoes. "You think Waffles wants any of these?" She holds up a red high heel, the sole worn thin. "They're not as cool as my sneakers, but he could start a collection."

I laugh at the image that springs to mind as I yank the sheet off a wardrobe. The inside contains little more than a few wire coat hangers and a toy horse at the bottom. The horse is made of metal, so it's clearly been around a while. I show it to Holly, who regards it with a practiced eye.

"If this were in my parents' shop, we could get forty bucks for it, easy," she says. "It's early 1900s, American made." Her eyes widen. "Maybe it belonged to one of the Arrington children! Hey, Cath—"

I shake my head, hoping Cathy didn't hear her. The older volunteer is making twice the progress we are, and there's no point interrupting her over a little horse. "Quinn said the Arringtons only lived here for ten years," I explain. "They would have left around 1880, before this thing was made."

"Since when did you take such an interest in history?" Holly grins. "I thought you were only looking for facts on Atheleen." She gives me a knowing look—I guess my feelings for Quinn haven't been as subtle as I thought. "What? I think y'all would be cute together!" she adds as my face turns pink. "You two are, like, the same flavor of weird."

"Dare? Holly?" Cathy calls. "Everything all right back there?"

I have no idea how much she just overheard, but she's right: we need to make a dent in this mess. So far, I've seen nothing that looks like it might have been Atheleen's.

As I unwrap pieces of a doll's bone china tea set carefully preserved in layers of tissue paper, I realize I'm still feeling off, though my blood sugar is a happy 102 and Waffles isn't giving me any warnings. I grab my water bottle in case I'm slightly dehydrated, remembering my promise to Mom to drink lots.

The water doesn't seem to help; maybe it's the humidity, which has curled boxes of someone's meticulously kept Walmart receipts into little bits of confetti.

Or maybe it's the attic itself. Maybe we're intruding where we aren't welcome.

I need a distraction. "If you could have gone anywhere this summer for free, where would you have picked?" I ask Holly as I toss the receipts and collapse the box. "A beach somewhere? To see the Great Wall? Eat pizza in Italy?"

"I . . . I don't really know. They all sound good, I guess," Holly admits, a sigh ghosting over her lips. "I just know *this* can't be all there is."

She looks around the attic as another tendril of cold slithers across my neck. If she feels it, too, that we shouldn't be here, she doesn't show it. I don't know what's caught her gaze in the deeper shadows between the draped giants of unwanted furniture, but I can't follow.

"I'd go to Japan. No—Australia. Or maybe I'd spend a few weeks in Prague. Think of the ghost-hunting potential." I force a laugh, still needing that distraction as I examine a pouch full of river rocks. The cold touch on the back of my neck lingers as I tentatively put the rocks in the "keep" pile; maybe Quinn or Rose can find something to do with them. "Not that I'll have a lot of time to travel—college, then veterinary school," I explain.

"Figures you have a plan." Holly tugs open the stubborn lid of a wooden chest that turns out to be full of hats from another decade—maybe the '70s, though I'm no expert on fashion. There's also a bright-pink princess-looking dress, the skirt made of billowing layers of silk and chiffon that wouldn't be out of place on prom night.

"Knowing me, I would have gone to the beach and then wished I were somewhere else the whole time. I'm always doing stuff like that. I used to be really into ice skating, and then dance team and prom court—haven't touched the skates in years. I'm trying to stick with running, but it's actually really hard to get up in the mornings around here . . ."

As I uncover a steamer trunk, I let the rest of Holly's words wash over me without fully hearing them, though I can't say exactly what it is about the old container that's captured my attention so fully. There are stains on the coffee-colored leather, but they don't seem to have reached the inside.

I shiver as I crack open the lid; there's a draft, at least back here where the light from the window doesn't reach. But the chill, like Holly's voice, retreats to the back of my mind as I realize what I'm staring at: papers, dark with age, some partly decayed but others still legible in places. Gently, I lift one to read.

These are letters, some dated 1870—the year the Arringtons moved in—and others from later years.

I pick up one dated 1871. *I was sorry to hear about your misfortune, and my heart has been heavy for days at the loss of your darling* . . . The handwriting gets less legible. *Your darling girl?* At least, I think that's what it says. The words are dappled with water that's smeared the ink. *I do not know how you carry on as you have, and wish the Lord had blessed me with a fraction of your strength,* the letter writer continues. Whoever they are, they'll have to remain anonymous because the paper is torn in two.

I am afraid every day. Every night, too, and I don't know what it all means or if there is any hope of escape. I've begged Father to consider moving us back to the city, and I'm not the only one, but he won't hear of it. Ever since the accident, he says we've begun taking leave of our senses, but I fear he's the one who's abandoned reality in his desperation to see her *again,* another scrap reveals. Beneath the words, in newer, brighter blue ink, someone else has written: *From the diary of Anne Arrington. c. 1874?*

These are too old to belong to Atheleen, but they're interesting all the same.

Beneath the stack of crumpled papers, which I set aside to read thoroughly later, there are a few blurry photographs. Three boys, their knees knobby and their faces solemn, sit on the porch steps of the estate. Though their individual features are hard to distinguish, as a group I recognize them from the portraits on the stairs—the Arrington children.

There's a grainy picture of Mrs. Arrington standing beneath the apple trees out back, one hand clutching a shotgun and the other on her hip. Maybe she wasn't the bored, frail creature I'd first conjured in my mind when I saw her portrait.

I carefully retrieve more photos: A girl in a lacy dress with a high collar, gazing steadily at the camera like she doesn't realize she's got actual dead birds fastened to her hat. There's a shot of one of the boys, a little older, standing stiffly in his father's uniform, or perhaps his own. Then there's a larger photograph, one I know we'll need to preserve and hang downstairs along with the portraits: all seven of the Arrington sisters lined up on the dock in the frilly, awkward dresses that passed for bathing suits in the late 1800s. Though they aren't smiling, they share parasols for shade like they're glad to be together. All but the pale-haired girl, the one who looks most like her mother. She stands apart from the rest, fully exposed to the harshness of the sun, her arms crossed as if impatient with whoever was taking the photograph, or perhaps like she's trying to shield herself from view.

"Whoa!" Holly says over my shoulder. "Daguerreotypes—cool!" She picks up the photograph of Mrs. Arrington and swears under her breath as she examines it. I'm pretty sure she's a little jealous; she was so eager to volunteer for this project, she must want to find something worth displaying, too. "These are amazing, but we shouldn't touch them too much. Mind if I give them to Cathy?"

I nod, handing over the photographs, though I tuck the papers out of sight. I don't know what they can tell me about the house—maybe they'll reveal who's in the grave beneath the orchard—and I don't want to share them until I've had a closer look. For now, I stash them beside my EMF meter, its faintly glowing screen reading 0.00.

As I cover up my contraband with a moldering cushion, a bell chimes overhead, twice, in quick succession. I flinch and glance around, startled, but I have enough self-control to turn on the digital recorder camping out in my back pocket.

"Where did that come from?" Holly rushes toward me with Cathy beside her. "Did you kick a toy that still had batteries in it?"

"She didn't," Cathy answers for me, arms crossed over her cheerful blue T-shirt from a vacation to Bermuda. "It's . . ." She glances between us, her lips pressed together as if unsure how much she should say. "That was the servant call system. There's a box just there," she points to the far wall. "A few of the maids would have slept here, and the family would have wanted to be able to reach them at all hours. But Rose told me all the wires had been disconnected."

"You've heard it before, then?" I ask as nausea twists my stomach. Part of me wants to run downstairs to the kitchen, as far as I can get from this cramped, oppressive place.

"Only a demonstration of a working system, at another house in the area," Cathy says slowly. She doesn't seem scared; she's just perplexed. "I suppose . . . it's possible a few wires were missed.

Rose and Quinn are working downstairs—someone must have bumped one of the call buttons. Talk about a wake-up call." She pats her heart and forces a laugh. "Now, can one of you help me take a second look at the donation pile?"

I shake off whatever unsettling feeling has come over me and manage to nod, but Holly waves us off, already immersed in another stack of boxes.

This is what I've wanted all morning—the perfect opportunity to talk to Cathy alone. I edge toward her, starting to pick through the piles on her side of the attic.

I've been waiting for a chance to ask Cathy some questions since she returned my camera, when she let slip that she knew I was looking for ghosts. I've thought about it since, and I can't think of any way she would know about my interest in Atheleen— unless she's been listening to *Attachments*. And it's a long shot, but maybe, just maybe, she's even the type to leave a comment under a cutesy screen name, like the one warning me about Miss E. After all, she's lived in New Hope her whole life, and she's in her sixties, at least. She's the right age to have known Eileen Brown pretty well. And if so, maybe I can get her to tell me more.

As I rewrap and stack doll teacups near the front of the attic with her, I ask, "Do you know anything more about Captain Arrington and his family? Why did they leave after just ten years here?"

Cathy arches a brow, as if surprised by the question. "I know the captain had a business partnership that soured unexpectedly. They had a meeting at the estate after which his partner stormed off, and they never spoke again. That must have had something to do with it."

She hands me a stack of black-and-white pictures of Arrington, inviting me to keep one if I'd like as a souvenir of my time here. But I'm not sure I want to see this place after I'm gone, not with the way the attic seems to be breathing down my neck.

It's not proof of anything—just a feeling. Easily dismissed. People want to *see* the paranormal, not hear about some girl getting chills in the kind of house that would spook anyone with its damp air and dark corners. And I'm sure it's nothing, anyway.

Determinedly ignoring my lingering unease, I sift through the donation bin, neatly stacking things while also searching for a key small enough to fit the gold-plated lock on the hidden door. "Who bought the place after they left?"

"That would be the Lawrence family," Cathy says, shifting a cracked flowerpot from the donate pile to the trash. "Old money. Not many Lawrences around here anymore; I think they went north, to Boston. After that, the Arrington Estate became a boardinghouse for many years. The landlord, a woman named Marilyn Adams, was quite something—she had a reputation in town for smoking and cursing, things that were frowned upon back then, but she scraped by with her few boarders. After that, the house fell into disrepair until the Tarver family came from out of town in the '60s and began renovations—they're the ones who added central air-conditioning," she adds with a small smile. "The house sat empty for a number of years before being purchased by the Bell family, and then, as you know, came into the care of Eileen Brown." Cathy's gaze sweeps over the attic, her green eyes a little sad. "This place has seen some good times over the years, but also a lot of neglect."

I'd started questioning Cathy with the goal of finding out

more about Eileen, but suddenly another idea occurs to me. "Would anyone—the Tarvers, maybe—have made or found blueprints of the house while they were renovating?" I'm careful to keep my tone casual. I don't want Cathy to realize just how interested I am, in case she suspects what I'm after: another way to figure out where the locked door leads, since I don't seem any closer to finding a key.

"Oh, I'm sure there are blueprints," Cathy says, "but you'd want to talk to Rose about that, not me. Here," she adds, producing a sleek black wool hat from somewhere and handing it to me. "This would be cute on you."

I try it on, and can't help smiling as Cathy nods her approval. She seems to be warming up to me; maybe she's ready to talk about Eileen.

"I heard the last owner used to take pictures of the lake and stuff. Is that what made her want to buy the house? Her photography business?"

Cathy pauses midway through sorting a stack of Polaroids—someone's forgotten Christmas party shots, likely the Tarvers', judging by the abundance of flared skirts and permed hair. She tosses the photos aside and sits on a finely carved rocking chair, probably an antique, and that's when I realize I've asked the right question.

"I never liked Eileen," she begins, with a faraway gaze. "But I could never get away from her—small towns are like that, you know. She used to babysit when I was little, and she was such a stickler for rules. Anyhow, after the Tarvers moved away rather suddenly, she was never quite the same, always at the lake, always alone. I've wondered for years if she was there the day that girl drowned. And if she was, why didn't she help? Or say something? Sure, she didn't know Atheleen, but how could a stranger's life—a life!—matter so little to anyone?"

"Watching someone drown would be pretty cold," I agree, a leaden feeling in my stomach. "Eileen was capable of that?"

"That's the thing," Cathy admits. "I don't know *what* she was capable of. She kept to herself, and most folks wrote her off as a harmless oddity without really getting to know her." Her distant look returning, she adds, "I saw her kill a mouse once, when my parents were out of town. She suffocated it, but slowly. It might have just been my childish imagination, but I remember thinking that she liked seeing it suffer."

"That's awful," I say. "But it's helpful to know more about her. Thanks for the intel . . . SewSweet412." Cathy's cheeks turn brilliant pink beneath her blush. "It's you, isn't it?"

She nods. "I gave myself away with the camera, didn't I? I saw the look on your face when I mentioned Atheleen that day." A new chill shoots down my spine, and Cathy shivers before turning to me, eyes wide as if she, too, senses something off with the attic. Recovering herself, she says, "The podcast is really impressive so far, Dare, but if you want to know more about Eileen, I'd suggest reaching out to her daughter, Megan. She still lives in town. Just . . . don't be surprised if you hit a dead end. This town likes to keep its secrets to itself." With that, she stands, brushing away dust bunnies that have stuck to her clothes. "It's nearly time to break for lunch. You must be famished!"

I thank her profusely and go look for Holly.

She hasn't moved much from the spot where I last saw her, deep in the shadows at the back of the attic. She's cradling something in her lap. "I did it!" she says, sounding oddly cheerful when she hears me approaching. "I found what I'm going to restore for the museum."

It's the most unfortunate-looking doll ever. Its remaining gold hair, which I'd guess used to be in curls, has the consistency of cobwebs: thin and clinging together in patches, the rest having been ripped out in chunks. Its lacy white dress reminds me of the ones that the Arrington girls wore in their portraits, though torn and muddied. There's a greenish tinge to the doll's once-white skin, and a gash in the side of its face, near the nose—a gaping cavern offering a glimpse of its blackened insides.

And, oh yeah, its eyes are missing. Twin sockets that once held painted glass irises stare blankly at me, the holes now too large to hold anything, having chipped and cracked over the years. More fractures spiral away from the empty eyes on all sides like dark veins pulsing across the remains of the doll's pale face.

"Don't you think it's going to scare little kids away?" I know she's been looking for something worth salvaging all morning, and I've had more luck despite knowing nothing about antiques, but restoring this monstrosity seems like a stretch.

"If they're scared of a doll, should they really be allowed in a museum?" Holly counters, gingerly fussing with the moldy harbinger of death as she climbs to her feet.

A rattling sound within the doll makes me flinch; the glass eyes must have fallen inward, not out, and now they're rolling around in this thing's innards.

I extend a hand reluctantly, but I can't say I'm too disappointed when Holly doesn't surrender the doll for a closer look. I can see it just fine without touching.

The letters stitched into the bottom of the doll's dress in blue thread catch my eye. "A. I. B."

"Wow. I think this belonged to Atheleen!" I shake my head, amazed that out of all the things the Bell family left behind, it had to be this. "It must have been a gift from a relative or something. She was probably too busy for it, working out with her Skip-It or obsessing over New Kids on the Block or whatever people our moms' age used to do."

Holly shrugs, more concerned with the doll than what I'm saying.

"Is that—mold?" I cringe as she dabs green spatter from a porcelain cheek.

"No, I think it's paint or something. Look, I know she's in rough shape, but give me a week and I'll make her good as new," Holly vows, smiling at me as though caring for a plague-ridden doll is a totally natural and fun thing to do.

"Dare?" Cathy calls. "I've got Megan's number for you, dear."

"Thanks—be right there," I answer, unable to shake the cold that envelops me as I turn for a final glimpse of Holly staring lovingly into the doll's ruined face.

EIGHT

THE CELL SIGNAL IN the house isn't always great, so after stashing the old papers I found in my bedside table drawer, I take Waffles outside and head for the lake. It's easier to get a signal at the end of the dock, and I have an important call to make.

Rose is halfway back to the house, apparently returning from a visit to the lake herself. When she sees me, she smiles and waves me over. "How's it going with the attic?" she asks, glancing at the house behind me. "Find anything exciting?"

I think of the papers I don't want to share yet, and Holly's broken doll. "Nope. Not unless you're into Christmas wreaths and fashion from several decades ago." Then I remember the pictures we gave to Cathy. "Oh! We found some really old photos of the Arringtons—Holly knows what they're called—and we're thinking they'd be a nice addition to the museum."

"Must be daguerreotypes. Interesting," Rose says in her usual cool, offhand manner. Only her eyes betray her enthusiasm. "Life out here wasn't easy back then, but they tried for a long time before they gave up and moved back to the city. I don't think rural living suited them the way they'd hoped."

"Dare."

I turn at the slightly muffled sound of my name, gazing up toward the sunroom that overlooks the water, expecting to see someone watching us. Quinn, maybe, or Holly. But the glass-paneled room is visibly empty. I try to swallow, but my mouth has gone dry, my tongue a heavy, dead thing stuck between my teeth as I search for whoever called out.

There's no face in any of the lakeside windows, but I know what I heard.

"That's Henrietta's room," Rose explains, gazing toward the sunroom after me. We still haven't gone in there yet, thanks to the abundance of shattered glass, and we can't clean it up until next week when repairs are done. "It's the only room in the house named after one of Captain Arrington's daughters instead of sea life. It must have been special to him."

"Huh. You'd think the captain would have been fairer; he had a lot of kids, and plenty of rooms to name," I say hoarsely, recalling the portraits on the stairs. Finally tearing my gaze from the house, I manage to swallow, giving my throat some relief. Quinn must have called for me but gotten distracted; whatever it was can clearly wait.

Of course, the voice didn't sound entirely like hers, but I guess the distance distorted it somehow.

"I get the impression that Henrietta was a bit of a favorite of the captain's, much to the irritation of his growing family." Seeing my confused look, she smiles. "When I acquired the Arrington portraits for the house, it was from a distant cousin of theirs who gave me a lesson in their history."

Overhead, midday clouds break apart, scattering sunbeams across the lake. The water, an innocent shade of washed-out blue today, dances at Rose's back, coming alive. She turns to watch it as we talk, Waffles sniffing the grass by our feet.

"Pretty, isn't it?" she remarks. "Paradise is a natural lake, though people usually think otherwise because of its size."

That means the lake was here long before people were, and will be here long after even the memory of us ceases to exist. It's not exactly a comforting thought, maybe because the sun at its brightest still seems unable to pierce more than a few feet into the lake. Like the attic, it wants to be left alone, pushing out the intrusive light.

"You should be careful with beauty, Dare," Rose adds softly, her eyes steady on the water. "It's just a mask, meant to draw your attention away from whatever lies beneath."

I'm not sure I'm quite following. "You mean from what's at the bottom of the lake?"

"I mean the dangers of the lake in general."

She reaches into her pocket and pulls out something to show me. A tiny object rests on her palm, and I lean in for a better look. It's about the size and consistency of a fingernail, the color of bone, slightly translucent in the sun.

"That's a cottonmouth fang," Rose explains. "Most snakes are harmless, but not these. I found this on my walk a short while ago—one of the many reasons I don't want you girls going in the water."

Maybe it's my imagination—after all, I don't see much of Rose, and I haven't quite figured her out yet—but I detect an edge to her voice. Does she know about the party? Did we miss a cup, a pair of sunglasses, something that gave us away?

"Yeah, I'd rather not get poisoned and put New Hope's medical care to the test," I agree, keeping my tone light and carefully watching her face for some sign that we've been found out. "And then of course, there are the rip currents."

"And parasites, bacteria, and blue-green algae," Rose adds, a laugh in her voice. She quirks a brow, the heat of her gaze settling on me as if she's just now truly noticing me. "You've been reading up on lake safety, I take it. I know it's tempting to go for a swim, especially in this humidity . . ." She dabs her glistening brow with her sleeve; this is the first time I've seen her break a sweat despite all her renovation work inside. "But trust me. It's not worth it."

"And trust *me*, drowning isn't on my list of things to do this summer."

Rose clears her throat and presses her lips together, gazing out over the water.

I guess I could've chosen my words better in light of what happened to Atheleen. Maybe she's afraid of the same thing happening to Quinn, or herself. Plenty of people don't like large bodies of water, and a lake this size doesn't feel much different from the ocean when you're standing on one shore.

"I'd better head in," Rose says a moment later. I must not have offended her too badly, because she's still smiling, though her eyes are elusive as ever, hiding her thoughts. "The glass company should be here around two, and if I don't eat something before then, I'll crash."

I nod appreciatively; it's nice to know even Rose the Machine has limits.

As she turns toward the house, I call out, "Do you know if Captain Arrington ever had a skeleton key made?"

"What?"

My face is already getting hot, but I had to ask. There has to be a way to access the hidden door. Hopefully, Rose will chalk my reddening cheeks up to nothing more than the sudden intensity of the sun.

"We found a couple of locked trunks in the attic," I say quickly. "But no keys. I figured a skeleton key might do the trick, but don't worry about it. They're probably full of moldy clothes and old scraps of paper like the ones we did open."

The last thing I need is Rose going up to the attic and poking around just to find out that I'm a bad liar.

Rose gives me a long look, blinking against the harshness of the afternoon sun. "I don't know of any skeleton key," she says at last. "I'll let you know if one turns up. That's exactly the sort of out-of-the-box thinking Quinn always does for me," she adds with a touch of pride. "Great work, Dare."

I feel like I've just passed some sort of test. As Rose's petite form is swallowed up by the house, I take a shaky breath and say to Waffles, "That was close, huh, buddy?"

But he's not there.

Deep, booming barks and growls draw me to the far side of the narrow beach, near the spot where a worn-in walking path through the bracken begins.

A flash of movement between the trees catches my eye.

Wavy brown hair. Pale skin. The white heel of a sneaker.

Atheleen.

But when I blink and look again, there are only branches swaying in a slight breeze. There's no way I just saw what I thought I did. It was too quick, a glare from the sun in my eyes distorting my view. But when I try to convince my fingers to wrap around my phone so I can take a picture of the spot where she disappeared, my hand hangs limply at my side, unable or unwilling to move.

A hint of the nausea I felt in the attic returns, bubbling in my stomach as I search for another flash of brown or white. Nothing stirs. It had to have been my imagination, a waking dream willed into existence, the result of hoping too hard for too long. It's not evidence of anything yet. But then again, isn't evidence what I'm after? The whole reason I'm here?

Waffles's barking finally unfreezes me from the spot where I stand, shivering despite the oppressive heat and humidity. He's crouched in what looks like a wild blackberry thicket, heedless of the thorny vines digging into his fur.

He never growled or fussed like this before coming here. Maybe it's this place, upsetting people and animals alike.

I kneel beside him in the thicket, thorns nipping at my bare arms, and peer into the water, trying to see what's frightened my big baby this time. A few sleek minnows and a muddy, whiskered catfish dart around near Waffles's large paws. If he's this freaked out by a few fish, he's definitely not cut out for country living. Good thing he's a city dog.

The breeze gusts, stirring the water, and the minnows scatter. Waffles keeps growling, though, and as the warm air lifts stray hairs from my damp forehead, a stench like rotten meat invades my nose and throat.

The first place my mind goes is the paper mill in town, but this definitely isn't like rotten eggs, and there's no way the smell could have made it all the way here anyway. We're too far out. Aren't we?

I scan the area around us, searching for the source, one hand on Waffles's sun-warmed back. His growls vibrate up through my arm, making me a little twitchier than I would be otherwise on a blazing summer afternoon.

A mosquito whines in my ear, and I slap it, wiping away the blood on the end of my shirt. There's nothing on the lake's surface that could cause such a rancid smell; a few feathery blooms of green algae float by like otherworldly jellyfish, but their stink of brine is something else entirely.

Waffles backs out of the thicket, and I absently pull a few thorns from his dark fur before he takes off, heading up the narrow footpath.

I quickly check my blood sugar—130—to reassure myself that I'm okay to follow him.

He doesn't go far.

Once again, he darts through the bracken until he's at the water's edge, and this time, since there are no obvious thorns, I stick with him. He stands with his front paws in the water, his ears and tail raised.

We aren't alone out here after all.

There's a body in the water, tawny fur dappled with white and a pale belly exposed to the merciless sun. It's a deer, or what's left of one, floating in the shallows a few feet away, her eyes now a prize for the fish or perhaps the forest birds who rustle their wings like fragile paper above our heads.

Her skin is stretched taut over her ribs, as if she couldn't find enough to eat in the summer forest, which makes no sense.

Could this have been Holly if Quinn hadn't saved her?

I shake my head to chase away the thought. The heat is clearly getting to me more than I realized. I put a hand on Waffles to guide him gently away from the area and the smell until we're in view of the house once again.

Seeing it doesn't make me feel any better.

I take a moment to look up, wondering who might have called out to me earlier, but there's no sign of Quinn or Holly. I scan the house's many windows, but stop short when my eyes roam over the one in my bedroom. I double-count to make sure I have the rooms right, and then do it again.

That's definitely my room. But the nearest tree is too far to reach the house even in a windstorm. My head spins as I realize that whatever has been scratching at my wall at night can't be branches.

So what is it? Something living, like a rat? Or something else that wants attention?

The intrusive thought makes it harder to breathe. I try to calm myself the usual way, with logic. Every noise, every shadow, everything has a reasonable explanation; I'm just not thinking clearly enough right now to come up with the answers I need.

My phone buzzes in my pocket, making me jump. Waffles leans into me, his warm fur and solid presence steadying me as I read the text from Max. *Mom wanted me to make sure you're alive. You should probably call her soon.*

Reminded of why I came out here in the first place—to call Eileen's daughter, Megan—I head for the dock, this time taking care to keep Waffles at my side. I tell myself it's because I don't want him accidentally swallowing any algae or parasites, or getting attacked by a snake, but part of me just wants the company.

I sit on the edge where Quinn and I almost kissed, dangling my legs over the water as I take out my phone.

My mind must still be fuzzy from the heat and the reek of decomposing deer because from here it looks like the water level has risen since the party; the old boat tied to the dock seems closer, like I could almost step into it, where before I would have had to jump down to reach it. The strip of rocks and sand that makes up the beach is smaller, too, a waning crescent moon where the lake laps greedily against land.

Either my mind is playing tricks on me, or the storms we've had lately fed the lake more than I realized.

I'm sure Rose would say it's yet another reason not to swim; more water, more problems.

Making sure Waffles has settled beside me, I put the lake out of my mind for a moment as I dial the number Cathy gave me.

A woman answers on the third ring.

"Megan Wilks? Hi. I'm Dare Chase, host of the show *Attachments*. I'm at the Arrington Estate right now, and I was hoping you wouldn't mind answering a few questions on the record . . ."

NINE

THE REST OF THE day passes in a blur as Holly and I clean our finds from the attic with Quinn's help. We found more than I realized—or rather, Cathy did—so we sit in the empty dining room and talk as we rub silver polish on teaspoons and gently rub dirt out of delicate hand-painted teacups using soft bits of sponge.

Thankfully, Holly's doll doesn't make an appearance. I guess she plans to restore it in her free time, sort of like me working on my podcast in our off hours, but I don't ask. I'm kind of hoping she'll forget about it if no one reminds her.

Megan and I made arrangements to meet at the Mystic Teacup in downtown New Hope on Saturday, three days from now, so I have some time to consider my questions. I want her to open up to me so I can learn as much about Eileen as possible—and maybe even learn where I can find the former homeowner herself.

Holly must have slept better last night, because she's full of energy as we work, asking me to tell her stories of famous hauntings—I can state the facts on them all—and walk her through some of my old Strange Virginia cases.

Quinn is clearly interested, too, though she keeps sneaking nervous glances at the doorway as though she expects her mom to appear and lecture us all.

When my blood sugar goes low amid dusting and polishing, Quinn leaps up to grab me a glass of orange juice to correct it before I have time to react. Waffles follows her, proudly wagging his tail when Quinn hands me the glass as though he personally squeezed the oranges and poured the juice himself.

"Is this okay?" Quinn asks as I sip it. "I mean, I know you can get things yourself. I just wanted to help."

There was a time when I was newly diagnosed that this sort of gesture would have only made me feel more helpless, like people thought I wasn't capable anymore. But the way Quinn looks at me when she thinks I'm not paying attention has already shown me exactly what she thinks of me, and I decide to accept her kindness for exactly what it is.

"This is perfect," I tell her, downing the rest of the glass. "I'll feel better soon. By the way, did you pick those tomatoes yet? I was thinking I could make tomato pie to go with whatever Cathy's planned for dinner."

Quinn beams. "Is food a love language?" she asks. "Because if so, it's definitely mine."

"Food *is* love," I agree, shooting her a smile. "Or I just really love food. As far as I'm concerned, it's officially the sixth love language."

"Y'all, I'm still here," Holly groans. "And still sadly single."

"So are we," I say quickly.

When I sneak a glance at Quinn, she's looking determinedly at the antique dog in front of her, the one she's been cleaning for the past half hour.

"Hey—is that a Staffordshire dog?" Holly asks excitedly, coming over to examine the tall porcelain figure. It has a mean, frowning red line of a mouth, a copper collar and chain, and raised eyebrows that give it a stern, judgmental appearance—

exactly the sort of thing someone like Captain Arrington would have enjoyed, I bet.

"You mean a Wally dog?" Quinn grins. "We have a pair at home."

I shake my head as the two of them start geeking out over antiques, but can't help smiling at their excitement. Their happy chatter makes it easier to not think about what's been scratching the outer wall of my room at night, and the inevitable darkness that will fall over the house in a few hours, changing and reshaping its familiar contours, while I lay awake flinching at every small sound.

After dinner, we manage to get the TV working. It's an older model that only picks up basic cable, and somehow the absence of Netflix and Hulu and all the ways I've grown used to watching shows makes me feel farther than ever from DC.

We shut it off after just a few minutes of an old sitcom. Holly and Quinn press in on either side of me on the sofa so we can watch *Gravekeepers* on the little screen of my phone—Holly's first introduction to the world of the unexplained.

She seems to be enjoying it, but we call it a night after just a few episodes; we have to get up early tomorrow to start painting the dining room, an all-day project.

Before I head to bed, I check on the digital camera I've placed inside a corner of the antique fish tank, hoping it's hidden well enough this time. The glass is clear enough that the lens should have no trouble picking up even a hint of movement.

Back in my room, I glance out my window at the lake, where the water is a dark mirror, reflecting the vastness of the sky. It looks empty tonight, the new moon a thin sliver of a hangnail.

Unlike Waffles, who sprawls on the bed beside me, I can't sleep. You'd think I'd be getting used to the stillness and the deeper darkness by now, and maybe I am. But the gentle scratching against the outer wall starts up, as I knew it would, so I wait with my back pressed against the headboard and camera in hand, ready to capture whatever's making that sound.

Squinting into the dark, I don't see so much as a shadow. Maybe I'm just hearing the rats in the walls; Cathy's traps might not have caught them all yet.

I might as well look over the papers in my bedside drawer, but when I turn on my lamp, it flickers and pops, refusing to shine steadily until I finally give up and turn it off. I'll have to ask Rose about getting the electricians to look at it whenever they arrive.

Boards pop and creak in the hallway, and when my doorknob rattles, I nearly drop the camera before realizing what's happening. "Holly. Q. Come on in. I want you to hear this," I manage to say after a few seconds, licking my dry lips.

But the scratching has stopped, the rats apparently having moved on for the night. I just wish my imagination wouldn't play it up—I can't help but think it sounds like they're at the window, scrabbling to be let in.

It's just Quinn at my door tonight, wearing a thin pair of cotton sweatpants and an oversized shirt advertising some band I've never heard of. Somehow, she makes even old pajamas look amazing.

"Did I interrupt an investigation?" she asks, half teasing, eyeing the open drawer of my bedside table and the camera in my hand with open curiosity.

I quickly shut the drawer and scoot over, nudging a drowsy Waffles to one side so Quinn can join us. "Not really. None of my equipment has caught anything here so far," I admit as she lays her head on the pillow next to mine. "Though that's actually not un-common. A lot of investigators have a way of making small things seem like a much bigger deal. Little noises—"

Quinn puts a finger to my lips. "Listen," she urges.

My shoulders tense, anticipating the sound of sharp nails on wood and glass. But the scratching hasn't returned after all.

Someone or something in the forest is crying.

The irrational side of my brain jumps to the little grave marker I found in the orchard. Sam. Are they lonely?

Waffles hears the wailing, too. He jerks fully awake, hops down from the bed, and trots over to the window, ears pricked up like little satellite dishes, no doubt catching nuances of the sound that we can't.

My blood runs cold, sluggish in my veins as the cries rise and fall. It takes me longer to place the source of the noise with Quinn so close, the scents of garden sage and lavender clinging to her hair that brushes my cheek.

"Wolves," I say at last. "No, wait—coyotes. They must be hunting." I think of the skeletal deer at the water's edge and my stomach clenches. It looked like a bad way to die.

"Can I stay here tonight?" Quinn whispers, her lips an inch from mine, if that. "Just to sleep, of course," she adds, as if anyone had suggested otherwise. Her mouth is practically on mine as she adds, "It's just . . . I feel safer in here. With you."

I touch her cheek with a shaking hand. I've never been so close to a girl, not like this—not that I haven't imagined it a million times. "Sure. Anything you want. I want . . ." My words trail off into the barest whisper as my mouth suddenly goes dry, but she understands.

She kisses me, her orange lip balm sweet on my tongue, letting me know I'm not dreaming. There's also the taste of *her*: new, inviting, thrilling in a way that makes my stomach swoop. I kiss her back, the heat building between us more than making up for the slight chill creeping into the room.

Later, when we're just lying nose to nose, I whisper, "I wanted to have it all figured out by now—the haunting. So you'd feel better about this place." It feels like I can confess anything in the fraction of space between us. "But there are a lot of things I don't know yet. Too many. I'm starting to feel like I have no idea what I'm doing here."

Quinn smiles and runs a hand along my back, pulling me in closer. "No one's expecting you to have all the answers. You're trying. You're here. That's enough for me. And hey, no more ghost talk tonight—not with that noise outside."

"It's better than the scratching," I murmur drowsily.

The coyotes' cries grow more distant, seeping into my subconscious.

Later, when I wake from a vivid dream about the lamp beside us flickering again as though the bulb is about to die, the room is frigid. Waffles has crawled up next to me for warmth, and I pull a blanket over us all, wondering if we missed a storm.

TEN

THE LAKE IS SHROUDED in mist when I take Waffles outside to do his business first thing in the morning, making it impossible to judge the water level from this distance. A cold front must have swept in overnight.

Something stops me from getting any closer to the shore, though Waffles whines and pulls at the end of his leash, trying to take me down there like he's suddenly got an urge to go swimming. There are shadows in the mist, dark blurs like bodies, like trees. I know it's the latter, but the way the mist shimmers and billows in thick swirls like smoke, it gives the impression that the shadows are moving.

I take advantage of being up early to review more silent, unmoving footage from both cameras and make muffins for Quinn—well, for everyone, of course, but she's on my mind as I whip up the batter with flour from the questionable remains of a bag I found in the butler's pantry.

Holly slips past me out the back door, her hair in a messy bun, her eyes half lidded and still heavy with sleep.

"Back soon," she promises, pausing only to sniff the muffin batter longingly. "Trying to make this morning-running thing a habit."

"Want me to save you one?" I call after her, but she's already disappearing into the mist.

After breakfast, I head upstairs to put on my work uniform for the day: an old shirt and ripped jeans I won't mind getting paint on. Holly isn't back from her run yet, so I figure I finally have a few minutes to look over the papers I stashed in the drawer.

I can't explain why I didn't want to share them yet, not even with Quinn, or even what I'm searching for in them as I stretch out on the bed with Waffles to read.

Something skitters along the wall, two scratches in quick succession. Glancing up reveals nothing but wall, window, and the sky outside still hazy with mist. The rats must be on the move again, though I can't figure out why the sound only seems to come from outside.

On the top of the stack of papers is an invitation dated May of 1871 for Captain and Jane Arrington—his wife?—to join friends for a getaway that July in New York, where, the letter writer insists, the weather is much more favorable in the summer.

Another, dated August of the same year, begins:

My dearest Anne,

How is your health faring since the accident? I've been grievously ill myself for weeks following a bout of scarlet fever, but now that I'm back on my feet, I find I'm longing for company my own age. And so, dear cousin, I have a proposal for you: come live with me in Philadelphia for a year, or for a span of months, if that's agreeable. We'll look to put the unhappy incident behind us and seek out all the joys our youth has to offer.

Yours,
Mary Riggins

What was this accident? Did one of the Arringtons fall off a horse or something?

A few of the papers are mostly illegible thanks to large splotches of water; I thought I'd tossed most of the water-damaged ones back in the trunk yesterday while in the attic, but evidently, I missed a few.

One of the scraps I salvaged seems to have been torn from a diary, frayed at the edges and lightly water stained. This is much more interesting than the letters.

> *Hettie was an absolute terror today, and Father, of course, took her side. He didn't even punish her! She scratched me so hard, she drew blood. But when I scolded her, she just said that's how coyotes play. Our dear governess tried to argue my side, but Father wouldn't hear it. I found her crying later, too; I hope she isn't being sent away.*
>
> *Hettie loves wild things so much. More than her own sisters. Sometimes I wish she'd move to the forest and join them. None of us would miss her. Not even sweet little Polly, not since the incident with the snake at the lakeshore—and Polly likes everyone.*

The handwriting is neat and precise, belonging perhaps to someone close to my age.

I can't help smiling as I read; I like the sound of Hettie despite the writer's frustration; sometimes I like animals more than people, too.

Cathy's voice drifts up the stairs. Holly must be back, which means it's time to get to work—I'll have to read the rest of these later. I quickly stuff the papers back in my drawer before heading down to the dining room.

As we spread drop cloths across the floor and carefully apply painter's tape to the dark wood trim, Quinn sneaks a glance at me and smiles. Warmth sears my cheeks as thoughts of last night come flooding back. Still, I can't help noticing that Holly seems exhausted, accidentally dripping paint down the front of her shirt with a roller before we've really gotten started.

"What's up?" I ask, choosing to help her with the left wall.

"I'm worried I swallowed some lake water when I went under at the party," she confides in a low voice as we streak the wall a dusty teal color that Rose chose from a line of shades honoring historic homes. "I think that lake is diseased."

"You saw the deer this morning?" I guess.

Holly turns to me, her lips parted in surprise. "What? No, not a deer—there were a couple of fish floating belly-up out there. I'm worried I got a mouthful of whatever killed them." She taps her fingers thoughtfully against the handle of her paint roller, adding, "A New Hope resident being sickened by the area's natural beauty would really drive the tourists away, wouldn't it? Oh, wait." She rolls her eyes. "There aren't any to begin with."

Remembering Rose's talk of parasites and bacteria, I wince. "You should keep an eye on how you're feeling. Drink lots of water," I suggest, my mom's solution to everything.

She nods and dutifully heads to the kitchen. When she comes back, I take a break to rest my arm and gaze around at the progress we're making. Cathy and Quinn are working on the wall opposite ours, which leaves two to go. The eight-armed chandelier has been moved to a safe location by Rose while we paint, so the only light comes from two tall windows at the back of the room. It gently illuminates the fresh stains that dapple the ceiling in a strange, sort of artful pattern, like a watercolor made on a soaked canvas.

Quinn sets down her paint roller, glancing up; she's noticed it, too.

"I should get my mom," she says to Cathy, biting her lower lip as she takes another look. "I don't remember all this water damage being here yesterday."

"Oh, no!" Cathy sighs, now joining us in examining the ceiling. "You're right, Quinn. You girls keep working; I'll go tell her. She said she didn't want interruptions this morning—she'll be madder than a long-tailed cat in a room full of rocking chairs when she sees this . . ."

She pauses at the threshold to the kitchen, taking another look at the damaged ceiling over her shoulder. Just as she did on her way out of my room a few days ago, she shapes the sign of the cross over herself. I imagine she's praying for strength in dealing with the problems that seem to be never-ending in a house of this size and age.

"It must be from last night's storm," I say as Cathy disappears.

Holly turns to me and frowns. "Can't be. I was up most of the night, and I never heard a storm. Just the coyotes."

"You could've come to my room, like before," I tell her.

Holly glances quickly between me and Quinn, so fast I almost miss it. "Uh-huh," she says with a faint grin. "I appreciate it, but I'm good. I watched some more of that *Gravekeepers* show on my phone instead of catching up on *The Bachelor*—y'all might have made me a fan."

Quinn smiles shyly at me, then reaches for my hand. "Glad

to hear it," she tells Holly, her eyes still on me. "We know a good thing when it comes our way." She drops my hand and goes back to painting, but I'm so busy wondering if she'll want to stay with me again tonight, to kiss me again, that it catches me off guard when paint splatters my face and hair.

"Ooh, the teal spots look good with your blue," Holly giggles.

She stands with her arms crossed in a poor attempt to hide teal-covered fingertips, one of the paint pans at her feet and mischief in her eyes.

"It's like that, huh?" I laugh, flicking a few drops in her direction. She shrieks and dances out of the way.

Quinn has her back to us, resolutely continuing to paint—but not for long. Holly and I ambush her together, flecking her glossy hair with teal.

She whirls around, her eyes wide, apparently torn between annoyance and wanting to join in. I run a hand through the paint and dab some on the end of her nose, then onto her cheeks, making little freckles. "Grab your phone and take a look," I urge her with a giggle as she feels the paint on her face, smearing it around. "Don't ruin it—they're cute!"

Quinn's lips twitch on the verge of a smile as she swipes a glob of teal onto my cheek, her finger sketching a heart. "This is cuter."

"Y'all are going to give me a stomachache with all the sweetness!" Holly groans, showering us in paint.

We fire back, ducking and covering using the drop cloths, grabbing paint pans to use as shields. It's clear no one's going to hire Holly and me to work on another historic home any time soon, least of all together—we bring out each other's wild side.

We laugh ourselves breathless, Quinn snapping photos of our

misadventure until we're tired and covered in cracked, drying paint. Quinn's glasses are so thick with teal that for once, she can see better without them.

Waffles looks like a different dog with his new spots.

From somewhere upstairs comes a bang—a door, I think, opening or closing. It's enough to startle Quinn into taking a good look around, her face shadowed with worry. I'm sure she's thinking of her mom's disapproval if she comes in here to inspect the damage and sees us covered in paint meant for the walls.

"Don't worry," I say quickly, the warmth that had filled the room quickly retreating in the absence of our laughter. "We'll get this cleaned up—we know how much this work means to you. We'd better clean ourselves up first, though."

Luckily, Cathy seems to be having a hard time finding Rose; no one is walking down the stairs, which means we still have a chance to tidy up before anyone realizes how much we've been messing around.

I don't think I want to see Rose angry.

We head up to our rooms to quickly shower and change. Holly, who's collected the most paint from head to toe, goes first by unspoken agreement.

The shower cuts on, the pipes gurgling reluctantly as Quinn heads to her room, and I hurry into mine, hoping for a few minutes to go through more of the old papers.

Quinn's scream echoes through the hall.

I race out of my room, Waffles on my heels. Quinn is in the hallway, her back against the wall like it's all that's keeping her standing as she gazes into her room.

The water in the shower keeps pounding the ceramic floor

of the tub; Holly must not have heard anything.

As I get closer, I realize Quinn is crying, and my heart starts beating double at the sight. She hastily wipes her paint-speckled cheeks with the back of her hand and leans into my shoulder. "Someone dumped my watercolors all over the carpet," she says softly, clenching her hands into fists at her side. She wants to fight whatever's made her so afraid, and I admire her for it. "And they wrote—well, go see for yourself."

Goose bumps rise along my arms at her tone, but I start to do as she suggests. Waffles hangs back against the wall with Quinn, and lays his head on her lap when she sinks to the floor.

I peer inside, cringing at the reaction I can imagine Rose having to the rainbow puddle on Quinn's once-white carpet. Metallic tubes of paint are scattered everywhere, a professional artist's watercolors that I'm sure cost Quinn a small fortune, shriveled and empty with their paste all squeezed out. Water soaks the rug, mixing the paint colors, though there's no sink in the room and no leak from the ceiling; it's like someone took a bucket and dumped it in the middle of everything. On the wall above her dresser, where her *Gravekeepers* poster proudly hung, someone has written in big, angry red letters:

THE GIRLS ARE NEVER GONE

It must be paint, given the mess on the floor, but whoever wrote this chose a color dark enough to resemble dried blood. More puzzling is the message itself: What girls? We're completely alone, in the middle of nowhere, and we're the only girls here. Yet what else could it mean? And why does my heart start beating out of control every time I read it again, hoping to spot something more that will help it make sense?

A few minutes later, Holly emerges from the bathroom. The three of us crowd Quinn's doorway, no one really interested in entering the room until we figure out who was having fun with paint at the same time we were. Waffles hangs back in the hallway behind us, tail between his legs, seeming more wary of the room than we are.

Holly looks thoughtfully at the lab as he paces and pants. "Could Waffles have—?"

"He was with us the whole time," Quinn says quickly, and I love how readily she jumps to his defense. "I never saw him leave the room for a second."

"And," I add pointedly, "he hasn't exactly mastered the art of writing."

"It can't have been any of us," Quinn says firmly, chipping bits of paint off her glasses. "Everything was fine when I went downstairs, and I met you on the way down, Dare. Holly was in the kitchen coming in from her run—she came straight to the dining room with us to paint."

"So that leaves Rose or Cathy—but this is Rose's house, and I'm pretty sure if she saw this mess, she'd break off her French tips punching whoever did this to her property," I say as Quinn nods her agreement.

"Cathy, then?" Holly asks, frowning as she thinks it over. "Why would she want to do . . . this?" She gestures at the wall. "Whatever this even is."

"I don't know. Maybe it's a warning?" I suggest weakly, wiping my clammy hands on my paint-smeared shorts.

"That makes no sense," Quinn argues, her eyes still lingering on the message. "Why would Cathy paint on the walls instead of talking to us herself? And what could this even be warning us about?"

"Well, whatever it means, Cathy has to be the one," I insist. "Rose wouldn't destroy her own property or scare Quinn, and we know it wasn't any of us. We should probably tell her before this escalates any further."

Close to my ear, someone laughs, breathy and a little frantic.

"What was that?" I ask, rubbing the top of my ear. That kind of tickled.

"I didn't say anything," Holly says, arching a brow. "I guess you're right, it has to be Cathy. She's the only one who had time, and—"

"I don't think that sweet woman did anything," Quinn says, staring at the paint-spattered glasses in her hands. "You're both ignoring the obvious. I've been telling you this house is haunted—a spirit did this. I didn't listen when it tapped me on the shoulder in the bathroom, so now it's trying to tell us something another way." She takes a breath and glances up at me, hope shining in her gaze. "Dare, can I help you grab your stuff—your recorder, the meters? Maybe we can do an EVP session before we clean all this up, in case the spirit has anything else they'd like to say."

"EVP?" Holly looks slightly lost.

"Electronic voice phenomena," I answer automatically. "Ghostly voices we sometimes can't hear with our ears, captured on a digital recorder or other audio device." I can't take my eyes off Quinn as I explain. There's no way she's going to spend another night in this house if I don't show her there's nothing to fear— nothing incorporeal, anyway. "Look, Q, I can go get my gear if you really want, but we won't find anything. Because . . . there are no ghosts here. Or anywhere."

Quinn stares at me. "What?" she asks softly.

"Trust me. I've looked. I've asked them to hit me, even. They're not real," I clarify. "Rose is right about that." It feels so good to be honest that even as something in Quinn's expression shifts, I can't hold back. "When we die, we die. Ride's over. That's all there is—and it sucks. It really sucks. When I think too much about the people I miss, and never seeing them again, it's so final that sometimes I don't feel like I can get through the day. But the *good* news is, there's nothing in your room that science and misguided human intentions, probably Cathy's in this case, can't explain."

"Says the girl wearing crystal bracelets," Quinn says slowly, her face falling as my words sink in.

"Just a gift from a friend."

Why are Quinn's eyes glistening like that? I just wanted to take away her fear. And now she looks so sad that I wish I had bit my tongue and grabbed my equipment like she asked.

"So Strange Virginia . . . ?" she asks tersely. "*Attachments* . . . ?"

I did that—made her voice tight, her eyes damp. And since I can't eat my words, I answer the rest of her unspoken question as honestly as I can. "Look, ghost hunting is part of my life. I think it comes from living with anxiety; I'm always curious, and I crave the truth about everything. I want answers, just like you. Those answers just happen to have natural, scientific causes, no matter how much I hope I'll find just one totally unexplainable thing.

Because that one thing would mean all the other paranormal stories I love have a chance, even if it's a small one, of being real."

"Ghosts *would* make the world a lot more interesting." Holly's gaze darts between us like she senses a storm coming, one she has no idea how to shelter from.

Quinn takes another deep breath, and doesn't say anything for a few minutes. The rainbow puddle in her room seems to be spreading as water soaks into the carpet and floor.

"I appreciate what you're saying," she says at last, choosing every word with care. "I think what's bothering me is that when I told you everything I'd experienced here, you acted like you understood. Like you believed."

"I want to believe. I want that more than anything—I've spent my life wanting it. Chasing it, even when I thought it was hopeless," I say as Quinn's face becomes a blur. "I still am, or I wouldn't be here. And I never lied to you."

"No, maybe not. But it feels like you did." Quinn pulls her hand away and stands. "Look, I've got to clean all this up before my mom sees."

"I'll help," I declare, leaping to my feet as my phone buzzes with an alarm: my blood sugar is rising. Good old stress.

"Me too," Holly says.

But Quinn hastily shuts her door in our faces. "Thanks," her muffed voice says. "But I'd rather do this on my own. If you two can clean up downstairs, that'd be great."

We stand in silence for a moment. "Sorry." Holly puts a hand on my shoulder. "And I'm sorry I didn't hear anything while Quinn's room was getting trashed. I'm the worst ghost hunter ever."

I laugh, though it's short-lived. "I can point you to several TV shows that will change your mind about that."

Holly smiles. "Well, if you say so. You're the expert." She says it so casually, but an expert is the last thing I feel like right now. Quinn's words made me feel like a fraud.

"You sure you're okay?" Holly presses, studying me with a slight frown. I nod. "All right. Then I'll start on stuff downstairs. You go shower." She sniffs the air and scrunches her nose. "No offense, but you stink."

I take a last look at Quinn's closed door. It feels so final. Like we're over before we ever really started.

She's so practical, so analytical in her thinking when she breaks down a *Gravekeepers* case with me. She mixes ratios of chemicals to feed her garden and paints shadow and light in hyperrealistic precision. She's got her future all planned out; she's got an enviable GPA—surely someone so smart can see that clinging to a belief in the supernatural, something no one has ever been able to prove, will only cause hurt and disappointment.

Look what it's done here.

I have no ghost, no earth-shattering podcast material—and no girl.

I came here looking for something I'll never find, and instead, I met Quinn. And now that I know her, I don't want to stop. But I guess that's not entirely up to me.

"I hate you," I tell the house and its ordinary, empty hallway, feeling like an idiot as the words leave my mouth. "Next time you want to pick on someone, I'm right here."

ELEVEN

WITH ITS LARGE, HAND-PAINTED sign—a witch's hat fitted on top of a teacup and saucer—the Mystic Teacup stands proudly apart from the rest of New Hope's depressing downtown.

It's flanked by an empty storefront on one side—FOR LEASE, with a sign taped to the glass advertising a farmer's market a few blocks away with Hanover tomatoes and the best ham biscuits in the state—and a small, cluttered antiques shop on the other. As Quinn parallel parks her silver Lexus against the curb amid a sea of pickup trucks and aging sedans, I peer inside the antiques place, hoping for a glimpse of Holly's parents.

The store is dark inside, and there's a sign on the door with a return date over a week from now; that's when I remember Holly said her parents are somewhere in New England, visiting family and attending a trade show.

"Thanks for the ride," I tell Quinn, still in the driver's seat, as I lean against her car. It's hard to believe I've only been at Arrington Estate for a week, but already I've kissed a pretty girl and maybe almost started dating her, and now I'm about to walk into my first exclusive podcast interview. If I'd gone to the beach instead like my friends wanted, all I'd have to show for it would be a new tattoo and a sunburn.

I check my hot-pink lipstick using the camera on my phone

and smooth the stubborn hair that took way too long to straighten. But for once, I don't adjust the sleeve of my white jersey-knit dress to hide the CGM sensor on my left upper arm. Whether it's showing or not, Quinn and Holly don't look at me any differently—it's made me realize my friends back home probably don't, either. I've spent too much time since my diagnosis trying to conform to somebody else's standard of beauty, and I have nothing to be ashamed of.

"You look great," Quinn declares, lowering her sunglasses a fraction so her eyes can meet mine. "And remember, after you and Megan are seated, I'll come in and sit a safe distance away. We've got this. You've got this," she amends, holding up her hand to high-five me like we're bros who never made out on my bed after midnight.

I sigh, but I high-five her and turn to walk into the café, my digital recorder making the small bag over my shoulder a little heavier than usual.

Holly was supposed to be here, too, which would have made the car ride into town less awkward. Quinn and I haven't spent any time alone since our fight outside her room a few days ago, and I've been hanging out with Holly—watching reality TV marathons and failing at yoga, mostly. She was looking forward to showing us both around town, so I was surprised when she dipped out last minute. She's gotten used to clean eating, whatever that means, and blamed her sudden stomachache on Cathy's rich Southern cooking. I left Waffles to keep her company, trusting my CGM to tell me if my blood sugar starts dropping.

I'm not sure if Quinn told Rose my suspicions about Cathy—I'm guessing not, as renovations have carried on like normal, and

Cathy has treated us the same as ever—but again, we haven't exactly been alone for me to ask.

As I reach for the door, a text comes through: *Relationships are overrated. Forget about Q and crush it today!* Deitra says, accompanied by multihued fist bump emojis.

If only it were that easy.

The bells above the door remind me of wind chimes, loud and musical as I walk in. The rich scent of fresh coffee beans mingles with the smoky-sweet aroma of vanilla and sandalwood incense, flooding my senses. Small wooden tables are arranged between a wide assortment of lush potted plants; from Quinn's rambles about gardening, I can name a few of the succulents and recognize the fiddle-leaf fig trees in woven baskets. Overhead, twinkly lights have been strung across the eggplant-colored ceiling, giving the feeling of a starry night sky.

Stepping in here is like wandering into an enchanted forest where clouds of coffee gently perfume the air. There's no other way to say it: the Mystic Teacup is totally Insta-worthy. It's the most modern place I've seen in a town that otherwise seems stuck in another decade.

About half the tables are occupied, and I get more glances than I'd like as I make my way through them all to reach the back, where an unsmiling woman in her early fifties sits alone, scrolling through her phone.

I know they're only staring because of my bright-blue hair, but in DC, most people didn't really give the color a second glance. Personally, I think my hair makes me look more at home in this oddly magical place.

"Megan?" I ask to get the woman's attention. She's clearly just come from work despite it being a Saturday morning, dressed in cheerful flowery nurse's scrubs. When she glances up warily, I put on my biggest smile and extend a hand, glad that Holly was feeling well enough last night to paint my nails for me.

"Hi, Dare." She has a firm handshake, though her skin is clammy, and a tremor passes through her arm before we drop hands.

"Don't be nervous," I practically plead, giving her another smile. "It'll make *me* nervous! This interview will be really straightforward; I just want to ask you some questions about Arrington Estate and how your mom came to own it, just like we discussed on the phone."

After we make our introductions, I insist on buying her coffee and something to eat. The cool barista on duty recommends their favorite pastry, a cheese Danish that's almost as big as my face, so I buy two of those along with a caramel latte for me and a large coffee, extra hot with two raw-sugar packets for Megan. I'm about to carry my bounty to our table when I notice Quinn has slipped in and seated herself near the front, pretending to be immersed in a book.

She's almost nailed the art of hiding in plain sight, except that she chose to wear a collared dress with a pattern of UFOs beaming up little shadow people for today's mission.

I try to guess what her favorite drink might be. "Help!" I beg the cool barista in a whisper, giving them a basic rundown of the situation. We decide together on an iced white mocha with whipped cream for Quinn, and the barista promises to bring it to her table. I tip extra and return to Megan's table, sitting opposite her so I'm facing the door.

"Oh, this is too much!" Megan protests, eyes widening when she pulls her giant Danish out of the bag. "But . . ." A smile breaks over her thin lips, and she admits, "These are the best in the state. I'm guessing you haven't tried them?"

I take a bite as I set up my recorder, and she wasn't kidding. I'm willing to give myself a lot of insulin for something this good.

Quinn catches my eye and raises her cup in thanks, having received my gift, and my heart beats double as we start the interview.

"Mom bought the Arrington place after it went up on the market for cheap while I was away at nursing school," Megan explains between bites. "She'd always loved the area; she would go for nature walks at the lake and take pictures of all the wildlife out there—deer, coyotes, rabbits, all sorts of waterfowl—to sell online in her shop. But actually buying the house was a midlife crisis, if you ask me; my parents had just gone through a bitter divorce, and Mom had big plans to turn the place into a gorgeous B and B, a place where tourists and her future grandbabies could play and stay all summer."

I nod encouragingly, taking small, careful sips of my latte; Megan still looks like a wrong word or look could send her barreling for the door.

"Well, after nursing school, I got married and wanted to move closer to home when we were ready to start having kids. Lisa and I settled in the city, about an hour from New Hope and Arrington, and had our first daughter." She smiles, but it quickly fades. "When she was a little older, maybe two or three, we brought her out to the estate for a visit to Grandma's, and . . . things started happening almost right away." Finished with her pastry, Megan balls the napkin up in her hands, twisting it until it tears.

"What kind of things?" I press gently. I give her another disarming smile.

"*Strange* things. But that's not what . . ." Megan reaches for her coffee, glancing over her shoulder toward the door; I'm not sure if she's worried who might be listening, or if she's looking for her way out.

"Are you all right? Can I get you something else—some water?" I ask. She's gone pale beneath her makeup; whatever memory she's holding back must be a powerful one, having such an effect on her years later.

Megan shakes her head, and I finally realize what she's watching: a younger girl and her two friends are inching closer to our table, all nervous giggles, bumping into one another. The one in front clutches a notebook to her chest, and she seems to be shaking. Maybe they're about to ask us for food money, or a ride home.

"Um, excuse me," one of the boys with her says as they continue their slow approach. "You're that girl from Strange Virginia, right?" He nods to the girl. "My friend is, like, your biggest fan. Would you sign her notebook?"

It takes me a minute to do more than stare. But when I recover myself, I beam at the girl. Her face turns red as she hands over the notebook, and I wonder if I'm supposed to apologize for making her blush, or thank her for watching, or what. This has happened a few times in DC, and once when I visited my cousin in Richmond, but never in such a small town.

"What's your name?" I ask.

"Ash," she says, following it up with a nervous giggle.

We chat for a minute or two while I write a message in the

front of her book, which turns out to be full of her poems and ideas. I sketch hearts and encouraging words on a few of them while the three friends look on with big, nervous grins.

Across the café, Quinn is watching over the top of her book, her lips hidden but her eyes smiling for her.

"You're really something," Megan says when they're out of earshot.

I glance up sharply from grabbing a bite of my pastry, unsure what she means by that, and find that she's regarding me with a sort of motherly pride that makes her blue eyes shine.

She leans across the table toward me, hovering just above the recorder. She still looks too pale, like she's going to be sick, but there's a determined set to her jaw now.

"I haven't told anyone but Mom and my partner about what happened on that visit, but I like you, so I'll say it—just once. I was giving Anna a bath before bed; it must have been around seven or eight at night. Anyway, I'd filled the old claw-foot tub upstairs with warm water, and Anna was splashing around with her little boats. I turned around for two seconds—just long enough to grab the baby shampoo—when I heard the faucet turn on. Anna couldn't have done it; the knob was stiff, hard to turn, and besides, I don't think she could reach." She pauses for a breath, steeling herself against what's to come. "The faucet was pouring murky lake water into her bath. All this green-brown filth . . ."

I'm not about to mess this up the way I did with Quinn. People open up more when you validate their experiences. I put a hand on the table near hers and murmur, "I would have been scared, too. And so grossed out."

"I was—well, more the latter at first. It was gross, but the estate is on well water, and it's so close to the lake," Megan explains, swallowing audibly. Maybe she's a bit more like me than I thought, looking for other answers before jumping to the paranormal. "But what happened later that night was too much for me. Around midnight, Lisa and I were getting ready to sleep, so I peeked into the bedroom where we'd set up Anna's little bed. She was there, giggling at something over her head—somehow, she'd gotten her toy sailboats out of the bathroom, and they were spinning in midair. When I screamed, they fell onto the bed, and Anna started crying. She said, 'You made her go away.' And when I asked who, she said, 'The skeleton girl.' But there were only the two of us in that room."

Megan drains the rest of her coffee.

"So what did you do?" I ask, trying to keep her on track, and—I'll admit—so swept up in her story that my palms are slick against the table. This is one of those moments where I love what I do, the rush of hearing a new story that almost makes me believe.

"We didn't sleep, that's for sure." Megan laughs, short and bitter. "After that, I pretty much refused to take Anna back there, even during the day—we would bring Mom to us instead. I think it really hurt Mom's feelings that we wouldn't come visit, but I didn't feel safe bringing Anna around, and honestly?" She sighs, as if it costs her something to admit, "I was too creeped out to stay there myself."

"Do you have any idea what Anna meant when she said 'the skeleton girl'?" I ask. Children sometimes say the freakiest things, after all—see a million examples on Reddit threads around Halloween.

Megan drops her voice even lower; thank goodness my recorder is sensitive enough to pick up most sounds. "I know about the death of Atheleen Bell, and how she looked when they pulled her from the lake—that's where my mind went, though I didn't ask Anna about it after that night. I didn't want her to start having nightmares. Anyway, when Atheleen drowned . . . it was pretty hush-hush. But it wasn't like I believed in ghosts or curses or any of that nonsense." She rubs her temples, like even now her experience battles against the logical side of her brain. "Still, I tried to convince Mom to move out. I said it was too much house for her, but she wouldn't listen. I tried everything—even fixed up a bedroom in our house so she could live with us and be more involved with her grandbabies." She looks tired as she continues, "But Mom wouldn't budge, and I had to watch the place fall apart around her."

"That must have been really stressful," I say, suddenly thinking of my mom, envisioning a day in the distant future when she might not listen to me and Max even though she needs help. Now that's a terrifying thought.

Sipping her nearly empty coffee, Megan adds thoughtfully, "Sometimes Mom would say she had a responsibility to stay at that house." Again, her laugh is brief, humorless. "Can you imagine? It's like the house had its hooks in her, and she was its puppet. When she started showing signs of dementia, I visited more often, and begged harder for her to let the place go. She'd tell me sometimes that she needed to keep the poor girl company."

"Do you think she meant Atheleen?" I ask, thinking of Quinn's insistence that someone had tapped her on the shoulder in the shower.

"No." Megan's eyes mist over slightly. "She thought she was seeing her friend, Scarlett. She disappeared from the Arrington Estate back in 1960. Her family were the Tarvers—they weren't from around here, and I'm not sure her disappearance even made the papers, so I expect most folks have forgotten by now. The last day anyone saw her, Scarlett invited Mom to swim at the lake while her siblings went into town with their parents, but Mom couldn't make it; she had the stomach flu. She was torn up about it for the rest of her life. She thinks Scarlett went swimming alone and drowned."

"That's awful," I breathe softly as the weight of another tragedy settles over me. "No one looked for her?"

"Just her family, and Mom. Since she was nineteen and an outsider, police considered Scarlett a runaway and weren't motivated to follow up. You'll find that law enforcement in this area has a selective memory and an even more exclusive list of those they choose to protect and serve." She sighs. "They laughed when Mom begged them to dredge Paradise Lake. The Tarvers moved away a year later, and Mom started going for walks around the lake, trying to remember the good times . . . and maybe looking for some sign of what happened to her friend. I would have."

So Atheleen wasn't the first girl to possibly meet her fate in the lake. I shouldn't be surprised, given the numerous dangers Rose listed off to discourage us from swimming, but my heart beats faster as Megan continues.

"One time, near the end, Mom seemed pretty lucid when she started telling me that Atheleen wasn't alone when she died. Then she said, 'None of them are alone.' When I asked who she meant, she said, 'The skeleton girls.' I remembered telling her what Anna had said that night at the estate, years ago, and thought it was the dementia talking. She used to say all kinds of strange things, those last few years—like 'She's not sorry.' That came up a lot, and it made me sad; I think she was talking in the third person. I think it meant she didn't regret buying the estate despite its problems."

Megan swallows audibly again. Without being asked, I jump up and get an ice water from the barista, along with a couple napkins.

After she takes a few sips and dabs at her nose, she says, "There's one more thing. One time, when Mom was rambling about Atheleen and the lake, she said, 'She was there. She saw everything.' I thought she meant somebody was there the day Atheleen died. I asked who it was, but I never got an answer. I was sure all of this was a sign that Mom needed to sell the estate and move to assisted living—I found a wonderful community, closer to my home so we could all visit with her, but she left this world just a week after leaving Arrington."

"I'm really sorry." I don't know how I'd navigate life without my own mom. As Megan finishes her water and checks the time on her phone, I try to quiet my racing thoughts long enough to figure out if I have any lingering questions that she might be able to answer before she leaves. "A friend of mine said that Eileen added a lot of security cameras to the property, and wanted to build a wall, even. Do you know why she would bother with all that if she wanted to make the estate into an inviting B and B?"

"She was worried about lookie-loos and teens out for a thrill accidentally damaging the house or grounds," Megan says, slipping her phone into her worn leather purse. "See, Arrington was something of a local legend well before Atheleen's time—before

Scarlett's, too, I believe. There was one woman in particular who kept coming around at odd hours, and Mom was troubled by it. And sometimes Mom seemed to think that her cameras could help her catch the person who was with Atheleen that night, like solving one death would ease her guilt over not being there for Scarlett the day she vanished. But . . ."

She hesitates, then presses on. "There was something she kept saying near the end, as we were packing up her things. She was worried the next owner wouldn't let the right ones in. Whatever that means."

She pushes in her chair and stands, offering me a hand. When I take it, she grabs on warmly, her hand no longer clammy like before. Maybe sharing this stuff with someone else was a bit of a release she hadn't expected.

"I'm sorry, I have to head back to work," she explains, picking up her purse. "I think I have an old picture of Mom and Scarlett, by the way. If I find it, I'll text you."

I wave away her offer of cash for the pastry and drink, and she bustles toward the door.

As soon as the bells chime, Quinn drops her book and hurries over, her eyes wide. "So is Atheleen our ghost?" she asks, leaning in close, the air around her sweet with whipped cream and syrup. "Or is it Scarlett, waiting for someone to find out what really happened to her?"

I don't know what to do with this new information about the Tarvers' daughter disappearing, especially if no police report was ever filed; that means no leads. Yet now we have two potential deaths, separated by a span of twenty-odd years.

Who was there when Atheleen died, if Eileen can be believed?

Who's the woman who saw everything—was it the same one who kept coming back to the property, scaring Eileen into getting more cameras? And did Scarlett ever really leave the estate? This could be huge.

As I wave goodbye to the barista and head out into the summer haze with Quinn, I'm leaving with more questions than answers.

TWELVE

LIGHTNING SHATTERS THE SKY over the lake as Quinn and I sit on the edge of Holly's bed, telling her everything we learned about Eileen from Megan: how Eileen thought Atheleen wasn't alone when she died, and that she may not have been the first to meet her end at the estate.

"Sounds like Cathy was way off with her suspicions about Miss E," Holly says in a sleep-roughened voice. "I'd probably act weird too if I thought someone was creeping around my house. Especially someone who might have seen a girl die and didn't go to the cops."

Holly doesn't look so great; in fact, she seems worse than when we left this morning. Her face is the color of the dead deer's pale stomach, her cheeks missing their usual healthy flush. Even her eyes seem different, blue irises washed out like paint with too much water. Still, she's fascinated by everything we've told her.

"Just think," Quinn adds, "Eileen believed her friend's spirit was here, so she stayed even though there were people coming onto the property who made her nervous and the house's creep factor kept her family away . . . That's horrible. She never even got closure about what really happened to Scarlett, and it sounds like she loved her a lot."

Waffles crawls further into my lap, sprawling across both me and Quinn in an attempt to get extra love. It works. His claws scratch once against the bed's wooden footboard, but thankfully, don't leave a mark.

"What if Scarlett is in that grave you found, Dare?" Holly suggests with a hint of her usual enthusiasm. "The one that you think said 'Sam'? Those could be initials—and they were faded, right? Maybe someone buried her here, hiding a crime in the most obvious place where no one would think to look."

"We'd need a lot more evidence before we have the police start digging in the orchard," I point out, inwardly cringing at the thought of involving small-town politics and its complications in our already brief time at the estate. "All I know is, we need to try to find this potential witness to Atheleen's death. It's time for her to break her silence, especially if it was more than an accident. For all we know, she might still be in the area."

"She has to be. No one born in New Hope ever really makes it that far." Holly sighs, shrinking back against her pillows.

"Until you," I say firmly.

"Do you think Scarlett's disappearance and Atheleen's drowning could be related?" Quinn asks as she twists a silver-and-opal ring around her index finger. "They're so far apart. For all we know, Scarlett hated this town as much as you, Holls, and went to start a new life. Hell, I hope she did. But . . . maybe there's something about this place and the people connected to it that we're not seeing."

"Beats me." Holly smiles wanly. "If there is, I'm not going to see it without a nap. Maybe I'll solve the whole thing in my sleep—has that ever happened on *Gravekeepers*?"

As I shut Holly's door, I catch a glimpse of something that stills the breath in my chest. That eyeless, moldy doll from the attic is sitting on top of her dresser. Why hasn't she cleaned it or thrown it away? I guess she hasn't had the energy yet, but I hope she does soon. I don't like the idea of sleeping just a few doors down from it.

Waffles growls as he leads Quinn and me into the hallway. Beneath his low rumble, a faint rattling echoes in my ears from somewhere at our backs—glass eyes rolling and knocking together in the doll's innards as Holly carries it to her bed? But I must be imagining things, because Quinn doesn't seem to notice.

She's frowning as Waffles glares at her, his lips pulled back, glistening teeth exposed. Why is it that he only ever growls at Quinn? Every time he's gone off like this in the house, she's there. Does she remind him of someone from his puppy days, a cruel caregiver from the few months before we met?

"It's okay," she says, quickly meeting my eyes—though I'm sure it's a lie. There's no worse feeling than a dog who likes everyone deciding that you're a threat. To Waffles, she adds lightly, "I'll grab you something tasty from the fridge tonight, and we'll be best friends again. Just you wait."

The sconces on the wall hum and flicker as usual, casting feeble light onto the dark-emerald carpet. I'm getting used to the shifting darkness, just like I am to the rest of the house's quirks—the way my bedside lamp occasionally pops on at night, the cries of the coyotes as they hunt, the long wait for water to sluggishly gurgle from any of the taps.

Quinn runs a hand lovingly along the stair banister as she heads toward her room, as if in the past week the house has become an old, familiar friend. It's quite a change from the girl who bought out the contents of some new age store at the first sign of odd happenings.

Maybe that's the approach I need to take; maybe if I befriend this place, it will start to spill its secrets.

This would all be so much easier if ghosts *were* real, and Atheleen could explain everything to me herself. But nothing's ever that simple.

A few days later, as I head to my room to change after several long hours of sanding and painting, a text arrives from Megan. The caption reads, *Mom and Scarlett.* It's a slightly blurry shot of an old Polaroid, but I can make out two girls in their prom dresses, their hair in big, loose curls, their lip gloss causing a glare. The dark-haired girl on the left is wearing a familiar dress—the bright pink one we found in the attic.

Cold washes over me as I stare at the picture and remember the feel of the silk fabric, the faint odor of citrusy perfume beneath the stench of mothballs. Whatever happened to her, Scarlett wasn't just a tragedy; she was full of dreams and plans and secrets. She was loved. She was human. If I can, I have to explore her story alongside Atheleen's.

Holly doesn't come downstairs for dinner—her stomach is upset again after a few days of seeming normal—so I tell Cathy I'll bring a plate up to her. I made spaghetti and salad for everyone, followed by cheesecake for dessert, but none of that seems fitting for an upset stomach. Instead, I heat up a packet of ramen and find some saltine crackers to put on the side while Cathy asks everyone if they've seen her elderberry jam. We all assure her we didn't take it—it wasn't very good—but that just seems to confuse her.

Thunder cracks open the sky as I leave the tray outside Holly's door. It's a merciless summer, the static charge of the storm raising the hair along my arms as I head to my room to check the podcast website. I don't like spending time in here, not after realizing the scratching I've been hearing can't possibly be from tree branches. But since the hosts of *Insomnia*, the most popular horror podcast around, shared yesterday that they've been loving *Attachments*, I'm so eager to see if their praise has started bringing new listeners that it's easier to ignore the way my stomach twists and my shoulders draw in tight as I step inside.

My blood sugar is high from the cheesecake—212—so I take a correction dose of insulin with a press of a few buttons before pulling out my laptop.

Someone knocks on my closed bedroom door, light and hesitant. Waffles's ears stand up toward the sky, pricked forward, and his tail wags a little.

"Can I come in?" comes Quinn's muffled voice.

"You've never had to ask before," I say, hoping she hears the smile in my words. She's been friendlier ever since we went to town together for the interview, jumping in to help when I accidentally switched two paint cans meant for different rooms and discussing our theories on *Gravekeepers* episodes while we work ourselves into exhaustion on the renovations, but she hasn't tried to be alone with me until now.

She enters, clutching a piece of paper to her chest, still in the paint-spattered sweats she wore for the day's work. She sits next to me on the bed, her back stiff, her shoulders heavy with all the things we've left unsaid since our fight.

"This is for you," she says brusquely, handing me the paper. "It's what I was working on when *someone* left that message on my wall. I finally finished it."

It's a watercolor of Waffles, his pink tongue lolling out of his smiling mouth, a crown of wildflowers on his head.

I hug it carefully, then set it on my bedside table. "I love it! Thank you."

"Good. Look, I . . . guess I overreacted a bit. I was so sure you believed in all this stuff that I built this image of you in my head, and I was disappointed when it turned out not to be real," she says, clasping her hands tightly in her lap. "I thought avoiding you would make things easier. But it turns out I was wrong about that, too." She raises her eyes to mine. "I want to keep getting to know you, but this time I don't want either of us to hold anything back. And . . . maybe it's better if we take it slow. No kissing. What do you think?"

"I'd like that." My face getting hot, I add, "I've missed this. Talking, just the two of us, I mean."

Mischief dances in her eyes as she leans closer, her hair brushing my cheek. "I've missed you, too." She traces a finger along my jawline in a way that sends sparks dancing across my skin. "But before I say anything else, you should really look at your podcast page. I've, uh, been keeping an eye on it for you. That shout-out from *Insomnia* was huge."

I shake my head to clear it, and open my laptop. It's too soon to think about kissing her again anyway. She's right; we should focus on getting to know each other.

When I open the *Attachments* site, my heart flutters at what I'm seeing. There's a sea of new commenters begging me to post the next episode, several from locals, even, who are thrilled to see the case receiving coverage. My subscriber count has soared since *Insomnia* boosted the show; I now have over three thousand downloads—so many people waiting to hear what happens next.

Quinn hands me my phone as the text notification chimes.

It's Max. *So now that you're, like, famous or whatever, will you buy me a new PlayStation?*

I have a few other unread messages.

Things are heating up! Lindsey texted. *What's taking so long with the next episode though? You back together with Q or something? I thought this was your No Distractions summer! P.S. Didn't get that tattoo without you. Amanda went with me, but she passed out when she saw the needle, so they asked us to leave.*

"Anything important?" Quinn asks, a slight concern shadowing her features.

I toss the phone aside, shut my laptop, and nudge her with my shoulder. "Only what's right in front of me."

She snuggles against me in the quiet; the rain is beginning to lighten. My pulse races at her nearness, but I also can't get all those downloads out of my head.

"This show could really take off," Quinn says dreamily, apparently thinking the same thing. "Before you know it, you'll be doing ads for weight-loss tea and mattresses and gummies that make your hair extra shiny or whatever."

I arch a brow. "You think I'll sell out, huh?"

"It's not selling out—it's embracing your success!" Quinn sits up, too excited to stay still. "Ooh, if you need someone to record your mattress ads in a sexy voice, I'm in!" She attempts an impromptu fake commercial that leaves us both breathless with laughter by the end. "I know it'll be a hit," she says more seriously, resting her head in the crook of my neck. "You'll go on late-night talk shows and I'll tell all my friends I knew you when."

"Or—hear me out," I say, my face aching from smiling so much. "The podcast takes off, you impress your mom with this museum project, and then, when you're on fall break, you can come to DC, or I'll visit you. We can introduce each other to our friends and maybe hang out in a run-down mansion for old times' sake."

"Savannah's got a haunting on every street corner," Quinn says enthusiastically, though I was kidding about the mansion part. "There's so much I could show you."

"If we have time," I say, my face turning scarlet.

"I see. Good point." Her smile is slow and sweet, dimples appearing on both her cheeks. "Oh! I know! We should fly to Bayamón and see my abuela. I don't know as much about life there as I should, just enough to warn you that you won't ever want to come back."

"Give me ten minutes to pack." I laugh. "I bet they'd miss you at school, though." I realize I don't know what she plans to do after she graduates, so I ask.

"This," Quinn says, gesturing around the room. "Arrington is more my sort of thing than my mom's. I want to preserve old houses by helping design accessible, hands-on learning in historic places. Museums, galleries, taverns, you name it. And . . . I guess I'd like to sell some of my watercolors, if people are interested."

"Then you will," I declare. "There's nothing you can't do."

"Except prove to you that we're not the only ones in this house, apparently."

I sigh. She can't seem to let it go, even though she might be trying. I don't want another fight. "I'm still here, aren't I? Still searching. That's all I can do," I say at last. "I take it you didn't say anything to your mom about Cathy's message on the wall?"

"That sweet woman didn't commit any crime worse than mixing up pasteles and tamales at dinner last night," Quinn says, a touch of heat behind the words. "Still, she can really cook for a white lady, and that says something. So no, I didn't tell Mom because I know Cathy didn't do it. Deep down, you do, too, or you'd have said something to her by now."

She takes both my hands, the cool metal of the silver rings stacked on her fingers pressing against my warm skin. "Listen. I know we don't see eye to eye on this—but I know ghosts are real, Dare. I've seen one. Not many people know this story besides Dad and Abuelita, but I'm going to trust you with it."

I squeeze her hands, ready for her to make me believe.

"When I was ten, our elderly neighbor passed away. He used to tutor me in math after school, because Mom insisted that I take algebra way before I was ready—typical—and he was a retired professor. He told the best stories. One afternoon, I got off the bus and walked to his place like usual. There were a couple cars in the driveway I didn't recognize, but I figured his family was visiting or something. I went in, and he was sitting at the kitchen table, smiling at me like always. He even pulled out a chair for me." Her lip quivers the slightest bit. "Then I blinked, and he wasn't there, but the chair was still pulled back from the table. I was so confused. I thought I'd blacked out or something, but then his daughter came out of the next room and told me he'd died that morning. My parents got in a fight when I told them, not that that was unusual—Dad has always believed, but Mom told me to stop making up stories."

I give her a knowing look; it sounds like exactly the kind of thing Rose would say. To a kid, that must have really hurt.

"I'm glad you told me," I say slowly. "But how do you explain that I've caught nothing, not even a shadow by now? I've been to every famous haunt in my hometown twice over, and I have nothing to show for it."

It's nice to imagine a kind man returning to say goodbye to his little neighbor, but accepting her story means my years of personal experience—or lack thereof—in the ghost-hunting department are a lie. And I can't let go that easily.

"Maybe the spirits don't like you because you always say they aren't real," Quinn teases. Growing serious again, she says, "I was raised on stories from people on my dad's side of the family who saw things, believed things you never will—some things I don't believe, even. And if you rule out the supernatural, you rule out half the possible explanations for what's going on here. How else do you explain Eileen seeing her dead friend?"

"Dementia. Megan said she was suffering, remember?"

"Or . . . maybe she was seeing Atheleen's ghost, and just thought it was her friend. She could have been confusing one dead girl with another, awful as that sounds," Quinn muses. "And since it wasn't Cathy, how about the writing on my wall?"

"I was thinking—remember the security cameras? Megan said that Eileen was worried about a woman who kept coming back to the property. What if the writing really was a warning—what if the person who saw what happened to Atheleen that night is the one who kept coming back? What if she came back to warn us about something?"

"Maybe," Quinn says, drawing herself inward with a little shiver. "But I don't love the idea of someone we don't know having access to the house and writing on my walls. Why not just talk to us? And I still don't understand what she'd be warning us about, anyway."

A reminder buzzes on my phone—I need to change my insulin pump infusion site tonight. The long needle that places the cannula, a thin piece of flexible material, beneath my skin still makes me sweat a little.

"I'll go get you some ice water," Quinn offers, briefly putting her hand on mine. "And another piece of your strawberry cheesecake. Want some?"

I shake my head. She slips out of the room, shutting the heavy wood door, and I'm instantly colder without her beside me.

Waffles jumps up onto the bed and licks my arm, apparently feeling the need to remind me that he loved me first.

I start pulling out the supplies I'll need—a vial of insulin, a cotton pad soaked in rubbing alcohol. As I press the button on the insertion device to deploy the needle over my left hip, a favorite spot where there are fewer nerve endings to sting, the bedroom door creaks open. No footsteps follow.

"Come in, Q," I call softly, in case Holly is still asleep. "Don't be shy."

I pull out the needle and close my eyes for a second, waiting for the flash of pain to fade. I don't mind Quinn seeing this part of my life. If anything, I'm more comfortable in my own skin when she's around. I know she sees more than my highs and lows.

Her long fingers stroke through my hair. As I lean into the touch, I wonder how she got this far into the room without a single floorboard creaking. "You're sneaky, huh?" I laugh as she runs a cold finger down my neck, opening my eyes and turning to face her.

"What are you talking about?" Quinn asks, her brows raised as she appears in the doorway, a plate of cheesecake in one hand and a glass of ice water in the other.

There's a shadow of someone else behind her, a twin to her own. When she strides into the room, it separates from her, stepping back into the deeper shadows of the hall.

I take an involuntary step back, slamming into my bedside table. The lamp wobbles precariously, and Quinn throws down her kitchen haul to catch it. After steadying the porcelain lamp base, she blinks a question at me, eyes wide and breathing hard.

There's no time to explain yet. I hurry past her into the hallway, my phone raised in pursuit of the shadow.

But as always, there's nothing there. No rustling of any person or creature, no light seeping from under the others' closed bedroom doors.

Relief and disappointment war within me. My eyes have played tricks on me before, like when I thought I saw someone disappearing into the woods a few days ago. But there was no glare of sunlight this time. I wasn't wishing to see something. That shadow was there, unasked for, unexpected. And no peculiar slant of light can explain the icy touch I felt when Quinn was all the way across the room.

"Dare . . . you're freaking me out." Quinn shuts the door and locks it once I'm back in the room. "What happened? What did you see?" Her fingers on my shoulder are warm, solid, real. But even being close to her doesn't chase away the lingering chill on my neck or calm my heart that bucks against my ribs like a horse trying to unseat its rider.

"It was nothing. Just . . . hit a nerve when I was changing my infusion site," I say in the most offhand voice I can manage.

Leaning against the dresser in case my shaking legs give out from under me, I drink my water and take some insulin. My blood sugar is hovering around 200; could a touch of blurry vision from high blood sugar explain Quinn's second shadow? As for what I thought was Quinn stroking my hair, maybe a strand was caught on something, and it pulled as I moved my head.

Besides, Waffles didn't growl this time. Animals are supposed to be more sensitive to the paranormal than humans, so wouldn't he have had something to say about a shadowy figure gliding into our room?

"You're lying," Quinn says, nudging me gently in the ribs. "You suck at lying. Tell me what really happened."

Reluctantly, I explain.

"Look, I don't know what high blood sugar feels like, or what it would do to my eyes, but isn't there a chance it's not that?" Quinn asks when I've finished. "I don't like thinking there was a spirit following me down the hall, either, but . . . I know. I'll order more crystals tonight. Maybe I just haven't found the right ones yet. I've only bought about half the store."

"I'm not rolling my eyes, but only because of how much I like you. There's an explanation for everything, Q, even if we don't know it yet."

"You can thank me later," she shoots back, pulling up a website on her phone.

I run a hand across the back of my neck until it starts to feel warm. I'm not sure how science would explain that icy caress. All I know is, it happened. Something touched me. But I'm not about to admit that to Quinn until I have answers—she doesn't need anything else to worry about.

Order apparently placed, she sprawls across the bed, but almost immediately leaps up again. "Ugh!" she shrieks. There's a big wet spot on my quilt, and it's coming from beneath the spot where Waffles has been lying since I started changing my infusion site.

I brace myself as I swipe my fingers through the faintly warm puddle and sniff. Definitely urine. "Not cool, buddy," I groan. "I would've taken you out again if you let me know. You just went, what, an hour ago?"

"It's in my hair," Quinn moans. "I know you didn't mean to, sweet boy," she adds to Waffles in a sugary voice. "Accidents happen," she assures me as she heads for the door. "But if you two will be okay, I need to go shower. Forever."

"Yes, go," I urge her. "Being peed on is the worst. I've walked enough nervous dogs to know that."

While Quinn heads for the shower, I whisk off the soiled quilt and rummage in the bottom drawers of the dresser for the extra bedding I spotted while unpacking.

Waffles comes over and nuzzles my cheek apologetically. I'm rubbing behind his ears when Quinn's scream shreds through the still, oppressive night air.

THIRTEEN

LIGHTS SWITCH ON, FLOODING the hall.

Holly staggers out of her bedroom, her hair mussed, her eyes heavy with sleep. Cathy appears in a pink bathrobe and fuzzy slippers, wielding a rolled-up magazine. She's trailed closely by Rose in a long silk nightgown, night cream giving her skin a fresh glow.

My bare feet squish through the carpet on my way to Quinn. I glance up just long enough to see another bloated spot on the ceiling outside the bathroom.

"I'm okay! Sorry!" Quinn stammers as we all crowd the doorway of the small bath. "It's okay." She clutches a robe tightly around herself, clearly still trying to catch her breath as Rose moves to her side. "It just startled me, that's all."

I follow Quinn's gaze to the claw-foot bathtub, where a dusty-brown snake with a pattern of deep-brown spots writhes and jerks. Occasionally, it lashes at the air as if seeking to punish someone for its predicament.

Rose's features harden ever so slightly at the sight; she must not like snakes. "You're sure, love?" She puts a protective arm around her daughter's shoulders. When Quinn nods, she says, "Good. Keep an eye on it, and I'll go get something from downstairs. Maybe a spade, or one of the saws—"

"No!" Quinn protests, horrified, shrinking back from her mom. It's the first time I've seen her so openly disagree with someone. "Mom, what the hell? Just—go back to bed. I can do this myself. Dare, would you hand me a towel?"

"What kind is it?" I only know it's not venomous; it lacks a pit viper's angled head, something I've seen in posters on Max's bedroom walls.

"Just a northern water snake. Harmless. I've moved plenty of them for my grandparents, when they used to live out in the country."

As Quinn kneels by the tub, I can't help thinking of Megan in that same spot, years ago, yanking her toddler out of a bath full of murky water as toy sailboats capsized around her.

"How do you think it got in here?" Holly asks, drawing me from my thoughts as Cathy and Rose talk in low, uneasy voices in the hallway. She looks more awake now, and—like me—curious, but cautious about our unexpected guest.

Cautious enough that she sticks close to me, her fingers gripping my forearm.

"The pipes," Quinn answers as she throws the towel over the intruder. "Has to be. We can check around for holes and rule out other entry points tomorrow, but I bet it's the plumbing—everything that's wrong with this place goes back to the plumbing."

"I guess it could have been worse—it could have been a cottonmouth," I say as Waffles and I escort Quinn to the shore. "They live around here; your mom showed me. I'm sure that's why she was, ah, so upset."

Trying not to think about the gory scene Rose would have caused, I hold the flashlight steady while Quinn gently releases the snake.

It snaps at her before slithering toward the dark water and disappearing below.

With everyone retreating to their rooms and a stifling hush falling over the house again, sleep seems a long way off despite my eyelids feeling like they're attached to anchors. I can't stop thinking—thinking about where Scarlett might be now, the possibility that Atheleen wasn't alone when she died, and whether the person who was with her, if she indeed exists, is still alive. The thoughts are a welcome distraction from worrying about what might have touched me earlier.

I pull out headphones and my laptop to edit the interview with Megan—comments keep popping up on the site, and I might as well satisfy my new listeners' need for more content. I feel a twinge of guilt that I haven't been able to get to it before now, but Rose and Cathy have kept us busy. I especially want to hear the last few lines of the interview again for myself—the part about the skeleton girls, and how none of them are alone. Was there once a serial killer in New Hope? Just thinking about it makes the hair on my arms stand on end.

I don't complain when Waffles jumps up to join me on the bed, even though he already ruined one quilt tonight. With his warm bulk squished against my side, it's easier to relax against my pillow and play back the audio.

Focusing on Megan's voice, I close my eyes. With the gentle clink of cups and plates in the background, it's almost like I'm back at the Mystic Teacup. Minus the delicious latte. When the interview nears the last ten minutes, I know what's coming:

Megan listing off the ramblings of a woman near the end of her life, the best evidence I have to go on so far.

But instead of Megan's voice, there's a crackling, static sound that's somehow *alive*. I don't know how else to describe it; it's pent-up energy pulsing through the headphones into my ears. Someone about to take a breath against the mic. But Megan and I were seated on opposite sides of the table, not close enough for the recorder to pick up our breathing.

"Leave, Dare," a voice hisses, harsh against my ears. "She won't save you either."

I jerk upright, my body reeling as though the speaker just dumped a bucket of ice water over me. Waffles's ears prick forward as he watches me skip back several seconds to play the moment again.

But this time, there's only Megan's voice saying now-familiar phrases.

I glance at the time on my phone. One fifteen a.m.

It's late, I tell myself; I had an early start, and if I wasn't imagining things earlier, I definitely am now. I take a deep, wavering breath. To prove a theory, you need to be able to recreate your experiment and achieve the same results many times over. Whatever I heard, or thought I heard, isn't proof of anything except that I'm not invincible, and haven't been sleeping enough. I just wish my brain would send that message to the rest of my body so it would stop shaking.

My blood sugar is a little on the low side for bedtime at 78, so I eat a granola bar before finally crashing, my recorder on the bedside table so I can pick up editing tomorrow.

But when I close my eyes, the voice slithers through my mind again. *Leave, Dare.* Except I'm not going to. Podcast aside, Holly and Quinn are my friends now, and I won't abandon them for anything. *She won't save you either.* Good thing I don't need saving, then. I can always count on myself when things get rough—if living with my disease has taught me anything, it's that.

Besides, what did the voice even mean—who is this person? And who did she fail to save the last time? No, I stop myself—it didn't mean anything. My subconscious just thinks of some weird stuff. I barely have time to roll my eyes at my twisted brain before I fall asleep.

I'm standing at the foot of a familiar set of stairs. Emerald-green carpet squishes between my bare toes. Above me, on the landing, the Arringtons stare down from their lofty perches, safe in their gilded frames as they survey their legacy.

In front of me, beside the old grandfather clock in the foyer reading 7:45, two girls appear to be having an argument. The taller one seems to be about my age, her light-brown hair cascading in waves down her back until it almost reaches the top of her denim cutoffs. She's clutching the shoulders of a shorter, younger girl with darker hair.

I can't see either of their faces clearly—just the suggestion of noses and mouths, barely defined, and dark pits where their eyes should be.

"You don't have to do this—don't go!" the older girl cries, gripping the younger girl tighter until her knuckles are white.

But the dark-haired girl tears herself away with surprising strength and moves toward the front door as if in a trance. The porch creaks with the weight of her steps, and now that the door is open, the hum of insects and frogs surrounds me. A summer night's chorus.

The older girl races after the younger, easily overtaking her.

I follow.

The tall girl leads me down to the gentle slope to the lake, her strides so long that I find myself running just to keep her in my sights. She heads for the long wooden dock jutting out over the lake, the churning green water so thick with algae that it's impossible to see more than a few inches below the surface.

There's a small rowboat floating there, and the tall girl unties it as if by muscle memory, her eyes never leaving the younger girl who's walking slowly to the lake's edge as if entranced. The water is turbulent, more like the Atlantic Ocean than a lake the way it slaps against the grassy shoreline, the rocky strip of sand where we had our summer kickoff party now several feet underwater, hidden.

As water strikes the younger girl's feet and wraps around her ankles, the older girl leaps feverishly into the boat, which rocks from side to side with the uneasy current of the lake, threatening to tip her out. She doesn't seem to notice. Her gaze is still on the younger girl, unwavering. She takes the frayed rope the boat was tied with and fastens one end around her waist and the other to the boat, anchoring herself.

I remain on the dock as she pushes off. I can't swim in water so deep and violent. For a second, I manage to tear my gaze from the girls to glance back at the estate; it hasn't changed from the way I know it, weathered and worn, but the lake has.

It's swollen, almost like it's devoured another lake and doubled in size; the shoreline is closer to the house than I've ever seen it, and it seems to be growing. As I watch, it inches up the grass, submerging the young girl to her waist, hungrily claiming everything in its path.

The dock beneath my feet is no longer visible either, greenish water oozing around my ankles, though I can still feel the boards beneath me. I hope they hold.

The older girl in the boat seems impossibly far from the younger one, though she's paddling so hard she must be breaking a sweat. I assume she's trying to reach the other girl before the water sweeps her away, but from here, it seems like she's heading toward the middle of the lake instead.

As the girls seem to slow almost to a standstill and the indigo sky darkens, I feel other eyes on me, and scan my surroundings.

There.

On the shore, several feet past the end of the beach, where long grasses hug the curve of the lake and blackberry bushes growing wild once concealed a dead, skeletal deer that my dog found, several girls stand in a row, arms linked. Watching me.

I slowly raise my eyes from their fish-bitten feet and calves toward their heads, dreading the sight of their faces. Their skin, a deathly gray-white, is pocked with hundreds of jagged wounds that have begun to fester. What skin they do have hangs loosely off their too-thin frames, as though there's no flesh padding their bones. But what stills my heart in my chest is the sight of their milk-white eyes, unblinking.

The wind whips my hair back, and as it does, I smell them. It's the stench of decaying organic matter, not just the algae but something else, sick yet sweet. Rotten roses.

They're wrong.

This is wrong.

I shouldn't be here, and neither should the two living girls in the lake, who seem oblivious to the dead things staring at us with their unseeing sea-foam eyes. The lake's daughters.

I scream and wave my arms, trying to make myself heard over a surge of water and wind. I need to get the older girl's attention.

She needs to know what's watching her, too.

But she doesn't so much as glance toward the dock as she continues rowing. It's clear now she's headed toward the middle of the lake, away from the young girl now up to her neck in murky, muddy water that reeks of what it did to those dead girls' bodies.

The older girl guides the boat steadily toward something—an eerie green light, as if someone is shining a spotlight underwater. Like the light I saw on my first day here. Once the boat is hovering over it, she drops an anchor and dives into the restless lake. A moment later, she pops up, gasping for air. The current immediately wallops her in the side of the head, punishing her daring.

There's something clutched in her hand I hadn't noticed before— a scrap of paper, I think, yellow-white and already soggy.

The older girl's head disappears again beneath the turbulent surface.

I have to do something.

I have to save her.

I try leaping into the water, but my feet are anchored to the dock. I can't move. I can only watch. "Do something!" I scream at the younger girl.

Neck-deep in the water, her eyes glassy as the lake on a calm day, the girl says nothing. She doesn't even look my way, or try to move as the water creeps up toward her ears. It's like she's content to be swallowed up.

"Why did you let her do that? Wake up! Snap out of it!" I

continue to yell at the younger girl. "Do something—she's going to drown!"

From the middle of the lake comes a muffled scream. A flash of a pale hand. The boat lurches and bobs.

What little light is left in the sky is growing dim.

"She's dying!" I shout. A plea.

But the younger girl's face is stony as the water caresses her chin. It doesn't seem to want to rise any higher, as though it already has what it wants. The wind softens, and with it, the current.

The water retreats slightly from the dock, exposing my feet.

"Atheleen?" the younger girl says suddenly. Then, "Atheleen! No!" Her voice carries, making her sound closer to me than she is. Her face, what I can see of it, is twisted, her words quick with panic, as if she's just realized what's happening.

Now I know what this is: the night Atheleen died.

I glance out into the water, now deceptively still, more blue than green, the way I remember it from my drive to the estate.

There's something moon-white floating toward shore. It could be a body, some of it concealed beneath the surface. Or it could be something alive. The gentle current draws it steadily toward me.

"What have I done?" the younger girl sobs from the shore, her cry so raw that it aches in my marrow.

I turn away from her; the white shape is nearly within reach.

Kneeling, I thrust a hand into the water.

My hand meets flesh—bony, cold flesh—and I pull.

Long waves of brown hair drift to the surface. There's the tip of a pixie-sharp chin, the sunken contours of a jawline.

I don't know if I'm ready for this. Seeing her face.

———

I startle awake, unable to sit up yet, boneless from the dream and what I almost saw. The face of a dead girl just after she drowned while someone else looked on and did nothing.

Water splashes my cheek, an icy drip from the ceiling.

Nothing should feel that cold when temperatures have neared a hundred every day this week. I glance up, still trying to catch my breath, but she steals what little air is left in my lungs: the girl plastered against the ceiling several feet above me, her face entirely in shadow, her long, wavy hair and sodden clothes—a T-shirt and jeans with ripped knees, absurdly ordinary—dripping rancid water onto my cheeks.

"Run," she whispers, her voice a scrape against my skin. "Go."

My bedroom fills with the sound of rushing water as the girl on the ceiling takes thick, gasping breaths, her chest heaving.

She slowly falls toward me, her white eyes wide and round, festering moons. As she gets closer, I can't stop staring at her muddy hands, missing several fingernails.

Throwing my arms above my head, I lash at the air, ready to fight her off. Preparing for the slimy feel of her skin on mine as we tangle.

I sit upright in bed, my heart pounding in my ears, my head aching. I'm finally awake; Waffles's gentle nudge of my arm assures me of that much, as does the lamp flickering on my bedside table. I must have forgotten to turn it off before I fell asleep. That thing on the ceiling was just a part of a dream that should have ended much sooner.

But why is my face wet?

Rubbing my cheek, I realize I must have been crying. I'm glad Quinn isn't here to see what a coward her ghost hunter really is.

I've read about sleep paralysis dozens if not hundreds of times, though I'd never experienced it until now. I'm sure that's all the girl on the ceiling was. And I'm sure Quinn would say differently, giving me a knowing look as she asked how I was able to move my arms, striking the air as the figure drew nearer.

Maybe it was an ordinary nightmare, then—one bad enough to make my skin crawl and leave me with a lingering sense of unease.

I grab my phone for added light, hesitant to touch the lamp while it's having a fit. Soon, the glow of my phone's flashlight illuminates the area around me. I force myself to check the ceiling, and of course, there's no one up there. No shadowy figure. Just the faint outline of a long, old water stain. One that might be called vaguely person-shaped—but that's what Quinn would say, not me, I tell myself.

Next, I check the quilt. No damp spots there.

I don't usually have to reassure myself like this after a nightmare, but I also don't usually remember my dreams. The few I do recall stand out vividly: falling from a balcony to a swimming pool far below, showing up naked and lost on the first day of middle school, a vampire clown chasing me with a knife on board a pirate ship. Those all had a cartoonish, surreal quality that made them memorable.

Nothing about my dream of the lake, or after, being in my bed with the girl hovering over me, felt very far from reality. That's what bothers me most. I can still hear the chorus of mosquitoes and frogs, still feel the wind that pushed my hair back, still smell something rotten in the throes of decay, something from the bottom of a trash can.

As sleep retreats further from my reeling mind, I realize the stench is real. It crawls down my nose and into my throat, choking me.

I hastily glance around the room with my phone light, but Waffles hasn't made a mess anywhere. His gaze is fixed on me, his eyes twin orbs of green witch light in the shadows. He whines softly and nudges my arm more insistently.

I try to ignore the smell and check my CGM as the unreliable lamp buzzes on and off beside me. The flashes of light throw disorienting shadows across the wall that sort of look like people dancing, twisting and undulating to a rhythm I can't hear. I keep glancing up sharply at the movement, unable to stop myself from feeling as though there's somebody else here.

My blood sugar has soared to 230. Figures. The adrenaline of my nightmare was bound to have some effect, and for some reason, the CGM alarm didn't go off—or I slept through it, too caught up in my subconscious's twisted version of Atheleen's final night.

I grab my insulin pump from the waistband of my pajama pants to take a dose, but the screen doesn't light up as it should.

I press a few more buttons, and nothing happens. My pump is dead.

After the way it's been burning through batteries since I got here, I shouldn't be surprised, but nerves flutter through me as I start my backup plan: first, a quick shot of rapid-acting insulin in my lower stomach. I'll be doing a lot of these in the near future, so it's a good thing they don't usually hurt.

Tomorrow morning, first thing, I'll have to call the medical company who supplied it and have them send a replacement.

The lamp on my bedside table finally sputters out, my phone now my only light. I scoot closer to Waffles, thanking him for letting me know something was up. I rub his ears as I scroll through Twitter and check my texts—anything to avoid thinking about the dream.

Between that and the stench in my room, there's no way I'll be going back to bed. I wonder whether Atheleen or Scarlett used to stay up late into the night, listening for the scrape of something unseen against their walls, or wake up breathless from nightmares about this place—the house, the lake. They seem to bleed into one another, two limbs of the same failing body. Maybe this room used to belong to one of them, my lost predecessors. The idea makes me feel closer to them, in a way, and sorry I haven't been able to learn more about them yet.

The only texts I have are from Quinn, memes of birds with human arms doing human activities. They're funny enough that I smile despite my lingering sense of unease, and I text her back a couple of my own, hoping she sleeps with her phone on silent.

That's when I realize I have to pee.

Awesome. Splendid, even.

I creep down the hall to the shared bathroom, motioning for Waffles to follow.

He watches from the doorway, head tilted in concern as I hastily switch on the light, checking for things that slither and crawl.

All is quiet and still while I quickly do what I came for, flinching at shadows as Waffles's silhouette stretches along the back wall of the shower.

I'm letting this house get to me. And if it gets to me, it wins.

Wait. What do I mean, it wins? A house can't win. A house can't want or scheme. It's just a building, not responsible for the actions or thoughts of the people within.

That's it. I'm going back to my room. The stench might have been some sensory thing left over from my nightmare, and if it isn't, an animal died in the walls and I'll have to tell Cathy or Rose when they get up. There's nothing to be afraid of. Who knows? I might even manage to close my eyes for a few minutes.

I reach for the bathroom light switch on my way out.

As the sconces on either side of the mirror go dark, something moves within the glass. A figure just behind me, glancing at its reflection. Thick hair falling past her shoulders, glasses, an oval-shaped face—I know that girl.

"Q?"

Or maybe I don't. Her mouth pinches in pain as she reaches for my shadowed reflection, her eyes draining of color until they're a luminous white, her muddy, bloodied fingers curling toward my neck as though she wants to grab me by the throat.

"What the hell?" I whirl around, raising a fist, but no one's there.

When I turn back, the mirror reflects only me, my eyes wide, nostrils flaring, blue hair plastered to my sweaty forehead. The girl in the glass—me—would be enough to startle anyone.

I look how I feel: like I had a bad dream and a worse night. My curious brain took everything from my interview with Megan and turned it into some dramatic re-creation of Atheleen's death, and this is the leftover result. That's all. Though it's hard to convince myself of that in the stifling dark.

"Atheleen?" I call out, feeling my face warm with the foolishness of what I'm doing. "Scarlett?" No one answers. No one's home. "You can talk to me, if you're there. You can trust me. Or you can be mad at me for taking so long to notice you. That's fine, too. Scream in my ear. Pull my hair. I swear, I can take it. Just—if you're there, I need to know. Show me. Give me anything. *Please.*"

Silence drapes itself around me like a wet, heavy blanket as I trudge through the hall.

There's only ever silence because as always, there's nothing waiting in the dark, only the wolves of our imaginations.

I still don't believe in ghosts.

But if I didn't know better, I'd say the house is trying to change my mind.

FOURTEEN

I DON'T GO BACK to sleep that night.

Instead, I grab my cameras and stare drowsily at the recording of the empty hallway, squinting extra hard at each shiver of static, each subtle shift in pixels as clouds skid over the moon. But there's nothing even close to what I saw on the ceiling in my dream. Not even a whisper of water falling onto the new carpet.

As a pale, pearly dawn breaks over the lake, Waffles and I head down to the dock, where I'll get the strongest signal for my phone call to the medical supply company.

With static-riddled elevator music playing in my ear as I wait to be connected with a representative, I scan the shoreline. There's no sign of the heron that watched me with its baleful yellow eyes on my first day here.

I try to remember the last time I saw any bird fishing this vast stretch of water since that day. I can't.

My gaze strays to the middle of the lake. There's no eerie light drawing me closer, no floating feathered bodies. Yet a little part of me wouldn't have been surprised to see them, not when I still can't explain what touched my neck last night. Or the face in the mirror.

Waffles sniffs the grass near the rising shoreline now creeping toward the house. This lake, the real lake, isn't nearly as sinister as the massive, restless one in my dreams; the water level must swell like this every summer when there's heavy rain, and my subconscious made it into something more.

Still, the water is closer to the dock than I've seen it, bringing the old rowboat almost level with the wood boards where I pace.

The boat, too, looks a lot like the one in my dream, which makes sense; my mind drew on familiar things to convince me it was real. Brains are jerks. It's a fact.

The rep picks up and begins to ask me questions. I mumble drowsily through my answers, my gaze now straying to the far shore near the blackberry thicket.

There's no one watching me. No sodden, decaying bodies. The dead deer is gone, too, likely dragged into the forest by hungry coyotes. Somehow, my mind must have turned the deer's corpse into the bodies of those girls, watching me because I hadn't taken time to call animal control or give the creature a proper burial or anything. Dream guilt—fun.

With each passing minute, the events of last night grow hazier, shrouded by distance and doubt. By the time I've hung up with the rep and my new insulin pump is set to arrive in a few days—New Hope is too rural for overnight shipping—I feel tired, but that's nothing unusual. At least, not for a type 1 diabetic who's used to making a hundred extra decisions a day and trying to predict the future for my own health. Not to mention the insomnia.

The sun warms my face, and I find an old tennis ball to throw for Waffles, enjoying the balmy morning air before heading back into the house's dim, oppressive interior.

Inside, only Rose is awake, if you can call it that. She stares blankly into a cup of matcha green tea, her hands wrapped around the mug for warmth.

"Everything okay?" I ask as Waffles and I trudge into the kitchen in search of food.

"I didn't sleep well," Rose admits, sweeping a short lock of hair back from her eyes as she meets mine. Her gaze remains sharp as ever, taking everything in. "I don't much care for snakes, as I'm sure you've realized. I was bitten by a cottonmouth when I was maybe seven or eight. It was perhaps the worst pain I've ever experienced."

She leans toward me, her face sincere, focused. No wonder Quinn is always worried about what her mom thinks; I wither under her scrutiny, fidgeting with the hem of my T-shirt, and I barely know her.

"How about you, Dare? You aren't usually up this early."

I explain about my insulin pump, and Rose seems concerned in her way. She asks me to keep her updated on when the replacement arrives, and makes sure I have everything I need in the meantime. She even offers to drive me into town if it will help.

That's the thing with Rose: she's intense, but she means well. She and Quinn are more alike than they realize.

Grabbing a Pop-Tart from Holly's stash and a banana, I head upstairs to see if I can detect any trace of something rotten in my room while I wait for everyone else to wake up and begin the day's work.

I smell nothing. Just a faint, acidic hint of Waffles's accident on the old set of sheets that are currently drying in the narrow hallway laundry closet.

With time to kill, I stretch out on my bed to finally, actually edit the audio from Megan's interview. I'm hoping to get the next episode of *Attachments* up today, especially with my fellow

Insomniacs now clamoring for more, too. When I reach the last ten minutes, my shoulders tense in anticipation. But there's no strange voice, no break in the clear, steady audio. I can even hear the barista in the background explaining drink sizes to someone.

As the interview winds down, I take off my headphones and put them on my bedside table. My eyes fall on the drawer, and I remember the scraps of paper I've been saving. I'd meant to read over the rest of them earlier, but with everything else going on, I'd forgotten about them.

I pull them out and spread them on the bed. There are four papers I haven't read yet that seem legible. The first appears to be another diary entry from the same writer as before, the penmanship again precise.

Something scratches the outer wall of my room once, then again—five, maybe six times in all, each motion drawn out like a kid dragging a Sharpie along forbidden furniture. Knowing I won't see anything but the lake out my window, I keep my head down and read:

> *Hettie's done it again. She broke one of Mother's beloved dogs, the handsome porcelain ones her family brought over from England. Now it has no friend to sit with on the mantel, and Mother won't stop crying.*
>
> *Worse—she blames me.*
>
> *I wasn't even home at the time. I was in town with Thomas, the boy who stocks shelves for his father at the mercantile. Hettie knew I wasn't supposed to be with him; Father has forbidden me from seeing someone so far beneath our station.*

That little rat knew, and she forced me to choose: admit
where I'd really been, or accept the blame for her wildness,
even though I've never broken so much as an eggcup in the
year that we've lived here.

Mother says to be patient with her, that she's a sunflower
that will only grow with love and patience. But I swear,
that girl was born wicked.

—Anne

Hettie's sounding a lot worse after reading this. I don't think we'd be friends. I wish I could find a date on the page, but there is none. I remember reading something else from Anne in the attic, a paper someone had dated around 1874. I wonder how the girl's diary got ripped to shreds in the first place—maybe this brat Hettie did it.

The next paper is written on Captain Arrington's official letterhead, addressed to a Mr. Andrews and dated September of 1871. He's trying to convince Andrews, a business partner, to buy one of his boats. He says it "betrayed him" and led to the darkest year of his life, but that in someone else's care, it could be seaworthy again.

Something stirs in the cobwebs of my tired mind, tugging at my thoughts.

Leafing through the other attic papers, I find the one where Mary Riggins invites her cousin Anne—Arrington, I assume—to come live with her in Philadelphia following some sort of accident. The dates are so close—August, September. They must be referring to the same thing: an incident involving the boat for sale.

As if I need more convincing to stay out of the lake.

I have to be especially careful with the next paper, which is so thin and wrinkled by time and water stains that I'm afraid it might crumble in my hands. Not daring to breathe on it, I quickly read the few legible paragraphs:

I turn sixteen next week, and Father has promised we can take the boat out on Paradise Lake for the occasion. But my sisters will surely find some way to spoil my birthday. I'm quite sure they won't even remember to get me a present. They spoil everything when it's not about them—I've kept a list.

—Anne: started a nasty rumor about me and everyone believes her.
—Lily: never thanked me for the gift I made her last Christmas.
—Nora: gives bossy advice I don't ask for.
—Violet: always brags about her good marks from the governess.
—Polly: won't clean up her messes in our room.
—Evie: cries too loudly when I try to sing to her.

You see? They are wicked girls who only care for themselves. They're so preoccupied with suitors and courtships and gossip from back home—they don't care in the slightest about this beautiful place Father bought to please them. Sometimes I get so lonely, I swear my heart might burst, or else shrivel up into a hard, bitter thing like the apples in the orchard in my attempts to care for them.

All I've ever done is love my sisters, but since we moved here, no one has once asked me to join them at play or invited me to share their secrets. They've all become islands, and I am unmoored—adrift, always alone. If they could see me, would they bother to reel me in?

One day, I'll curse them all. And when they beg for mercy, I'll let their screams and their tears give me strength until I drain them dry.

The words leave a sour taste in my mouth—they're heartbreaking, but also selfish, the ramblings of someone young, privileged, and unhappy despite it. Glancing around the room, I realize the scratching has stopped, though Waffles stares toward the window and whines softly. Not seeing whatever has captured his attention, I read on.

The final paper is another, slightly messier diary entry, the letters tangled together as if the writer was in a hurry, or maybe in distress.

August 15, 1872

Sam finally turned up today, after two whole months of searching, though not in the way we wanted. Violet found him floating in the lake, starved to death, from the look of things; she's been in floods ever since. We're going to bury him in the orchard because that was his favorite spot. He was the best cat anyone could ever have.

I'll try to write again soon. Mother wants to move, but Father won't hear of it; there's so much to tell you.

Love,
Lily

So Sam wasn't a person after all; the grave I found on my first day here belongs to someone's beloved pet, not to Scarlett Tarver. Maybe I should feel relieved. But I don't. I'm holding the half-drowned remains of two diaries that make me feel like I've just walked into a room where I don't belong.

This house has seen its share of tragedy, almost from the very beginning. If it could feel, I bet it would be wary. Disappointed. Maybe even angry.

"Dare."

Someone calls my name, faintly muffled—it must be coming from the hallway. I open the door and poke my head out, but find no one. Unease prickles my spine. Holly's door is finally open, though, and so is Quinn's; one of them must have called out to me as they headed downstairs.

Impatient to catch them up on everything, I slide all the papers into my jeans pocket and race after my friends.

But just like when I heard my name at the lakeside, my stomach rolls uneasily.

How did they move so quickly, and without making a sound?

When I get downstairs, Cathy and Rose have plans for us, none of which involve reading the old letters in my pocket over coffee. It's time to renovate the Sunfish room, or as anyone who isn't the eccentric level of rich would call it, the family room.

After giving instructions, Rose disappears to order table settings for display in the Kraken room. Somehow, despite getting more paint on each other than the walls, we did a good enough job in there that Rose is moving forward with the next stage of decorating.

"Adding the beauty marks," she explained fondly.

With Cathy's help, the rest of us haul the leather sofa to the top of the driveway, where it will wait for a scheduled large trash pickup. Next goes the TV, off to be donated to a nearby senior center. I hope they enjoy it more than we did, though honestly, I'm sure they, too, would rather have Netflix.

We buff dents and dings out of the original pine flooring and lay down new rugs, covering holes and scrapes as best we can. We cut open boxes, unpacking new chairs and lamps designed with the Gothic feel that Rose has chosen for this place, blowing Styrofoam bits all over the downstairs in the process until it looks like Christmas in July.

"Keep it up, girls," Cathy urges. "I'm parched. I'll go make us some lemonade—sugar-free, of course."

"And some of your cookies to go with?" Holly asks hopefully as she collapses a box, her blue eyes once again free of the shadows that have been lingering beneath them. She must have actually gotten some sleep for once.

Quinn flinches and glances upward as a drop splashes her leg. There's a puckered, bloated spot on the ceiling. A new one. Before I can figure out which room is above us—there must be yet another leaky pipe somewhere—she turns to me and says in a low voice, "I need to show you something. Both of you, actually. Come here, Holls."

Quinn's hands glisten with sweat as she pulls out her phone. It's warm in here—the historical society only has so much money to pour into this place, so they keep the AC on seventy-eight, but the press of her lips tells me it's more to do with nerves.

Keeping an eye out for Cathy's return, she shows her screen to me and Holly. "Take a look, and then tell me we shouldn't leave this stuff about Atheleen's death alone. Tell me we shouldn't leave, period."

There she goes again, acting like she's terrified of this place. But half the time, she seems to love it. How can so much fear and care exist together?

I swallow, pushing the thought aside, and glance at what Quinn wants to show us.

It's a picture of the three of us, covered in paint and laughing, Waffles rocking teal spots in reverse dalmatian fashion. Holly and I are wielding paint rollers like lightsabers, while Quinn feigns a shocked expression.

"Cute," I say, a little unsure. I must be missing something.

"Not us. Look there." Quinn taps the screen, making the area in question larger.

There's a misplaced shadow behind us, a tall one, solid, positioned as though it's gazing out one of the windows, its back to the room. It can't be any of ours, based on the angle of the light and where we're standing. It shouldn't be there.

But it is.

My body recoils slightly as I push the phone back toward Quinn. "Something must be wrong with the app, or your phone lens."

"Let me see," Holly says, leaning across me for a look.

"That shadow isn't in any other pictures," Quinn counters, her voice hushed. The way her eyes dart to the corners of the room, I don't think it's Cathy she's worried will overhear. "We can at least agree there's no simple explanation," she presses.

"I'm with Quinn on this one." Holly swallows hard, like she's fighting back a wave of nausea, averting her gaze from the phone.

"That picture . . . it's wrong." Lowering her voice, she adds to Quinn, "I still can't decide if I believe in ghosts. You know me, queen of indecision. But—sometimes . . . sometimes I think this house isn't good. Does that make sense?"

Quinn nods gravely. "I feel it, too. I think there's a spirit here, an unhappy one, and it's trying to tell us something we aren't getting. I wish I knew how to listen better."

"I'm not so sure," I say, recalling the dining room from memory in search of something that could have caused such a startling shadow. "There's always another explanation, even if it's not so simple—come on, I'll prove it."

Quinn and Holly follow me to the dining room, where Rose is comparing color swatches and talking quietly to herself.

A quick glance into the room reveals the antique coatrack on the right wall, which casts a long shadow between the two windows.

"The angle's all wrong," Quinn whispers, not wanting to disturb her mom.

As we head back to the family room, I smile; I have an answer for that, too. "The coatrack was moved to the center of the room for painting, and had a sheet over it, remember? I bet I could recreate the shadow in that picture if your mom would let me move the table again."

Quinn's shoulders relax slightly, even as Holly bites her chapped lower lip and glances back as if she expects we're being followed.

"You win—this time," Quinn says, brushing her fingers over mine.

The small gesture sends a thrill through me. I'm glad I could do this one small thing to chase away some of her fears.

"But you've got a long list of other claims to debunk," she points out, her eyes glinting with the challenge. "You never figured out what keeps tapping my shoulder in the shower. Or what knocks on the walls—and don't you dare say 'rats.'"

"Or why my room is always freezing compared to yours," Holly adds unexpectedly.

"Give me time," I say with more confidence than I feel. "And rats are a totally reasonable answer. Speaking of answers," I add, digging out the papers I found, "I have something to show you, too. Apparently the lake has a long history of tragedies, going back at least to when Arrington was built."

I spread the evidence on top of a large, unopened box for Quinn and Holly to examine. They press in close on either side of me for a look.

Holly finishes reading the scraps before Quinn, but it's hard to tell what she thinks; she's glancing over her shoulder again, seeming lost in thought, distracted.

Soon, Quinn puts down the final entry. "I don't usually call girls this, but Hettie sounds like she was a real—" Quinn's words are cut off by the chime of a bell.

The servant call system.

FIFTEEN

THE BELL RINGS A second time, as though someone is annoyed with us for not responding faster.

Quinn hurries to the foyer, studying the brass bells and their corresponding numbers. Rose explained the call box system to me in more detail the other day: each bell is assigned to a particular room, and the one with a tiny dropped flag beneath it indicates a summons—in this case, a bell on the top row. A call coming from one of the rooms upstairs.

"I wish I'd spent more time figuring out which number matches which room," Quinn frets as Waffles and I start toward the stairs. "Hey, wait for me!"

She hurries after me, shoes slapping against the scratched wood of the foyer floor.

Last night, even if it was all in my head, I felt like a rabbit in this house. Hunted. Now it's my turn to pursue whatever's causing that noise. I'm an investigator. A ghost hunter. I run toward the unexplained, not away from it, and debunk what's happening until I can rationalize every phantom sight and sound.

"Girls—where are you going?" Cathy calls from one of the downstairs hallways. "I brought cookies! And I fixed all this lemonade . . ."

"Be right back!" I shout over my shoulder.

As I reach the top of the stairs, the chime echoes once more from below.

"Oh, that infernal bell system." Cathy sighs from out of sight.

Waffles hangs back on the final stair, tail hovering near his legs on the verge of fear, gazing up in a clear invitation for me to walk toward the unknown first.

"Chicken," I tell him, and he owns it, waiting for me to move before trotting reluctantly after me. Quinn is close behind him, with Holly bringing up the rear.

We search the rooms one by one, starting at the dead end with the wardrobe and working our way along the hall toward the antique aquarium and stained-glass windows. So far, nothing is out of place. Not even in my room.

That leaves just Quinn's to check.

Once more, we find ourselves gathered at the threshold of her open doorway. That's where we stop, staring at what's been scrawled across the walls this time.

They look like mermaids.

There are six in all, crude figures of people with long hair floating around their heads and bodies that end in fish's tails. I can't help but shudder as I think of the figures in my dreams, nightmarish mermaids of a different kind.

Beneath them are new words in a rich shade of blue:

THEY'RE NEVER SORRY

A tube of ultramarine watercolor paint oozes the last few drops of its contents onto the floor at the base of the wall, crumpled as though squeezed by a fist.

Cold ripples down my back as the words continue to drip, the paint runny and thin.

Near the discarded tube of paint, someone has smeared dirt into the rug. There, too, are shards of a ceramic pot and the remains of a torn-up plant: Quinn's peppermint that she brought inside from the garden. The soothing aroma of the crushed, ripped leaves isn't nearly enough to calm my nerves right now.

"That's it," I declare around a lump in my throat, striding into the room to pick up the tube before any more paint spills out. Quinn joins me, leaving Holly in the doorway with Waffles. "Someone is seriously screwing with us. And they seem to be picking on you in particular, Q. Does your ex-girlfriend know where you're spending your summer?"

Quinn shakes her head, running her fingers over the wet paint in disbelief. "And even if she did, Britt couldn't draw a mermaid to save her life—not even one this sloppy."

"Which again leaves Cathy—" I start to say as something sharp crashes into the wall, not an inch from my head.

Another tube of paint.

Black, this time.

It was thrown with enough force that it explodes on impact. Dark droplets spatter the mermaids, rivulets coagulating as they run down faces and bodies. I know it's paint, but it looks more like blood. The metallic odor only adds to the illusion, and I have to swallow to hold back a wave of nausea.

We all freeze, looking at each other, not sure we can believe our eyes.

Quinn holds up her shaking hands. "It wasn't me."

"I know. I was looking at you." I instinctively move closer to her, breathing hard as I wipe flecks of paint from my face. I want to protect her, even though my heart is tapping out a warning that right now, I can't even protect myself. If that paint had hit me, it could have really done some damage—I don't even know how much force you'd need to put into a throw to get a tube of paint to burst like that. "Holly, did you—?"

"No!" She flinches away from my wide-eyed gaze as though stung. "Are you serious? Of course I didn't!"

"We're sorry," Quinn says, her voice hushed. "Both of us know you'd never do anything like that. Right, Dare?" She shoots me a pointed look.

Still trying to catch my breath, I nod. "Right."

Cautiously, I study the distance Holly would have needed to cross to reach the paints, turn, and whip a tube across the room in the second my eyes weren't on her. I don't think it's possible, seeing as she's not the Flash. But the tube had to have been thrown by someone—a living, breathing person. Maybe whoever painted the walls was waiting for us to come inspect their artwork and properly freak out before ambushing us. If so, they can't have gone far. I just can't figure out who would want to paint some mermaids on a wall and write a cryptic note like this. "They're never sorry"?

As I mull it over, my mind flashes back to the audio I edited earlier this morning. "She was there. She saw everything," Megan claimed her mother would say. "She's not sorry." Megan thought Eileen was speaking about herself in the third person, but what if she wasn't? What if she was talking about one specific person? "She was there. She saw everything, *and* she's not sorry." What if whoever witnessed Atheleen's death also caused it? And if so, that person is probably still in the area because as Holly pointed out,

New Hope is a tough place to leave. Could she be in the house with us right now?

Holly notices my expression. "What's wrong?"

When I explain what I'm thinking, quietly enough that the other two have to crowd close around me, Quinn frowns. "We would have seen someone throw it. She would have had to get pretty close—close enough for Waffles to run over and check her pockets for treats."

She has a point, but this is the only way to explain a lot of other things. Like the person I thought I saw disappearing into the woods when I was out by the lake with Waffles. Like the voice that's been calling my name. Maybe even the scratching on my wall.

"*Someone* put that snake in the bathtub," I insist. "Someone's made the bell system ring by pressing buttons when we're not in the room. And wasn't Cathy missing something from the fridge the other day? Some elderberry jam no one wanted?"

"It's a stretch, but . . . we should probably check it out if we ever want to sleep again," Quinn agrees with a little shiver. "I really hope you're wrong on this."

I turn to Holly. "I know I was a total jerk, but will you help us search the house? It'll go faster with three—four," I amend as Waffles hesitantly wags his tail.

"Sure. *If* you'll do yoga with me for the rest of the week," Holly says with an attempt at a smile, hurt still glistening in her damp eyes. "It'll be like that one episode of *Gravekeepers*—what was it, 'The Hidden' . . . ?"

"Season one, episode eighteen. 'The Secret Roommate,'" Quinn says helpfully. "Where it turns out there's a man living in the walls of this girl's apartment, stealing snacks from her pantry one at a time so she wouldn't notice. He was even letting her dog out to go to the bathroom when she wasn't home."

"Thanks for the reminder," I say through suddenly dry lips.

Quinn heads downstairs to sweep the first floor. Since Cathy and Rose are there, it seems like the safest place to start, so she declines my offer of sending Waffles with her.

I start opening every door upstairs, Waffles poking his head around my legs to sniff at things, while Holly makes her way toward the attic with a baseball bat in one hand. I don't know where she found it, but she carries it like she played on a team at some point. Which she probably did.

The most exciting thing Waffles and I find is a very large, very dead moth, though I do note that Holly was right: her room is colder even than mine or Quinn's.

The others meet me back near the staircase where we started a few minutes later, equally unsuccessful in their searches. That leaves just one place where someone could be hiding: the locked room at the end of the hall.

"We have to get that key," I tell them, slightly out of breath from my search. "If there's someone else here, we need to know. We need *proof*."

"If there's a skeleton key, it'll be in my mom's room. She has a separate key ring for all things related to the house," Quinn says, her eyes gleaming with the same curiosity that burns in me. "If you two can make sure she's distracted, I'll sneak in and grab her keys. There are so many—one of them has to unlock that door."

I raise my eyebrows at Holly. "You in?"

She frowns. "I don't know, y'all. It sounds risky, and I really need this week to go well. Besides, wouldn't someone need to have the key to be hiding in there? How would they be putting the wardrobe back every time without help?"

"There could be another way in and out of that room we don't know about," Quinn says after a moment's thought. "We won't know for sure until we check it."

She shoots me a worried look, and I share her feelings; Holly has been a little distant lately, especially since she had to miss the trip into town. I hope she isn't feeling left out, or like Quinn and I are excluding her. I reach to touch her shoulder, but she shrugs my hand away. It's so unlike the girl who's quick to hug everyone that I pause to take a closer look at her.

The circles under her eyes are still there after all; she's dabbed concealer over them.

"I just want to make it through the rest of this internship, get my recommendation letter, and go home," Holly murmurs with the cadence of a well-practiced speech. "Does that sound dumb?"

I know how much getting out of New Hope means to her. She's clearly thinking past the internship to the rest of her summer, the rest of her year, but all I can think about are girls whose futures were ripped away from them.

I need to know what's in that room. Especially if there's someone in the house with us—a murderer sleeping a few doors down—who could tear away our futures, too.

"It doesn't. But Holls, this is important. It could be—"

"Dare, I don't think she's interested," Quinn interrupts, her hands tightly gripping the wood banister at the top of the stairs; she hates conflict. "We can handle it on our own. And I'll have to tell Mom, of course. But Holly—at least promise you'll stick close to my mom or Cathy for the rest of the day. And lock your door tonight if you don't want to stay with us."

Holly gives a quick nod before she turns and heads down the stairs. It's like she can't wait to get away, either from the locked room or from us. I can't tell which.

"At least she left us this," I mutter, picking up the baseball bat and handing it to Quinn. "You take the bat, and Waffles. I need to do something really quick, and then I'll help you clean up the new mural in your room. I have to say, I like your art much better than our uninvited guest's."

"I know that look," Quinn says, making me pause with a gentle touch on my arm. "What are you planning?"

"I'm going to record a message asking my listeners for tips about Arrington—we have plenty of local subscribers now. I want to get the names of people who worked here during Atheleen's time, or even earlier. And then I'm going to post it with the new episode."

If there are spirits here—which I highly doubt—they aren't talking to me. So it's time to see what the living can tell me about the dead.

SIXTEEN

"ANYONE IN THE MARKET for an artificial pancreas?" Quinn calls through the family room door.

It's early, sun glowing hot and bright against the curtains, and it takes me a moment to clear my head enough to rise from the lumpy sofa where I'm stretched out, taking care to step around Holly's empty sleeping bag below me. Once again, Rose and Cathy have been working us so hard over the past few days that the three of us have barely had time to shower or do more than watch a little TV on one of our phones before we all fall asleep in here, the door locked against intruders. None of us want to sleep alone.

We've been looking for the key as much as we can, of course—with the threat of a potential murderer lurking in the house, there's not a moment to waste—but no luck so far, and it's hard to avoid the laser-sharp gaze of Rose no matter where we go in this house. If I didn't know better, I'd say she suspects we've been searching her room for something, and she's finding ways to keep us busy—but the house does have a lot of problems, all of which are very real. And half our tasks seem to come from Cathy, besides.

When I open the door, Quinn stands before me holding a cardboard box in one hand and wearing a gray printed dress with a full skirt and a pattern of chomping sharks. It's such a Quinn outfit, I can't help smiling.

"Morning," she adds cheerfully, sweeping into the room with Waffles. "I gave my friend here his breakfast and took him on a walk so you could sleep in."

"You're the best," I murmur appreciatively, still tempted to crawl back to the sofa. I hardly slept, listening for footsteps in the hall as Quinn tossed and turned beside me.

Then I realize she's holding the box containing my new insulin pump, and the urge for more sleep vanishes. Doing injections for every meal and correction sucked, my lower stomach getting tender from all the pinching and sticking. Technology—oh, how I missed it.

Quinn perches on the nearest arm of the sofa, petting Waffles while I program my basal rates—the small amounts of insulin I take per hour as a baseline—into the new pump.

"Holly went for a run, by the way. I saw her heading for the path around the lake when I took Waffles out. My mom wants us all to meet in the dining room at nine, so we have a little time," she explains, glancing at her phone. The screen shows it's just past eight. "She said it's important." Whispering, she adds, "I checked her car for the key first thing this morning, but it wasn't there, which means she really doesn't have it. Maybe Eileen took it with her when she moved out, so for all we know, it could be in a Goodwill somewhere by now with anything else Megan didn't want."

I tuck my insulin pump into the waistband of my pajamas and turn to her, disappointed—but also impressed with the thought and effort she's putting into this. "You'd make an excellent spy. I know we agreed to get to know each other better before we jump into anything, but you should know that I'm wildly attracted to you right now."

Quinn's smile lights up the room.

"So, what do you think your mom wants to talk to us about?" I ask.

"Probably something to do with the company she called this morning—there are more plumbing and electrical problems." A faint line of worry creases her brow. "Hopefully the fixes aren't too expensive."

"Hopefully," I agree, starting toward the door. "Be right back—I need to run upstairs to grab the cameras. I always review footage in the mornings; you can help if you'd like."

Quinn leaps to her feet. "I'll get the thermal."

Back downstairs, the family room door shut for privacy, we sit on the sofa and arrange the cameras so that we can watch play-back from the two feeds at once.

"Remind me what I'm looking for," Quinn says, adjusting her glasses.

"On the digital camera, you'd hope to see orbs—big, fast-moving balls of light, not little specks of dust. Old places like this are always dusty, no matter how much anyone cleans." I grin at Quinn's expression—the intensity of her gaze, focused on the screen, reminds me of a look I've seen on Rose's face many times. "With the thermal, we're looking for anything cold. A spirit, in theory, would manifest in shades of blue and purple, cool colors, instead of having a heat signature like a warm body."

But when I press the playback button on the digital camera, nothing happens. Same with the thermal. I try again. There's no footage for them to display, which makes no sense—I make sure they're on every night before bed, and they both had almost full batteries last night.

The uneasy silence is broken only by Waffles's tail thumping as he watches something move through the curtain-covered windows.

"Someone erased all our footage," I say at last, reluctant to admit it out loud. Somehow, that makes the situation feel more real.

"You mean someone who might be hiding in the locked room?" Quinn whispers.

"Unless ghosts know how to work cameras, yeah."

I glance into Quinn's wide eyes as this latest possibility sinks in. The living are always scarier than the dead.

"I hate this," she declares. "The not knowing. But there's no point bringing it up to my mom again until we have evidence—you remember what she said last time."

How could I forget? She told Quinn it was impossible. That she was imagining things. Rose wasn't even bothered enough to check around, and convinced Cathy it was pointless, too. She made it clear that she disapproved of us abandoning our rooms upstairs as well, but at least she didn't try to stop us.

Glancing at her phone, Quinn sighs. "Speaking of Mom, it's eight forty-five, and she expects people to be early for everything; we should go."

Reluctantly, she pulls away, leaving me shivering in a slight draft.

I quickly check my phone before following her out of the room with Waffles. There are a few texts waiting that came in overnight or early this morning. One is from Deitra, who must have listened to the latest episode of *Attachments* because all it says is: *OMG!!!* Followed by several screaming emojis, naturally.

Hope you get a ton of tips today, Lindsey said. *I don't know how you're sleeping there at night. I couldn't.*

There's even one from Max: *Congrats on not being as lame as I thought you were. Where's my PlayStation?*

The last one, from Mom, just says: *Call me!*

That will have to wait until after the morning meeting.

I trudge across the foyer after Quinn, absently playing with the elastic of the gemstone bracelets on my wrist. The Arringtons silently judge me from their frames above us on the landing, their stares making my skin crawl until we reach the next hallway and disappear from view.

Cathy and Rose are waiting for us in the dining room. Rose looks ready for anything in her designer jeans, sleek hair pulled into a high ponytail, her blouse partly covered by a simple black blazer. She isn't smiling, but that's not unusual.

What's strange is the way Cathy paces in front of the room's black marble fireplace, her hands clasped, shadows under her eyes, and frown lines gathered around her pink lips. Her cheeks are missing their signature blush, as though she got dressed in a hurry.

Holly is there waiting, too, sitting in one of the newly refinished chairs. She reaches down to pet Waffles and smiles a quick greeting as Quinn and I drop into seats beside her, the cushions stiff with their new mint-green fabric.

"Thank you for coming, girls," Cathy says. "I know you haven't even had breakfast yet, and I apologize. There's a coffee cake in the kitchen for when we're done here."

I catch a slight waver in her voice—did someone die? I anxiously wait for her next words as she collects herself.

"We're going to have to end the program early, I'm afraid.

Dare and Holly, I need you girls to make arrangements to be picked up in the next three days."

They're ending the program almost two weeks early.

Rose stands with her arms crossed, listening intently to Cathy's words and nodding after each phrase. But when Cathy shoots her a pleading look, apparently too saddened by this news to continue, Rose jumps in.

"Unfortunately, as you may have noticed, we have major problems with the plumbing here. Problems the contractor can't fix with people staying in the house. There are also some electrical issues that—"

"With the bell system?" I interrupt, recovering from my initial shock.

Rose tilts her head, confused, but Cathy knows exactly what I mean.

"No, dear," she says, the waver in her voice becoming more pronounced. "I, ah, had the men take a look at that this morning before they left. They insisted all the wires were cut, just as we were told when we had the first inspection done."

Rose starts talking again, but I can barely hear her over my heart's sudden pounding. I don't understand—the workers must have missed something. There's no other explanation. I need them to have missed something, because we all heard those chimes.

Rose's next words are louder, sharper, cutting into my thoughts. ". . . the lake has become too turbulent. This isn't how we wanted to end the program, especially not so soon, but it's for the best."

Too full of nervous energy to keep sitting, I leap out of my seat and cross the foyer, heading for the side of the house that overlooks the lake. The windows in the study and family room offer partial glimpses of the water, but it's best seen from the slimy walls of the sunroom. Henrietta's room.

Glass crunches under the delicate soles of my flip-flops as I step lightly into the room. The stench of brine and dead organic matter is strong in here, and the overgrowth of algae on the intact panels blocks most of the light, but several of the busted-out sections offer a clear view of the water.

Something brushes my ear as I lean to peer through an opening—probably a mosquito. Annoyed, I swat it away and focus on the water.

Under a secretive gray sky, the lake churns with small waves of its own, lapping at the grass mere feet from the house. The narrow crescent-shaped beach where we had our party is now completely underwater. So is the spot where Waffles and I played ball the other morning.

No wonder Rose chose the dining room, with its view of the trees and distant mountains, for our meeting; it looks like one more storm would send the water creeping into the house.

I hurry back to the others, my mind racing as I think of leaving so soon. As much as a part of me is relieved to know I won't have to stay here much longer—won't have to keep staying up all night to listen for a stranger's footsteps—a bigger part of me screams that I have too many unanswered questions; I can't go now. Not when the right tip could come in at any moment. Not when there's still a room full of secrets at the end of the upstairs hall.

Besides, I know she's long gone from this place, I know it isn't possible, but—sometimes I can almost sense Atheleen—an echo of her, at least, like a coat someone discarded at a party that still smells faintly of their perfume. It makes me feel like I know her, like I owe her some closure.

I know it's probably just this old house playing tricks on me, but I hate the thought of leaving without finding answers for her.

"Everything all right, Dare?" Cathy asks, misty-eyed, as I return. "We really are sorry to see you go. But you can visit the museum for free when it's open, anytime at all. Your families, too, of course," she adds, glancing between me and Holly as I take my seat.

Quinn slips a hand over mine under the table, and my fingers tremble slightly in hers. I'm not ready to let go of her, either.

"Now that all our unpleasant business is out of the way—who wants coffee cake?" Cathy claps her hands together excitedly.

To my surprise, Holly, who's been quiet this whole time, suddenly stands; I figured she would turn down baked goods in favor of her usual poison of choice, the last pack of Pop-Tarts. She turns away from Quinn and me, jerkily motioning for Waffles to get out of her way.

I quickly call him to my side as Holly doubles over and vomits a pool of murky water onto the freshly polished floor. I'm pretty sure the greenish, wiggling bits in there are just strings of algae, but they look like little green worms.

My stomach does a backflip at the sight.

Cathy cries out in alarm and sweeps over to Holly, putting a comforting arm around her shoulders. "Oh my dear, let's get you upstairs and I'll help you clean up . . ."

As Cathy ushers Holly from the room, Quinn sucks in a breath beside me. But she's not looking at the puddle of sick on the floor. She's looking at her mom.

Rose's eyes are wide, her mouth slightly open, her breathing rapid. She's terrified. It's rolling off her in waves. She strips off her blazer like it's suffocating her, tossing it over the back of one of the dining room chairs, and then collapses into the seat.

"Girls—go. Just—I need a minute. Please," she says tersely, running a hand through her tightly styled hair.

I frown, not sure whether she's worried about Holly or about her dreams for the big house she bought slipping away as the water rises.

Quinn touches my arm, and the two of us take Waffles and head into the foyer.

The servant call box chimes.

This time, I'm standing so close that I flinch, my ears ringing with the force of the sound. One of the flags for an upstairs room has dropped.

I try to take a deep breath, but it doesn't stop my head from spinning as I stare at the little flag; when did the air in here get so heavy? Part of me wants to run to Rose, to have her call the electricians back so I can watch them inspect every part of the call system.

I want the satisfaction of hearing their embarrassed confession when they find the wires intact. They just weren't looking hard enough.

"I worked on mapping these flags out a little before you woke up," Quinn says, running her slender fingers over the glass meant to keep visitors from touching the bells. "I think . . . the one that dropped is for Holly's room."

She blinks a question at me, one hand still on the glass covering the flags.

I want to yell for her to stop touching it. But that would mean meeting her in a place where anything is possible and the world is so much more than we can perceive. I shake my head at myself. "Electricians make mistakes like everyone else. They missed something—I'd bet money on it." Before she can argue, I say, "Let's go check on Holly."

As I climb the stairs, Waffles behind me, Quinn catches up and takes my hand. I squeeze hers, smiling—I need to make the most of these last few days with her. But as we turn the corner on the landing, I can't help casting a last glance down at the call box, hoping I never have to hear its impossible ringing again.

SEVENTEEN

"OH, GIRLS, DON'T LOOK so worried!" Cathy declares when she sees our faces. "Holly's going to be fine. Her stomach feels better already. But I told her not to drink the tap water anymore. Apparently, she hadn't been using the filtered pitcher in the fridge."

I guess we still look skeptical because she motions toward Holly's door in invitation. "Go see her. And remind her that she's not to do any work today! Neither are you two, for that matter. Dare, let me know if you need any help arranging your ride home, dear."

I gently push open Holly's door. She's sitting upright in bed, the pillows propped behind her, rebraiding her long blonde hair. She smiles lazily when she sees us, looking so much like the girl I met on my first day here—energetic, approachable—that the knot in my chest loosens just a fraction, making breathing a little easier.

"Oh em gee, y'all, I swear that woman means well, but her cooking is going to be the death of me," she jokes. "Dare, can you make me some plain toast? Pretty please? I won't make you do any more yoga if you say yes."

"Of course," I agree, relief continuing to wash over me like sunshine on a cold day. Downstairs, she looked like death. It must have been the house again, toying with light and shadow.

"I'll stay here till you get back." Quinn settles on the end of Holly's bed and pulls out her phone to show her something— probably a meme, knowing her.

I turn to head back downstairs to the kitchen, but something stops me. "Hey, Holls—the call bell for your room went off a few minutes ago. Did you happen to push it . . . ?"

To my surprise, Holly grins. "Cathy's butt did. She backed into the button while insisting on fluffing my pillows." She points to the brass plate on the wall near her headboard, but I can't quite bring myself to laugh along with her.

Neither can Quinn.

I know what the look she's giving me over the top of her glasses means, why her red lips are quirked: if the wires are cut, those buttons shouldn't do anything. This is the proof I've been after; she's waiting for me to admit that she's been right about this place all along.

But as much as I want her to be, the bell chiming for the right room at the press of a button is proof that wires somewhere are running just the way they should. That the world might still be ordinary. Safe.

So why does the damp air keep pressing in tighter around me, smothering me even here, now, with my friends by my side?

Once again, I turn to go, and this time my gaze sweeps over Holly's dresser. The sightless doll sits atop a stack of books as if on a throne, spatters of green on its face. Either Holly has given that thing freckles, or there's fresh mold growing out of the hole in its cheek.

I wouldn't be surprised if a mold allergy has caused Holly's health problems, rather than Cathy's cooking or even the questionable tap water—though I'm not sure I completely trust Rose's reassurances that there's no lead in the pipes.

After I bring Holly a tray with her toast and she starts bolting it down, Quinn and I return to the hallway with Waffles.

"I should probably call my mom," I admit, my phone heavy in my back pocket. She'll be worried when she hears that the program is ending early, because that's what moms do, but I don't have much time to reassure her.

I wish we didn't have to go so soon, not when I'm this close to—something. I'm not sure what, exactly, but there's a filmy coating on my tongue from the humid air and a dark, electric current running along my skin, promising answers to questions I've been asking for years if I just look a little deeper.

"This changes things, doesn't it?" Quinn studies me through her long lashes. "Leaving so soon."

"What do you mean?" My heart skips and stumbles as I try to read her face.

"It's just, I thought we had more time together. I know you've got the podcast to finish—assuming you can rush the ending—and we still haven't found that key, but do you think we could take a minute? Just us?" She moves closer, and at my quick nod of permission, puts her hands on my waist.

"I . . ." I want to say yes. But the key to the locked room could be everything. That key could be hiding someone who shouldn't be here. Someone dangerous.

Quinn shakes her head; she seems to sense where my thoughts have strayed. "The more I think about it, the more I agree with Holly. There can't be anyone in a boarded-up room. Mom or Cathy would have noticed something by now, too."

"Haven't they, though?" I ask, my mouth a little dry as we lean into each other. "Cathy crosses herself every time she leaves a room. Seems like a person who's on edge to me."

"I don't think that's something people do when they're worried about the living."

She has a point. But someone hiding in the locked room is the only explanation for a list of incidents that's growing with alarming speed. "I'm just saying, we can't know for sure that we're alone unless we get in there and look for ourselves. Otherwise, how do you explain the missing camera footage?"

"I can't. Not in any way you want to hear." Quinn gently tucks a strand of blue hair behind my ear, understanding glistening in her eyes. "Everyone needs to believe in something, whether it's a spirit, a deity, a piece of art, or an intruder. I know that as well as anyone. I guess I'll go see what my mom—"

"Wait!" I draw her back as she starts to pull away.

It's been three days, and whoever is in the locked room hasn't attacked anyone yet—a few hours with Quinn won't ruin my chances of finding the key. Just like I need answers, I need to explore whatever it is I feel for her before we're forced to leave.

"I was thinking—the family room hasn't been touched yet. And now that we've moved the TV out, there's space to set up a picnic in there since going outside doesn't seem like an option." I run my fingers through her glossy hair, trying to distract myself from the sweat that's breaking out across my brow at the thought of what this could mean for us. "It'll be like a real date, or whatever."

"Or whatever," Quinn teases, her fingertips twisting the fabric of my shirt—I'm not the only one who's nervous. "If you're sure you've got the time . . . I'd like that."

We don't see Rose or anyone else as we tiptoe around the quiet downstairs, scrounging up a large wool blanket and an assortment of candles from the supply closet near the parlor entrance. Quinn takes charge of food while I use the empty study to call my mom.

"Can't wait to see you," Mom says excitedly through a crackle of static. "Max has insulted my frozen-food-heating skills so many times in the past week, even he's ready for you to come home. His guinea pig got loose the other day, did he tell you?"

As Mom catches me up on what's happening at home, I realize she hasn't listened to *Attachments* yet. I'm sure she will, but she's always the last to catch on to any trend thanks to her busy schedule, and for once I'm glad. If she knew everything going on at Arrington, she would probably insist on picking me up today.

When we hang up, I enter a room that's been transformed into something like an enchanted garden—the shadowed stacks of boxes stretch and sway like trees when glimpsed out of the corner of my eye as the flames of candles leap and twist. Quinn sits on the wool blanket we spread across the floor, a generous chunk of Cathy's coffee cake laid out on a plate with two forks. There's a bowl of berries beside the cake, and even a few small apples.

I shut the door and quietly lock it before sitting opposite her.

"How did it go with your mom?" Quinn asks uncertainly, keeping her voice low.

I notice her gaze stray to the speaking tube on the nearest wall—we still don't know who might be listening, and this moment is just for us. "All good," I tell her. "The food looks amazing, by the way." I take an apple and turn it over, examining its dappled red-and-green skin in the flickering light. "I didn't know Cathy made another grocery run."

"She didn't." Quinn smiles proudly at the bowl. "These are from the orchard on the grounds. They're loving all the water. The garden's flooded, though. I picked the few veggies that were ready, but I'm not sure anything will survive out there if the lake keeps rising."

"I'm so sorry. I know how hard you worked on it."

A fleeting smile touches her lips as she grabs a small knife and an apple for herself, and I find myself reaching out a hand to stop her.

"Don't," I say, the back of my neck prickling for reasons I don't fully understand.

Quinn arches a brow. "Why not? There are no chemicals on these. I washed them, just to be safe. No pests—"

"Still. Don't. For me?" I think of Quinn in her shark dress, thick mud sucking at her sneakers as she trudges to the graveyard of an orchard near the rising lake, and shake my head. "I can't explain why, but I'd feel better if neither of us ate anything else that grew here. I'm a little worried something in the food is making Holly sick." Not to mention the water.

Quinn slowly puts the apple back in the bowl and nods. "Okay. I wasn't that hungry, anyway. I'm just glad you're here."

She pushes the food aside and snuggles against me. I put an arm around her and breathe in the perfume of lavender and sage that clings to her.

"I've changed my mind, by the way," she announces, a whisper against my ear. The candlelight makes her eyes glow like molten honey, sweet with a hint of danger.

"About what?" I murmur, distracted by the way she's running her fingers over my back.

"Kissing you."

When our lips meet, the shadowed room around us melts away. There's only me and this smart, talented, beautiful girl who sees something in me that draws her closer. I don't know what the science is behind why her kiss tastes so good. For once, I don't care.

Nerves dance in my stomach as her hands wander to the hem of my shirt. I don't want her to stop, but I'm out of my depth, and afraid it shows.

I start to draw back, but realizing just how cold it is in here, I lean into Quinn's embrace instead. "Remember when I told you I had no idea what I was doing here?" I confess, my lips against her ear. "I still don't. The only thing I'm sure of is you."

When you have a body with a history of letting you down, the last thing you need in your life is a person who does the same. I can't say for sure yet if Quinn is someone I can rely on, but unlike the rest of the happenings at Arrington, I have a good feeling about this. About us.

Quinn turns her head, catching me off guard with another kiss. This one is so intense, it's like the first and last time all at once, neither of us willing to come up for air. Her lips touch my hair, then my neck—at that, I grab her shoulder, digging my fingers in. I must press a little too hard, because she flinches, and I quickly drop my hand.

"Oh my god, I'm sorry, Q. What—?"

"I don't know," she says quickly, pulling at the collar of her dress until she exposes her bare shoulder to the room. "Oh, shit," she says. There's a bruise dappling her skin, four long marks like fingers.

"Did I just—?"

She gives a quick shake of her head. "People don't bruise that fast." Her words are hushed with worry as she lets the collar of her dress snap back into place. "I think it's from my shower this morning, after I took Waffles out. Something pushed me. Or tried to."

"Why didn't you tell me?" I ask, gently touching her face until she meets my eyes.

"I didn't think you'd believe me," Quinn says simply.

But this is evidence; those marks are real. Something hurt her, whether of this world or another. And I would do anything to protect her.

"Q, I don't—"

"Shh. It's just a bruise. Let's talk about it later." She leans in, brushing the tip of her nose against mine, and grabs the bottom of my shirt. "I have something better in mind than talking right now, anyway," she says, her eyes dancing, as she kisses me again.

She wants me. I've let her see a few of the scars I never show, and still, she keeps getting closer. And when she touches me like this, fingers tracing the lines of my face like I'm a work of art, I'd take a hammer to my remaining walls for her without stopping to think twice about it.

Moments later, she whispers, "I want to try something," setting every nerve in my body on fire. She slowly untangles herself from me, climbing to her feet, and offers me her hand. "Dance with me? It's dumb, but—I never went to any of the dances in high school. I never cared. But for some reason, I do now." She grins, at once shy and daring. "You can sing for us, right? I've heard you in the shower, so don't even think about pretending you're no good."

My head is spinning from the sudden change of pace, but I like it. I let her pull me up and wrap my arms around her waist. "Am I doing this right?" I laugh, feeling a little shy myself as her hands cling to my back.

"You're doing all the things right," she whispers, and I don't know how I keep singing and swaying with my knees turning to water at her words.

As my voice fades and we hold each other in the near dark, Quinn says, "I've been thinking about what you said the other night, by the way. About fall break. I'd like to come see you."

"Really? I'd love that." I can't remember smiling this much since before I first stepped onto the overgrown lawn of Arrington. "Does this mean . . . you want to try the whole long-distance thing?"

"Oh I want, very much," Quinn says, sealing the deal with the soft press of her lips on mine. "I just wish we didn't have to start the distance part so soon."

A sudden gust of wind snuffs our candles in a merciless blow.

We had shut the curtains over the windows before starting our picnic to hide the view of the rising gray water, so without candles, we're left in hazy darkness.

"It's okay," I say quickly, starting toward the nearest window. "We must not have shut one of these all the way."

Something hits my cheek. The back of my hand. My chest.

Quinn screams and jumps back; she feels it, too. "Gross!" By the light of her phone, I can see greenish water raining down on us from the ceiling.

Crossing to the window, I happen to glance into the mirror Rose recently hung on the opposite wall. The flash of Quinn's phone sweeps over the room, and within that beam of light, I see a girl trapped within the glass before me.

Her skin is mottled with years of decay, her waves of hair limp and dripping, her eyes milky white, but I know her from my dream.

Atheleen.

She's here.

She extends a bony arm, the curved talons of her fingers reaching toward me as she smiles too widely, a smile that grows until it splits her face open. It looks like she's laughing, her lips parted to expose mossy teeth, her face twisted in ghoulish delight.

Water pours out of her mouth in a rush, spilling over the cracked skin of her lips and onto her sunken neck, soaking the front of her shirt.

The beam from Quinn's phone dies. She mutters a flood of curses as darkness wraps a cold fist around us, the echoes of impossible laughter gurgling in my ears.

EIGHTEEN

QUINN HASTILY FLIPS ON the overhead lights, and the laughing apparition vanishes like smoke, leaving only a faint, lingering haze where she stood. It's gone when I blink. I can tell by Quinn's expression—slightly frazzled by the water, but otherwise calm and purposeful—that she didn't see what I did, which means maybe Holly isn't the only one who feels unwell in this house. I'm now seeing things others can't, which is never a good sign.

It can't have been real. If Atheleen's spirit had really been in that room, Quinn would have seen her, too. After all, she saw her dead neighbor, and that's more experience than I have.

A few of the bulbs above us buzz and flicker weakly; the water stain spreading across the ceiling is practically the size and shape of Texas, and some moisture must be seeping into the fixtures. Another problem that's going to drain Rose's dwindling funds.

As we clean up our picnic and try to soak up the water using rags from the supply closet, I decide I'll only brush my teeth with filtered water for the last few days of my stay. I don't trust the water here, and I refuse to let this place get to me any more than it already has.

If Quinn notices that I'm quieter than usual as we make more toast to bring up to Holly, she doesn't act like anything's wrong. She even steals a kiss before we knock on Holly's door, and her warmth lingers, pushing away the cold terror of what I saw, the nagging voice in the back of my mind suddenly full of doubts and more questions than ever.

The night passes quietly except for the breath of the lake lapping against the shore as it creeps ever closer to the house. With Holly still upstairs in her room, we forgo the family room sofa to be closer to her, Quinn joining me in mine. She seems on edge— about the idea of someone living or dead in the locked room, I can't tell which.

We stay up half the night talking, unable to do much more than that with Waffles deciding to sandwich himself between us. I'm not sure when we fall asleep, but the next thing I know, I startle awake to the buzzing of my phone near my head.

At first, I assume it's my CGM letting me know about my blood sugar, but I'm 109, in range. Then I see an email notification flash across the screen, and remember: I changed the settings for email alerts to vibrate after I posted the new episode of *Attachments*, not wanting to miss a tip.

To: AttachmentsPodcast
From: IvyBeanArt
12:15 A.M.
Subject: Officer Brian S. McDougal

Look into Brian. He's one of the first responders who arrived at the scene when Atheleen's accident was called in. He knew the family pretty well. He used to grab drinks in New Hope on Thursday nights with Mr. Bell, and his wife divorced him within weeks of the Bells moving away. There must be a story there.

The message isn't signed, but they did provide a phone number for Officer McDougal. Sitting up, I glance at the spot next to me on the bed, a stretch of cold, empty space where Quinn was sleeping. Waffles isn't there, either—she must have taken him for an early walk again.

I pull out my laptop to thank the anonymous listener, and openly beg them to tell me any other little thing they might know.

From behind me comes a faint scratch, just one, like someone rubbed a fingernail against the wall as they passed.

But when I glance over my shoulder, there's just the headboard, the wall unblemished.

It's impossible. Yet I know what I heard.

Maybe Holly was right when she said this place isn't good; maybe it's not us but the house itself that's infected, a damp, locked tomb beginning to fester. It's a ridiculous thought, but I can't shake it.

Finally, I manage to refocus my attention on the email and start typing. But as soon as I do, the door creaks open. "Hey, Q," I call without glancing up. "How was it out there? Lake rise any more last night?"

"You have no idea," a voice answers as someone steps into the room. But it's Holly, not Quinn who's entered, dressed for a run in her usual branded athletic wear. "I felt a little better this morning, so I was going to go for a run, but I only got as far as the kitchen—the downstairs is flooded." She gestures to the bottoms of her yoga pants; they're soaked to the ankles, her footsteps into the room leaving behind a glistening trail.

"Oh, no," I murmur as our eyes meet.

We both know what this means: the internship is just a few

weeks for us, and whether or not all our hard work is ruined, we get to go home soon and enjoy the rest of our summer. But for Rose and Cathy, it's a whole summer of wasted effort and a massive bill to try to address the damage. I think of Rose and Quinn, each with their own shiny car, and wonder how much of a loss they can afford to take on this place—appearances can be deceiving, after all.

"Rose is on the phone with the insurance people now," Holly says, shaking her head as she glances around my room and rubs her arms. "Is it always this cold in here?"

"Sometimes," I say as her gaze falls on my laptop. "Maybe more than that, but I wouldn't know—last night was the first time I've slept in here in a few days."

"How's the podcast stuff coming?" Holly asks, sitting beside me. Before I can answer, she says quickly, "I'm sorry I was weird about the key. Quinn told me you haven't found it yet. It just seems like the house is trying to tell us to back off, you know? It's pretty hard to ignore literal writing on a wall."

"I think we should be more worried about the house falling down around us, at this point," I say with another glance at Holly's sodden footprints on the floor. "And about whoever's here with us."

"I really don't think—" Holly begins, cutting herself short. She takes a breath. "You know, it's almost time to head home. Before we do, I was thinking it might be fun for you, me, and Quinn to go into town. We can visit the Mystic Teacup again. Plus, I have a key to my parents' shop—you can watch Quinn geek out over old stuff with me and tell her how cute she is."

I smile. The idea is tempting, but the email in front of me is the most important thing right now, and I can't ignore it. "I want to, but—I'm sorry. I can't. I have to chase this tip I just got. It's the number for one of the officers who responded to the call the night Atheleen died."

"Cool!" Holly's eyes light up as she leans forward to read the email. As she finishes, her face darkens. "Dare," she says seriously, "you might have gotten me into *Gravekeepers*, but you're not thinking like them right now. How do you know some random person isn't sending you into a trap with this? What if whoever wrote this wants to hurt you? Look, you're strong as hell—I wish I were more like you that way—but you're not invincible."

"I know that," I insist.

"Do you?" Holly turns slightly to reveal the plum stains of a bruise on her pale shoulder, four long lines running down her neck into the collar of her leopard-print tank top. "Because you seem to be ignoring some dangerous signs. I'm starting to think Quinn's right—Atheleen's ghost doesn't want us here. I got this in the shower yesterday while I was washing the puke off, and I'm pretty sure it's her way of saying 'Go home.' Maybe it's time to accept that some things are better left unknown."

I can't stop staring at the bruise, so similar to Quinn's in size and shape. Almost like something has marked them.

"So you—believe?" I rasp, my mouth suddenly dry.

Holly looks pointedly at me and nods. "This house would make anyone believe."

Not me. "Atheleen isn't here. She's dead. She's past caring what we do," I say firmly, thinking of the apparition in the family room vomiting water all over the floor. Water I mopped up with my rag. I dig my fingernails into my palm, grounding myself in reality with the sudden sharpness. Just because I can't explain it doesn't mean there isn't an answer.

But my list of questions keeps growing. The wolves of my imagination are hunting, conjuring shadows to make me shake and cower—but I don't have time to be scared. I only have two days left here.

Holly reaches for my hand, wrapping it tightly in hers. Despite how sick she's been, her grip is strong, her fingers slightly chilled. "Come with me. Let's find Quinn and go into town. You can bring your laptop and call whoever-it-is in a safe, public place, with us to back you up if it gets weird. And trust me, if we're talking about somebody from New Hope, it'll be weird."

"I don't know . . ." There are answers waiting for me. All I have to do is call the tip number. "I guess you're right. I can call Brian from anywhere."

Holly beams at me and lets go of my hand, but not before I feel a slight tremor in her fingers. "Good. I feel better already—I might even get a Danish at the Mystic." She hops off the bed and crosses to the door. "I'll be right back. Just need to change into dry pants."

I save Brian's number in my phone and type him a quick text introducing myself just as Holly rushes back into the room.

"That was fa—" The words die on my tongue; she hasn't changed yet, after all.

"Come with me," she gasps, out of breath, eyes wide. "You have to see this."

I quickly pull on yesterday's socks and my sneakers, following her out of the room.

The aquarium at the end of the hallway is flooded. Thick green water bubbles and oozes from the pipe at its base that feeds it. The stone diver in his astronaut gear floats on top, facedown, surveying his watery prison from above.

As I take pictures for the podcast's Instagram feed, Holly wanders toward a small, grimy window overlooking the swollen lake.

"Dare, come quick!" she shouts suddenly, pressing her hands against the glass. "Look out there—it's Quinn."

A dark-haired girl wades into the lake, water soaking the hem of her paw-print-patterned dress, an empty leash and attached collar dangling from around her wrist. Slate-gray water sloshes around her knees as the current rolls toward the house. There's so much lake now that from up here Quinn looks doll-sized in comparison.

What is she doing out there? And where is Waffles?

"Help," I plead, tugging at the bottom of the stubborn window.

Holly and I tug upward, and finally with our combined strength, we force the reluctant panel to budge. Cool air wafts toward us as we stick our heads out the window and scream Quinn's name.

She doesn't turn around.

She doesn't even flinch. It's like she can't hear us.

She can't even hear Waffles barking at her from out of sight. He sounds close to the house, as if he fled in terror when Quinn headed for the water.

We race down the stairs, keeping close together as we splash through the damp halls. Rose and Cathy are nowhere to be seen.

We fling open the door at the back of the kitchen and run outside into a sunny but windy day, our shoes and socks already soaked through thanks to the soggy carpets inside.

By the time we get to the lake's edge—maybe ten feet from the house, too close—Quinn has waded out farther, water inching up past her thighs.

Holly and I crash into the churning waves, spraying water everywhere, even onto Quinn. Absently rubbing her shoulder, she stares toward the middle of the lake as though she can't feel the cold kiss of droplets on her face. Water sucks at my waist as I finally reach her side, taking one of her arms while Holly takes the other.

Waffles barks, loud and insistent as he finally charges into the water, making laps around us as if to guard us from something. With a few lessons, he'd be a strong swimmer.

"What are you doing down here?" I demand, shaking Quinn's arm to get her attention. "How did Waffles get out of his collar? What's going—?"

I don't get to finish my question. Something grabs me by the ankles, and I get only a brief glimpse of Holly holding on to Quinn, of Waffles yelping and paddling toward me, before I'm yanked under so hard that my head hits the bottom of the lake.

NINETEEN

THERE'S NO TIME FOR the highlights of my life and loved ones to flash before me—there's barely time to fight my way free before I'm out of air. But whatever grabbed me now presses down on my chest, trapping me beneath the surging water.

I can feel fingers digging into my skin, nails sharp and jagged. But when I blink my eyes open in the filthy, stinging mix of mud and water, there's no one holding me down. Only the sensation of two hands pushing with everything they've got, of bone and skin pulsing with violence as I struggle in their hold.

There's a commotion as someone fights their way toward me, gripping under my arms and pulling me up, forcing whatever was holding me to let go. It's Holly.

Quinn's face is still a blank canvas as she stares at me coughing and gasping, tears mixing with the water on my cheeks, as though she's completely unaware of her surroundings. Catching my breath in Holly's arms, I glance warily at the house. I almost think I see a pale face looking out of one of the upstairs bedrooms. But my eyes are blurry from the muddy water, and it's gone as soon as I blink.

"What happened? Did something grab you?" Holly demands as Waffles leans against my legs, shaking as badly as I am. Thank goodness my CGM and pump are waterproof. "You know what—

never mind," she adds with a hasty glance toward the blue-gray horizon. "We need to get back inside, now. Can you walk?" I hesitate, then nod. "Okay. Good."

She clamps a hand around Quinn's wrist as though scared she'll wander off again, lured by whatever brought her out here in the first place.

"La piña está agria," Quinn murmurs drowsily as Holly guides her to shore. Somehow, with help from Waffles, I follow unsteadily in their wake.

"What was that?" I ask Quinn as the burning in my lungs starts to subside. Holly catches my eye and frowns; she doesn't know what it means, either.

Quinn blinks, finally looking at me as though she's just realized she's not alone. "Huh? I . . ." She swallows, her brows knitting together, and for a moment I think she's going to faint. "I don't know. Did I say something wrong? You look upset." She sweeps her eyes over the grounds, confusion flitting through her gaze. "Why are we outside? What time is it?"

"You . . . don't remember?" I ask her. Seeming embarrassed, she shakes her head, and I do my best to fill her in between labored breaths.

With every step we take toward solid ground, the clamoring of my heart in my ears fades a little more, until at last the rush of the water is louder than my racing pulse.

"Do you think it was another rip current? Do you feel sick at all?" Quinn asks softly. Typical—she's more worried about me than herself.

"That's the last thing on my mind," I tell her, though it's not entirely true. I can still feel the memory of those hands pushing down on my chest, like an invisible weight has lingered. "How could you get all the way out here without knowing it?"

Quinn shakes her head, helpless. Gazing down at the leash and collar dangling from her wrist, she gasps. "I don't know how he got loose, Dare. I'm so sorry." Turning to Holly, she adds, "I'm sorry to everyone. I didn't sleep well last night—maybe I was sleepwalking?"

Holly presses her lips together. "Maybe," she agrees a moment later. "But awake or asleep, none of us should let the others go anywhere near the lake. Nature talks, if you listen—and this place is telling us it doesn't want us here. We should go pack. Today."

Her words echo what she said in my room: Atheleen doesn't want us here.

The lake wants us gone. The so-called spirit wants us gone. Holly wants us all to leave now, too.

Even if she's right, I can't. Not when I'm so close to getting answers—for Quinn, for me, and in a way, for Atheleen.

As the water clings to our ankles, reluctant to release us from the shallows, Quinn shivers and seems about to fall backward. I raise both hands to steady her, and the elastic on my gemstone bracelets snaps. Little bits of amethyst and obsidian scatter into the water like colorful pearls, rapidly vanishing from sight. That's what I get for playing with them too much. I'm not about to try to dig them out, not with dead fish and snakes and who knows what else floating around in here.

The next step we take is more mud than water.

"Waffles, we don't need a weather update—we know the lake is dangerous," I shout over a sudden burst of his growling as the wind rakes through my messy hair.

I glance down to give my dog a warning look. He tucks his tail between his legs, apologetic, but growls at Quinn, showing teeth.

Or maybe not her, but the extra shadow behind her, a twin of the same height floating on the surface of the lake.

I blink, and it doesn't vanish, but seems to merge with hers until I can't tell where the shadow ends and she begins.

"What?" Quinn asks, anxiously searching my face.

I'm not about to admit my eyes are playing tricks on me again and give Holly even more reason we should all leave today, so I quickly say, "Just worried about you. We should see if your mom—"

"No!" Quinn gasps. "Please, don't tell her. You know how she is, Dare. She'll say we're all imagining things like a bunch of kids. Just—I'll be fine once I take a shower and clear my head. This won't happen again. I swear." Leaning closer, her warm copper eyes looking deep into mine, she begs, "Trust me?"

"I do," I say, ignoring Holly's faint headshake.

Waffles calms down once we get inside, wagging his tail contently as Quinn recovers herself enough to pet him.

"You said something earlier in Spanish," I tell Quinn as Holly makes everyone some tea. "What does it mean?" I repeat the phrase from memory.

"Oh," Quinn laughs, a startling sound in the damp graveyard of hard work gone to rot. " 'The pineapple is sour'—Dad loves that expression. It means 'times are hard.' "

Even in her dreamlike state, she wasn't wrong about that.

As I sip my tea and put Waffles's collar back on, I try not to think about the fingers that dug into my skin as two hands held me under the lake. I don't think that's how rip currents are supposed to feel, but what do I know? Very little, apparently.

My stomach rumbles. The tea I'm sipping is a cloudy color, brown tinged with gray, and it makes me wonder if Holly remembered to use the filtered water like Cathy said.

But when I open my mouth to ask, lake water and bile gush past my lips, splattering the table and floor.

The house is infecting us all.

I'm not sure where the thought comes from, but I don't disagree.

As Holly helps me clean up the watery vomit with a rag and Quinn ties my hair back, making a fuss, I notice both my friends occasionally running a hand over their wine-dark bruises and wincing as if they ache deep beneath the skin.

How long until the house marks me, too? What does it want with us?

After our poor attempt at warming up with tea, we walk Quinn through the flooded lower floor toward the staircase. She gazes around as if seeing the damage for the first time, her pupils still slightly dilated. "All that work for nothing . . ." she sighs. "La piña está agria. I'm sorry again—for all of this. For bringing you both into such a mess."

"Stop," I insist. "None of this is your fault. I'm just glad you're okay."

I haven't been able to stop shaking, but I'm not sure if it's more from the thought of almost losing Quinn, or what I saw reflected behind her. It was just like my vision of Atheleen at the picnic, like the face in the window as I coughed up lake water: there and then not.

Quinn asked me to trust her, but I'm not sure how much I even trust myself anymore.

We trudge upstairs past the cold stares of the Arringtons, each as emotionless as the last. The girls' pale lips and bloodless features, the anemic look of long-ago wealth and status, make them nearly impossible to tell apart but for one's white-blonde hair and the slight, arrogant curl of her lip, as though she reviled whoever painted her. This is surely Hettie, the cruel girl whose diary page I found; she looked much the same in the decaying images we unearthed in the attic, always apart from the rest.

"I'm going to pack," Holly announces as Quinn heads for the shower. "Y'all should, too, if you have a lick of sense. Dare, give me a hand? I . . . don't really want to be alone right now."

I watch Quinn head to the bathroom, shutting the door behind her. My heart beats out of sync as my muscles tense, waiting for her to scream—another snake in the tub, an unseen hand reaching out, anything. But a minute or two later, when it doesn't come, I inhale deeply and quickly change into dry clothes before going to help Holly.

She's got a duffel bag open on the bed by the time I show up, and she's shoving shirts and shorts into it. "Hand me the socks in the top drawer, would you?" she asks.

But I can't look away from her bedside table.

There, next to her pillow, is the moldy doll from the attic. There's definitely a spread of new green across its face, not paint as Holly first insisted. It's not safe or sanitary for such a thing to be in the house, much less in someone's bedroom, so close to their face while they sleep. We have to get rid of it.

I reach for the doll, but Holly dives across the bed, beating me to it. She snatches it up and clutches it against her chest as its insides rattle.

"What are you doing? That's covered in mold!" I gasp, more startled by the hawkish look in her eyes than by the way she clings to the soft, mildewy body.

How can she bring herself to care so much? I can't stand the sight of it, its face too ruined to be a reminder of beauty or innocence or happier times; if anything, it's going to mean someone's death thanks to whatever spores are breeding in its hollow innards. My mind flashes back to the pigeon hitting the attic window, feathers and blood bearing a bad omen.

"That thing belongs in a dumpster!" I tell her, not sure why she doesn't seem to understand. "Ideally one that's on fire."

"It's mine," she says stubbornly. "I told you, I'm going to repair it for the museum."

"But I thought you were leaving early?"

"Right. Like anyone ever leaves this house!" Holly huffs as she slams the doll on top of her dresser, well out of my reach, seeming on edge from the simple question.

She's not the only one. The doll slumps forward, its weight unbalanced on the lip of the dresser and from Holly's sudden movements, and begins an ungainly swan dive.

Holly shrieks and tries to snatch it out of the air, but it soars past her grasping fingers.

The clink of breaking porcelain rings through the room as the doll hits the floor and its china head shatters. Holly's eyes water, and for a minute, I think she might actually cry. Then she shakes her head as if clearing away cobwebs. "This town. I—I meant to say nobody leaves this town. I'll go get a broom." She tries to laugh, but the sound is hollow, lacking any sort of humor or cheer. "There goes another project I'll never finish."

As Holly strides to the door, Quinn appears, out of breath and wide-eyed, her skin glistening from the shower. "What happened? I heard a crash—" She stops short, her gaze landing on the mess.

"I was just going to get a broom," Holly sighs. "Be right back."

"I think we've done more harm to this place than good," I tell Quinn as we crouch over the porcelain shards. Holly's footsteps retreat down the hall behind us. "Serves it right, too. I'm starting to hate this house."

Quinn scowls at me. It's such an unusual sight that it takes a moment for my mind to make sense of things—I had no idea her face could contort like that.

"How could you say that?" she snarls. Softer, she adds, "This poor old place needs love, and more money and care than we can put into it." She runs a hand tenderly along the scuffed floorboards. It's like she wants to protect the house, the gentleness in her eyes and voice suggesting it's not all about her mom's investment, either. I've seen her look at me that way before, when we were dancing by candlelight.

She loves the old estate. Quinn, who's too afraid to sleep alone at night, who winces when she rubs her bruises and puts crystals in every windowsill, loves this place more than she fears it.

Me, I wouldn't be sorry to see it burn.

A glint of gold catches my eye as I return my gaze to our latest disaster. Cautiously pushing past chunks of moldy porcelain and two marble-sized glass eyes, the irises colored a milky green, I reach for something small and metallic among the rubble. It's short and slender, about the length of my pinky finger, its top decorated with swirls of filigree forming shapes of skulls and birds, the bottom a series of crooked teeth. This is what was making the rattling sound as it banged against the eyes in the doll's innards.

A golden key for a golden lock.

TWENTY

ON OUR WAY TO the end of the hall where the old wardrobe with lion-headed knobs hides a long cut in the wallpaper, I duck into my room just long enough to grab my digital recorder. Waffles whimpers as I leave the room, unwilling to follow, and curls up on the bed.

By the time I reach the hidden door, Quinn has already pulled aside the empty wardrobe and has started prying away the remainder of the boards barring the door. It helps that the wood is soft and slightly damp, with a faint odor of something wild beneath.

As the boards fall away, Holly sees what we're doing and drops the broom and dustpan in the hall, hurrying to join us. Quinn gestures for me to do the honors.

The golden key clicks softly as it lands at home.

I push, but the door doesn't budge. My friends join me in throwing their weight against it, forcing it to give from the frame where it swelled over time with neglect and weather. Breathing hard, we stumble forward into a bedroom as perfectly preserved as a fly trapped in amber.

Quinn and Holly both meet my eyes, and I guess their thoughts at once. There are no other doors in this room. No way someone could be getting in and out, no signs that this place has been inhabited in years, maybe decades. Only a pair of windows stuck hard in swollen frames, inches of dust gathered on the sills.

My chest tightens, but I try to ignore it and push into the room with a little help from Holly, who gives me an encouraging nudge.

Several strands of small twinkly lights are strung above the double bed, its chipped white headboard resting between windows that overlook the withered apple orchard out back. The bed itself is neatly made up with a sunny-yellow comforter and violet throw pillows. A woven carpet brushes the bottoms of my bare feet as I wander toward the bed, trailing my fingers lightly over this graveyard of white wicker furniture and bookshelves still stocked with someone's favorites—old paperbacks of the Baby-Sitters Club, a few Saddle Club titles, and Nancy Drew books; like me, the reader must have loved a mystery.

I pick one up at random, thumbing through the delicate pages, and a school picture of a guy around my age falls out. Someone was using it as a bookmark; they've drawn little hearts around the guy's face, and I smile because some things never change.

The shallow two-door closet is stuffed with clothes that smell faintly of lavender despite an overwhelming musk of neglect; there are a few old scent sachets on the floor, along with a broken CD. Holly sifts through the clothes almost reverently, gingerly removing and trying on a fuzzy knitted scarf.

A delicate purple flower encased in clear glass hangs from a wire cord in front of the left window, glowing as it catches the scant morning light allowed in by the years of grime coating the glass. Quinn reaches for it cautiously, as if afraid it might burn her.

From the walls, posters of wolves and fairies and trees with faces watch us silently, their edges curled with the weather they've endured.

On the dresser, amid aging perfume containers, bottles of nail polish, and hair ties, someone has arranged several plastic horses of various colors and sizes into a neat row. There are a few porcelain figurines of cats and dogs, too; whoever lived here loved animals.

Quinn eyes the dead flowers on the corner desk, fragile husks still arranged in a bouquet inside their vase. Stacked beside the vase are homework sheets and textbooks on subjects like algebra II and biology. The rest of the desk is covered in framed photos.

"Dare," she chokes out, the first word spoken inside this room in who knows how long. "Holls. Look."

She points to the photos, and when we join her, she grabs my arm. She's shaking.

On first glance, the pictures are remarkable only for how ordinary they are: Two girls on horses, their smiles wide, their brown hair frizzy from the summer heat. A family of four out for ice-cream cones. A girl and her friends getting ready for prom. Two girls again, standing on the front porch of Arrington, suitcases in hand.

I know one of the girls right away: Atheleen. She looks just like she did in the photo I found of her hugging her cat, the one that was run in the local papers with news of her death.

Which means this must be her bedroom.

I can watch her grow up in these pictures if they're in the right order, but I know they'll stop when she reaches seventeen. Her story ended too soon. Maybe someone selfishly ended it for her.

But the other girl, the smaller girl hugging Atheleen's mom and dad, handing her sister a birthday present, holding her sister's hand at the familiar lakeshore, showing off a fairy-themed Halloween costume, is unrecognizable. Someone has scratched the young girl's face out in every last picture.

Why would Atheleen want to erase all these memories of her sister?

Or did someone else do this?

Part of me wants to grab Holly and Quinn and finish packing right now. There's no one here but us, which should make me feel safer, but it's just the opposite; a damp, heavy feeling steals over me as I stare at the scratched-out face in Atheleen's family photos. Too many things have happened that can only be explained by another person hiding in the house.

The room is tidy, if dusty, and full of cheerful, cozy things—yet I've never felt more unwelcome anywhere in my life.

But this is what I came for, after all. Answers. Swallowing my unease, I turn on my digital recorder and begin describing the room for my listeners, from the bookshelf's offerings to a detailed description of each family photo.

That's when it hits me: I saw Atheleen's sister in my dream. Her face was blurry there, too, but she had the same slim stature, the same dark hair, the same pale skin. But I'd never seen a picture of her before today.

Quinn and Holly sit on the floor, pulling boxes from under the bed and sneezing as the resulting dust wafts over them. Quinn puts a hand on the lid of the first large shoebox and hesitates. "Maybe we should go get my mom and Cathy . . ."

Holly and I exchange a glance, and at my nod, she rips the lid off the box—there's no telling whether Cathy and Rose would let us see whatever is inside.

It's full of old CDs.

"Oh, I know this one!" Quinn says excitedly, holding up an album called *Sunshine Station*. "My parents use to play it in the car for me when I was little. Apparently, it helped me stop crying when I was worked up."

She recognizes several more discs as she sorts through Atheleen's collection, as does Holly, but I'm ready to move on to the next box. I set my digital recorder down on the rug between us, letting it run as I continue to narrate our findings.

The second box contains sketches and paintings—some in charcoal, some in pencil, others done in watercolor. Each piece is carefully stacked with a layer of tissue paper between it and the next, and I'm surprised someone our age took such meticulous care to protect their work. Of course, when that work is as good as what I'm seeing, maybe that's just what you do.

"Wow," Quinn breathes, handing the rest of the CDs to Holly when she notices what I'm holding. Peering over my shoulder, she stares at a watercolor of the lake, its shoreline much closer to the house than it was when I first saw it—much like it is now.

Atheleen has titled it at the bottom: *High Tide*. She even signed it A. I. B.—Atheleen I. Bell—and dated it June 17, 1990.

The next piece we unwrap is a watercolor that looks disturbingly like the art we found on Quinn's wall—so much so that I can't bring myself to say it out loud. Glancing quickly at my friends' pale faces, I realize there's no need. They see it, too.

The Mermaid Girls, Atheleen called the piece, dated April of 1989. On the paper, four underwater creatures with scales in muted blues and greens and grays stare mournfully toward what I assume is the surface of their home, their arms ending in claws that grasp at a bare human foot just visible at the top of the page. Despite the title, they aren't quite *girls*, their features too pointed, their eyes all pupil and no iris, their faces too sunken to have ever been glimpsed on land. One of the creatures has dark, curly hair, reminding me of someone I've seen before—someone I've seen recently—but I can't quite figure out who it is that's tangled with this wraithlike image in my memories.

I start unwrapping the next picture with shaking fingers.

The Skeleton Girls. February 21, 1992. The year she drowned.

Quinn presses her fingers to her lips to stifle a gasp.

Four dead girls rest on the surface of a lake. Paradise Lake—whoever thought to call it that clearly never visited. Their smudged charcoal-etched features are pinched with sorrow, their bodies seemingly drained of blood and flesh, of life, leaving behind only skin stretched tight over bone. Hollow corpses, pale corpses, floating like sailing ships.

Bile rises in the back of my throat as I shove the drawings away.

But Quinn, who has somehow steeled herself to keep looking, mutters a few moments later, "These are really good. She was even better than me."

Reluctantly, I skim over the images she's selected—painted apple trees, their growth stunted and twisted, reminiscent of the orchard behind the estate; a blood-red cardinal on a tilted fence post; horses in a pasture; brown coyotes in the summer woods;

the lake in different seasons, surrounded by a ring of fiery trees in fall and somehow diminished in winter, frozen and retracted, burying its secrets in ice.

"We liked painting a lot of the same stuff, too," Quinn says softly, gathering up the sketches and returning them to their box. "But now I'm even more confused about why she's been trying to scare me. Maybe she doesn't realize how much we have in common." She grabs the CD she first held up. "I'll play this tonight. Remind her of happier times."

I don't answer, afraid that if I open my mouth, it'll attract the army of dust bunnies under the bed. And maybe something more.

Holly spots another box deep in the shadows, one that she and Quinn somehow missed the first time around. It's shoved so far toward the wall that she has to crawl beneath the mattress frame, cold metal scraping her back, to grab it.

"Let's see what Atheleen was hiding," she says eagerly as she cracks open the lid.

The smell of the attic hits us first: musty and damp, with a hint of mothballs.

Inside are photographs in various states of decay, spanning decades, if not the last century. No wonder we couldn't find much when we were sorting through the piles of junk; Atheleen beat us to it, salvaging the bones of the past and storing them here.

The first picture shows us the jet-black curls and prom-queen smile of Scarlett Tarver. As soon as Holly picks up the photo, I realize: that's the face I was remembering—that's who the mermaid in Atheleen's painting reminded me of.

Next is a black-and-white shot of a much younger girl with blonde hair in an old-timey, frilly dress, clinging to the hand of her mother and staring openmouthed at the camera as though she's just seen a ghost. Behind mother and child looms a stray shadow that can't possibly belong to either of them, too lean and too tall. The spidery, faded-blue writing on the back of the picture says *Liv*.

Then there's a picture of a girl close to my age, wearing a long gown and clutching a large bouquet of flowers, her sepia-toned features warm and alive—a bridal portrait? This one has more detailed writing behind it: *Mercy Elizabeth Lawrence, March 11, 1913.*

The youngest girl, Liv, shows up in another photo, too, this time on a grandparent's lap on the front porch of Arrington. There are several of Scarlett at the lakeshore with her siblings and a shy-looking girl with a camera on a strap around her neck. That must be Eileen Brown. Miss E.

I pass the pictures to Quinn and carefully dig out the next item: four newspaper clippings. The oldest proclaims, "Respected Veteran Captain Arrington Loses One Daughter, Another Hospitalized." Henrietta Arrington drowned in a boating accident on the day of her sixteenth birthday. The article lists the names and ages of her surviving brothers and sisters, too—Alexander, twenty-four. Levi, twenty-one. Anne, nineteen. Lily, eighteen. Nora, seventeen. Violet, twelve. Polly, eight. Marcus, six. Evie, three.

The next newspaper clipping details the suspected suicide of a bride-to-be in 1913 who jumped into the lake a week before her wedding. Then there's an article about an accidental drowning in the late 1930s. Last, there's a brief clipping about Scarlett's suspected disappearance on the afternoon of August 28, 1969.

"What's that?" Holly asks, gently nudging me in the side.

Glancing down, startled from my thoughts, I realize I'm also holding a folded piece of notebook paper. The handwriting is Atheleen's.

> *Henrietta Arrington. "Hettie." Sixteen years old.*
>   *Died July 20, 1871.—The first?*
>
> *Mercy Lawrence. Seventeen years old. D. March 12, 1913.*
>
> *Olivia Welch. "Liv." Eight years old. D. November 30, 1938.*
>
> *Scarlett Tarver. Nineteen years old. D. August 28, 1969.*
>
> *Augusta Bell. "Gussie." Twelve years old. 1992—she's next.*

TWENTY-ONE

IN MY HANDS I hold evidence of four dead girls. Four skeleton girls. Drownings separated by decades—forty-two years here, twenty-five years there, then another thirty-one. Scarlett's name among them, written confidently in Atheleen's hand. I scan the numbers, the dates, looking for a pattern. As always, my mind searches for order, logic.

It's when my gaze lands on the article in Quinn's hand, the one about the boat accident, that I finally see it. "The girls' ages," I whisper. They all match up.

I put the newspaper clipping and Atheleen's list of names on the floor side by side as Quinn and Holly look on. Mercy Lawrence, seventeen years old—just like Nora Arrington. I point to both girls' names. Liv Welch was eight, like Polly Arrington, and Scarlett Tarver and Anne Arrington were both nineteen.

Each of the victims after Hettie was the same age as one of her sisters the year she drowned. Even Atheleen, at seventeen. It all fits.

"Megan's daughter was three when she saw something she called a skeleton girl," I say at last, my tongue scraping against my dry lips. "And look—Hettie's youngest sister, Evie, was three when the accident happened."

Quinn whispers, "So it's a spirit who's been killing all these girls? Does this mean Hettie is our ghost, then, not Atheleen?"

I press my lips together, unsure. This does make it look like there's something more going on here than random bad luck—but can I really say that this proves there's a ghost in this house? My whole life, I've believed that there's an answer to anything, no matter how unexplainable it looks from the outside. But now that I know there's nobody hiding in this room—nobody living, at least—I don't know what to think anymore. Is Quinn right? Is Hettie Arrington's spirit behind these deaths?

"Think about it," Quinn urges. "It fits. We all saw the diary entries; we know Hettie was a spiteful thing with her list of petty grudges. I don't know how cruel she was in life, but maybe death has twisted her mind." She lowers her voice. "Made her ruthless. Made her try to drown anyone who reminds her of her sisters."

Holly puts a hand over mine. "Y'all realize we're the same ages as her sisters, too, right? No matter who the ghost is, I think we're in trouble." Her words are rushed, sharp; the room doesn't seem to like that, the air turning harsh with a sudden chill.

"Why wasn't her picture in the box with the others?" I ask in a hush. "Hettie's, I mean."

Holly shakes her head. "It wouldn't be a picture. Look at the date—in her time, they would have used daguerreotypes. I bet anything she's in the ones we found in the attic."

At her words, I recall an image with startling clarity: a pale-haired girl standing apart from her sisters, reluctant to take part in their pose in which they all wore old-fashioned bathing suits and twirled parasols by the lake. Atheleen must have missed the contents of the steamer trunk when she explored the attic before us, or else it would be here with the rest of the evidence; she was a thorough researcher.

Atheleen thought her sister was in danger from something in this house—from the ghost of Henrietta Arrington?—but something went wrong, and Atheleen herself died instead.

"I think I saw it happen," I murmur, glancing around the room for the source of the persistent cold—the windows are stuck shut, as before. "Atheleen's death." I try not to let my friends' increasingly grim faces unnerve me any further as I give them the details of my nightmare and what I saw on the ceiling when I woke up. "I hate to say this, but . . . I can't explain it. Any of it."

As Quinn puts a concerned hand on my back, I continue, "But how could I have dreamed something that really happened? How did I know Atheleen's sister was there, and that she was in danger, too?"

"Wonder where her sister is now," Holly adds, frowning down at the papers between us on the floor, her gaze lingering on the list of names. "And who scratched her face out in all those pictures? Atheleen, or someone else? Whoever it was, they must have hated her."

Holly's frown deepens as she runs her fingers over her shoulder—the faint discoloration of a bruise just visible through her T-shirt.

Quinn spreads her hands out before her in a helpless gesture.

The three of us have been talking almost nonstop for two weeks, and suddenly we have nothing to say. None of us have answers, least of all me. What if I've been ignoring signs of a haunting, the very thing I was searching for, all this time? And why? Is my mind trying to protect me from a truth I thought I could handle? I lean into Quinn because she's the only thing in my world that makes sense right now.

"Looks like we missed something," she murmurs, and I follow her gaze to the shoebox of Atheleen's careful research. There's a slim journal at the bottom. I wipe my sweaty palms against my shorts before pulling it out.

I recognize Atheleen's handwriting on the first page.

To the next owners of Arrington Estate,
whoever you might be:

This house was cursed long before we arrived. If I can't stop it, I fear the curse will continue long after we're gone.

Something wasn't right from the moment we moved in. I knew it, and my sister knew it, but our parents ignored our suspicions for years.

At first, it was little things. Cold spots. A stray touch when one of us was alone. Water on the windowsill, the floor. Stains on the ceiling. My boom box turned on by itself all the time, and never to one of the good stations.

Lights would come on when none of us were home. The lights Dad and I hung above my bed would turn on sometimes in the middle of the night, too, but I didn't mind that as much; I liked the way they flickered like fireflies. It was like a game at first. A joke only me and the house were in on.

The ghost in this place travels by water. That's how it gets inside.

I think of the water stains on the ceiling, the walls, of the green gunk that came out of the taps when I tried to do the dishes on my first night here. Atheleen was the kind of investigator I want to be, one who didn't miss a thing. I wish I'd known her. I keep reading:

Gussie found puddles in her bed, and Mom thought she was having accidents brought on by night terrors. By the girl in her mirror. Gussie said the mirror-girl had curly hair, milk-white eyes, and the bluest lips she'd ever seen. She wore a princess dress. The girl in her mirror watched her with those luminous eyes every night for years.

Bells chimed in the house so often that Mom and Dad had the old system disconnected, making sure the wires were cut. But the bells kept ringing, and Dad wrangled a partial refund from the electrical company, claiming poor workmanship.

I started researching everything I could find about Arrington—the attic was a lot of help, at least until I got pushed down the stairs for touching her picture. The one of her and the sisters she hated so much.

I'm fine. At least, for now.

But in the past few days, the pipes have taken to regularly choking up chunks of algae, or something, that Gussie calls slime. She's started sleepwalking, which she never used to do, getting closer to the lake each time. And now, the water is rising too fast to ignore. I think . . . it's hungry. And I'm afraid it won't stop until whatever evil lives within its depths takes my sister away for good.

Henrietta Arrington was the first to drown, and it's my theory that her spirit controls everything here—the lake, and the ghost that's been haunting us: Scarlett Tarver.

Hettie is using Scarlett to get what she wants: Gussie, a new companion to keep her company in the lake. I don't know why she needs somebody new—maybe it's for once she's finished using up what's left of Scarlett, or maybe she just wants another girl to add to her collection. I don't know if Hettie remembers what it was like to be a girl anymore, or if all that's left are her own worst fears and cruelest wishes— the blackened heart of the lake.

And it's not just a theory anymore. I know I'm right. The last time I went to pull Gussie back inside after one of her sleepwalking adventures, I saw her. Scarlett floated in the middle of the lake, watching us, gaunt and pale, more skeleton than human. But just behind her was a second girl, a golden, glowing girl, her face flush with life, her eyes full of hate.

I blinked, and they were gone, but I was sure I recognized that second face—and a trip up to the attic confirmed it. That's when she made Scarlett push me, because I suspect I was too close to the truth.

This place worms its way into your most private thoughts. It finds your weakness, commits it to memory, then uses it to tear you apart. And so, dear reader, I beg you: run as far and fast as you can from this place. Because if you're reading this, then I failed. I tried to stop her, to starve her, and if I'm gone, then it didn't work. And perhaps that means it never will.

If I fail, maybe I'll be trapped in these walls in Gussie's place, stuck doing Hettie's bidding to find her a new life to

*consume and destroy, but that's a risk I have to take. No one
is going to hurt my sister while I stand by. I'll fight to the
death for her if that's what it takes.*

The rest of the journal is blank.

I set it down, my body humming with nervous energy as
Atheleen's words sink in.

Henrietta Arrington was an unpleasant girl at best. I know that
much from the surviving bit of her diary. She died. I know this,
too, from the newspaper articles and letters from the Arringtons'
friends and family. There have been four drownings since hers—
Mercy, Olivia, Scarlett, and Atheleen. Four victims. I have proof
for most of this as well, all but Scarlett's. But where are these facts
leading me?

As I clutch the journal between sweaty palms, mind reeling,
another disturbing memory nudges its way to the open. Megan
said Eileen kept repeating something near the end about "letting
the right ones in." The right ones for *what*? Did she know about
Hettie, too, and that the ages of the girls who drowned over the
years matched up so perfectly with the Arrington sisters'? Did she
suspect that the house was counting on her to draw in girls of a
certain age, impossible as it seems? Or was it just the rambling of
a tragically fragmented mind?

Either way, I have no tangible evidence. It's just another frustrating, mind-twisting, infuriating mystery I'd need more than a
few days to solve.

"The water is rising now, like it did the summer Atheleen died,"
Quinn says slowly, her voice thick and heavy with dangerous

words as she stares at the journal in my hands. "And there were six mermaids on my wall. One of the spirits here must be Atheleen, but the other—"

"Could be her sister, or someone new. It could be a warning," Holly adds, thinking along the same lines as Quinn. She dabs sweat from her forehead with the edge of her shirt. "She'll come for us next. We need to go, just go now. If this thing—Hettie—"

Her words are cut short by the ringing of a bell somewhere downstairs.

The servant call system.

I hastily grab my recorder and hold it out in front of me. "Atheleen?" I ask around a sudden lump in my throat. My heart is stuck there, quivering like a caught rabbit. Then, feeling slightly foolish in the midst of my panic, I add, "Hettie?"

This could be the moment I've been waiting for my whole life; I can't walk away now, no matter what I'm about to see or hear. Like a math test, it's time to show my work; without evidence, only the desperate will believe what I say, even if it's the truth. Without evidence, I won't believe me, either.

Another bell joins the first, this one fainter; I think it must be coming from the call box in the attic. They keep chiming, one after the other, picking up speed.

"Hey—I know that song!" Quinn says suddenly. "It's from the CD I showed you."

The bells stop abruptly.

In the silence, I think I hear someone's heartbeat. Mine, yes, but an echo of someone else's, too.

"Hettie, we know you're there!" Holly shouts, glancing uneasily around the room. "Why have you been pushing us around? What do you want?"

"Why can't you just let Atheleen go?" Quinn adds, her eyes flashing. Masking her fear with anger. "Did you kill her sister, too? Are you sorry? Why are you doing this?"

A poster rips itself from the wall.

Then another, this one slashed as though by invisible claws.

Static raises the hair on my arms and neck. The house seems to draw itself inward. Bracing for what's to come.

By the desk, just out of reach, an image flickers to life as I blink: a girl in torn jeans and a faded T-shirt, sodden clothes clinging to her skeletal frame. Thick waves of brown hair hide most of her face, but the sliver of pale, decaying cheek and the curve of a smile splitting bloodless lips is enough. More than enough.

One look at Quinn's and Holly's faces tells me they see her, too. All that's left for me to do is accept the mounting evidence that's been piling up since I walked through the old oak doors: the Arrington Estate is always haunted by its latest victim, always under the control of the vengeful spirit of Henrietta Arrington.

Ghosts are real. And there's one here, right now. It took five dead girls for me to see the truth. I just didn't know how to look past my brain's attempts to protect me from my nightmares. The mind is a weapon whether you believe in anything or not; faith and denial, they both cut deep if you hold on too tight. Both can be fatal, preventing you from seeing what's true until there are hands around your throat, wringing out your last breath.

"Ath—Atheleen? Is it really you?" Quinn chokes out.

I'm not hallucinating, though I'd almost prefer it.

Atheleen was on my ceiling that night.

Water rolled off her rotting face and splashed me as I lay help-less in bed.

She was in the mirror in the bathroom.

She was at our picnic, vomiting water that I mopped with my own hands.

And I think she's the extra shadow at Quinn's back, watching. Waiting.

She's really here. But as quickly as she appeared, the figure by the desk is gone. Yet somehow, it doesn't feel like she's left us. Just disappeared from view.

Suddenly, I have a whole new level of respect for ghost hunt-ers whose shows I've mocked and flipped past with sarcastic com-ments. Some of them are out there searching because they know the truth, like I do now. Imagine facing all that ridicule while wrestling with the terrible knowledge of what hides in the dark.

I *know* what hides in the dark.

Water, seemingly from nowhere, slides down the walls as though the room is weeping.

As I watch, my body screaming for me to tear out of the room, out of the house, and never come back, framed photos slide off the desk one by one and shatter on the floor until there are none left standing.

The three of us cling to each other in the center of the room as more posters drop off the walls. A mounted butterfly in a wood frame follows suit as if flung by a careless hand, the colorful corpse it held now floating in a sea of glass.

Still clutching my recorder, I raise my voice, narrating what's happening over the sound of the crashing. There will be those who won't believe me. Who, like me, will dance around the truth even though they long for it. But I'm recording for them, too, so that one day, when they have an experience they can't deny, they'll listen and feel seen.

Books start flying off the shelves. Pages tear themselves out, a flurry of paper snow raining down on us, a few delicate edges slicing my face and hands. A book sails toward us, and Quinn darts in front of me before I can react. Though she throws her hands up, it strikes her on the cheek, raising an instant welt.

As more books hurtle through the air, I position myself in front of Quinn and Holly, trying to shield them. But Holly is the one who manages to strike several of the books down before they can reach us.

"Atheleen? Can you hear us?" I stammer. "How can we stop what's happening here? Help us—help us succeed where you failed."

The books stop fluttering.

The room goes utterly still. It looks like a hurricane ripped through here.

I can feel a presence nearby, the unseen fourth person in the room with us, each slight movement of air like angry, heaving breaths.

Someone else's pain and fury crackle across my skin, and Quinn must feel it, too, because she grabs my hand and holds tight. That touch conveys more than words ever could about what I now know, what we all know.

Most ghosts are hoaxes, but this one isn't.

It's the exception: The one that makes you pause and consider a story you'd otherwise laugh at. The one that lingers in your mind and makes you ask, "What if?" instead of moving on with your day. The one that means any other ghost story could be true.

I thought I would feel comforted knowing that none of us are ever as alone as we think we are—that's how I always imagined it would be in my search for the truth. So why, instead, do I feel like spiders are scurrying across my skin?

This new understanding is nothing like I hoped for, nothing I wanted. The three of us exchange nervous glances, our chests heaving with the effort of breathing in the hostile air. No one seems to want to be the first to make a move for the door, let alone a sound; who knows what might set the spirit off again?

A soft noise breaks the silence for us.

Footsteps, deliberate and wonderfully solid, climbing the stairs.

TWENTY-TWO

JUST AS WE MANAGE to slide the wardrobe back over the closed door to Atheleen's bedroom, Rose emerges into the upstairs hallway.

Something in our expressions must give away how frightened we are, because Rose's face falls as she and Quinn stare each other down. Does she know about the door? Does she suspect where we've just been?

"What are you doing?" she asks, her steady voice revealing nothing. "Did you girls hear the bells again, too?"

My eyes are damp, my skin flushed with the horror of what I've just realized to be true, one hand tightly grasping Quinn's. I have to think fast. Ghosts or not, Rose would be livid that we've opened up a wall without permission.

"We did. But Holly isn't feeling well—we were just going to help her pack so she could go home early," I say in as normal a voice as I can manage. The words come out too breathy, but hopefully Rose takes it as concern, not fear.

Holly catches my eye and gives the slightest nod, willing to play along. I wonder if I'm as pale as her after what we just saw; her skin is the color of curdled milk.

"Oh?" Rose peers closely at Holly, her slight figure somehow seeming to block the hallway. "I'm sorry to hear that. Is there anything I can get for you? Are you nauseous again?"

She's too concerned, too interested; we aren't getting past her with just that one line.

"A little, actually," Holly says, her voice faint.

I raise a brow when I'm sure Rose isn't looking, impressed; Holly never told us she was such a good actress.

"I'm sure I'll feel better once I'm back in my own bed," Holly adds, her expression pinched, her features growing more ashen by the second.

Rose rushes forward and takes Holly by the elbow, pulling her away from me and Quinn as if to guide her to her room. "Let's get you into bed here, for now. You don't look like you're in any shape to travel right now, even a short way. And aren't your parents out of town until tomorrow? Who's going to call for help if something happens?"

"My brothers, if they're around—look, I'll be fine," Holly insists. "Home is exactly where I need to be right now."

With that, she collapses in Rose's arms.

Quinn and I exchange a look; this doesn't feel like acting. Not the way Holly slumps like a rag doll in Rose's surprisingly strong hold, and not the utter terror on Rose's face as she gasps, "Girls, help me!"

We hastily move Holly's half-packed suitcase off her bed and draw back the sheets, tucking her in. I squeeze her hand, hoping she'll signal back that this is all an act, but her fingers are limp and still as cold as they were in Atheleen's bedroom.

"She just needs rest; she'll be fine in a few hours," Rose declares, settling on the end of Holly's bed and taking out her phone. "But I'll stay right here until she wakes up, in case she needs anything— that's a promise."

Quinn and I linger in the doorway, reluctant to let our friend out of our sight. What we saw in Atheleen's room seems to have been too much for her, which doesn't surprise me; I'm not sure how my feet have carried me this far.

"Mom? I think we should close down the estate tonight. It's just one day early," Quinn says, not looking at me. "There's so much damage to this place already, and the lake just keeps rising. Wouldn't it be better if we all got rooms at a motel? There are plenty of vacancies. Plus, we could take Holly to urgent care in New Hope if she gets worse."

Rose seems to consider it a moment, but then she shakes her head. "I've got a contractor coming first thing in the morning to try to save the work we did downstairs. I have a lot of money tied up in this place, sweetheart. I can't just walk away because things aren't easy." Her eyes hardening, she adds, "But you can go, if you really don't want to finish out the project. I'll understand. This line of work isn't for everyone."

"No!" An unsettling blankness slides over Quinn's face, like she's suddenly gone somewhere else and left behind a shell. "I'll stay," she says firmly. "I . . . want to stay." It's like watching a stranger wearing my girlfriend's face.

This house is twisting us, turning us into the worst versions of ourselves with whatever plague it carries. Maybe we really should leave tonight, with or without answers; maybe, if we stay long enough, we'll start to rot from inside like Holly's moldy doll until our eyes sink into our skulls and cracks appear in our faces, trying to let light back in.

A moment passes before Rose glances up from her phone, just long enough to give her daughter a slight, approving nod. "Good.

Then see if you can help Cathy," she says, making it clear we're dismissed.

"Q, what the hell?" I demand as soon as we're out of earshot. "You think it's safe to spend another night here with Hettie? We have no idea which of us she wants for the lake—I don't want any of us ending up like Atheleen!"

"I never said it was safe," Quinn whispers sharply as we head into my bedroom, where Waffles greets us like he thought he'd never see us again. As Quinn pets him, the light slowly returns to her eyes, and when she speaks again, her voice is stronger, warmer, sounding more like herself. "Hettie wants us either gone or dead, and I know which I'd choose. But . . . I have to protect my mom. I can't just leave without her. If you want to go, I'll understand."

She leans into me, her fingers brushing my cheek. "I'd feel better and worse if you left now—if that makes sense. I wish I were as brave as you."

"Who says you aren't? You came here knowing all this stuff was real; I don't know if I could have done that. And I'm not going anywhere," I tell her firmly, lacing my fingers through hers. "I won't leave you."

What I've learned here has changed my world, and any proof I can gather with my equipment will mean so much to others, too—but I've got to be here for that to happen. And I only have one more day to do it; how can I turn away now? Even if the podcast didn't exist, I wouldn't abandon Quinn. Not for anything.

Hettie is using her spirit to scare us, but aside from the bruises on my friends' shoulders, she hasn't hurt us. Yet.

Does that mean there's something of Atheleen left despite Hettie's hold on her? Is Atheleen trying to warn us, frighten us into leaving before Hettie forces her to drown one of us, the way she drowned in place of her sister?

My phone buzzes—probably my CGM. But when I pull it from my pocket, it's a text. From Brian McDougal, the police officer my anonymous tipster connected me with. With everything I learned about Hettie and Atheleen, and the other girls, I'd already forgotten about him. My first thought is to ignore his message—now that I know our murderer is a ghost, how much help could the police really be?—but a second later, I reconsider. Maybe he knows where Atheleen's sister is now; from the list Atheleen kept, it seems Hettie only claims one victim at a time. Of course, maybe that changed when two girls, both the right ages, walked up the creaky front steps of the estate.

I've heard ghosts usually stop haunting once their story is told in its entirety. Maybe Hettie and Atheleen will both rest once the truth of the Bell family is out. Atheleen deserves to be free of this place. Now that I have all the work she did, I owe her that much.

Can you meet tomorrow? he writes. *Two p.m. There's an auto-repair place just down the road from the estate—turn right after you cross the bridge. I can tell you all about Atheleen and Augusta Bell.*

I text back to accept. If Atheleen's sister is alive, she could be the key to stopping this whole thing. She might have the answers we need.

"Where'd you go?" Quinn asks softly, her eyes seeking mine.

I quickly put my phone away and return my attention to her—my girlfriend. My sweet, artistic, amazing girlfriend. I wish I could take her far away from here, somewhere we could be alone without the weight of Arrington bearing down on us.

"Nowhere," I say, holding on to her so I can watch her eyes

light up; she likes being close. "Just wishing I could protect you. You know, put a whole ocean between us and Hettie."

As I stroke her hair, my gaze strays to the water stains on the ceiling, vaguely person-shaped, and I hastily look away. It reminds me too much of the apparition of Atheleen's corpse splashing my face as she plummeted toward me. It also gives me an idea.

"There's one thing we can do to stay safe. It's a little gross, though."

Quinn draws back to look at me. "Name it."

"Since the spirit uses the water to come inside the house, we shouldn't take any more showers or baths here. We're all leaving tomorrow night, anyway."

"Then the next shower I take will be at a New Hope motel," Quinn says, mustering a smile. "And I'm never coming back here, no matter what my mom says. I'm going to make her listen to me for once."

I give her an encouraging hug, which somehow turns into another kiss.

"We'd better check on Cathy," Quinn sighs against my lips, too soon. Cathy and Rose aren't the right age to join the ranks of Hettie's victims, but they could still get hurt in one of the spirit's outbursts—a pipe breaking, a piece of ceiling falling in. "But we'll have to stick together, and bring Waffles—there's a *lot* of water down there."

She doesn't have to explain further. Reluctantly, I nod, and Waffles jumps off the bed to follow us downstairs. Before I step out of the room, I grab the digital camera. I'm not going anywhere without it again.

When we reach the house's damp lower level a few minutes later, we find Cathy working steadily, listening to something on her phone that she quickly shuts off at the sound of our footsteps splashing toward her. She's happy to have our help in her war against the flooding, so we slosh around the drafty mausoleum of a house, carrying lamps and decorations to airtight boxes where they'll be stored until the contractors finish the bulk of the repair work.

"Ugh," Quinn sighs as she helps me move an expensive antique chair from the study, "That smell is giving me a headache."

It's the stench of mildew and decay, intensifying as the lake inches closer to the house. It's so strong now that I swear it's under the floor and in the walls, but I know neither Rose nor the historical society budgeted for ripping everything open and starting over.

I keep my digital recorder and camera within reach, ready to investigate at the first sign of Atheleen's return. But now that it knows I'm searching for its ghosts, the house seems to be retreating, scuttling away its secrets into places I haven't yet thought to look. Once again, I glance around the watery halls with resentment; I can't leave my listeners without proof, not when I'm this close.

Hopefully Brian can help me solve the mystery of Augusta Bell tomorrow before my mom comes to take me home. I can't leave Atheleen's tormented spirit to rot in this watery tomb without trying to help her, and her sister might be the key. I just need time—with the mystery, and with Quinn. I wish I had more.

After moving another load of boxes, I decide to take Waffles outside for his potty break. We leave through the front door this time and head toward the grassy space closer to the woods, the area that will become the museum's parking lot.

Waffles prances around me, finished with his business and wanting to play. I let him off leash and throw his ball for him, careful to keep it on the side of the house farthest from the lake. I don't even want to look at the restless water, its surface cloudy even on a sunny day.

Suddenly, Waffles gives a single bark and darts across the driveway.

"Your ball's over here! Come back!" I shout, chasing after him.

He bounds toward the lake, and as he crashes into the water, my heart sticks in my throat at the thought of a snake or a rip current—or worse, a pair of greedy, bony hands—stealing away my best friend.

He doesn't seem to hear me as I continue to shout his name, too focused on whatever has caught his attention. He dips his whole head underwater as I rush in after him, but by the time I've reached him, he's up again and hastily paddling toward shore.

Soaked up to the edge of my shorts and shaking, I guide him back to the porch and refasten his leash to his jingling collar. "That's the last time you're going off leash for the next ten years," I tell him sternly. "Then you'll be too old to try anything, anyway."

He lies down on the sagging porch and wags his tail, oblivious, chewing on whatever prize he found in the water.

"What's that, buddy?" I ask him, crouching beside him for a better look. My legs weren't doing a great job of holding me up, anyway.

It looks like a deer bone—I don't want him chewing on anything that might splinter in his powerful jaws and choke him, or give him some sort of bacterial infection from the lake. It takes some coaxing, and a trade: one of my flip-flops for his prized contraband, but finally I succeed.

As he licks the straps of my shoe appraisingly, I turn his chew toy over in my hands.

The door creaks open.

"There you are!" Quinn sounds out of breath. "I've been looking everywhere; we just agreed we'd stick together! Hey, is that—?"

The words die in her throat as we both stare at the thing in my hands. Long, sturdy, yellowed, and mottled with age, it's definitely a bone.

And there are still a few human-looking molars attached.

TWENTY-THREE

"**YOU DID THE RIGHT** thing, calling this in so quickly," Officer Owens assures a jittery Cathy as everyone talks in the kitchen over coffee and tea. The officer is a young Black woman in her late twenties—too young to have known about the Bell case, so I can't dig for more information.

Owens and her partner already bagged the jawbone and packed it in their car to take to the station, but they had a few questions for Cathy and Rose first, and then Holly started fixing drinks for everyone.

She came downstairs when the officers arrived, guided by Rose, a little color returned to her cheeks. She keeps making faces at me every time she catches me looking worriedly in her direction, trying to reassure me she's fine.

"Lake sure looks angry," Officer Owens's partner says, gazing out the window. He's a tall man, built like a linebacker, but he looks somehow diminished with the vastness of the lake behind him. "You ladies need anything before we go?"

Rose stiffly insists that we don't, and sends the officers on their way.

I tell her I'll lock up behind them, and hurry to keep pace as they stride to the door. It's like they can't get outside fast enough—not that I blame them. "Wait," I say quickly as Officer Owens grabs the doorknob.

Both officers turn to me, unsmiling, clearly not pleased with the delay.

I switch on my recorder without taking it out of my pocket. "I just wanted to ask you about one of your fellow officers—Brian McDougal. Do you know him?"

Quinn will be much cooler when I tell her about tomorrow's meeting if she knows that this officer checks out with his coworkers.

"Sure. He retired from the force a while back. Nice guy, by all accounts. Sorry, we've really got to go," the male officer says dismissively. "Unless you wanted to share anything else about what your dog dug up here?"

I hesitate. The officers said they plan to try to identify the body using dental records, but that will go a lot faster if they have somewhere to start. I don't know how seriously they'll take me, but I work up the nerve to try.

"Yeah, I . . . think that bone probably belongs to Scarlett Tarver. Or maybe Atheleen Bell's younger sister, Augusta." As the officers' eyebrows start to climb, I hastily add, "I've been doing research. For a podcast."

"Oh!" Officer Owens says. "*Attachments*, right? My sister won't shut up about that. But Augusta Bell didn't die here. She moved away with her parents."

I try to hide a grin. So she is out there somewhere, maybe holding on to important information we could use to bring her sister peace.

"Podcasts," the male officer grunts. "Why not just listen to the radio?" He shakes his head, marching out the door without a goodbye. Officer Owens follows with a wave. At least she doesn't seem to think I'm a total idiot.

So, Brian McDougal is the real deal. It's actually a good thing he's retired, I think. That means he'll be less guarded, talk more because he won't be afraid of losing his job if he lets the wrong thing slip.

Back in the kitchen, Quinn says, "I can't believe they aren't going to dredge the lake or anything. The rest of the body has to be down there still."

"It's too deep, darlin'," Cathy says, her back to the restless water. Rose seems to have vanished into another room—moving furniture, from the sound of things. "They're not going to risk lives over one that's already been lost."

With that, she turns to leave the room, probably following after Rose.

Holly, sitting at the kitchen table, glances uneasily out the window. Maybe she feels it, too, the push of the house as though it wants to reject us, to suck out the poison of the intruders in its walls.

"I thought you were packing up and leaving as soon as you felt up to it," I say, sliding onto the bench beside her. "I wouldn't blame you."

She pushes around a mug of tea, now cold, and shakes her head. "It's only one more night. And I bailed on so many things before I came here. So many friends, too. But I can't leave you and Quinn with an angry ghost. I like you too much."

She leans against me, her head on my shoulder, and I have a feeling she'll be in my life forever. Not just because of what we've been through, or all the shows we have to talk about—it's more the way she just fits there without a second thought.

After I quickly edit and upload the audio from Atheleen's

bedroom to the podcast, the three of us spend the rest of the day helping Cathy secure the more valuable furnishings so the contractors can do their work without fear of breaking anything, and it's such exhausting work that I barely notice when the last of the light leaves the sky.

We all head to bed early, none of us willing to risk showering off the grime of the day. Holly makes a half-hearted joke about being a third wheel as she climbs onto my bed with me and Quinn, but she seems more grateful not to be alone than anything.

I set up my digital camera facing away from the bed to record the rest of the room while we're sleeping. Settling against my pillow, I absently reach to remove my gemstone bracelets, then remember I lost them when we rescued Quinn from sleepwalking into the lake. Not that the gems seemed to give me much protection from the ghosts of Arrington anyway.

I wonder what my friends and listeners will think of the discoveries we made in Atheleen's room, what they might hear that I missed. Or if, like me, they'll find their thoughts constantly straying back to the bone I pried from Waffles's mouth—the ending of this latest episode. Soft scratching above my head sends me off to sleep, or maybe it's not real, just a memory. The beginning of a dream.

I'm back at the lakeshore under an indigo sky, an early summer's evening wind lifting my hair. Just like before, there's a body floating in the water—skeletal, facedown, long hair fanned out and writhing like snakes, the only part of Atheleen that's still alive.

I brace myself before glancing at the person standing to my right, just visible out of the corner of my eye. I know the same young girl from before, Atheleen's sister, will be next to me.

But as I turn, the person beside me grows taller, changes shape. It's Rose.

Her hazel eyes burn into mine, her face pale as death.

Just as before, the body in the water drifts toward us. I know what I have to do. I need to save Atheleen. I need to help her. I reach for her hand, the swollen, waterlogged flesh of her fingers tangling with mine, and start to pull her from the water.

But the dead girl I've dredged up isn't Atheleen anymore.

It's Holly, her hair unbound, her milk-white eyes unblinking, the beautiful misty blue of her irises leeched of all color from her time in the water. Her body is just skin shrink-wrapped over bones; I count her ribs as my heart beats in time with each number.

Her face is grotesque, twisted in shock.

I scream, and turn to Rose, but she's gone.

In her place is Quinn, wearing a false smile that shows too much teeth, making her momentarily unrecognizable.

"Q?" I choke out.

Her smile widens impossibly far, splitting her pretty face in two. She shoves me into the water.

The night grows darker as the lake closes over me and a strong current sucks at my skin, dragging me away from light and air and everything familiar.

Above me, another body floats by, eyes wide and staring as I plummet to the depths.

Cathy.

I try to shout for her, but only bubbles rise from my lips. Everything goes dark.

———

I sit up with a start in a dark room, alone and gasping for air, sloshing water everywhere. Where am I? Why can't I take a deep breath? It feels like there are hands around my throat, but when I touch my neck, the sensation vanishes.

As my wits return, I use the scant light of the hallway to study my surroundings; I'm in the hall bathroom, sitting in the claw-foot tub, lukewarm water gushing steadily out of the taps.

I quickly stand and turn them off; the tub was in danger of overflowing.

The ghost in this place travels by water. The words of a dead girl echoing in my ears, I grab a towel and wrap myself up tight. I have to move, but my limbs don't feel like they belong to me, my feet getting tangled with each step. How did I get here in the first place? Am I sleepwalking now, like Quinn? Like Atheleen's sister?

As I flick on the lights, my gaze lands back on the tub. It's full of murky green water, the sudden smell of brine filling my nose. And bobbing in the muck like a dead fish is a handheld silver device—my digital camera. Any evidence it caught tonight is lost forever.

I scream and stumble backward, my feet sliding on the slick tiles.

"Dare!" Quinn's voice sounds impossibly far away, but she rushes through the dark hall with Waffles at her heels, reaching my side a moment later. "What happened? What are you doing in here?"

"I don't know," I choke out as she wraps me in a warm embrace.

"I don't know," I repeat, swallowing a sob. "I don't know anything anymore."

Is this how Atheleen's sister felt leading up to what would have been her final days had Atheleen not intervened?

"It's okay," Quinn tries to reassure me. "Neither of us has been sleeping nearly enough. That's all it is. You're okay. I'm here now."

But my brain can no longer accept such a rational answer. I shake my head, barely able to move, or speak. What would have happened if I hadn't woken up when I did? Could I have drowned without even being in the lake?

"Don't—" I gasp, watching Quinn move toward the tub.

But the water is clear now. Maybe it always was. Maybe Hettie has chosen me to join her in the lake, and I've just seen my future. Maybe she doesn't care which of us she drowns, just as long as someone the right age joins her.

Anything is possible.

I still have the paper cuts from the flurry of books in Atheleen's room to prove it.

As Quinn kneels, pulling the drain stopper and fishing out my ruined camera, something scratches the wall behind me. Just once. Torn nails scraping dry paint. There and gone. Atheleen's spirit, twisted by Hettie's cruelty, letting me know she's with me.

She's always been with me, from the day I arrived.

It was her scratching on my wall, nails skittering across the windowpane. There were never any rats, only a dead girl, unseen, watching me. Trying to figure out how to lure me into the lake so she can drown me. Do I remind Hettie of the sisters who failed to save her?

Waffles nudges my hand with his cold nose, a trusted old

friend anchoring me to the present. I put a grateful hand on his head and rub his ears, focusing on controlling my breathing until it slows a little.

The water drained, the floor mostly mopped of the mess I made, we take the waterlogged camera and head back to the bedroom. While I change, Quinn double-checks that the door is locked and barred in case anyone else tries to go somewhere in their sleep.

In fresh pajamas, I climb in beside Holly, who somehow slept through the entire ordeal.

Quinn is a great girlfriend. She stays awake with me, whispering soothing things in my ear, but it's all I can do not to flinch; her wicked smile in the dream as she shoved me into the water is too easy to picture now. Too familiar. Too real.

TWENTY-FOUR

I DON'T SLEEP MUCH after that, even with Quinn and Holly beside me. Especially with Quinn beside me, thanks to my nightmare in the bath.

As I grab my phone, my fingers brush the frigid wood of the bedside table, and I hastily withdraw my hand.

My phone notifies me of two important things as I swipe left on the home screen. One, my blood sugar is in range and stable at 115. Two, my interview with Brian is this afternoon, and I still haven't told Quinn where I'm going, or made arrangements to borrow the historical society van from Cathy.

So much is riding on today's interview. I know Holly is worried about me meeting a stranger, but I need Brian to help me figure out who Atheleen's sister is, where she is now, and everything she knows about how Atheleen tried to stop Hettie.

My friends and I aren't safe here. Atheleen's spirit has made that clear. But I've been putting pieces of this puzzle together in real time for an audience that—according to Deitra's latest text—is now growing by the hour, and I don't want to let them down. Though it's more that I don't want to let Atheleen down, no matter how much she's scared us already.

She isn't herself.

After last night, waking up in a bath I could have drowned in, I know how that feels.

I open the *Attachments* site and scroll through the comments, more than I've ever gotten on any episode of Strange Virginia.

I'm going to give my listeners what they want—an unforgettable story. Not just for them, though. I'm in too deep to turn away now. It's that constant itch, the need to know. Anxiety and fascination intertwined.

The light streaming in through my window is tepid at best, the sun obscured by clouds. Patches of hopeful blue sky break through here and there, but the clouds are thick, bound to burst with rain at some point today. Wind turns the leaves on the trees, whipping the lake into a frenzy.

I turn to say good morning to Quinn and Holly, but it's Waffles snuggled up against my back. On his other side, Holly is sleeping soundly, an arm flung over her eyes to shield them from the early sun. But Quinn isn't here.

A sick feeling scurries through me—could she be walking into the lake in a daze again? What if Hettie wants her, not me?

As a text comes in from Quinn, I try to calm my breathing.

Helping Cathy downstairs. Lots to do! Join us when you can. Mom went into town on an errand. Contractor was a no-show.

The message is followed by a series of colorful heart emojis. I smile, and try not to picture Quinn's cold sneer as she shoved me into the lake in my dream. It keeps flashing to mind at inconvenient moments, and I don't know how to stop it.

There's so much Atheleen learned, but so much she left unanswered.

I pull on my standard work outfit, jeans and a clean T-shirt. I'm torn as I consider waking Holly. She should be safe enough for a few hours until the sun gets her up—if she starts sleepwalking toward any water like I did, we'll hear her thanks to the hopelessly creaky floors—and someone deserves to be well rested for a change. No reason we should all suffer.

Downstairs, I volunteer to help Cathy move the chaise lounge out of the parlor, where a steady drip from above has soaked the velvet fabric while the water on the floor slowly erodes the chair's carved wooden legs. As we move it to the foyer, where we've put down waterproof tarping, the absence of a now-familiar sound sets off alarm bells in my mind.

The grandfather clock has stopped working, its hands frozen on 7:45.

"Can't say I'm surprised," Cathy sighs, following my gaze. "This whole project is starting to feel doomed. Maybe it was foolish of me to think we could make this place into anything other than a Halloween attraction . . . Anyhow, did you need something, dear?"

"I've been meaning to ask you—could I borrow the van today? Just for an hour or so. I have my license," I add quickly as Cathy's brows begin to rise. "I need to run into town this afternoon for a few diabetes supplies before my mom gets here tonight. I used a lot more than I expected; stupid mistake, I'm supposed to pack double what I know I'll need."

"Oh!" Cathy reaches for her phone. "I'll just call Rose and have her—"

"No, no, they're too hard to describe. It'll be less frustrating for everyone if I just run to the pharmacy myself after lunch. I've never gotten a ticket or anything," I press as Cathy's expression wavers.

Quinn arches a brow, taking in every word, and my face immediately gets hot. I need to tell her where I'm headed; I can't put it off much longer. I'm just worried she'll try to talk me out of it. If I don't go, we could miss out on information we need to save what's left of Atheleen's spirit. To save ourselves, and the next girls.

The phone in Cathy's hand vibrates with an incoming call.

"All right," she sighs, answering me at last. "Keys are in the kitchen, hanging on the wall near the old phone. Now, I'd better take this."

I grab a clean rag and then wipe down the legs of the rescued chaise lounge so I can listen in on Cathy's call, guessing it's Rose on the other end. What was so urgent that it drew her into town when the contractor bailed? Maybe she's getting supplies to try to fix the plumbing problems herself. I hope not. That could lead to even bigger disasters.

"This is she," Cathy says politely, her tone all business.

Not Rose, then.

I don't catch much—just the name "Tarver"—but it's enough for my stomach to sink.

Scarlett never left the estate, just as Atheleen suspected. Her body is in the lake.

In a daze, I sit on the edge of the soaked chaise. I think of Scarlett's prom dress, her wardrobe packed away and forgotten in the attic over our heads, now on its way to Goodwill. Her friends and her dreams. All the things she could have been and done.

It isn't until Waffles licks my cheek and whines that I realize I'm crying.

"Oh, honey," Cathy sighs, sitting heavily on the chaise beside me and putting an arm around my shoulders. "I know. It's awful."

Quinn comes back from the kitchen, takes one look at our faces, and she knows.

Cathy says briskly, "The officers called just now. The dental records on the bone from the lake match Scarlett Tarver, who went missing back in 1969. I was just a girl then myself, so I don't remember it well—but that doesn't make it any less sad. You know what? I have an idea." She leaps up and strides purposefully toward the stairs. "Be right back."

Quinn takes the spot she vacated, wincing at how wet the velvet fabric is. "The museum . . . this place . . . it was such a mistake," she sighs. "Maybe Mom's biggest one ever."

"It kind of feels like the walls are going to start falling down around us, doesn't it?" I wipe my tears, then—despite a small flare of panic as the remnants of my nightmare intrude—let Quinn take my hand.

"I don't know what my mom's going to do," she mutters, staring at the wrinkled tarp on the floor now hiding water-stained boards. "She was seriously freaking out this morning, so I guess she doesn't know yet, either." Softer, she confesses, "She's just in too deep. No one would buy this place now—waiting on workers to fix it is our only hope, ghosts and all."

"Maybe all Atheleen needs is some closure," I suggest with more optimism than I feel, staring at the frozen hands of the grandfather clock. "But I don't know what to do about Hettie. I'm not exactly an expert in breaking curses. I might have a lead on Atheleen and her sister, though," I add in a small voice.

"Why do I have a feeling I'm not going to like this?" Quinn

takes a long look at me, urging me to speak as the silence grows between us. "Spill."

I tell her about my meeting with Brian in a few hours at a nearby auto-repair shop, unable to meet her eyes.

"You *what*?" she groans. "Please tell me you won't be alone there. Do you know if the auto shop is even open today? I want to know where Augusta Bell is now as much as you do, Dare, but it's our last day together, our last few hours, and . . ."

She falls silent as Cathy jogs back down the stairs, a palm-sized silver cross clutched in her right hand.

"Would one of you grab me a hammer and nails?" she asks, selecting a spot on the wall to the right of the grandfather clock. "Ah, thank you, Quinn." As she lines up her nail, she mutters, "I'm usually just a Sunday Christian, and I certainly don't believe *every* word in the Bible, but this can't hurt, can it? You girls might not think I've noticed, but the strange noises have kept me up at night, too."

"What noises?" I ask, pulling out my recorder and switching it on.

Cathy raises her hammer, but pauses, glancing at me over her shoulder. "The ones that come out of the speaking tubes, dear," she says matter-of-factly. "They sound like dripping, or like— bubbles. Like someone screaming underwater." She blinks, then titters nervously. "I'm sorry. What an odd thing to say."

Quinn shoots me a pained look as she sits beside me again. I don't know how I'm going to make it to my interview now—I shouldn't have told her, but I can't bring myself to lie to her, and she would have noticed my absence immediately.

The sound of Cathy's hammer echoes through the house like gunshots. Methodical, deliberate.

Beneath it, faintly, something scratches at the walls around us. "You should get a refund on those rat traps," I tell Cathy, feeling a sudden urge to laugh and howl and never stop. Hysteria. Brought on by lack of sleep, perhaps, or breathing too much damp air. "There aren't any. Or if there were, they're dead. Haven't you noticed the way things seem to die around here?" I'm babbling, and I know it, but I can't seem to stop.

Waffles growls softly, sniffing the briny air.

When the hammering stops, the scratching just gets louder.

"Of course I have, dear. But we have a secret weapon," Cathy says, a hint of pride in her voice. She turns to us and pulls something from the pocket of her oversized cardigan—a baggie of fine white powder about the size of her hand. She walks toward the front door and begins sprinkling some in a line across the threshold.

"Is that—salt?" Quinn asks, surprise evident in her wide eyes.

"That's right. To keep unwanted spirits out of the home." Color creeps into Cathy's cheeks, darker than the blush she wears. "It, ah, works for the boys on *Supernatural*."

I can't hold my laughter in any longer. Quinn glances sharply at me, concerned, but a dam has burst inside me and I have to let it out.

Even Cathy is scared, trying fictional ghost protections she saw on TV. If only the Winchesters could see us now.

A drop of water lands on my leg, cold and stinging, like it fell from up high; the shock of it is enough to make me swallow the rest of my laughter. Another drop strikes the top of my head. Then another. I glance up to a shaking ceiling, the gemstone-studded jellyfish chandelier at its center dancing with each vibration.

The droplets begin to fall hard and steady, a foul storm stinging my eyes as I try to find the source of the water.

Cathy cries out, dropping her bag of salt and running for shelter.

But Quinn just stands beneath the rocking chandelier, arms crossed, frowning like she hears something other than the rain and scratching that the rest of us can't.

Waffles growls again. Maybe he hears it, too, whatever has captured Quinn's attention so thoroughly. Or maybe he's sensed all along what we can't—that Hettie has chosen Quinn to be her next companion at the bottom of the lake.

It would explain why he never growls at anyone else.

"Get away from there!" I jump to my feet, not sure what exactly I'm going to do—how do you fight something you can't see? I have no idea how strong Atheleen's ghost is, but if she wants my girlfriend, she's going to have to pry her out of my arms with her bony fingers.

I've only run halfway to Quinn when the chandelier gives way.

TWENTY-FIVE

CATHY SCREAMS AND DUCKS into the parlor doorway. Waffles barks like a maniac. But Quinn doesn't make a sound as she's thrown off her feet like a puppet, a bit of fabric and string.

She lands hard on her back, the air likely knocked from her lungs, sprawled out in the left-side hallway near the study.

Behind her, a shadow flickers in and out of view. White eyes flash from the shadows, made sightless by the water but somehow taking in everything. Atheleen.

I have just enough time to shield Waffles and me behind the chaise as the chandelier hits the tarped floor and shatters in a crashing wave that leaves my ears ringing. Waffles keeps barking, but he sounds disoriented now, less brave.

Bits of crystal shower the room like hailstones, a diamond rain.

The cross Cathy nailed up moments earlier hits the floor with a dull thud, and for a moment, I think she might faint.

I call out to her, but my words are muffled, and I'm not sure how much she hears because she's still looking toward the dark space where the chandelier hung.

Trusting Waffles to stay put, I crawl toward Quinn. Droplets spatter my back as I creep along the wall toward the hallway, staying clear of the worst of the shattered glass.

I kneel beside Quinn and help her sit up—she's shaken, and

she bumped her head, but she isn't acting like Max did when he had his concussion. "Can I get you anything?" I ask, though once again, I can't tell how loudly I'm speaking.

She shakes her head and blinks, disbelieving, at the scene in the foyer as water begins to gush like a tidal wave from the gaping hole in the ceiling.

I'm busy staring behind Quinn, where I saw Atheleen's ghost appear. She just saved Quinn from a world of hurt—but why? Just so Hettie won't be deprived of her next victim? Or is there a little of her left despite Hettie's years of influence over her spirit, some sort of lingering humanity? I can't be sure, which means I can't trust it.

Across the foyer, Cathy is on the move. "A burst pipe, of all things! I'm going to shut off the water—stay put!" she shouts to us over the roar of water.

As if there's anywhere we can go that Atheleen won't follow. As if anywhere is safe from Hettie's whims.

At least the scratching has finally stopped.

With Quinn finally back on her feet, I hurry to fetch Waffles. He's already on his way to me, tail between his legs.

"I know, buddy," I tell him as the three of us head to the kitchen. "I agree."

I manage to make tea for us using bottled water—I don't even trust the filtered pitcher anymore—while Quinn sits at the long wooden table, petting Waffles. I add a bottle of water to his bowl for good measure.

Breathing in the steam from the old kettle revives me a little, enough to wonder when Holly will rush down the stairs; that crash would have woken even the heaviest sleeper.

"She saved me. She was there . . . I felt her grab my shoulders. Did you see her?" Quinn rubs a tender spot at the back of her head, not so much as glancing at the mug I put in front of her. I nod, answering her question, and she says softly, "I want—I hope we can help her finally be free. I mean, she's family, you know? Maybe if I go out there and talk to her . . ."

"Out where—no!" I slam down my mug as I realize belatedly what she means, sloshing hot tea over the side. A few drops burn the back of my hand near my thumb, but I barely feel it. "No one's going anywhere near the lake. We agreed."

"I don't think she's going to hurt me—we just saw that she can fight Hettie's influence," Quinn says, her gaze slightly unfocused as she stares out the window at the churning gray-brown water. "And besides, I have to try. Your family's future isn't tied up in this place, but mine is. And the house deserves love. It deserves someone devoted to making it shine."

I can't believe what I'm hearing. It's like there are two people battling for control of whatever comes out of her mouth at any moment.

"Quinn." I put my hand over hers, hoping to snap her out of this. "Last night, you begged your mom to take us all to a motel, remember? You didn't want to spend another night here. You can't wait to leave. We're going to get out of here and if there's nothing left of Atheleen to save, then that's a shame, but Hettie isn't getting any more company." My words don't seem to reach her; I press my fingers a little harder into hers. "Quinn. Come with me to meet Brian. It's too dangerous for you here."

She presses her lips together, annoyed. "I'm not going anywhere until we have to."

I try a different argument. "You'll be helping Atheleen if you come. We're going to see what he can tell us about her sister and figure out if there's anything we can do about Hettie. You don't want me to go alone, so, come. Wait in town while Rose and Cathy close up—"

"Is everyone all right? No lumps to the head?" Cathy asks over me as she appears in the doorway, her posture drooping under the weight of the pressure this place has put on her. "Quinn, sweetheart, you took quite a fall back there."

"I'm fine. Promise." Quinn smiles wanly, then returns her gaze to the window, making it clear our discussion is over.

Seeming relieved, Cathy slumps onto the bench beside her and grabs the spare mug I set out. "Oh, this looks great. Thank you, girls. I got the water shut off and texted Rose. She's in town right now trying to find somebody who can help today, so until then, we can't use any water other than the pitcher and bottles in the fridge. Got it?"

Quinn nods, still watching the rising water.

If my guess is right, she's in more danger than any of us. But I can't make her do anything she doesn't want to. All I can do is what I always have; search for answers, and hope I find some way to stop Hettie so Quinn will be safe anywhere she wants to be, even here. Even in this unloved house that sometimes hungers for a spirit to sustain it for a few more years, one not yet worn thin by life's many small cruelties.

I have to go talk to Brian, even if it means leaving Quinn behind. I won't be gone long. And with the program ending, this is my only chance to fully understand what's happening here. I have to try.

"Hey," she says softly, leaning across the table. She reaches forward and gently plucks something from my hair—a crumb of glass. "We should check Waffles over, too."

"Already done," I assure her, my face warm with her lingering tenderness.

She smiles, and my nightmare surfaces once again—her sneer, the force of her hands and the lake pulling me down—and I'm torn between a sudden wave of revulsion and the urge to kiss her until I forget who I am without her.

My phone buzzes with an alarm I set, reminding me that it's one thirty. I don't have far to drive, but I shouldn't keep Brian waiting. Not when so much is riding on what he has to say about Augusta Bell.

There are two key rings on the wall-mounted rack by the old phone; one I recognize as Quinn's by the silver *Gravekeepers* logo dangling alongside her car key.

I slip the other, battered set of keys into my pocket and call softly to Quinn, "Stay inside. Keep an eye on Holly, and I'll be back before you know it."

Blood pounds in my ears as I return to the foyer, guiding Waffles carefully through the water and around the spray of glass to the front door. Brian had better not disappoint me with what he knows—or doesn't.

I'm just closing the door behind us when something pulls from the other side and it swings back open.

Quinn stands there, eyes flashing, a hand on her hip. "You're really doing it? What if this guy is dangerous? And what about us? What about sticking together? This is insane."

"So is staying in a house that's literally falling down around you, when you have to leave in a few hours anyway and you could be riding with your girlfriend to make sure she doesn't get attacked by some weirdo," I counter, heat prickling across my cheeks.

"You don't have to go anywhere." She tucks a strand of dark hair behind her ear. "Stay. Let's do something fun with these last few hours . . ." There's a hint of suggestion in the words, but none of Quinn's usual playfulness. I wonder if she knows what she's saying, or if it's Atheleen who doesn't want me to leave.

She touches my arm, her fingers a warm relief after the oppressive chill of the house.

I wish I could say yes. I love how her face lights up when something goes her way. But she isn't herself right now—she doesn't truly want to be here. She needs help fighting Atheleen's unhappy influence, but I won't be able to help her if I sit inside this shipwrecked house pretending nothing is wrong.

Heart sinking to the worn porch floor, I step back, retreating from the house—and Quinn.

"I can't. I'm sorry. I have to do this. Stay close to Cathy and Holly," I beg. Unlike Rose, at least Cathy realizes something is wrong here. "I need you to be okay at the end of this."

"You, too, you reckless, infuriating, amazing person." Quinn starts to shut the door, then changes course and steps outside, grabbing the front of my shirt and pulling me toward her for a kiss that lasts several seconds and somehow still isn't long enough.

Maybe because it feels like goodbye.

With her, the world is full of light and shadow, contrasts that create depth. Tiny moments worth capturing with the press of a button. A palette of colors both tender and loud.

I never saw it that way before.

I want to drink her in, to drown in her, this—us.

She smiles sadly as she draws back, and the door swings closed.

This time, my mind doesn't immediately flash to the twisted version of her smile, to her hands on my shoulders shoving me into the lake.

There's just Quinn, sweet and beautiful and real, there and then not.

I turn and head down the porch to where the white van with the society's logo is parked, Waffles at my heels.

Despite Quinn's worry that I'm walking into this meeting completely vulnerable, I do have some protection with me other than my friendly, goofy dog: Pepper spray. Military grade. A gift from my dad when he went through his prepper phase.

The van coughs and sputters to life, and soon I've convinced it to start limping down the bumpy driveway.

The back of my neck prickles, causing me to tap the brakes and glance over my shoulder, but there's only the house. The door is closed, the porch empty.

Upstairs, in the attic window, a light blinks on and off. A message? Or a game?

It flashes in my rearview mirror until I round a bend in the road. From the back seat, Waffles gives one short whine, a question: Am I going to have to sit here long?

"It's not too far," I tell him, injecting as much enthusiasm into my voice as I can muster. I earn a single tail wag for my performance.

The bridge buckles and sways in the high wind as I coax the van across it. Last time, I tried not to look down, but this time I force myself to take a good look at the rushing, rising water. Does the lake swell every summer? Or only when a girl the same age as one of Hettie's sisters arrives at Arrington? And why hasn't the town taken action—are there just too many years between each drowning for collective memory to categorize the girls' deaths as anything more than senseless tragedies? The stuff of lore and fascination, a status generally reserved for missing white girls— but never a tangible threat, they might think, not here, not now.

Perhaps there's something about the lake itself that repels locals and visitors alike, though they never fully realize it; it's certainly big enough to be a tourist destination, yet there's not a single water-sports rental or cutesy crab shack lining its untamed banks.

Soon, the water is at my back, and tension melts from my shoulders. I put on the radio, listening to a pop song through a crackle of static for the five minutes it takes to reach the fork in the road where I veer right, toward the auto-repair shop.

The main building and adjacent garages are all shuttered, the windows dark. A few are boarded up. I approach the front door and knock—pepper spray in hand—while Waffles waits in the van.

Is this even the right place?

It appears to be completely deserted. The only tire marks in the dusty lot are my own.

The faint sound of another car turning down the unpaved road, wheels crunching over twigs and gravel, grows louder as I look around.

That must be Brian.

I stand by the driver's side door to the van, just in case he's not who I'm expecting—a grayer-haired version of the white man in the photo I found on the New Hope PD website honoring his time on the force.

The car that pulls up is an SUV, its navy paint job recently refreshed, silver rims flashing in the slim rays of sun that manage to pierce the clouds.

I know that car.

It's not Brian's.

The person behind the wheel is Rose.

TWENTY-SIX

I DIDN'T SEE THIS coming. This piece of the puzzle doesn't fit.

I stand taller, bracing myself for whatever's about to happen as Rose swings wide into the parking lot and skids to a stop at an angle behind the van. It's not like her to do anything so haphazardly.

She hops out of the driver's side and gestures to the garage directly ahead of us. "Dare!" she calls. "Thank goodness I caught you in time. Come with me," she says briskly, already striding into the knee-high weeds that separate the parking lot and garage.

"What's—what's going on?" I force the words out, one hand turning the cap on my pepper spray as I search the surrounding trees for an intruder, or some other reason Rose is moving like she's in a house on fire.

All I see are heavy clouds rolling in, oil-black and streaked with menace.

"I need to show you something," Rose says, waving a hand impatiently even as I hurry to catch up with her. "It's important; it's about Brian."

"You know him? Wait, did Quinn say something?" I ask, feeling more lost than ever as Rose slides the metal door up, revealing shadowed workbenches, the covered bulk of a car, and a faint smell of motor oil.

"In here," she says, motioning for me to enter. "Brian's an old family friend. He can't be here today, so he asked me to tell you about Augusta, but we don't have much time. Hurry!"

As I step into the shadows, the garage door slams shut behind me.

Heart clanging in my ears, I shout, "Rose?" I pull at the bottom of the heavy door, trying to slide it back up, and tear a fingernail in the process. "Help—it's stuck!"

Or something is holding it down.

The living are the ones to be wary of. That's what I always believed.

I scream a curse and bang a fist against the metal, making it shiver. "What the hell? Why? Let me out!"

"I'm sorry it has to be like this, Dare," Rose says coolly from beyond the door. "But I need you out of the way—just for a little while. You'll be safe in here. I'm the one who emailed you about Brian, by the way; he's not coming. He's busy enjoying his retirement on a beach somewhere in Florida."

"You know about the podcast?" I ask stupidly, trying to buy time while I figure out why Quinn's mom would have impersonated a retired cop and planned to trap me here.

"I've dedicated myself to thinking about Atheleen. Reading about Atheleen. I've built my life around the one she never got to have. The one that was stolen from her. And your podcast is all over the internet; I couldn't have missed it."

I take deep breaths of stale air as my eyes adjust to the dim. There's a window in here, but it's so caked with grease and filth that it hardly lets any light in—not that there's much sun peeking through the gathering storm.

Without AC, the small building is oppressive; at least I left the van running so Waffles won't get hot. The realization that I don't know when I'll see him again makes my knees weak. I slump against the door, my mind reeling.

Why would Rose dedicate her life to Atheleen? Unless—she said in her email that Brian was a friend of the Bell family. And she said it again before she locked me in here, calling him an old friend.

A family friend.

Despite my skin being slick with sweat, the realization hits me like someone pouring ice water down my back. I switch on the voice recorder in my back pocket.

"You're her, aren't you? Augusta Bell?"

Even in my nightmares, her face wasn't clear. Until now. Rose's face. I've finally put it together, too late to help anyone.

Quinn is right. I *am* reckless. I should never have come here.

The door shakes as Rose does something to it, and I stumble back. Who's going to find me out here? Holly doesn't have the address, and Quinn's mind has been twisted by the spirits, too preoccupied with the house to consider leaving; no one else knows I'm here. Several miles of forest lie between me and town.

There's no point in screaming. But I do anyway. Hopefully it shatters a little of Rose's infuriating calm.

Eventually, Cathy will want her van back and ask questions—but what will happen to me by then? What if my blood sugar goes low? There's nothing I can use to treat it in here.

"Why are you doing this?" I shout, stalling. The longer I can keep her here, keep her talking, the better my chances are that someone drives by and hears me.

"I would have thought that was obvious, Nancy Drew," Rose

says from beyond the door, the words sarcastic but without any real bite as the scrape of metal on metal rings through the charged air; she's locking me in, or else barring the door somehow. "The lake is connected to the spirit of Henrietta Arrington. She always claims a victim the same age as one of her sisters; last time, Atheleen died instead of me, and became the spirit's new plaything. I came here to make it up to my sister, to free her, but she wouldn't appear without someone the right age in the house. That's where the internship came in."

"Fresh bait?" I stammer. "Including your own daughter? Wow."

"I'm not going to let anyone die, and never was," Rose says calmly; everything's always under control in her world. "At first, I thought the lake had chosen Holly; I was sick like her, once. But then Quinn started sleepwalking—I saw her on your cameras, very helpful by the way—and now I'm not sure which of them is the one."

She obviously hasn't heard about my sleepwalking episode with the bath. She must have also missed her daughter nearly drowning when she walked into the lake, unless that was part of her plan and I ruined it.

"So, what? You're going to dangle one of them over the dock until your dead sister pops out of the lake and tries to grab them? I didn't think anyone was that selfish." As I talk, I pace the small two-car garage, looking for anything I can use to break out—a tire iron, or something sharp enough to shatter the window glass.

"No! You don't know me, and you don't know—never mind. We're done here," Rose says in a low voice, the words clipped and heated. "I'll come back for you when it's safe."

"Wait!" I plead. But I have nothing to bargain with.

The sound of another car turning down the road makes my heart skip. "Help! In here!" I shout, banging my fists on the door as tires grind to a stop in the gravel-strewn lot. "Please, let me out!"

"Mom? What are you doing? What's in there?"

Quinn's voice sends a thrill through me. In the end, she didn't let me come here alone. Whatever she feels for me must be stronger than the spirits' hold on her.

"Quinn! She's locked me in!" I shout. "It's her—your mom is Atheleen's little sister! She's Augusta Bell!"

"What are you talking about?" Quinn calls. "Dare?"

I wish I could see what is happening out there. The door rattles briefly, and then Rose murmurs something too low for me to make out.

Quinn's voice is sharper, higher. "What are you going to do? Hit me?"

A moment later, the garage door rolls up and weak daylight floods the room. Rose stands several feet away in the weeds, arms crossed, shaking her head—she definitely didn't plan for this. Quinn throws her arms around me, her hair windblown and her eyes flashing.

"Did she hurt you? Are you okay?" she asks against my ear.

"I'm fine, but listen—we have to get back to the house and get Holly. Now. Your mom is Atheleen's sister. She knew about the curse. She lured me and Holly here so her sister's ghost would appear. She let *you* stay there knowing you could be the next victim, too."

A punch of thunder shakes the sky, clouds colliding to blot out the last shard of sun.

I start running toward the van, trying to pull Quinn with me, but she stands in the open garage doorway with her hands dangling limply at her sides. She turns toward her mom. "Tell me Dare is confused. You don't have any sisters. Your last name was never Bell—it was Olsen before you met Dad. Olsen," she repeats, like saying it again will make it true.

Rose looks back and forth between us for a moment, as if she's deciding what to say. "Dare is right," she finally says in a much gentler tone than normal. "My name was Augusta Rose Bell—Gussie for short. My parents divorced after everything that happened in that house; Dad's refusal to accept what really happened tore them apart, and he died shortly after he moved up north. Mom remarried and took her new husband's last name, and so did I—anything to distance ourselves from the past."

"No," Quinn says, not seeming to notice as the wind changes direction and tugs strands of hair across her face. "No. I don't believe you. You're lying."

"Listen," Rose pleads. She takes a step toward Quinn, but her daughter darts toward the parking lot where I stand, pepper spray at the ready.

"Whatever you have to say to me, say it from over there," Quinn demands, a tremor in her voice.

Rose nods. "Fine. It's time I told you everything." She rubs her temples, looking skyward—the drop in pressure from the coming storm must be giving her a headache.

Refocusing her gaze on Quinn, she says, "You need to understand what it was like growing up with only my parents and sister for company. I was often lonely, at least until I met the girl in the mirror. We played princess tea party—she always had on the prettiest gown—and talked until dawn. I told her all my worries about starting our homeschool program and living in my sister's shadow. Atheleen was better at everything, you see. The mirror girl was a good listener; I didn't care that her eyes were the color of spoiled milk or that her skin was falling off in a few places. I knew it was unkind to point out others' differences."

My gaze darts between Rose and Quinn, searching my girlfriend's face. She's a blank canvas, eyes shuttered so no emotion can escape. "Go on," she says, looking steadily at her mother.

Rose nods, but is quiet for a moment, as if summoning the will to continue. "As I got older, nearing my twelfth birthday, the mirror girl stopped being fun. She was moody and withdrawn, and I bore the worst of her tantrums: Floods on my floor. In my bed. Water stains on the walls and ceilings as she went throughout the house. I was constantly sick to my stomach, and then the sleepwalking started. I had nightmares about drowning in the lake, about Atheleen pushing me in. Our parents didn't believe me, but Atheleen did. She was seeing things by then, too, and when she found the bodies by the water, she became convinced we were haunted."

"What bodies?" Quinn demands, her voice thick with emotion.

"Squirrels, mostly. A rabbit. A coyote, once—that was the worst," Rose answers. "All skeletal. Bizarre. Atheleen told me she thought whatever lived in the lake was feeding on them—not just their bodies, but their spirits, using their energy to keep itself strong."

"She figured everything out when she looked through the attic, didn't she?" I cut in, unable to stop myself. "She even knew what Hettie wanted—for you to take Scarlett's place as her companion in the lake—but not how to stop her from draining you dry like the poor animals she found. Isn't that right?"

Silence winds taut as a bowstring through the parking lot as wind shakes the trees. Rose, pale beneath her tan, finally nods.

"She found some old belongings of Hettie's, gifts she was given, and brought them to the lake. She had a theory—she thought the curse would end if Hettie was reminded of her sisters' love. But whatever is left of Hettie isn't capable of such emotions." She pinches the bridge of her nose between her fingers, closing her eyes. "The night Hettie tried to take me, Atheleen rowed out into the middle of the lake to confront her, and got pulled in instead. She scratched at the boat, fighting not to go under; her nails were torn to bits when they found her floating the next day. Sometimes, I can still hear it when I try to sleep. That scratching."

"How am I supposed to believe anything you say, now?" Quinn cuts in, raising her voice over a peal of thunder. "You've been lying to me this whole time—my whole life!" She paces the gravel beside me, her heels kicking up a mini dust storm. "Why come back here at all if it's so dangerous?"

Rose holds her daughter's gaze. "For Atheleen, of course. To free her. I owe her everything. I've been trying to reach her for years, since before we sold the house. I pleaded with my parents to stay; I could sense her nearby, watching me, as we packed our things, but she never appeared to me. When they boarded up her room, I hid the key inside her favorite doll—it was easy, as the eyes had fallen in years earlier—hoping the next owner wouldn't be able to disturb her things. To give her spirit a safe, familiar place to wait for me."

I laugh, dry and cold. "Safe and familiar? Then why did you scratch your face out of every photo in the room?" I raise my voice, making sure the recorder will catch every word. "You're a coward. You didn't want anyone who might enter the house to recognize you, to tie you to Atheleen's death because you're responsible."

Rose blinks. "What are you talking about? I never—I didn't— I haven't been in that room since it happened," she stammers. "Holly found the doll before I could, and I only realized this morning when I saw the pieces in the trash. I never had the key."

"Then I guess Atheleen isn't very happy with you. Wonder why that is."

Inside the van, Waffles whines. I shoot him a pleading look, a finger to my lips.

"I know why," Rose says, trying to disguise the tremor in her voice. "And she has every right to be angry; it's taken me far too long to rescue her. When Eileen Brown bought Arrington, I visited the grounds every chance I got, searching for Atheleen. I begged the old woman to sell me the house, but she refused; I could tell the house already had its hooks too deep in her, controlling her thoughts and using her to lure more girls the right age, so I did the only thing I could: asked her to keep caring for the place, so at least Atheleen wouldn't be alone. And when Eileen moved out, I finally had my chance to make things right."

"How thoughtful of you, *Augusta*," Quinn says through gritted teeth, crossing her arms as she studies her mom with new eyes. "What a great sister."

Rose reaches a hand toward Quinn, as if a simple gesture can bridge the distance she's created between them, but doesn't come closer; she seems aware that one wrong move will send her daughter speeding away in her silver convertible. "You're so much like her. Like Atheleen. Our parents called her Ivy-Bean, after her middle name—remember when I used to call you my bean? You both love music and art; she was a painter, too. She had a way with animals like you, too. People and creatures were just drawn to her."

A smile flickers and dies on her lips as she sees her words are having no effect on Quinn.

"And you're both fiercely protective of those you love," she adds, softer. "You don't know what it was like, growing up in that big, drafty house, being scared to turn a corner because you never knew what you'd see or hear—"

"Shut up! Just shut up!" Quinn yells. "I do know because you let me come here! You're supposed to protect me, remember? I'm not Atheleen, and I'm still here. But you've made it clear which of us you really care about."

She takes a few steps back, gaining more distance, her heels crunching gravel. "My whole life, I've craved your approval like air, even when it meant blowing off my friends to take an extra AP class in the mornings, or staying late after school to volunteer. I barely had a life until this year when I moved out, but I thought this would be the perfect chance to bond with you. To impress you. Only, I don't care what you think of me anymore! You're a liar. And you're dangerous. Just like that house."

She seems to be thinking much more clearly away from Atheleen's influence.

And so am I.

I jump into the van, signaling for Quinn to do the same. She jumps in on the passenger side, wiping her glistening cheeks, and I lock the doors behind her.

Waffles beats his tail against the back seat, overjoyed.

"Wait!" Rose shouts. "Where you going, Quinn? Did you not hear anything I said? You can't just leave—the lake has risen too far! We need to act now!"

Safe in the van, I ignore her and check my blood sugar. Figures—209. Hello, stress. I take a couple units of insulin to bring it back down before I start getting a headache.

I turn the key, and the van shudders to life as Rose bangs a fist on the glass.

"Stop!" she screams. "You don't know what you're doing—I need her! Quinn!"

I throw the van in reverse and steer toward the main road, driving in white-knuckled silence as the wheels eat up the mile to the fork, jostling us all the way.

Waffles sniffs Quinn's hair, and she turns to him, crying quietly into his fur.

As we reach the fork, I hesitate. I only have a few seconds—Rose isn't far behind. I could turn right, put us on the road to New Hope, and go somewhere safe and dry where I never have to see that lake or the house slowly rotting away on its banks again.

"Wh—where are we going?" Quinn asks as I cut the wheel to the left.

Cathy is still at Arrington. Holly is still there.

Maybe Hettie planned to feed on Quinn's energy, to drain her dry to keep herself going until another girl just the right age came along, but I'm willing to bet Atheleen will lure Holly instead if that's the only option. Hettie accepted Atheleen in Rose's place, after all. She would accept me, too, as my nightmares have shown.

But just like Holly didn't leave us for a single night, against her better judgment, I'm not abandoning my friend to haunt that place. I know Quinn wouldn't want to, either.

I step on the gas, speeding toward the bridge.

In my rearview mirror, Rose does the same.

TWENTY-SEVEN

I PULL MY RECORDER out of my pocket and rest it in one of the van's empty cup holders. "I'm sorry you had to find out this way," I say over a burst of thunder that drowns out the rush of the AC and Quinn's quiet sobs.

Outside, the restless sky swirls with shades of indigo and rotten plum, a bruised color almost as dark as night.

"Are you okay?" I ask, though I know from the shaky sound of her breathing that she isn't. "Sorry, that was stupid. Of course you aren't." Her pain cuts me, too, but what hurts worse is knowing I can't do anything to make this better for her. Still, I say the things her mother should have. "I'm sorry she lied to you for so long. And I'm sorry I didn't listen to you—about the haunting, and about that stupid meeting. I really screwed up."

"Stop. Stop apologizing—this isn't your fault. She locked you in a garage like some wild animal, and for what? It's just . . ." Quinn sighs, resting her chin on her hand. "I've never yelled at her like that before. And actually, it felt kind of good to be heard for once. I don't know what to make of that, or any of the rest of it. I just didn't know what else to do."

She grabs a bottle of water from the backpack I brought. Type 1 diabetics are like Girl Scouts, always prepared with snacks and drinks. After she takes a few shaky sips, splashing water down her chin, she wipes her mouth with the back of her hand and says,

"*I'm* the one who should be sorry. I'm sorry my mom brought you here. I can't believe . . . What was she thinking? Was she going to let Atheleen drown one of us?"

I shake my head, forcing myself to keep my gaze on the road. Whatever Rose's intentions, there's no way she could control her sister's spirit. Not with Hettie already pulling Atheleen's strings, making her into a wicked thing like herself.

"I'm glad I recorded that conversation, at least," I tell her proudly. "I got every word."

"What?" Quinn sounds so anguished that it's all I can do not to pull the car over and let Rose pass us while I comfort her. "You can't post that! Never. My mom sounds crazy—she'll go to jail or something! She talked about being there when Atheleen died. You can't." She's right—I can't. I nod, promising her that I won't, but she doesn't seem to notice. Resting her head against the cool glass of the passenger side window, she adds softly, "I . . . I never should have left that comment on your channel."

Icy tendrils of doubt snake around me as her words sink in. Quinn, not her mom, is the one who really brought me to Arrington—or lured me. Maybe her distress is all for show. Maybe she knew exactly who her mom was and what she was doing.

Did Quinn want me to be next so her beloved aunt would go free?

It's a good thing I skipped lunch, because my stomach is churning. I would have done anything for Quinn. I would have stared down a murderous ghost for her. Was anything she ever said to me real, or was it all lies? The way she nurses plants back to health and catches bugs in cups to put them safely outside—is it all an act she put on to lull me and Holly into a false sense of calm, to gain our trust?

"It's my fault you're here," she murmurs, her cheek still resting against the window. "I can't regret meeting you, but—I regret putting you in danger."

I want to believe her. I want to believe she didn't know about her mom's secret, about the lake's curse and the skeleton girls.

But while my instinct is to trust her, my instincts have been wrong before. After all, I used to be so sure there was no such thing as ghosts, only tricks of the mind and environment. Look where that got me.

Maybe I'm wrong about more than I realized.

And still, as her breathing changes, keeping pace with my racing heart, I want to make everything okay for her. I can't. But I really wish I could.

I swallow around a lump in my throat, resisting the urge to give Quinn any sort of reassurance I don't mean. I won't lie to her, even if she's lied to me. I blink away the pain and keep my eyes on the road as my phone begins to buzz.

Mom's calling.

She isn't due to pick me up until dark—true dark, around eight—but maybe something came up. I let the call go to voicemail, but she tries again.

The third time my phones goes off, Quinn half turns and asks, "Are you going to answer that, or . . . ?" Her eyes meet mine for the briefest moment before darting away. My face must betray some hint of my thoughts despite my efforts to keep it blank as a new canvas.

Putting the phone on speaker so I can keep my hands on the wheel, I say, "Hey, Mom. Now's really not a great time. What's up?"

"I listened to your podcast." Mom's voice crackles with static, erasing any hint of emotion I might be able to glean from her words. "I'm on my way to get you right now. I'll be there in three hours, sit tight and—"

She's gone. The signal must have dropped.

She doesn't call back, and there's no time to text her. She doesn't believe in ghosts, but if she gets here soon enough, Arrington will change her mind.

As we turn up the long driveway to the waiting house, lights flash in every window, putting on a show for us. The sight chills my blood, and I turn down the van's AC.

I park on the side of the house opposite the lake, among the ground-up stumps of trees that were sacrificed for a parking lot. I doubt that will happen now. Or who knows? Maybe Quinn and her mom will go through with the museum, hiring young docents to find the perfect candidate for the lake's next sacrifice.

Holly, Cathy, and I are getting out of here. Now. And Quinn, too, I hope.

I reach for the door handle, but Quinn puts a hand on my arm.

"Don't go back in there," she pleads. "If you ever felt anything for me at all, do this one thing for me. I can't stand the thought of something happening to you in there. I'll go get Holly and bring her right to the van."

Maybe she would. Or maybe she would grab Holly's hand and lead her to the water so her dear old Aunt Atheleen could go free. I don't know if I can trust her, and the thought feels like a knife in my chest, digging through layers of muscle and sinew. A hurt that can't be mended.

I glance sideways at her, wondering if at just the right angle of light, I'll see the shadow of someone else behind her.

Her aunt's shadow.

The reason Waffles sometimes growled at Quinn instead of greeting her with tail wags.

Has Atheleen been controlling her this whole time? Was Quinn even herself all those times she kissed me? Either way—whether she's a pawn of the ghost's or her mother's, or both—I can't trust her anymore.

I don't even know if I can trust my own perception.

Waffles scratches at the back door, as eager to be let out as I am to get out of this van and away from Quinn. I need to make sure Holly is okay.

"Stay here," I tell her, the words a little sharper than I intended. "Please. I just—need you to stay here. I'll be right back."

"Dare!" Quinn cries as I throw open the door. I haven't known her long, but the way she's looking at me twists the knife in my chest a little deeper. "Look, I get what's going on here. Since I'm the one who reached out about the house, you think I'm part of whatever game my mom has been playing. But no matter what you think of me, I don't want to lose you. Not ever, but especially not to this place."

Tears mingle with her mascara and eyeliner, streaking down her face like ink.

"If you lose me, it won't be because of anything that happens in there," I promise. It'll be because I learn the truth of her involvement in her mom's plan. Of how much she knew when she asked me to come here. And I hope it isn't true, but right now I don't know what to think.

I've survived coming out to my family, a broken heart, a life-changing diagnosis, and now a haunting. I face my biggest fear every day when I pick up a needle and push it into my own stomach. I used to think my disease made me weak, vulnerable, but now I realize there's something it's taught me: I can rely on me. Those needles, my doses, all the decisions are in my hands. And so far, I have a pretty good track record when it comes to keeping myself alive. I have the resilience that's kept me here, kept me hoping and dreaming when just getting out of bed sounded impossible.

I don't need Quinn or anyone else to save me.

I'm not going to be taken down by that house, a monument to the wealth and arrogance of a family long dead.

I've got me, I've got Waffles, and we're going to save our friend.

"I'm coming with you," Quinn declares, reaching for the passenger side door.

"If you really want to help, you'll stay there!" I know she won't listen, but I have to try. I leap out of the van and open the back door for Waffles. He bounds excitedly at my side as I run through the tall grass toward the house.

The last thing I need is for Quinn to follow me inside when she isn't herself; who knows what Atheleen might make her do? Or, if I'm wrong, and she's still the girl I've come to care so much about, I can't watch both our backs.

Somehow, I don't think the lake, or Hettie, will let us all go that easily.

I pick up my pace, cursing myself for not taking Holly up on joining her for a jog. I'm not exactly in the best shape of my life, but I put on a burst of speed that widens the gap between me and Quinn by a few more feet, Waffles at my side.

I've just run up the porch steps where the Arrington children once posed for a picture that may well have been their last together when the whole house seems to buckle and sway beneath my feet. The crash of breaking glass pounds against my ears as the house's windows explode, and the flashing lights within go dark.

For a moment, the house holds its breath; if a place can hate, this one does.

Somehow, Hettie's spirit has become fully entwined with the decaying structure, one no longer able to be separated from the other by even the most precise surgeon's hand. When the walls creak, her bones ache; broken windows needle her like open sores, oozing mold and stale air, and when the house remembers, it cuts so deep it lays bare the howling fury that lives in the place where her heart should be.

Lake water bursts out of every opening, green-brown and chilled, reeking of brine and dead, decaying things. I don't know how it's possible. But I have to trust myself and what I'm seeing, and that's a house with windows like miniature waterfalls.

The house is infested. The lake is a disease—sick with Hettie's anger—and there's no cure.

I wish I still had my camera; no one is going to believe this. All this time, all this effort, and no one will believe me. If only I could get a T-shirt or something to prove I was here, I survived, and it was all real.

The air around me vibrates with Hettie's hatred. We've made her mad, avoiding Atheleen's attempts to drown us and give her a new companion for too long, it seems, and now she's having a tantrum. No amount of hanging around after dark in old hospitals and cemeteries prepared me for this.

I grab Waffles and stagger back, tripping as I misjudge the distance between the first step and the ground.

Pain flares in my ankle; I may have sprained it. But instead of trying to figure out what to do for it, I glance around for Quinn. I can't help that it would kill me if anything happened to her, no matter what she did or what she knew. Halfway between the porch and house, she's wiping her glasses frantically on the bottom of her dress.

She's also much closer now, having run toward me as the water burst from the house.

Would someone being controlled by a ghost do that?

There's no time to consider it. I need to find Holly.

Thunder rocks the sky again, an angry cracking sound like the estate collapsing in on itself; the storm is here.

Either Holly and Cathy are drowning with the house, or they're somewhere else—and I know exactly where Atheleen would make Holly go.

I sprint toward the lake despite the protests of my swollen ankle as the bruised sky breaks open and rain begins to pour.

Waffles barks a warning.

The lake, swollen beyond recognition, churns and crashes against the side of the house. Henrietta's room, the sunroom with its broken glass panels, is just visible over my shoulder. Though the rest of the house is dark, the sunroom pulses with a faint, greenish light.

Narrowing my eyes against the onslaught of rain and wind, I

gaze toward the middle of the vast lake on the horizon and spot the same green glow. I've seen it before. It's been here for over a hundred years, and if I don't do something to stop it, it will be here long after me.

Waffles growls and nudges my leg, trying to push me back toward the driveway.

"I can't, buddy. I wish I could."

I'm not leaving without Holly and Cathy. Wiping my eyes, I scan the lakeshore.

Someone's scream pierces through the cannonball bursts of thunder—Quinn. She followed me down here, searching in the opposite direction to cover more ground.

I follow her gaze to the end of the dock, the boards nothing more than a long shadow now buried beneath a foot of raging water.

My heart momentarily stills.

Holly stands with her toes curled over the edge, swaying dangerously as another wave pummels the dock and crashes into her legs. Her long, blonde braid swishes at her back as the wind gusts around her.

She doesn't flinch at the sound of Quinn's scream.

She doesn't turn when I shout her name.

She doesn't even seem to feel the bite of the wind or the sting of the water lashing her bare legs, or even the electric current running along everyone's skin as lightning forks over the middle of the lake.

TWENTY-EIGHT

IF I DON'T DO something now, the lake is going to take Holly. Henrietta Arrington's spirit has become something monstrous, feeding off the suffering and sacrifice of others.

Atheleen tried to stop it, and now it's my turn. I still don't know how to finish what she started, but as I focus on the spot where the lake turns from a stormy gray-brown to an angry olive green, I try to think of something.

Did Hettie know how to swim? Did her sisters try to save her when the accident happened, or even want to? Did anyone? Or did the family just watch her go down with their boat because losing her was easier than living with her?

None of those things really matter now.

Rose seems to think Hettie's spirit is twisted beyond recognition, past the point of forgiving what happened to her. So since I can't convince Hettie to let go of this place and her anger, we have to get away and never look back.

Make Rose seal up the estate for good.

Sacrifice her sister's spirit so that Hettie, deprived of new energy to steal, will finally starve and dissolve on the waves.

Waffles paws at me, the tags on his collar jingling as the wind surrounds us.

He's alerting me—my blood sugar must be dropping.

Sure enough, my CGM says my blood sugar is 90 and starting to drop a little quicker than I'd like. With a frustrated growl, I shove three glucose tablets in my mouth—all I have left from the sleeve of them I keep in my pocket. It'll have to work.

I kiss Waffles on his nose in thanks, then order him to stay, to not follow me.

My blood freezes as Quinn screams from the dock. As I run toward her, time seems to slow; Holly falls into the surging water, eyes closed, the tips of Quinn's fingers managing to grasp our friend's T-shirt, but not to hold on.

Clutching at air, Quinn stares wide-eyed into the lake. "I can't see her!" she shouts.

"Go wait for me where it's dry. See if you can find Cathy—I'll get Holly back," I pant as I reach the edge of the dock.

Remembering what Atheleen did in my dream, I look for the boat that's always been tied to the dock. I'm going to tie a rope around myself, securing myself to the boat, and row out to the middle of the lake where Hettie lives. That's where I'll find Holly, in the bony arms of Atheleen or perhaps the young Arrington herself.

It's time for her to let go—of the house and the spirits she's trapped.

But the boat isn't in its usual spot.

Someone has stashed it in the thicket of trees and bracken where I found the dead deer with its eyes plucked dry.

I start to run toward it, and Quinn follows; Waffles, remembering my instructions, whines a protest that carries on the wind.

My sandals slide through the mud as I near the blackberry

bramble. I'm almost to the boat. But now that I'm close enough
to peer through the curtain of rain separating me from my way
to Holly, I realize there's already someone else untying it from its
new mooring.

Rose.

I pause, letting Quinn catch up with me. "Distract your mom,"
I whisper, hoping she can hear me, or at least read my lips through
the swirling rain. "I need that boat. I don't think I can get to Holly
without it."

It's a big ask. She might say no. After all, trust is what I wouldn't
give her when I ran toward the house to look for Holly. But I don't
have much choice right now, and besides, she really seemed like
she was trying to help Holly on the dock—and at risk to herself.
She could have been knocked under in the surge, too.

"What happens if it tips?" Quinn asks in a low voice.

I shrug helplessly. "Then I'll swim to her."

Quinn shoots me a worried look.

Three weeks together and she can already see right through
me—it thrills and terrifies me. I hope my suspicions about her
were wrong.

"I'm coming, too," she mouths. Then, raising her voice, she
runs toward Rose as the boat inches free of its tether. "Hey! Mom!
What the hell do you think you're doing? Where are you going in
that thing—were you just going to leave me here?"

Rose's eyes widen. "Quinn, no! You need to get away—go
back to the car!"

With Rose distracted, I creep around behind them using the
path Holly always took on her runs, hidden behind bushes, and

make my way toward the boat from the opposite side of where Rose stands with one hand on the wood siding.

I start to swing a leg over, but Rose whirls around in time to push me over the side.

"I can't let you go out there!" she cries as I hit the shallow water. "You shouldn't have come back here, Dare! And you shouldn't have brought Quinn!"

"I thought you needed her and Holly to help you reach your sister!" I splutter, tasting the lake on my tongue. I quickly check my pockets, making sure my insulin pump is still there, but my phone is gone. It must have toppled out when I fell. I frantically search for it on the muddy lake bottom, but I can't find it.

And I don't have time to keep looking, not with Rose breathing down my neck and Holly in the water, depending on us.

At least my recorder is still wedged deep in my back pocket. If it survives being submerged, maybe there will be something worth hearing on it.

Pushing myself up, I scramble to the side of the boat and tug it free of the bank where it's beached. I take one of the oars, holding it between myself and Rose like a weapon.

"Dare," she says tersely, extending a hand. "You need to give me that. You girls both need to get out of here right away."

"Not without Holly." Quinn takes up the other oar and stands beside me, knee-deep in the surging water. With her free hand, she gently touches my shoulder. "Do whatever you have to. Get my mom out of the way. I—I'll understand. Holly needs us."

A flash of lightning throws the trees into sharp silhouette. For a second, I see a shadow just an inch off from Quinn's, but this time I can't be sure if it's Atheleen's spirit or if there's too much rain in my eyes.

The oar shakes faintly in my hands—I can't tell if it's the effects of low blood sugar, or if it's fear. Fear that we're already too late, that Holly has gone deeper than we can follow.

The sandy lake bottom sucks at my sandals, stubbornly anchoring me in place, so I kick them off and crash my way deeper into the churning water as another streak of lightning cracks open the night-dark sky. Feeling drained, like I've just run a marathon, I flop onto the front seat inside the narrow boat.

Quinn takes the back bench, her oar raised, ready to help push off.

The greenish aura on the horizon glows faintly, beckoning us closer.

"Girls, *wait*!" Rose begs, grabbing at the back of the boat as Quinn shakes her head. "I thought I needed whoever the lake had chosen to help me draw Atheleen out. But I—I saw her when I came for the boat. Out there. I'm afraid there's nothing left of her to save. Just Hettie, wearing her face like a mask. And if that's the case, none of us will be safe on the lake."

She points to the horizon, shielding her eyes from the wind flinging rain in her face—or perhaps it's too painful for her to look for long at that otherworldly light beneath the surface.

For a moment, I feel a shiver of sympathy for the woman trying to anchor our boat. She was Hettie's victim, too, in a way.

But she never should have let any of us come here, least of all Quinn—she risked our lives to help someone who's already gone. How can someone so levelheaded not see how reckless that plan was?

Rose tightens her grip on the boat as I stick my oar into the water, and I feel another tremor race through my hand. This time, even without my CGM, I know what it means: this is the start of a low blood sugar episode. The glucose tablets I took must not have kicked in yet; how much time has it been? In the wind and rain, it's impossible to tell.

"I can't let you girls go out there!" The embers in Rose's eyes become flames, her posture rigid with determination as she clings to the boat. "It's my fault Atheleen became part of this evil thing. I can't let another girl drown out there. I thought I would have reached her before now. I thought she was stronger. I thought this would be so different. I *never* wanted to hurt of any of you." Rose looks from me to Quinn, her face desperate, wilder than the storm. "Least of all you, love. Forgive me. Please."

Quinn's face crumples. She looks away, and when she next meets her mother's eyes, something in her gaze has darkened. "You put me in danger—you played with my life! And my friends'! How could I ever forgive you for that?"

Rose grips the edge of the boat tightly as Quinn and I try to paddle, going nowhere.

I think I understand why Rose wants the boat now; she's trying to sacrifice herself. She's arrogant enough to assume her death could break the cycle, I guess. But she's not the right age, and Holly is.

Desperate to reach her before it's too late, I shove Rose with the end of my oar, and she falls back into a watery bed of leaves with a startled cry.

Quinn takes us out of the shallows, and we begin paddling against the defiant current to reach our friend. The lake doesn't want us here, just like the house resisted our intrusion; the waves shove us back a foot for every few inches we manage to gain with both of us using our full strength at the oars.

There's no sign of our friend yet, but that doesn't mean the worst—I hope. The storm makes it hard to see more than a few feet away on any side of the boat.

Waffles's barking back on shore gradually grows fainter; we're at least headed in the right direction. At the murky point where the water turns from gray to green, Quinn loses her grip on her oar, and before she can snatch it up, it sinks beneath the waves.

She slumps over, exhausted. "I can't do this," she gasps. Tears mix with rain on her cheeks as she stares into the lake's glowing center. "Where is she?"

"I know you're there, Hettie!" I shout. "I know you've been killing all these girls because you're lonely, and you're angry at your sisters, but guess what? Sisters fight! But they can still love each other, too. You were just too stubborn to see it. Laying blame somewhere else is just a tactic to avoid dealing with your own shit; who keeps a list of dumb things their siblings do to them, anyway? You don't have to do this—you can let Holly go!"

I don't know what I expect to happen. I just know I want justice for Atheleen, for all the lost souls wrongfully claimed by one selfish girl. But there's no reasoning with ghosts—there's nothing reasonable about them in the first place.

Holly is still nowhere to be seen, and the glow in the center of the lake doesn't diminish at my shouting; if anything, it begins to widen, creeping like blood from a slowly leaking wound into the outer reaches of the water.

Worse, the jittery feeling in my limbs convinces me that my

blood sugar is getting too low. The glucose tablets must not have been enough, and I won't be any good to Holly or anyone else if that's the case. I might even put Quinn in more danger being out here with her—she should bring me back to shore. "Quinn, maybe we should—"

A wave slams into the side of our boat, stirred up by the wind, cutting me off.

Our little vessel rocks violently, forcing me to cling to the seat for stability. I pass Quinn the remaining oar; she told me once that she has years of experience on the water with her dad. I trust her to get us out of this. She got us this far, after all, so her loyalty must be with me.

But sometimes trust isn't enough.

Quinn doesn't control the lake—Hettie does—and as a second, higher wave crashes into the boat, it spills us out.

Water closes over my head. The ever-present current punches me in the chest as the lake invades my nose and mouth, punishing me for daring to enter the place where Hettie lives.

I've been in the house where she once lived, but now I'm in her territory.

At her bitter mercy.

TWENTY-NINE

CHOKING DOWN A MOUTHFUL of foul water, I kick toward the surface, scratching pointlessly at the edge of a boat I'm not sure I can flip over with my shaking hands. Low blood sugar has officially set in, and I have no way to get help until I'm back on shore.

This is a nightmare come to life. My head spinning, my thoughts a muddled, panicked fog, I can't tell what's real and what's not as I cling to the boat like a life preserver.

Is that really Quinn surfacing several feet away, choking out a mouthful of water as she swims toward me, her glasses missing? The waves, at least, are a harsh and persistent reality, slapping our faces as the current continues trying to wash us out like stubborn stains.

I can't see Holly anywhere, but I do see something bobbing in the water nearby: a fox, its insides sucked dry, matted fur barely concealing its bones.

Shutting my eyes, I use the overturned boat to shield myself from another wave. When I open them again, three hazy figures are circling around me, barely formed shapes that seem cut from the spray of water and rain. Two are tall, the third barely half their height.

As their faces become clearer, I realize I know them. Scarlett. Olivia. Mercy. The other victims of Hettie's undying anger, now free of her parasitic hold on them, but somehow still tethered to this place. They watch me with sad, gentle eyes set deep into their gaunt faces, surrounding me with a pale flicker of light as a fast-moving current begins to tug at my ankles, trying to separate me from the boat—my lifeline.

Quinn, rummaging frantically in her dress pocket with one hand as she holds on to the boat with her other, doesn't seem to notice what's happening.

Wincing as bony fingers dig into my skin, I start kicking and twisting out of what must be Hettie's attempt to pull me under. The effort leaves me shakier than ever, even a little sweaty despite the chill of water that should still be summer-warm.

At least I can't feel Hettie's grasp anymore.

As the upside-down boat rocks in the turbulent water, I close my eyes, suddenly filled with Scarlett's peace. With Olivia's. With Mercy's. All the girls who went before me, who can't save me, but still showed up to comfort me.

I could die out here tonight. We all could.

But the thing is, I don't think we will.

I've spent my life wanting to believe in ghosts. And now I do. But even more, I believe in a girl who loved art and horses and her sister. I believe in the small smile Quinn can never hide when she's proven right. I believe in a girl who doesn't know the extent of her own power yet. I believe in the strength that's helped me battle a demanding disease.

I believe that no matter what strange things the wind blows our way, no matter how fierce the storm, my friends are going to carry me through.

It would be easy to let go of the boat, to let the water and the darkness claim me.

But I've never done things the easy way. I'm not about to start now.

"Dare? Dare!" The way Quinn shouts my name makes me wonder if she's been doing so for a while now. "Here, take these!" A triumphant look on her face, she presses something into my free hand, a sealed plastic tube with orange-colored candies inside.

Glucose tablets. Instant sugar.

I chew and swallow several quickly as she explains, "I put these in my pocket for you when we left the van. You looked like you needed them. How shaky are you? Can you tread water for a second?"

With very little help from me—the tablets take time to kick in—Quinn manages to turn the boat right side up.

The three misty figures are still there, watching over us, though their features are even less defined now, blurred by rain as the storm intensifies. I whisper my thanks for their help.

Quinn swears, ripping my attention away from the figures and back to her. Immediately, I understand her frustration: we have no oars. The lake either carried them out of reach or sucked them into Hettie's lair in the depths.

Still, being in the boat is better than our legs dangling in the murky greenish water where sharp hands can grab us, so we clamber in.

As we wring out our hair and blink against a combination of wave spray and rain, searching for Holly, Quinn gasps and points toward the center of the lake, the brightest green. "There, I think I see her! Just her head—oh."

It's not Holly.

Those long tendrils of dripping hair are all too familiar. So are the white-yellow eyes like spoiled milk that stare a challenge at us as she rises from the center of the lake. She wants us to see her. The entity wearing Atheleen's chapped, skeletal face glows blue like she's made of water, or perhaps electricity. A being of violent, raging energy testing its boundaries.

Rose was right; there's no trace of Atheleen left, just a gross mockery of her face after death. Hettie, or the lake entity that used to be Hettie, isn't going to listen to anyone. It's past helping, too powerful, too consumed with its own needs to notice anything around it.

Atheleen glides toward us with alarming speed, hovering just a foot away from the front of our helpless vessel. Has she changed her mind about taking Holly? Well, I won't let her have Quinn either. "Don't touch her!" I scream, throwing out an arm to shield her.

Undeterred, the apparition thrusts out a bony hand, her fingers just grazing my chin. The spot burns with a cold fire, but I don't give it the satisfaction of reacting.

The boat wobbles precariously, and a smile splits Atheleen's cracked lips. Now I understand: she's using the lake to try to drown us. Not to be her companions, not as the one Hettie chose, but just to get us out of the way while she drains the life from Holly.

This can't be it for us.

"Help me balance!" I tell Quinn, showing her where to put her weight as another wave rocks us. I'm not going back in the water if I can help it.

"Aunt Atheleen!" Quinn shouts over the roar of water and wind. "I know you can hear me! If there's any part of you left that cares, you can still stop this. Fight her! Or does she own your soul now?"

Despite everything, I smile.

If there's one thing I trust, it's the power of the girl beside me, holding her head high, her darkly lined eyes boldly issuing a challenge to the rotting apparition hovering at the bow of our boat.

I believe a girl can be fierce as a storm, her own force of nature.

Quinn is a hurricane, and I'm the wind that rips trees from the ground and sends rooftops flying. Now that I know she's on my side, we aren't going to let this thing have our friend without a fight.

A small figure appears through a break in the waves as though our thoughts summoned her: Holly. It's really her this time.

She swims with the quiet grace of a selkie, a sea-creature-turned-woman reclaiming her watery birthright. As she glides toward the grinning specter of Atheleen, the entity reaches out a hand, beckoning our friend like a doting mother greets her precious child. If that doting mother had drowned and was wandering around as a shambling corpse, that is.

The closer Holly gets to Atheleen, the brighter the glow in the lake becomes, until it stings my eyes and makes them water.

But I force myself not to look away. I've spent too much of my time here ignoring what's been right in front of me all along.

The glow isn't really a light at all; it's Hettie, looking just as she did in her portraits—skin the color of curdled milk flushed with a hint of life, eyes cold but bright, full lips unsmiling, the lace collar of her dress stiff and high, not a single hair out of place despite the howling wind.

In her diary, Hettie said something about wanting to "drain them dry." This must be what she meant, what Atheleen had guessed: sapping away her victims' flesh, their life, and eventually their spirits so that she can be immortal while the others are whittled away to nothing, skeleton girls becoming half-formed shapes in the mist.

The dead deer I found floating at the lake's edge swims to the front of my thoughts, uninvited, the small gravestone in the orchard surfacing in its wake.

Hettie liked animals. I guess that's why she draws them in when they get too near the water—for their company, for their energy, just like the girls.

Every time Hettie moves a hand, Atheleen's apparition moves with her, a true puppet unable to break her strings. Hettie's laughter ricochets around the lake, carried on the wind, seeming to stir the waves to new heights.

Quinn starts trying to paddle us toward Holly using her hands. Now that my blood sugar is rising, the fog in my head clearing, I can help her. But our efforts are more pathetic than they were when we had our oars.

We won't make it to her in time.

I grab Quinn's arm, stilling her motions and pointing as movement at the corner of my eye draws my gaze. There's another head peeking above the waves, sleek dark hair plastered against her pale skin. She isn't at home in the water like Holly. It's a struggle for her to hold her own against the current. But she's fighting.

Blinking against the rain, the spray of the churning waves, and the blinding glow of the sun beneath the water, it's hard to make out exactly what's happening.

Rose reaches Atheleen and Holly, putting herself between the two before our friend can grab the skeletal fingers awaiting her.

"Mom! No!" Quinn screams.

Rose takes both Atheleen's hands in hers, sweeping her frail body into an embrace. As they touch, the wind dies, the noise of the rainfall drops to a hush, and everything goes dark.

THIRTY

THERE'S NO MORE GLOW in the lake. No more Hettie with her cruel smile.

There's also no sign of Rose, Holly, or Atheleen.

The three filmy figures of the girls hovering behind our boat become more solid, their toes just skimming the water as they hang in the air, watching us. I nudge Quinn, not wanting her to miss their round, smiling faces. Mercy's wedding gown is no longer in tatters. Scarlett's hair is glossy, her skin healthy and smooth, no longer stretched taut over bone. Olivia, hugging a stuffed puppy to her chest, waves shyly at us and steps behind Scarlett, who puts one arm around her and the other around Mercy.

I don't think they can speak, but their faces say enough. They're free. No longer bound to this place. They can go home.

Quinn grabs my hand and holds tight as the girls become shapes in the mist once again, and a gust of wind blows them away.

"I saw," she whispers hoarsely. "That has to be a good sign."

Does this mean Atheleen is free, too? Is Hettie gone for good, her power over this place finally broken when Rose stopped her sister from claiming a new victim?

Until we know for sure, we still need to get away from the water as fast as we can.

As my vision adjusts to the semidarkness, I spot an oar floating nearby. Quinn and I paddle toward it, and I manage to grasp the end and pull it into the boat.

"Mom? Holly?" Quinn shouts, the wind-tossed trees throwing her words back to us in an ever-softening refrain.

I still my breath and strain my ears, hoping for an answering cry, but none comes.

The rain softens to a drizzle, the clouds parting slightly as we search the water for two figures, one with blonde hair, the other dark. The thunder gives a faint parting growl before the rain stops entirely.

As a shaft of sunlight strikes the dock, I realize the waves are no longer surging over it. The water gently lapping at our boat is a beautifully ordinary blue-green, and there's a touch of warmth to the air, reminding me that it's still summer. The wind is cleaner, too, no stench of decaying matter clawing its way down my nose as I inhale. No electric current of pent-up energy crackles along my skin.

All the signs of Hettie's presence are vanishing, the lake healing itself in her absence.

Even the water level is retreating; already, I can make out the half-moon of rocky beach where we had our party.

I lift my gaze to the house in time to see Waffles, tail wagging, amble toward the front porch. There's no longer water pouring out of the windows, but I still don't want him going in there. I call out to him, but he doesn't seem to hear me. He's as stubborn as I am, I swear; it's why we get along so well.

Anxious to get back to shore—I don't care how safe the lake seems, I'll never trust it—I scan the sun-dappled surface for any sign of Holly or Rose, still daring to hope.

Quinn gasps and touches my arm.

I follow her wide eyes to the retreating shoreline. A body lies in the wet sand, her long blonde braid draped across her chest, her face toward the sky. The glare of the sun makes it impossible to tell if her eyes are open or closed.

"Holly!" I shout, starting to row us back to shore.

Quinn grips the side of the boat, keeping a silent vigil for some sign of her mother in our wake. She doesn't cry or protest as I steer us into the shallows alongside Holly; I'm no expert, but I think she's in shock.

There's nothing more satisfying than the feel of solid ground beneath the bow as I run us aground a few feet from Holly.

"Is she breathing?" Quinn asks, her words slow, dazed, her eyes still on the lake.

I drop to my knees in the mud beside Holly just as she stirs and coughs up water. Putting an arm around her shoulders, I carefully help her sit up.

Hettie didn't get her new victim after all. Even if Rose was taken by the current, she wasn't the right age. The cycle has finally been broken.

Holly takes one look at me and bursts into tears, throwing her cold arms around me so hard, she almost knocks me over. She definitely seems like the Holly I know, no longer under whatever influence the lake had over her. "I told you this town was the worst," she laughs, touching my face, then her own, as if trying to reassure herself that she isn't dreaming. "Now do you see why I wanted to leave?"

"That might be an understatement," I agree, smiling slightly as Quinn kneels next to me for her own enthusiastic greeting from Holly.

Still, Quinn's eyes never leave the lake. Watching and worrying. Hoping.

I hurry toward the house to find Waffles, dreading the thought of stepping foot inside even if Atheleen and Hettie are, as I suspect, gone like the rest.

But I don't have to look far.

My big, beautiful, goofy dog bursts from around the corner of the far side of the house and into my arms, followed by a dazed and slow-moving Cathy who leans against the side of the house for support as she tackles each forward step. "You know, I've never liked dogs much," she admits as she moves away from the house to join me in the long grass, unsteady on her feet.

I offer her my arm.

"But your fella here has me convinced I ought to adopt one. He came to find me and woke me up."

"You were asleep?" I don't quite know what to make of that. "In there?" I nod toward the front door, confused, remembering the water that cascaded from the shattered windows.

Cathy shakes her head with an air of bewilderment. "I was outside, behind the house. I was trying to shut off all the breakers because lights were flashing in every room like crazy, but then something hit me in the back of the head."

She presses her lips together as she gingerly touches the spot where she was struck. "That wind was really something. Must have been debris from the storm."

Or Holly, under Hettie's influence, did something she would regret.

But that's all over now, and there's no need to alarm Cathy.

"Where's Rose?" she asks as I guide her down to the shore,

Waffles gleefully bumping against my legs every other step. "I need to tell her I'm leaving—I've tried to stick it out, but the society can't be involved with a house this costly. Not to mention hazardous. And I'd better call my family doctor to take a look at my head while I'm at it."

As we move toward Quinn and Holly, still sitting together near the boat, I keep my voice low as I explain to Cathy, "The storm was really bad. Holly got in some trouble, and, uh, Rose went in after her. I . . . haven't seen her since. She didn't come out."

"What?" Cathy's hand flutters to her heart. She tries to quicken her pace to reach the others, but she stumbles and reluctantly leans more of her weight on me. "We need to call someone. The police. My phone is still in the house—"

"The cops won't dredge a lake this size, remember?" I whisper as we reach the shore. "But maybe she's out there."

I hope Atheleen's final embrace with her sister was meant to lift her up, not to drag her into the depths. But it's hard to say, not knowing where Hettie went.

Holly leaps to her feet and hugs Cathy. "Dear, you're half frozen!" the older woman admonishes, touching Holly's hand, then Quinn's. "All of you are, and no wonder—you'll catch your death in those wet clothes! I'm sorry, Dare, but we do need to call someone—I'll have a friend bring us some blankets and hot drinks while we take what we can salvage from the house, and then we'll start getting you all home."

My shoulders sink in relief; for once, I'm glad to just follow directions and go along with someone else's plan. I don't want to think anymore. Not for a long time.

Sitting in the sand beside Quinn, I spot a familiar gleam of black stone. A bead from one of my broken bracelets. I pick it up and put it in my pocket, just in case I ever need a reminder of what happened here. What I now know.

As Cathy starts toward the house in search of her phone, leaving the three of us clustered like lost seagulls on the shore, the last of the clouds roll back.

Sunlight gilds the house in rich, syrupy light that hides its cracks and dented corners, turns shards of broken glass into crystal treasures.

Two girls appear from behind us, near the dock, walking hand in hand toward the house. The taller one has long waves of frizzy brown hair and a big smile; the other, younger girl has a sweet, round face and glossy, darker hair cut around her shoulders. I never saw her with such clarity in my dreams, but Rose's eyes are the most familiar thing about her. A small black-and-white cat scampers at their heels, weaving between the girls' bare feet.

Their hair lifts in the breeze, looking impossibly solid, impossibly real.

Cathy freezes.

Quinn begins to shake, her body racked with silent sobs. I hold her close as the sisters climb the porch steps, their feet creaking against the sagging boards, and disappear through the closed front door as if flesh melting through a solid barrier is the most natural thing in the world, talking and laughing about something only they can hear.

Like the others girls, Atheleen is finally free, at peace. And Rose is with her.

Hettie, if she's still here, is all alone. And I'm going to try my best to make sure it stays that way until we know for sure she's become nothing more than a bad dream, a memory that will serve as a warning.

It seems fitting that a selfish person like Henrietta Arrington was finally made powerless by the only thing that's stronger than death: love. Sappy as it sounds, our proof just walked up the porch. Love can be a gift, a motive, a weapon. It's powerful stuff.

I'd like to think that if Max had been the one trapped in the lake, I would have done for him what Rose did for her sister.

"Mom," Quinn whispers urgently, her voice cracking over the words. "The last thing I told her was that I could never forgive her."

"She's forgiven you, though," I say gently.

"You saw how happy she looked just now," Holly says, reaching out as Quinn's face crumples and she collapses into herself, hugging her knees to her chest and bowing her head—maybe to avoid having to look at the lake any longer.

As Quinn's body shakes with sobs, Holly and I lean in on either side, anchoring her as grief threatens to tear her apart.

Cathy glances between us and the house, her mouth hanging open. Waffles nudges her hand with his nose, trying to be comforting and get some petting out of the deal at the same time. Judging by her glistening eyes, Cathy understands more than she was letting on; she definitely recognized Rose.

"Forget the blankets," she stammers. "Let's just go. We have the van. Quinn, you'll come stay with me, at least for tonight, and Dare, your mom can pick you up from my house when she gets here. Holly, dear, we'll drop you off first. We'll call the police once we cross the bridge—they can look around out here without us."

She strides toward the van, moving faster than before, ready to put this place behind her and never look back.

As for me, I think I'll be doing a lot of looking back, analyzing the details to uncover what I missed, what I should have seen sooner.

But I can do all that from the comfort of home. My home. With a mom who would never put me in danger, the brother I've missed being annoyed by, and the friends who will stay up all night with me to distract me from the worst of my thoughts without me even having to ask.

I leap to my feet, ready as Cathy is to leave this place behind.

Quinn takes a last look at the house and then stands. She brushes away a fraction of the sand that clings to her sodden dress as tears continue to wash her face clean of any lingering trace of the lake.

I hold out a hand to help Holly up, but she shakes her head, waving me off.

"Go on, y'all. I'm going to walk home, actually. It's just . . . my parents will be there, and I need a lot of time to myself to think before I start answering a million questions." She glances toward the house. "There's nothing I need to grab from in there—I have too many clothes and shoes at home anyway."

I don't really want anything I left in there, either. And the thought of going back inside and finding the remains of that moldy doll, or anything else from our time here, must be too much for Holly. It's too much for me, too.

As for Quinn, I'm not s°ure she knows where she is right now, but she lets me put an arm around her shoulders and guide her away from the water's edge.

"Message us when you get home, at least?" I beg Holly as she wrings out her hair. "My phone is super dead, but it shouldn't take long to get a new one."

"I will," Holly promises.

"And don't be a stranger. We'll still talk all the time, right?" I ask quickly, torn between saying my goodbyes to Holly and helping Quinn get into the van before she collapses.

"Duh," Holly says, "but only if you watch the next season of *The Beach* so we can discuss." A hint of a grin appears on her face before the sounds of Quinn's grief wash it away, and she hugs us both tightly before turning to go.

She heads toward the faint dirt path around the lake, which eventually diverges somewhere I've only seen on maps, the right branch leading into the back of the neighborhood where Holly's parents live.

That leaves me and Waffles to help Quinn up the path Rose's and Atheleen's spirits took just a few minutes ago.

The van's motor wheezes to life; Cathy is impatient to get going. And so am I.

Holly turns and waves one more time before disappearing into the trees.

As Cathy steps on the gas, Quinn gazes quietly out the window and Waffles sprawls across my lap. Somehow, by nature or by accident, Quinn's hand and mine find one another on the middle seat. We hold on. She gives me hope. And for now that's enough.

Arrington Estate is silent and still as we put it in our rear view. No lights flicker through the shattered windows.

No shadow stirs where there should be none.

No bells chime within those water-stained halls.

But there's no erasing the things I've seen. The things I've felt. The next time I reach out into the dark, I'll be careful. I'll be ready for the slightest possibility that something cold as death could grab my hand and refuse to let go.

ATTACHMENTS

S1, E6

Intro music fades in. Violins play a slow, eerie melody.

In my brief time at the Arrington Estate, I learned that some mysteries are better left unsolved.

Atheleen's story, though, deserved to be told. After all, ghost stories are human stories, brimming with life, with history, drama, and personality. They're as enduring as we are. I'm not sure that I was the right person to tell her tale, or that I did it in the right way to honor her memory—the way she would have wanted. I have no way of knowing her wishes. What I do know is that Atheleen was a reader who loved stories as much as I do, and now she is one. Immortal. I hope you all think I've done her justice in the telling.

I've been doing a lot of looking back lately, like I thought I would. And there's one thing all of us, even Rose, got wrong about Atheleen at some point: she wasn't entirely gone, at least, not until the storm. Most of the time, there was some shred of her goodness left. She used Quinn's paints to warn her away in a language they shared: art. I think she tapped Quinn's shoulder in the shower repeatedly, trying to get her attention to warn her away. Same with Holly. And when the chandelier in the foyer fell, she used all her energy to throw Quinn out of harm's way. She fought to protect her niece until Hettie took her over completely.

As for Henrietta Arrington, her side of things is less clear. What happened to make her so angry with those closest to her? And how did she become such a powerful entity, feeding off others and trapping them in the lake? I'll never forget the pulsing green light at its center. But what haunts me more—still—are the living. In this case, the townspeople of New Hope. The girls who drowned and disappeared were largely outsiders, yet that doesn't mean no one noticed what happened to them. It's easy to pretend something isn't real when it isn't happening to you, and the town chose easy; they looked away, looked after their own, and never questioned what was happening at the estate. Never bothered to warn the next girl. If they had, I wouldn't be telling Atheleen's story; maybe she would be writing her own, a tell-all memoir about how she grew up in a haunted house—and got out. Her and Rose.

I didn't go to Rose's memorial. Quinn sent me a video, though, and it was beautiful. There were roses in every color of the rainbow, even ones that couldn't be natural, yet it was nothing short of elegant. A merging of Quinn's boisterous style and her mom's more reserved one.

For those of you who've been asking—no. We're not together. Maybe we will be one day; who knows? Right now we both need space to heal from what happened. Quinn especially. But we're forever linked by what we saw, what we know. We have plans to meet up this fall somewhere, about a week before Halloween. I'd be lying if I said

I wasn't counting the days. No matter what our futures hold, we'll always be in each other's lives because we both need someone who understands.

Deep down, part of me still clings to the hope that there's some other explanation for everything that happened this summer. Some kind of mold that makes people hallucinate, maybe. My new therapist and I are working through it—she says my need to rationalize is part of how I cope with my anxiety. She's probably right.

I also talk with her about the complicated feelings still lingering after my diagnosis. I'm getting involved in some advocacy work online, too. Greater visibility and education are the only ways we're going to end the misconceptions and stereotypes. But no matter what's happening in your life, I personally guarantee that talking with a qualified professional can help. And you can start today. Here's how:

Commercial break.

And we're back!

For all the Waffles fans out there, he's doing great. Shout-out to everyone who has sent him shoes for his collection—I'm a little behind on thank-yous, but they're coming. Waffles himself is busy with his new hobby: swimming lessons. You can follow his progress on Insta @WafflestheWonderDog. He's predicted a couple of late-night low blood sugars lately, too. My mom says he's like a fine wine, improving with age. I say all this fame is just going to his head—he got recognized while we were grocery shopping the other day. I guess I did, too. Shout-out to Angie. I love that there are so many of you out there excited to share your experiences with me. I promise I listen more carefully than I did before.

As for Cathy, we keep in touch by email, and she recently started a local paranormal investigation group called New Hope Haunts. They're currently closed to applications for new members after a surge of interest—can't imagine why—but they should reopen this winter. And she wants me to make it absolutely clear that, no, her group will not now or ever be investigating the Arrington Estate. The water damage inside the property was so extensive that after Rose's death, the bank took ownership, and who knows what they're going to do with it.

If it winds up on the market and one of you listening out there is brave enough to buy the place, I hope you'll reach out. It seems Arrington and I have some unfinished business.

A pause, followed by a sigh.

This is the part I've been dreading. Our last day at the estate was also the last time I ever heard from Holly. She ghosted Quinn, too. And I mean, at first I was like, I get it—things got so tense, maybe she wants to erase all memories of the estate. Maybe we're too painful a reminder. But it's not just that she never texted or reached out anywhere else—all her posts on her social media just . . . stopped. Last week, I worked up the nerve to call Holly's parents; they never saw or heard from her again, either. Apparently, they found a college rejection letter in her bedroom trash and think she had a nervous breakdown on her way home. The police think she finally made good on her life-long goal of leaving New Hope, but her parents fear the worst. So do I, but I don't think Holly took her life in the woods or anything.

I'm afraid that when she washed up on shore that day, she was already gone. I'm afraid she took Atheleen's place in the lake. Holly was eighteen, the same age as Lily Arrington; it fits the pattern. Maybe Hettie had already drowned her by the time we saw Rose reach Atheleen, and letting the other spirits go free was just a distraction. I'm afraid all isn't well at the Arrington Estate, and maybe never will be. One day, I hope to be ready to face the house and the lake again and finally put things right. I owe it to Holly, even if she's mostly gone. But I'm not there yet.

You're not alone in the dark. That's the truth. I used to watch ghost-hunting shows just to point out all the stuff they were faking. A lot of it—most of it—probably is bull-shit, but remember: it only takes one. One true story to blow a hole in the world you knew and make you rethink every possibility, every "what if." That's why they step into the dark and ignore the ridicule. And now, that's why I do, too. I've started doing some investigations again with a small team of my own—nothing I'm ready to share yet, but watch this space for updates. There are other compel-ling stories waiting to be explored.

And that, dear listeners, concludes the true account of how I solved the mysterious death of Atheleen Bell and finally saw a ghost. More than one.

This has been *Attachments*. Thanks for listening. Sleep tight.

ACKNOWLEDGEMENTS

As always, this last section will tend toward the frightfully long, as I have many wonderful people to thank! Strap in.

First and foremost: huge thanks to Katelyn Detweiler, who is both my agent and yet still my dream agent—a talented advocate, author, business partner, and friend. Whoever says you can't have it all or do it all clearly hasn't met her.

Endless gratitude also goes to Lucy Carson, the first enthusiastic champion of this idea.

To the stellar team at Razorbill and PenguinTeen, most especially to Gretchen Durning, Alex Sanchez, and Julie Rosenberg for their tremendous input and insight that helped shape this story. Many thanks also to Marinda Valenti and Rebecca Blevins for polishing this book with care and the best commentary. Thank you to Kristin Boyle and Marko Nadj for creating an unforgettable cover. And thank you to Jayne Ziemba, Patricia Brown, Rebecca Aidlin, Ashley Spruill, Felicity Vallence, Kara Brammer, Ruta Rimas, Casey McIntyre, Emily Romero, Shanta Newlin, Elyse Marshall, Carmela Iaria, Alex Garber, Christina Colangelo, Bri Lockhart, Felicia Frazier, Debra Polanksy, Jen Loja, Jocelyn Schmidt, and Jen Klonsky for all your support and the roles you each took on to help bring this book to life.

To Christy Mershon, Rhiannon Martin, and the amazing

board members and volunteers who pour so much time and hard work into the Glenn House—thank you for striving to tell my great-great-grandparents' story and maintain their beloved home with such care. Tell the spirits I said, "Behave!"

To Grant and Reanna Wilson, Kristen Luman, Mustafa Gatollari, Brandon Alvis, Daryl Marston, Brian Murray, Richel Stratton, Kaylen Hadley, Nina Giannelli, and the whole team at Ghost Hunters, thank you so much for welcoming me into your world and treating my family's ancestral home (and all its denizens, seen and unseen) with warmth and respect.

Huge thanks to my amazing author friends like Allie Christo, Astrid Scholte, Kelly Coon, Shea Ernshaw, Eve Castellan, Gwen Cole, Kelly McWilliams, Jenny Howe, Teresa Yea, and, of course, the one and only K.T.; it's our calls, texts, emails, D&D sessions, etc. that keep my head above water many days.

To Bry, who reminds me of the fun to be had in writing, that it's better to be a happy phantom than a sad elf, and who isn't afraid to embrace the chaos! Long live the trio and all their haunted, messy, glorious (probably, if Al's telling the tale) shenanigans in Middle Earth.

To my pottery family, who are excellent (and patient!) company for this endless talker who loves to tell stories while we throw.

To my impressively well-read friends, including the fabulous booksellers at One More Page Books, Fountain Bookstore, Bard's Alley Bookshop, and Chop Suey Books; passionate educators like Jamie Marsh, Jordan Frederick, and Deidre Cutter; as well as bloggers spreading the word about great new reads like my dear friend Tiffany Lyann (secondhandpages), John Clark (JCReads), Monica Laurette (pawed_pages), Lili (utopia state of mind), Brittany (brittanysbookrambles), Becky (booknerdbecky), Melanie Parker, Mireille Chartier, all the amazing folks at TBR and Beyond Book Club; Heather (velarisreads), Destiny (howling-library), Leelynn (leelynnreads), Melanie Parker (meltotheany); Eloise (eloisewrites), Bethany Pullen (beautifullybookishbethany), Rosina (lacedaggerbooks), Jami (jamishelves), Allie (themystical-reader), Thais (tatalifepages), Delly (dellybird), Diana Muñoz Carbonell (mydreamabyss), and Dez from the fabulous *Bingeology* podcast—plus way too many more to name here! Thank you all for championing my work with such enthusiasm; without you, I wouldn't feel seen, and the words wouldn't flow quite so well.

To Chris and our zoo, always, with endless love and gratitude. I can't believe it's been ten years—and what an adventure it's been so far!

To my family: Mom, Dad, Lindsey, Team W, and the one and only Papa Bear. You're my world.

To my excellent friends, most especially the Richmond Pokémon family (hi, Josh!), plus Lenore Bajare-Dukes, Joe Sparks, Erin Oliva, Megan Placona, and Melinda Allen. I don't know what I'd do without our family dinners, adventures, phone calls, and all the memes.

And in memory of my incredible, hardworking, book-loving Nana—I hope wherever you are now, there's a beach and endless cocktail hour. See you on the other side.